:d with a poor sense of direction and a propensity
ıd, **Annie Claydon** spent much of her childhood
n books. A degree in English Literature followed by
eer in computing didn't lead directly to her perfect
-writing romance for Mills & Boon—but she has
grets in taking the scenic route. She lives in
on: a city where getting lost can be a joy.

and raised just outside Toronto, Ontario,
Ruttan fled the big city to settle down with the
ry boy of her dreams. After the birth of her second
Amy was lucky enough to realise her lifelong
ı of becoming a romance author. When she's not
ısly typing away at her computer she's mum to
wonderful children, who use her as a personal taxi
hef.

THE BEST MAN AND THE BRIDESMAID

ANNIE CLAYDON

A REUNION, A WEDDING, A FAMILY

AMY RUTTAN

MILLS & BOON

First Published in Great Britain 2020
by Mills & Boon, an imprint of HarperCollins*Publishers*
1 London Bridge Street, London, SE1 9GF

The Best Man and the Bridesmaid © 2020 by Annie Claydon

A Reunion, a Wedding, a Family © 2020 by Amy Ruttan

ISBN: 978-0-263-27988-7

MIX
Paper from
responsible sources
FSC™ C007454

Printed and bound in Spain
by CPI, Barcelona

THE BEST MAN AND THE BRIDESMAID

ANNIE CLAYDON

MILLS & BOON

CHAPTER ONE

HE *WAS* HANDSOME. It was the first thing Andrea Allinson noticed about Cal Lewis, when he stepped into the hotel foyer. Maggie had gone into some detail when describing him, and the dark blond hair, tawny eyes and broad shoulders were all present and correct. Along with an indefinable quality that made Andrea catch her breath…

The hotel staff were homing in on their three newest guests like bees around a honeypot. The manager appeared from her office and shook everyone's hand, declaring that everything would be perfect for the wedding. Maggie looked dewy-eyed and excited, as any prospective bride should, and a little pink cheeked from the ride up here on the funicular railway. Her fiancé, Joe, caught her hand and raised it to his lips.

But Andrea couldn't take her eyes off Cal. He was standing a little to one side, allowing Maggie and Joe to be at the centre of everyone's attention. Smiling and… Handsome didn't really cover it. *Very* handsome, maybe, but that didn't account for the tingle that was running down Andrea's spine. *Love at first sight* might describe it, but Andrea was immune to that kind of thing. It was more likely just a severe case of physical attraction at first sight, which was awkward, but far more manageable.

Maggie caught sight of her, and broke away from the party, running towards Andrea and practically falling into her waiting arms.

'I'm so excited!'

Andrea hugged her friend tightly. This moment had been a long time coming, but now Maggie and Joe's wedding was just twelve days away. They'd met here, at the hotel in the Italian Alps where Andrea was the in-house doctor, and Joe and Maggie had decided that it was the perfect place for their wedding. In a little over a week's time family and friends would be arriving, but for the time being the wedding party consisted of just Maggie and Joe, along with Cal, who was Joe's best man.

'Everyone's been so kind.' Maggie's eyes were dancing with happiness. 'We had champagne on the plane, and then the man who operates that gorgeous train gave me this...'

Maggie displayed a red rose that was pinned to her coat, which had been a little squashed by the embrace. Andrea set it to rights, and then couldn't resist giving her friend another hug, which crushed the petals of the rose all over again.

'It's going to be perfect. I've got everything arranged at this end.' Andrea had been liaising with the hotel staff for months, determined that everything *would* be perfect for her friends.

'You're more worried about this than I am. It'll all be fine.' Maggie displayed an enviable optimism about the arrangements for her wedding, maybe because she'd been through so much to reach this point. 'As long as we're all here and we're happy and healthy, what can go wrong?'

Andrea had a list of all the things that could go

wrong, but she wasn't about to share it with Maggie.
Her friend had a point. As long as everyone was happy
and healthy, what more could anyone want?

'And we'll have more than a week together before
the big day to relax. I'm so looking forward to it…'
Maggie hugged Andrea again, taking the opportunity
to whisper in her ear. 'What do you think of him? He's
rather lovely, isn't he?'

Maggie had already made it quite clear that good
looks were just the tip of the iceberg. Besides being
handsome, Joe's best man was kind and had a good
sense of humour. He had a fascinating job and was a
doctor too, so he and Andrea would have lots in common and plenty to talk about. Maggie had been to his
flat in London and considered it comfortable and styl-
ish. And he was single…

That final detail made Maggie's intentions very clear.
A flutter of romance between the head bridesmaid and
the best man might be considered par for the course,
but Maggie had obviously decided that Andrea needed
a little shove in the right direction. As far as Andrea
was concerned, Cal Lewis's best attribute might be his
ability to turn a blind eye to Maggie's hints, because
she wasn't interested.

'He's…you're right. Very handsome.' That was more
than obvious, and saying anything different would be
the kind of lie that attracted suspicion from her friend.

'And he's a really lovely guy.' Maggie's bright blue-
eyed gaze searched Andrea's face. 'The kind someone
might move on with?'

'Don't you worry about me. I have moving on in
hand.' Andrea squeezed her friend's hand. It had been
three years since Judd had died, and Maggie had been
quite right when she'd gently suggested that maybe he

would have wanted Andrea to move on with her life. But moving on was easy to wish for, and hard to do.

Maggie grinned at her. 'Well, in that case—'

She jumped as Andrea nudged her hard. Cal and Joe had been relieved of their cases, and were heading towards them. Which was a relief because it meant Andrea didn't have to listen to any more of the ways in which Cal was wonderful, and a new challenge because now she was going to have to look him straight in the eye.

'Andrea...' Joe greeted her with a hug. 'It was nice of you to get the welcoming committee out for us.'

'Everyone loves a wedding.' Andrea smiled up at Joe. He'd been a rock for Maggie over the last two years, and their shared concern for her had brought Andrea and Joe together and made them firm friends.

'And *this* is going to be the best wedding ever.' Maggie smiled up at her fiancé. 'Because *I'm* marrying *you*.'

Joe chuckled and kissed Maggie's cheek. 'We'll take the lovebirds thing elsewhere in a minute, before we bore everyone to tears with it. Andrea, meet Cal...'

Andrea ignored Maggie's excited smile. It was bad enough trying to dismiss the little thrill of excitement that coursed through her, and she was sure that any moment now she was going to blush...

'Andrea. It's a pleasure to finally meet you. Maggie's told me so much about you.'

He had a nice voice—soft and deep, like rich honey. Andrea took his outstretched hand, feeling the warmth of his fingers. As handshakes went, this one was pretty spectacular, as well.

She *was* blushing now. Maybe it would be better if she stopped trying to ignore the unwanted feelings that gripped her. Just take them for what they were—

a momentary thrill—and hope that he would manage to do something unattractive enough to make them wither and die.

'Some of it good, I hope.' Andrea tried to make a joke, but it just sounded as if she was fishing for a compliment.

'I've been hoping all the way here that you might have just one or two faults that Maggie didn't mention. This is my first time as a best man, so I'm feeling my way with it.'

It was said with the kind of smile that turned it into a very nice compliment. Andrea swallowed down the lump in her throat.

'It's my first time as a bridesmaid too. I guess we'll just make our mistakes together, and hopefully no one will notice.'

This conversation was going in entirely the wrong direction. The thought of feeling her way with Cal and making a few mistakes was all-consuming.

But Maggie was looking extremely pleased at the way things were going. Smug, even. Andrea couldn't deny her this small pleasure.

'Why don't we all go for coffee? I'm sure you could do with one.'

Joe nodded, clearly about to agree, and Maggie grabbed his arm.

'We'd love to, wouldn't we, Joe?' Maggie gave an exaggerated look of dismay. 'But I was up really late last night packing, and we had an early start this morning. We've hardly slept, and I can't keep my eyes open. I just want to go and lie down for an hour.'

Joe smiled, clearly unable to deny Maggie anything. 'Yeah, now you mention it...' He took Maggie's hand, looking around for someone to show them to their room. 'Can we take a rain check?'

Cal nodded thoughtfully. Obviously he had something on his mind, and Andrea swallowed down the impulse to wonder exactly what he was thinking. Better to leave his thoughts out of the equation and concentrate on what she needed from him to make this wedding perfect.

'Would you mind if I took a rain check too? I have some emails that I really need to answer...'

'Cal! I thought you said that you were going to have a *holiday* with us!' Maggie shot him a reproachful look and then turned to Andrea with a confiding air. 'He's very important. Very busy...'

Cal winced. 'I'm not that important at all. My patients are, though; I'm sure Andrea understands that as well as I do.'

Would he just *stop*? Stop saying all the right things and do something that made him less...likeable. Wantable, if that was even a word. Andrea wasn't picky, anything that would harden her heart against him would do.

'Of course. I have a clinic later on this afternoon, and there are a few things I should do beforehand.' Not very important things, but no one needed to know that. 'I'll catch up with you all this evening...'

The steep, uphill path was caked with snow, which crunched under Cal's boots. He had woken early, and in the bright morning the mountains seemed to be a welcome reminder that the world kept turning, without any regard for his own small preoccupations.

He'd reckoned that he had everything under control. That was the way he liked things. Two weeks off work, during which his bosses had suggested he consider their offer of a promotion. He'd get in a little skiing, help out with the wedding arrangements, and then have the pleasure of seeing his best friend marry the woman who made him supremely happy. If Maggie had teased him a little about how well he'd get along with the head bridesmaid, it was just a little harmless fun.

Then he'd seen Andrea. It was as if the busy hotel foyer had suddenly lost focus, and the only thing that was clear and bright was her. When the porter had tried to take his case, Cal had realised he'd been clenching his fingers so hard around the handle that his knuckles were white. He'd apologised and smiled at the man, then followed Joe over to where the women were standing.

He thought he'd seen the suspicion of a blush on her cheeks. Maybe the temperature *had* actually risen and the sudden warmth in his chest wasn't just the result of his racing heartbeat.

Cal had thought himself relatively fearless. But when faced with Andrea's blue-grey eyes, her soft, dark curls, and the feeling that somehow he'd known her all of his life, he'd run away…

Yesterday evening, he'd sent his apologies to Joe and Maggie and ordered dinner in his room, writing a string of emails. This morning, he'd left the hotel early for a walk, telling himself that a little solitary exploration was what he always did when he found himself in a new place. These excuses were beginning to wear a little thin.

Climbing higher, he could see the hotel below him, the low sun glinting in the large windows that made the most of the stunning views. People were beginning to circulate on the veranda, and early morning skiers were heading for the slopes that surrounded the building. The funicular railway, that ran high over the rugged terrain between the hotel and the village at the foot of the mountain, seemed to glisten in the morning light.

Here, of all places, it felt as if he'd found something precious. Something he didn't understand. Cal had spoken with Andrea for a total of maybe five minutes, and yet every word, every glance, had embedded itself deep in his consciousness.

Cal shook his head and turned, lengthening his stride as he made his way up the steep path. It didn't matter if this was just a passing impression, or something real, his way forward was exactly the same. His inability to commit to a relationship had already hurt a very dear friend. He was bad news, and liking someone was no excuse for breaking the rule he'd made that relationships were best left alone.

He would, however, have to spend a fair bit of time with Andrea since they had a wedding to organise. And now that a little exercise had worked off the shock of feeling something—feeling so much—when he'd first seen her yesterday, he knew he should stop avoiding her. They would work together on the wedding, maybe share a quiet toast with each other when everything went off smoothly, and that would be that.

Piece of cake.

Cal's absence from dinner the previous evening had been half expected, but when Andrea joined Joe and Maggie for breakfast the next day and found them sitting alone, she couldn't help but feel a little disappointed.

'He's gone for a walk.' Maggie turned the corners of her mouth down. 'And then apparently he has to make some phone calls. I can't imagine what he finds to say that takes so long.'

Andrea glanced at Joe, for help. He understood...

'You know this job isn't a nine to five.' He gave Maggie a smile. 'Would you want things any different?'

Maggie shrugged. 'No. Dedication's a very attractive trait. Within reason, I suppose...'

Andrea laughed. 'Dedication doesn't always listen to reason.'

She'd been dedicated once, to the work that she and Judd had shared. It had seemed a perfect match, living and working together, sharing the same ideals. It had started slowly, as a friendship, and then turned into love, gradually growing together, their work and their lives dovetailing neatly.

And then the accident had ripped everything away. She'd been unable to save Judd, and had lost, not only the one man who meant everything to her, but her own confidence in being able to make a difference. Coming here to take up a job that didn't stretch her professionally amongst people who were little more than acquaintances had helped her to heal and given her a measure of peace.

'You won't go back, will you? To Africa...' Maggie's face was suddenly serious.

'No, I don't think I will. Going to Africa was just... it was never really a choice; it was something I just knew would happen. I'll never regret it, or the things that I was able to do there. Or meeting Judd. But I'm not going back.'

'You did more than most of us, Andrea. This is your place now, and that's good too.'

Joe was a doctor, and he knew what her work here consisted of. He must also know that most of her days consisted of bumps and sprains, with the odd broken limb or case of flu to break the monotony. The sense of achievement in the face of heavy odds wasn't so great, but it was all that Andrea could do now, and it *had* to be enough.

'It is what it is. I like it here.'

'I still worry about you, stuck away up here in the mountains. Never meeting anyone…'

'Maggie…' Joe's voice contained a hint of warning. He clearly had his reservations about Maggie's new role as matchmaker.

'It's okay.' Andrea grinned at Joe. 'It's what friends are for.'

Maggie nodded in agreement. 'Of course it is. And Cal is…well, naturally Joe didn't choose him as his best man on that basis, but since he's here…'

Joe put his face in his hands, in an expression of fond exasperation. It was time to surrender gracefully, before Maggie managed to wring any definite promises from her.

'Okay. I heard you. And if I *do* manage to catch up with Cal before the wedding, I'll keep it in mind.' Andrea reached for the folder in her bag. 'And meantime, this is for you. All the arrangements for the wedding.'

'Ooh!' The folder had the desired effect of changing the subject and Maggie flipped through the pages. 'Thank you. This is *so* amazing. Look, Joe, there are stars…'

'The stars indicate who's supposed to be organising what. Pink are for you, Maggie, and blue is for Joe.'

Joe watched as Maggie turned the pages. 'They're all purple and green.'

'Look, here's your stag night. There's a blue one.' Maggie consulted the index and turned to the page.

'Oh, right.' Joe read the entry. 'So…apparently I just have to turn up?'

'That's right. The green stars are for Cal...or...who-ever's up for organising it.' It seemed suddenly too presumptuous to ask anything of him.

'He did promise to do something. I think he'll appreciate the list of venues.' Joe smiled. 'Thank you so much, Andrea. This is fantastic.'

'I *told* you Andrea had everything under control.' Maggie gave him a bright smile, flipping the pages. 'There you are, see. You have to turn up to the wedding, as well.'

Joe chuckled. 'Yeah. I'll be doing that, don't you worry...'

Cal. Green stars. The first had to be introduced to the second at some point. But it seemed that when Cal wasn't holed up in his room, writing emails, or going for early morning walks, he was on the phone. Presumably on calls that lasted a while, because he hadn't joined them for lunch, either.

There was only one conclusion, and it was inescapable. Since Joe had confirmed that his friend wasn't a hermit, and that he'd had several conversations with him since they'd arrived here, Cal must have caught wind of Maggie's matchmaking intentions and was avoiding her. Andrea couldn't help a sinking feeling in the pit of her stomach, accompanied by the sharp tang of disappointment. They were actually two very good reasons why she should keep her distance.

But the wedding wasn't going to organise itself and she was going to have to seek him out sooner or later. Andrea decided to leave that until after her afternoon surgery.

'Andrea.' For once, she hadn't been thinking about him, and the deep, honey-soaked sound of his voice took her by surprise. The bunch of keys that she'd just taken from her handbag to lock the door of the medical suite dropped to the floor with a clatter.

'I'm sorry. I didn't mean to startle you.' Andrea had been about to bend for the keys, but he was there first. As he rose, she caught a hint of his scent. Soap-fresh and yet somehow carrying with it an image of hot nights. Her limbs entwined with his... Andrea swallowed hard as Cal dropped the keys into her hand.

'You didn't. Thank you.' It occurred to Andrea that he might be here for the medical suite, and not her. 'Is there something you needed? You're not sick, are you?'

'Actually, it's you I need.' He frowned suddenly, as if that was a little too blunt for his liking. 'I'm sorry I haven't been around much. I know I need to touch base with you over the arrangements for the wedding, and Joe tells me you have a folder.'

'Yes, I have.'

Good. Cal and the folder. Green stars. Forget about everything else.

'Maybe I could get you a coffee? Whenever you have a moment.'

'Now's good. I only had two people on my list for my surgery and so I have the rest of the afternoon free. I can go and fetch my folder, and join you in the main coffee lounge.'

He nodded. 'Thanks. That's good of you.'

As soon as she'd pointed him in the right direction for the coffee lounge, and watched him turn the corner out into the reception area, Andrea made for the back stairs, and the small apartment that was situated above the medical suite.

Even when he was relaxed and moving slowly, Cal had a kind of energy about him. It was evident in his face and the way he moved, and it held the tantalising promise that anything might be possible. Anything and everything.

Andrea made for the bathroom, splashing cold water onto her face. Anything and everything extended as far as Cal's duties as best man, and no further. There was no place for her wildly beating heart, nor for her fevered imagination; now more than ever she had to be cool and collected. If she showed Cal that she was just as immune to him as he was to her, they could find a way to work together and make sure this wedding went without a hitch.

'Okay.' She squinted at herself in the bathroom mirror, resisting the impulse to put a little lipstick on. 'You know what you have to do. Stop being such a teenager about it.'

The comfortable coffee lounge offered spectacular views of snow-capped mountains, reaching up towards a clear blue sky. Cal was sitting by the window, and Andrea hoped that the panorama would have its usual calming influence on her. Maybe even provide a topic of conversation, if there were any awkward silences.

He was just as mouth-wateringly handsome as he'd been ten minutes ago. Maybe more so—it was difficult to quantify it exactly, particularly when she was trying to ignore it.

'Joe tells me you already have everything well organised.' He rose, waiting for Andrea to sit down before he lowered himself back into his seat. 'I'm planning on following your instructions to the letter.'

Nice. He was obviously keen to lay down a few ground rules, and this one would make everything easier.

'Nothing's set in stone, and I don't want to tread on

your toes, if there's anything that you were planning.'
Andrea bit her tongue. Just a *thank-you* would have
done; it wasn't necessary to invite any further discus-
sion.

Cal nodded thoughtfully, turning with a smile to the
waitress who brought their coffee. Foamy cappuccino,
just the way she liked it. Andrea remembered that his
parting shot had been to ask how she wanted her coffee, and he must have already ordered.

'How did you meet Maggie?' It seemed that Cal was
just as keen as Andrea was to keep the conversation on
the topic of their friends, which was a relief.

'We lived on the same road when we were children.
We've been best friends since we were six. I hear you
met Joe at medical school?'

'Yes, that's right. And you're the in-house doctor for
this hotel complex…'

He stopped speaking, pressing his lips together as
if he'd made a faux pas. Being the doctor here was just
a fact, but the way they'd managed to veer into asking
about each other so quickly was unsettling.

'Yes. I…um…' Andrea took a breath. 'I've brought
the wedding folder.'

She reached into her bag, taking out Cal's copy of
the folder and putting it down on the low table between
them. He nodded, making no move to pick it up.

'It seems we've heard all about each other already.'
He raised one eyebrow, as if he could say more, but was
debating whether that was wise.

'Yes, I suppose so.' There wasn't much doubt that
Maggie had told Cal as much about her as she'd told
Andrea about him. She felt her ears begin to redden,
and wondered what on earth Maggie had found to say.

He was studying her face, and she felt a flush begin

to spread from the back of her neck. This was *very* awkward. Then suddenly he smiled and the ridiculous feeling that she'd known him all her life, and that it wouldn't do any harm to be honest with him, asserted itself. Andrea turned her attention to her coffee, picking up her cup. At the moment, distance seemed a lot less complicated than honest.

Then Cal spoke again.

'I'm getting the sense that Maggie hasn't confined her matchmaking efforts to just me.'

CHAPTER TWO

Cal had been wondering how he might drop this into
the conversation. Whether he even should. But he was
going to have to spend time with Andrea, and she was
clearly just as uneasy in his company as he was in hers.

Her reaction told him that he hadn't been wrong.
She reddened suddenly, and almost spilled her coffee
all over her sweater.

Watching her regain her composure was delightful.
She flashed him a look that gave the impression that
he'd taken her by surprise but it could all be laughed
off. She put her coffee down again, staring at it. Then
she turned her gaze straight onto him.

Beautiful blue-grey eyes. The kind that could reach
down into a man's soul. It felt as if they *were* reaching
into his soul.

'You've saved me the trouble of working out how to
mention it to you.' She gave him a little smile and Cal
felt his heart lurch, beating faster at her command. 'It's
a little awkward, but Maggie doesn't really mean anything by it… Think of it as one of those wedding tradi-
tions that we don't have to comply with.'

She quirked her lips downwards suddenly, as if
she'd said the wrong thing. Cal smiled, wondering if

it would ever be possible for Andrea to say the wrong thing to him.

'That sounds good to me. We can practise non-compliance.' Andrea's charm meant that he'd have to practise a good deal before he got it perfect, but at least they were on the right track now.

'Because I've no intention of...um... I mean...' Andrea reddened furiously. 'I didn't mean that as an insult. It's me, not you.'

It was tempting to pretend he didn't know what she meant. Cal reminded himself that she must be suffering from an agony of embarrassment at the moment.

'I feel just the same. I'm far too set in my ways, and too busy to do any woman the rank disservice of asking her to be more than a friend. Least of all you.'

Somehow it all came out in vaguely understandable sentences, which was a surprise. All Cal was able to think about was the delicate pink of her cheeks, and how much he wanted to touch her skin.

But he'd managed to make his meaning clear. She puffed out a breath of relief.

'Nicely put. I feel the same. Only, I'm not terribly busy, it's more...' She gave a little shrug, the colour draining from her face suddenly. 'Bad break-up.'

Cal nodded. However much he wanted to ask, he should leave it at that. 'We understand each other, then.'

'Yes, we do.'

Why did he feel so disappointed? This was exactly what he'd wanted to happen. Cal brushed the question aside.

'I guess Maggie and Joe are so happy together that they have a hard time imagining anyone would choose anything else.' Cal ventured the observation, and Andrea nodded, smiling.

'That's right. They met when Maggie came here on holiday to visit me. She said she knew he was the one and kept apologising for spending so much time with him and not me. But I was really happy for her.'

'I remember Joe saying something of the sort when he got home. He told me he'd met the woman he wanted to marry. And then two weeks later Maggie told him she didn't want anything more to do with him.'

'She had her reasons. Joe told you…?' Andrea shot him a querying look and Cal nodded. 'She'd just found out that she had breast cancer and she didn't want Joe to feel he had to stick with her.'

'He had no choice. Being there for Maggie wasn't something he even had to think about, he knew that was what he wanted. I told him if that was the way he felt, he needed to stop moping around and convince Maggie of that.'

Andrea chuckled, leaning back in her seat, suddenly at ease. 'And I told her that if she really wanted to be with him, she might consider giving him the benefit of the doubt, and believing him when he said he wanted to be there for her. So I guess we should both take a little of the blame for this wedding.'

That explained a lot. Why Joe had been so sure that Maggie wouldn't change her mind, and then suddenly she had. Cal felt the muscles at the side of his jaw begin to relax. It seemed that he and Andrea felt the same way about more than one thing.

'I'm very happy to do that.'

'Me too.'

'In that case…' He leaned forward, picking up the wedding folder. 'I think I have some reading to do, to catch up.'

'Perhaps I should leave you to it. We can meet up

again later.' It seemed that Andrea wanted out of here suddenly and she sprang to her feet. Having her close prompted much the same set of conflicting feelings in Cal's heart. He couldn't bear the thought of her leaving, but he knew that it would bring relief from having to constantly remind himself that he mustn't reach forward and touch her hand.

Whatever she wanted to do was fine with him. He should let her know that he'd be there when she wanted him, and not when she didn't. Cal supressed a smile at the irony of the notion. Allowing someone else to dictate his actions was new territory for him.

'Shall we discuss it a bit more over dinner?'

Andrea hesitated, and when she nodded, gratification swelled through Cal's heart. 'Yes, dinner would be okay. The hotel has a crepe bar and a pizzeria. The restaurant's nice too.'

'How about the restaurant?' He had no doubt that pizzas or crepes would be good options, but a restaurant implied three courses and a little more time to sit and talk. To drink in Andrea's way of getting straight to his heart.

'Yes, that's fine.' She didn't hesitate. It seemed that Andrea had no objections to spending a little more time with him. 'Eight o'clock?'

'That sounds good. I'll see you then.'

He watched her go. Not as a courtesy, in case she turned, but because he couldn't drag his gaze away from her, or from the entrance to the coffee lounge, until he was absolutely sure that she wasn't going to return.

Cal Lewis. Out of control and craving one last glimpse of a woman. If Cal had confided that to Joe he would have seen the irony of it too. Maybe made a smiling enquiry about whether this was love at first sight, which Cal would have rejected out of hand.

Because Cal had always been *in* control. His parents' tug of love with each other had turned into a tug of war when Cal was ten and they'd divorced. From then on it had been a matter of having to steer a centre course between two parents who had each wanted him to take their side.

Cal had learned to ignore their differing ambitions for him, and quietly pursue his own course. If love meant he had to live his life according to someone else's aspirations, then he wanted no part of it. He'd dedicated himself to his studies, and then to his work, never allowing a woman to entwine him in the sticky threads of commitment.

And then, Mary. She'd been a good friend, and Cal had thought they saw eye to eye. She knew his track record, and it was she who'd suggested their on-off relationship as being the obvious answer for two busy people. Then she'd fallen in love, and Cal hadn't.

He had no excuses for hurting Mary so badly. He'd cared for her deeply, but he hadn't loved her, and he didn't know how to give what she was asking of him.

'There's something missing in you, Cal...'

He felt Mary's words had been slightly unfair because the thing that was missing in Cal was the very thing that had attracted her to him in the first place. But the words could be forgiven, because they had come from a place of hurt, and they were true. Love took compromise, bending to fit with another person's life and values, and he just didn't have that in him. He would never hurt someone again the way he'd hurt Mary.

He flipped open Andrea's folder. Love was for other people, not for him. He might be a control freak when it came to guiding his own destiny, unwilling to compromise and unable to commit, but at least he knew what he was. And for the next two weeks, he was Joe's friend, here to help with the wedding.

Really? Andrea hadn't spent more than half an hour with Cal, and already it seemed she'd entered into some kind of collusion with him. She'd come dangerously close to mentioning the hurt that she never talked about, and which she'd come here to escape. And then...

Then he'd said they understood each other. And Andrea's agreement hadn't been born from a wish to be polite—she felt that Cal really did understand her, and that she understood him. Which was ridiculous, because she hardly knew him.

It's done now. Get on with it.

Andrea murmured the words to herself as she walked towards the large suite that Maggie and Joe were occupying. She didn't have to examine every little thing that they'd both said so closely. She should concentrate on the matter in hand.

She found Maggie alone in the suite, the crumpled bedcovers and the book which lay open on the pillows showing that Maggie was doing exactly what Andrea wanted her to: relaxing. But now it seemed that Maggie not only wanted to talk, she wanted every detail of Andrea's meeting with Cal.

'You're having *dinner* with him, then.' Maggie made it sound as if sitting at the same table while eating was exciting and seductive. Andrea had been trying to convince herself it was neither exciting nor seductive ever since the idea had been mooted.

'Someone's got to keep him company. And I'm

starting to feel that three's a crowd where you and Joe are concerned.'

'Never.' Maggie reached forward, pulling Andrea down to sprawl on the bed with her. 'Three's just right when it's you.'

'It's nice of you to say so. But you and Joe are on your own for this evening.'

'Hmm.' Maggie was clearly pleased by the thought. 'Where are you going?'

'What, so you can book a table and keep me under surveillance?'

'No!' The thought had obviously occurred to Maggie. 'So we can go somewhere else and leave you in peace.'

'You don't need to do that either. But we will be talking about the wedding, so you and Joe aren't invited. We're going to the main restaurant.'

'Very nice. Okay, so I think I fancy something light this evening. Crepes, maybe.'

'Or you could have room service. Oysters and champagne...?' Andrea teased her friend.

'That's a thought. Although Joe isn't a big fan of oysters, we might just have the champagne...' Maggie quirked the corners of her lips down. 'I'm being a pain, aren't I?'

'Yes.' Andrea leaned forward, hugging her friend. 'But don't ever give up on me, will you? I'd hate that.'

'I just want you to be happy. Cal's a lovely guy, but it's not really about him. You'll never know what you want if you don't get out and meet new people.'

Andrea swallowed down the temptation to say that it was *all* about Cal at the moment. All about that nagging feeling that maybe she was a little stuck, and that Cal had the power to pull her free. She already knew what she wanted, and it was her quiet little life here. Calm and uneventful, it had given her the ability to function when the world she'd known, the world she'd chosen, had been torn apart.

'It's all about possibilities.'

Maggie was all smiles now. 'Yeah. Possibilities…'

They'd already unpacked Maggie's wedding dress, and hung it carefully in the wardrobe, but a small second case still lay untouched on the luggage rack. Andrea got to her feet, and lifted it over onto the bed.

'You're going to Bridesmaidzilla me again, aren't you?' Maggie's grin told Andrea that she didn't mind in the slightest.

'Someone has to. I want to make sure you've brought everything, so I can tick a few things off my list.'

'You don't need to go and try on some options for what to wear for dinner?' Maggie shot her an innocent look.

'No. It doesn't take me three hours to decide what to wear for anything; my wardrobe isn't that big.' Something to take her mind off dinner, until Andrea absolutely *had* to think about it, was a much better modus operandi.

'Whatever you say.' Maggie sat up, unzipping the suitcase.

Cal had thought about wearing a suit, but decided that would be far too formal. When he arrived in the hotel's large restaurant, it was obvious that his choice of an open-necked shirt and sweater blended in with everyone else here, and waiting for Andrea to arrive gave him the opportunity to wonder why on earth he'd given the matter a second thought. What to wear didn't usually come so high on his list of priorities.

He saw her enter, stopping to speak to one of the

waiters, who pointed her in the right direction. Cal couldn't help watching as she hurried towards him.

The dark curls around her face, her blue-grey eyes, were a stunning and ever-changing form of beauty. Her dark blue top and trousers couldn't hide the way she moved, and seemed to be an exercise in understated perfection. She would have been perfect anywhere, wearing anything.

He rose as she approached and she smiled awkwardly, before regaining her composure. A waiter pulled back her seat for her, and she turned to make eye contact with him as she thanked him. Cal almost begrudged the man those few moments of her attention.

'Sorry I'm late. I've been helping Maggie unpack the rest of the things she brought for the wedding.'

'Everything's survived the journey?' Joe had almost knocked someone over in his eagerness to get to the luggage carousel at the airport, and reclaim the cases that held Maggie's wedding dress, and other unspecified items that were necessary for the wedding.

'Yes. We unpacked the wedding dress yesterday and it has a couple of little creases but they'll steam out. Everything else is all present and correct, so I can tick all of that off my list.'

Cal had spent the last few hours acquainting himself with Andrea's lists, and the folder she'd given him lay ready on the table. The first page covered the arrangements for yesterday, and quite a few details that had seemed to him to have happened by chance turned out to have been carefully planned: the hotel minibus that had turned up just at the right moment; the ride on the funicular railway that had been waiting for them at the station; even the rose that the conductor had presented Maggie with was there, and had been neatly ticked off.

Then there were pages to track the arrival of guests and family, which rooms were booked for them, along with dietary requirements and special arrangements for children and the elderly members of the wedding party. The cake had been made and was apparently stored in the hotel's kitchen. The venues for the wedding and reception, both of which were to be held here at the hotel, had been photographed and there was a seating plan, along with an itinerary for the wedding day.

'Your folder's impressive. You've done something like this before?' The whole thing smacked of maximum forethought and minimum fuss.

'No. But it's much the same as arranging anything, isn't it?'

'I suppose so.' The clinic that Cal worked for could do with the kind of attention to detail and organisational ability that was displayed here. If Andrea was as good a doctor as she was a wedding organiser, then her talents were wasted on sprains and bruises at a smart skiing resort.

'If there's anything I've missed…' The way her lower lip quivered slightly at the thought of something that had escaped her attention was delightful.

'I can't think of a thing. I'll follow up on your list of places to go for the stag night.'

She blushed a perfect shade of embarrassed pink. 'I…um… I didn't want to step on your toes, but I thought… Just in case you didn't already have somewhere in mind…'

'No, I had nowhere in mind. I was going to ask you for some suggestions, along with the number of a local cab company.' The relevant page had the numbers of three taxi services, typed in a clear, bold font, presumably in an attempt to counteract any blurred vision that might occur at the end of the evening.

'Ah. Well, it's all there, and you've got plenty of time to scout them out.'

Cal wondered if Andrea might be persuaded to go with him. As he turned the thought over in his mind, it seemed far too precious to dismiss entirely, and he decided to put it on hold in favour of ticking another few items off Andrea's list.

'I have the rings, they're locked in the safe in my room. And I saw your email about photographs. I have some old ones of Joe from our time at medical school.'

She gave him a thrilling smile. 'Perfect. I have loads of Maggie from when we were growing up, and it'll be nice to include a few embarrassing ones of Joe as well.'

'I'll let you sort through them.' Cal picked up the menu, raising one eyebrow. 'Any suggestions?'

She laughed, just as she was meant to. 'No, I'm not that much of an organisational freak. You're on your own with that.'

Ordering their meal, eating it, and discussing the arrangements set out in her folder carried them through the next hour, but coffee brought one of those awkward silences.

'So…' Andrea cleared her throat awkwardly. 'What do you do? Apart from being a doctor, I mean…'

She wanted to go there? Cal had kept the conversation deliberately impersonal in an attempt to make it clear that he wasn't about to embarrass her by going along with Maggie's plans for them. But her interest prompted a pleasant tingling feeling at the back of his neck.

'I work for an organisation based in London, which

specialises in helping patients worldwide who don't have access to the medical facilities they need.'

'Really?' Something ignited behind the cool blue-grey of Andrea's eyes. 'Tell me more…'

Maybe he shouldn't. Cal's work was the one area in his life he was passionate about, and he'd promised that passion should have no part in his relationship with Andrea. But he couldn't help himself.

'We have a two-pronged strategy. We have facilities for complex surgeries in London, and part of my work is to assess referrals from doctors overseas and care for patients there.'

Andrea nodded. 'And the other part?'

'Simple, everyday surgeries, available locally, can make an enormous difference. We work to provide surgical support to doctors and patients in their own countries. That's done partly by travelling surgical teams, but mainly by helping build facilities and providing the equipment that's needed. Along with maintenance, of course.'

Andrea smiled, suddenly. 'That's the crucial part, isn't it? Often it's the supply of spare parts for things like X-ray machines which is the most problematic.'

So she understood the issues. And she cared about them—Cal could see that in her face.

'Yes. We pledge to maintain the equipment we supply and a lot of our effort goes into that.'

'And what's your role exactly? Are you based in London?'

The desire to tell her everything about himself was as strong as the yearning to touch her. Stronger maybe, because it felt so much more personal.

'I spend about half my time in London, and half at

our projects worldwide. My role's a mixture of surgical work and patient care, along with planning and strategy.'

He could almost feel her gaze tingling across his cheek, before it dropped to his hands, and then retreated to her own fingers, resting twined together on the table between them.

'It sounds like a very rewarding job.'

'It is. It's difficult sometimes, not being in one place for any appreciable length of time…' He fell silent. The stock excuse for his solitary lifestyle felt awkward at the moment. As if it broke the connection that had formed between them.

'Yes. I imagine so. You chose your job over your personal life, then?' Andrea was looking at him now, as if the answer meant something to her.

'I guess so. Not consciously, but that's the way things have worked out.'

She raised one eyebrow. Maybe she saw straight through him, and knew that he'd thought about it more than he would admit. That he'd always struggled with relationships, and then when he'd hurt Mary so badly, he'd decided to back away from that side of his life.

'Consciously enough that you know you're not going there, though.'

Maybe she was looking for reassurance, that what he'd said about not wanting a relationship wasn't just a reaction to Maggie's matchmaking, but a decision that he stuck to.

'Yeah. Enough for that. What about you?' Quid pro quo.

'Me?' She gave a little shrug. 'I thought the world was full of choices when I left medical school. I had a great job and I was engaged to someone I worked with.

Then it all went rather badly wrong and… This is my happy place.'

Which rather supposed that everywhere else was Andrea's unhappy place. Cal wondered just how badly something had to go wrong for that to happen. The impression she gave, that everything was under control, seemed to be just a protective shell. Beneath it she was vulnerable, and that was one very good reason for Cal to keep his distance.

'It's…a beautiful place to be happy in.' Outside, the floodlights illuminated a winter's fairy-tale landscape, and during the day the view from here would be as spectacular as all the other views from the hotel's windows.

'Not always as fulfilling as I'd like. But yes, it's a beautiful place.' There was a sadness in Andrea's tone that seemed to betray a knowledge that she could do more. At least he still had a world full of good places, and it seemed a shame that someone like her should have settled for so little.

A little shake of her head indicated that she was done with that conversation, though. However much he wanted to pursue it, it was important that Cal respected her boundaries.

'Have you tried snowboarding?' She was staring out of the window.

'No. I'm hoping to get a little skiing in, though.'

'I've never tried it either.' She gave a little shrug. 'Which is actually quite outrageous, given that I've been living here for two years now. Maggie and Joe have a lesson booked tomorrow morning and I was thinking of going with them…'

The unasked question hung in the air between them. It suddenly felt that Cal had been missing out on something all his life, and that snowboarding was the one and only thing he needed to do tomorrow.

'Do you know if there's a spare place in the class?'

'I did happen to check.' She twisted her mouth in a flash of dry humour. 'Yes. There is.'

This was okay. He didn't need to avoid Andrea, as if she were some dangerous creature that could rock his whole world. Cal could get to know her a little, and still stay within the boundaries he'd set for himself, because she had boundaries too. He'd stuck to his life plan up till now, and he could keep doing so.

'It would be remiss of me to pass that opportunity up, then. What time tomorrow...?'

CHAPTER THREE

THIS WAS *NOT* a date. Andrea had that thought firmly fixed in her mind. Maggie and Joe would be there, and if three was a crowd, then four was a positive army of people. She and Cal were on the same page with this, neither of them were minded to take any notice of Maggie's matchmaking. It was going to be just fine.

Even so, the look in Maggie's eyes when Cal had mentioned over breakfast that he'd be joining them this morning had said it all. Learning a new skill that would likely end up with her falling flat on her face was perhaps best avoided if romance was on the cards. Even Joe had looked quietly appalled.

But then, this wasn't a date. When the class had been divided into two, it was okay that Maggie and Joe were in the other group. And Cal betrayed none of that eagerness to impress that might spark the tinderbox of Andrea's fears.

'Slowly…' She heard Francine, the instructor, murmur quietly as he tackled the downhill slope for the first time. He was almost at the bottom when he fell, prompting a shock of concern that made Andrea clap her hand over her mouth. But then he climbed to his feet, grinning, and brushing the snow from his jacket.

'Don't do it like that. Watch out for your shoulder,'

Francine reminded Andrea as she positioned herself at the top of the slope.

Andrea nodded. The temptation to forget all about the old injury to her left shoulder, and the craving for the same kind of fearlessness that Cal showed, should be resisted. She wasn't unbreakable any more.

But her shoulder was stable now, and she'd remembered to wear a support under her jacket, just in case. If the worst came to the worst, then at least there was a doctor on hand...

The thought of Cal having to snap her shoulder back into its proper position was far worse than any pain she might experience. That wasn't going to happen. She wasn't going to fall.

Her first attempt at the beginners' course was a little slower than everyone else's, but she managed to keep her balance. Cal was waiting at the bottom, and gave her a delicious smile.

'Nice one.'

Andrea quirked her lips down. She'd made it to the bottom, but not without compromise. 'I didn't go as fast as you...'

'Francine told us to go slowly for starters. I should have listened.'

'Is that an option for you? Giving it less than one hundred per cent?' The words slipped out. For some reason it was proving easy to treat Cal as if she'd known him all her life, and Andrea had to keep reminding herself that he was really just an acquaintance.

He chuckled as if they *had* known each other all their lives. They walked back up the slope together in companionable silence, but he'd clearly taken the comment to heart. When it was Cal's turn to try again, he shot her a conspiratorial smile, holding up seven fingers.

Giving it seventy per cent worked. He made it to the bottom without falling and Francine gave a nod of approval.

Maybe it was the thumbs-up sign he'd aimed in her direction from the bottom of the slope that had made her knees wobble with pleasure. Maybe it was because she sensed he was watching her every move as she prepared for her second descent. Or maybe she just hit a bump in the snow…

The feeling of falling dragged a panicked cry from her lips. She hit the ground, rolling over onto her shoulder, and a growling pain reminded her that she'd been tempted past the limits that she'd set for herself.

'I'm okay. I'm okay…' She felt a hand on her arm, and knew it was Cal's.

'Sure you are. Stay down for a moment and catch your breath.' His voice was very close, and very reassuring. Andrea opened her eyes, focussing on his face.

That gaze. The one that seemed to know her through and through, and which seemed to accept everything it saw. It was probably just an illusion, but it felt all too real. She took a breath, and as the shock of falling subsided, her shoulder began to throb.

'Anything starting to hurt now?' He was on one knee, next to her.

'Um… No, I think I'm all right.' Andrea's hand drifted to her shoulder before she could stop it and she saw that Cal hadn't missed the gesture.

'Your shoulder?'

'It's fine,' she replied quickly and he raised his eyebrows.

'Is that one hundred per cent fine?'

Andrea ignored him, sitting up in the snow. 'Give me an arm up, will you?'

He leaned forward, his arm coiling around her waist. That wasn't quite what Andrea had meant, but the feel of his body against hers was enough to silence any protest. And she had to admit that it was the most efficient way of propelling her to her feet.

'Okay?' Cal was very close, his arm still protectively around her.

'Yes. Thanks. Okay.' His scent rendered anything approaching a sentence out of the question. When he let her go, she couldn't step away from him for a moment. Cal's bulk, the sheer strength of his body, was mesmerising.

Then he stepped back. Andrea watched as he retrieved her snowboard, tucking it under his arm along with her own. One more small intimacy that only seemed to fuel the one massive intimacy that was growing in her imagination.

They walked together back up to the top of the slope. From here, they could see the steeper slopes, planted with yellow-and-black warning flags after last night's snowfall. And despite them, two figures were weaving their way down, their paths criss-crossing in the pristine layer of snow.

'Francine...' Andrea turned and Francine looked up, her face hardening as she saw the snowboarders.

'*Arrêtez...!* I told them to stay off that slope this morning, but some people just can't resist fresh powder.' Francine turned to the other instructor. 'Bruno, will you finish up here for me?'

But it was already too late. As Francine made for one of the skidoos that was parked at the top of the ridge, one of the snowboarders seemed to waver from the precise formation, crashing into the other. As they both fell, a layer of snow seemed to detach itself, sliding after them.

She heard Francine's curse as she ran for the skidoo. The snowboarders were tumbling down the slope, but couldn't stay ahead of the rumbling mass of snow that followed them.

Bruno had already reached the skidoos, and started one of them up. Francine jumped on the back, hanging onto him as he set off around the curve of the ridge. Andrea made for the second skidoo, knowing without having to look that Cal was hard on her heels.

'Did you see where they fell?'

'Right there.' Cal pointed to a spot at the bottom of the slope. He was waiting for her to take her lead, and his confidence in her chipped away at her own fears.

'Okay, keep your eye on that spot while I drive. It's easy to get disoriented, and we have to find them fast...'

No more explanation was needed. Cal nodded, grabbing one of the helmets that hung from the handlebars, and Andrea climbed onto the skidoo. She put her own helmet on, and twisted the ignition key, feeling the all too welcome warmth of his body as he climbed onto the narrow seat behind her.

She followed in the tracks of Bruno and Francine's skidoo, knowing that they'd be taking the safest and most direct route to the fallen snowboarders. As they neared the bottom of the steep incline, Andrea could see a bright red flash of clothing as a figure got unsteadily to its feet. It looked as if one of the snowboarders had escaped relatively unharmed, but she couldn't see the other.

'Help us... Help...' It was a man's voice, filled with panic and desperation. Francine stopped the skidoo next to him, and he almost collapsed into her arms. Bruno sat him down, talking to him.

'He says he's okay.' Francine jogged across to Andrea as she got off the skidoo. 'Bruno will make sure, while we look for the other one.'

'Okay. Cal...' Andrea turned to find him but he wasn't there. Cal was trekking away from them, in a determined line across the snow.

'Here.' He stopped suddenly, turning towards them. 'I last saw them here.'

Francine gave him a nod of approval. 'Good. Then we start looking a little lower down.'

'Have we called for reinforcements?' Cal returned to where Andrea was standing, and murmured the words to her.

'Yes, Francine's got an alarm pager that she uses if anything happens on the slopes. They'll be here soon. We have drills every month, so everyone knows what to do. Do you have your transceiver with you? You'll need to switch it off now.'

He nodded, pulling the small unit out from under his sweater, and fiddling with it to switch it off, so that its signal wouldn't override that of the person who was buried in the snow.

'Great idea to have the hotel give these out to anyone going out on the slopes.' He grinned at Andrea. 'Yours?'

His smile was good to have, especially now that her suggestion that the hotel made sure everyone was carrying transceivers might save someone's life. 'It's part of our new safety plan.'

'Can I assume that was your idea too? Since you seem to know what everyone's about to do next.'

She felt a blush starting to reach up from the back of her neck, towards the cool air on her cheeks. Cal had seen past the swift reactions to the carefully constructed plan that Andrea had put into place.

'It's part of my job. Prevention is always better than a cure.'

He nodded. Andrea had done everything she could to avoid facing another life-or-death situation alone, and there was something very reassuring about Cal's presence—the way he was so calm, and yet ready to throw off that relaxed way of his at a moment's notice.

Francine was skiing in a wide circle, trying to locate the transceiver signal from the person buried in the snow. It must be ten minutes now…

The vision of Judd, so badly injured that she'd been unable to do anything for him, brought tears to her eyes. Then panic began to seep steadily into her body, fuelled by the low throb of pain in her shoulder. She was losing it, letting her fears govern her actions.

'Do the skidoos carry something we can dig with?' Cal's voice cut through the visions in her head.

'Um… Yes.' Andrea hung onto the calm in his voice, feeling it pull her back into the here and now. 'I'll get the kits.'

Shaking, she unpacked the probes and shovels from the skidoo, handing Cal one of each. 'You know how to use the probe?'

'Right angles to the surface, and feel for soft resistance?' Clearly he did, but he was checking with her. Or maybe he'd seen her falter, and was checking *on* her.

'Yes, that's right. As soon as Francine gets a hit on the transceiver, we can spread out and probe…'

Francine's voice sounded, and Andrea turned to see her signalling from a spot ten metres further down from where Cal had indicated. He'd done well in remembering it so precisely; it had shaved precious minutes off the time needed to find the buried snowboarder. Bruno was running over to join them now, and the small rescue party spread out and began to carefully probe the snow.

'Got something.' Cal fell to his knees, starting to dig with his hands. Almost immediately, he uncovered what looked like a discarded glove, but when he took hold of it the fingers gripped his tight. Cal started to clear the snow with his other hand, and Andrea ran to help him.

He wasn't letting go. Good. His tight grip was the one thing that gave the person beneath the snow hope at this moment. Andrea dug frantically, ignoring the sudden pain in her shoulder, and Francine and Bruno ran to help her.

She uncovered the second arm, this one thrown up as if to protect someone's face. When she moved it, she saw a woman's features, dazed and frightened. She was struggling to breathe, and Andrea tried to move the snow that covered her chest, while Cal cleared the snow from her face.

Pain shot through her shoulder again, so bad this time that it momentarily paralysed her arm. Andrea groaned and saw Cal's gaze flip up towards her.

'Shield her face, while Francine and Bruno dig.' No questions asked. Just a quick assessment of the situation, and exactly what was needed.

Andrea shifted along, carefully protecting the woman's face as Cal and the others dug furiously. The woman's chest was quickly exposed, and slow, shallow breaths turned into a deep gasp for air. Then she began to cry.

'Okay… You're okay.' Andrea tried to comfort her, in English first and then French. When she tried Italian, the woman's eyes opened suddenly, frightened and imploring.

'She's breathing better now.' The woman's lips were blue from the cold and lack of oxygen, but now that the pressure of snow on her chest was removed she could draw breath.

Cal nodded. 'It looks as if she landed feet first. We'll have to dig down a little further to free her legs.'

They'd cleared just the first hurdle. The woman was alive and breathing, but there was no way of knowing what injuries she'd sustained. They had to get her out before the effects of shock and cold weakened her even further.

Cal and Bruno were shovelling snow, while Francine moved the quickly growing piles back and out of their way. Bruno was trained for this, but Cal kept pace with him, tirelessly. Andrea kept a tight hold on the woman's hand, shielding her face and speaking to her to reassure her.

She could hear the deep growl of the snow ambulance, distant at first and now closer. The fully tracked vehicle carried the rescue and medical equipment needed to get the woman off the slope and transport her back down to the hotel, and it had brought reinforcements too. Two men grabbed the shovels from Cal and Bruno and they both moved back, breathless from their exertions.

'That's enough.' Cal's voice sounded, and Andrea looked around as silence fell. The woman's legs had been uncovered, and everyone stood back as he reached down into the deep well in the snow.

His examination was quick, but as thorough as the conditions allowed. He could only check for the most obvious of injuries at this stage, and Andrea watched the woman's face carefully for any signs of pain.

'Can we move her?' Cal's gaze connected with hers

suddenly. With his expertise to help her, Andrea felt equal to the decision.

'Yes.' She looked up at the paramedic who had arrived with the snowcat. 'Tomas, we'll take spinal injury precautions.'

Tomas nodded. He already had everything ready, and passed a neck brace to Cal. Andrea reassured the woman, stepping back to allow Cal and Tomas room to work.

They'd done it. Together. She'd been so close to giving into the blurred panic that robbed her of her ability to help others, but Cal had been there for her, and Andrea had managed to keep functioning. The collective sigh of relief as the woman was lifted from the hole seemed to be a milestone for her, as well as their patient.

Andrea hesitated before climbing aboard the snowcat, reaching out awkwardly to grab the handhold with her right hand. Without thinking, Cal reached for her, boosting her up into the vehicle. Concern for the woman buried in the snow had driven everything else from his mind, but now that she'd been strapped into the carrycot and transported to the snow ambulance, he had a moment to think about Andrea.

The smooth, effective procedures were Andrea's doing. She was no stranger to taking on emergency situations, and when she'd faltered it hadn't been through any lack of experience. Too much experience, maybe. He'd seen the look in her eyes, the long-distance stare that focussed back onto something else, beyond the situation that had presented itself today.

'It all went rather badly wrong.'

He'd seen the evidence of her words, today. Not in

her actions, but in her face. Suddenly Cal wanted to know *what* had gone so wrong for her.

But those questions could wait. There were more pressing issues on his mind now. Tomas had taken charge of the other snowboarder, helping him into the snow ambulance and strapping him into a seat.

'How's your shoulder?' he asked.

Andrea was now bending over the young woman they'd lifted from the snow, reassuring her. If Cal had seen that this was hard for her, she'd given no suggestion of that to their patient.

'It's okay. An old injury...'

'You sit.' He indicated the spare seat, next to Tomas. 'I'll keep an eye on our patient on the way down.'

She nodded. Andrea knew her limitations, and that Cal would find it easier to grab hold of something to steady himself as the snow ambulance transported them down to the clinic. The feeling of being part of a jigsaw puzzle, and fitting neatly together with the people he worked with, wasn't new to Cal. But when it had happened with Andrea, there was a level of intimacy that he hadn't experienced before.

The woman was drowsy still, alternating between moments of extreme distress and listlessness. Cal was rather more worried about the listlessness, as distress was a natural reaction to the terrifying experience of being buried alive. The snow ambulance was well equipped, and he busied himself with basic checks on her status, trying to reassure her as he did so.

'Va tutto bene.' He heard Andrea's voice behind him, giving him the Italian words that he was struggling to recollect. He repeated them, and saw the woman calm a little.

The vehicle came to a halt and Andrea was first off,

climbing down awkwardly. He and Tomas lifted the
carrycot carefully and he found himself in a covered
area with swing doors at the far end. Andrea held them
open, and he helped carry the woman through into a
large and well-equipped medical bay.

Andrea spoke to a woman who came to meet them,
then turned to Tomas to ask him to take charge of the
other snowboarder. The she turned to Cal.

'The air ambulance will be here in fifteen minutes.
Which means we have some time to prepare her for
the ride.'

'Okay. Gentle warming and observation?'

Andrea nodded. 'Yes, I think so.'

She took charge of the paperwork, writing everything down in a neat, precise hand. The woman's name
was Giulia, and now that they were here Cal could see
that she was little more than a girl. She had no relatives
here at the hotel and had come with a group of friends,
who had all gone out to the local village this morning.
The hotel staff had called them, but they wouldn't be
back until the funicular railway delivered its next group
of passengers.

As warmth began to penetrate her body, Giulia began
to cry and Andrea comforted her tenderly. Cal kept a
close eye on the screen that displayed her vitals, and
when he removed her boots her ankle was a dark pur-
plish colour and began to swell almost immediately. Andrea pointed him towards a cupboard, which he found
held every kind of splint imaginable, and he chose a
temporary inflatable cast for Giulia's ankle.

She'd be in good hands. When the air-ambulance
crew arrived, they were kind and efficient, and Andrea
clearly knew them, so he was happy to leave Giulia in
their care. As the helicopter rose from its landing pad

on the roof, Andrea turned to him, scooping her curls back from her face.

'Thanks for your help.' She twisted her mouth down. 'So much for you being on holiday.'

'Holiday's a relative term.' He grinned, wondering if he could tease her a little. 'And Maggie told me the other day that she found dedication very attractive in a man.'

Andrea smirked, leaning towards him. 'Yeah, she mentioned that to me, too. I don't want to burst your bubble, but I think she's referring to Joe.'

Laughing out loud with her was so very easy, so natural, and it helped lift the remains of the tension that was still pressing on his chest.

'I thought as much. Although I'm suitably crushed.' He ventured another observation. 'Dedication's one thing, though. Putting together the procedures and training that make a rescue operation go as smoothly as this one is *really* impressive.'

He only needed to glance at Andrea to get the answer he was looking for. Her awkward smile betrayed her, showing that the slick organisation and thorough training of everyone involved was probably her doing.

'I'm guessing that you had a hand in that...?' When she didn't answer, he pressed a little further.

'The doctor who was here last wasn't very proactive. If there was an accident on the slopes, he'd step back and let the mountain-rescue team and the air-ambulance crews deal with it. I felt that there was a bit more that we could do in the time it took for those specialists to get here.'

Cal nodded. 'I think Giulia should be grateful that's your approach. It worked well.' No time had been lost in sending Giulia down to the hospital. She'd been brought off the slopes quickly and efficiently, so that she could be properly examined and prepared for the journey. Andrea's definition of a 'happy place' clearly didn't include just sitting back and going with the flow.

They strolled together from the helipad, taking the lift back downstairs. He saw Andrea wince slightly as she reached for the door of the surgery, and Cal reminded himself that she'd already brushed away his concern for her.

Suddenly he didn't care. He was on thin ice, skating dangerously close to shifting professional involvement onto a personal level. But she was hurt, and the only way he knew how to respond to that was with concern.

'Your shoulder's still bothering you?' He leaned forward, opening the door that led back into the clinic, and they both stood for a moment waiting for the other to go first. 'After you.'

Andrea grinned up at him. 'Nice manners. Dedication. No wonder Maggie's been getting all the wrong ideas.'

That sounded like a change of subject, which meant that her shoulder *was* still hurting. Andrea was heading towards the other treatment room, where Tomas was with the other snowboarder, and she didn't seem inclined to look back. That was okay. He could wait.

CHAPTER FOUR

CAL WAS GETTING more and more difficult to handle. Andrea had just about managed to blind herself to the fact that, not only was he very handsome, but he also had that indefinable quality that turned good looks into touch-me-now sexiness. She couldn't *quite* blind herself completely, but she had it under control.

Then he'd added his smile into the equation. His rock-steady presence, which had kept her focussed on the search for Giulia and not on the pain of the past. They'd worked well together, and Cal seemed to understand all her strengths and weaknesses.

No one could be expected to hold out against all that for long. And then Andrea remembered why she was here. Why she'd run away from everything and made a life up here in the mountains. Her happy place. Or, at least, the place where she could find a little peace.

Then Cal added one more entry to the list of things that recommended him. When she arrived back in the main treatment room, everything was spick and span, the mess of emergency medical treatment all cleared away.

'I thought you would have gone by now...'

'I was waiting to see whether you were going to give

me an answer to my question about your shoulder. And to see how Tomas's patient was doing.'

Cal's easy-going manner and his smile made his words sound less confrontational than they might have done. All the same, she ignored the first question in favour of the second.

'He's fine. He had a lucky escape. He was thrown clear and he's just got a few bruises.'

'I expect he's pretty worried about Giulia.'

Andrea twisted the corners of her mouth down. 'I told him she was on her way to the hospital and that she'd be well looked after there. He wasn't too concerned about that; he only met her last night. They had a few drinks together and he persuaded her to meet up with him again this morning for snowboarding.'

'Ah. So he won't be visiting her at the hospital, then.'

'I wouldn't imagine so. I'll wait here for her friends to get back, and I'll go down with them to the hospital if they want me to.'

'After you've done something about your shoulder, eh?'

His concern was chipping away at her defences. And the hint of male assertiveness was more than a little attractive. Andrea frowned at him and he pulled a face, frowning back.

'I saw how much it was hurting you. We could spend a moment exploring why you think that kind of pain should be ignored, if you like.'

'Or we could just get on and ignore it, without making so much fuss.' Andrea jutted her chin out at him.

'Yeah, we could do that. I'm not going to insult your intelligence by pretending to think that's okay...'

Please! Could he please just do *something* that made him seem less perfect? Just the once would be fine.

'I dislocated my shoulder in a car accident. It didn't heal well, and I had surgery to stabilise the joint last year. Sometimes it hurts a little...' Andrea lapsed into silence as he leaned back against the counter top, folding his arms. He was giving her the 'don't be a hero' look that she reserved for her most stubborn patients.

'All right, then.' She walked over to the treatment couch, sitting down on it. 'It *does* hurt. And I'd be grateful if you could take a look at it.'

He nodded quietly, clearly not feeling the need for an 'I told you so'. One more thing to like about him. Turning towards the sink, he started to wash his hands while Andrea pulled her sweater over her head.

'Ow!' Raising her arm hurt a great deal more than she'd thought it would. She heard his footsteps, and then felt his hand, gently steadying her arm.

'Just relax, would you...?'

There wasn't much choice. And relaxing against Cal, as he carefully disentangled her from the folds of her sweater, felt good. Great, even. His clean scent seemed to curl around her in remembrance of the pleasure that being close to someone could afford. Andrea pulled at the hook-and-loop fastening of her shoulder support, thankful that she'd worn a sleeveless vest underneath for extra warmth.

He didn't meet her gaze. Laying the sweater down next to her, he walked around the couch to adjust it to the right height for him to examine her shoulder properly. Then she felt his fingers, tender on her skin.

'Anterior dislocation...?'

He must be able to see that from the scars, one blotched and ragged from the accident, and a thinner, straighter one from the surgery.

'Ten out of ten.' She heard the sarcasm in her tone—

one last-ditch attempt to resist the things she didn't want to feel. 'Sorry. Doctors make the worst patients...'

'So I've been told.' He chuckled quietly.

She felt his fingers, light on her shoulder. Andrea squeezed her eyes shut, trying not to think about his scent and the warmth of his body against hers. *He* wasn't aware of all that; he was entirely focussed on the task in hand.

'Have you seen all you need to see?' She couldn't stand much more of this. She was either going to turn and embrace him, or slap him away, and the second felt like a much safer option than the first.

'You must be a really great doctor, because you're a terrible patient.' He didn't seem in the slightest bit fazed by the sharpness in Andrea's tone. 'Give me another moment. When did you have the op?'

Andrea puffed out a sigh. Cal was actually trying to help her, and she shouldn't be so confrontational with him.

'Just over a year ago. The accident was two years before that but my shoulder never healed properly. It slipped out again while we were doing a rescue practice, and I went home last summer and had it fixed.'

'Looks as if it's healed well; it feels stable.' His fingers closed around her arm and Andrea concentrated on not resisting him as he flexed her shoulder, testing the movement. 'It's a little stiff. Been doing your exercises?'

'I've been a little busy. With the wedding.'

'Right.'

Andrea waited for him to say that was a poor excuse. Or that keeping her exercises up, even after her shoulder seemed fully healed, was important. Since he obviously wasn't going to, she might as well say it herself.

'I know. They only take twenty minutes...'

'Yeah.'

'I'll make sure I start doing them again.'

'Yep. Some anti-inflammatories and a week or so spent building your exercises back up again will do wonders. But you know that already.'

'Yes, I do.' Andrea twisted around, to face him. 'Hearing it doesn't go amiss though, so...thanks.'

'No problem. Consider me available to tell you what you already know at any time.' He bent to press the controls on the examination couch, lowering it until her feet touched the floor, and then turned away quickly. Andrea reached for her sweater, pulling it back over her head.

He was staring out of the window at the mountains, hands in his pockets. The silence was worse than anything he could possibly say at the moment.

'Giulia's going to need a lot of help.' It wasn't clear whether Cal was talking to her, or himself. Since she was in the room, Andrea decided to answer.

'Yes, she is. The trauma of being buried and half suffocated...' Andrea shrugged, wincing as her shoulder complained at the movement. 'But she'll have that. The doctors at the hospital here are very experienced in dealing with avalanche survivors and they know she's going to have to do a lot of talking.'

He turned, his gaze searching her face. 'Did you talk...about your accident?'

If he was jumping to conclusions, then his instincts were unerring. Or maybe he just looked a little closer than most people did, and saw the things that Andrea tried to hide. She took a deep breath.

'Yeah, they... It didn't help much, to be honest.' She'd been through everything with her counsellor, and it had made her feel neither better nor worse. Nothing had been able to penetrate the guilt and despair.

'Perhaps you just weren't ready.'

'Maybe. It's behind me now.' Andrea felt her lip quiver. Time hadn't blurred anything. Pulling Judd from the car and finding he was so badly injured that she couldn't save him was just as clear as it had always been.

'If talking will help you commit to your recovery a little better…'

Andrea caught her breath. Not Cal. He was the last person she could ever talk to about it. And he seemed to know that.

'You should find someone. It doesn't matter who, just someone who'll listen.'

The distance between them grew suddenly. It was the same distance she'd felt with anyone who tried to reach her and talk about the accident.

'I'll bear that in mind. Don't confuse letting things slip a bit because I'm busy with the wedding, with being in denial, Cal.'

His gaze seemed to bore into her. 'No. I won't do that.'

He saw right through her. And he knew that there was nothing more to say. Cal caught up his coat and left the room, closing the door quietly behind him.

Andrea didn't see him at lunchtime, and she didn't want to. She'd careened, out of control, between rage and the suspicion that Cal was right. Conjured his ghost up out of thin air, and asked what gave him the right to think he knew her, and then tearfully acknowledged that he was right, but that she didn't want to admit it. It seemed that Cal had the ability to get under her skin, even when he wasn't around.

But she could ignore all of that for the time being.

News of the avalanche had spread around the hotel, and the manager was available in the lobby for anyone who needed reassurance. It was always important to take heed of the warning flags, but beyond that the slopes were safe. The snow patrol were checking them this afternoon, and the usual precautions were in place.

She called the hospital and got the good news that Giulia's scans had shown her back and head were uninjured. She had a fractured ankle, but she was recovering well from her ordeal. Then Andrea made the difficult call to Giulia's parents, adding her reassurances to those they'd already received, and telling them that someone from the hotel would meet them at the airport tomorrow morning. She'd go and see Giulia this afternoon, and call them again with an update.

Giulia's friends all wanted to visit her, and Andrea's suggestion that just two of them at her bedside was enough prompted a frenzied process of deciding who should go and who should stay behind. Finally, the decision was made, and they set off, Sylvia and Maria carrying presents and a card that had been signed by all of the group of friends. The half-hour journey on the funicular railway was followed by an hour's taxi ride, but finally they got there and found their way to Giulia's room.

'Would you like to wait here?' Andrea stopped at the door. 'I'll go in and see how she is first, eh?'

The two girls nodded. They'd started off in high spirits, but as they'd neared the hospital Sylvia had asked whether they should mention anything to Giulia about the accident. Andrea had told them that they should allow Giulia to talk, if and when she wanted to, but both girls seemed a little overwhelmed and afraid of saying the wrong thing.

But the first thing Andrea heard when she opened the door was the sound of quiet laughter. She stopped short in the doorway and saw Cal sitting by Giulia's bedside. He'd obviously been trying to supplement his schoolboy Italian with gestures and Giulia was smiling at his attempts to make himself understood.

'Oh…' Cal's hands fell to his lap. 'Sorry. They said it was all right for me to come and see Giulia.'

And he'd made her smile. That alone made Andrea want to forgive him for everything.

'Don't be sorry. It's good of you to come.' Andrea could feel Sylvia and Maria jostling behind her, wanting to see what was going on. 'How are you getting on?'

'Not very well. I don't understand much of what she's saying…' Cal flashed Giulia a smile. *That* she understood. Who wouldn't understand one of Cal's smiles?

'Tell him…' Giulia turned her head towards Andrea, speaking in Italian. 'Tell him I like the flowers. And…thank you.'

Andrea nodded, relaying the message to Cal. He smiled at Giulia, stretching out his hand, and Giulia gripped it tightly. She remembered. Cal's hand, reaching for her. Letting her know that she'd been found.

'Tell her it was my pleasure. Any time.'

Andrea didn't need to translate. She had a feeling that Giulia already knew that.

Sylvia and Maria pushed past her into the room, and sat down quietly next to the bed. They seemed almost afraid to speak to Giulia, and Cal leaned over, gesturing to the large bag that Sylvia carried.

That message got through as well. Sylvia opened the bag and produced a cuddly toy that had been bought from the hotel shop. She passed it over to Giulia, who hugged it, and soon the girls were talking animatedly. Cal slipped from his seat, joining Andrea in the doorway.

'Perhaps we should leave them to it. Fancy a cup of tea?'

'Yes, I do. You stay here though. I'll go and fetch some drinks.'

'Me? Stay here with three teenagers when I don't understand a word they're saying?' Cal shot her a pained look. 'Is this a subtle form of revenge?'

It might have been a few hours ago. But Andrea had seen the confidence in Giulia's face, and knew that Cal's presence had reassured her.

'I'd like to think I'd be far more imaginative if I wanted to take revenge on you.' Andrea smirked at him. 'Giulia's been talking to you?'

'Yes. I think she was talking about the avalanche, but I didn't understand what she was saying.' Cal rubbed thoughtfully at the back of his neck. 'Maybe that was the point.'

'I think it probably was. Just stay here with them and let them talk between themselves. I'll be back soon.' Andrea leaned a little closer, grinning up at him. 'Someone reminded me recently that talking's good. It seems that Giulia feels safe with you and able to talk.'

He pursed his lips. 'Okay. Point taken. Although she could have chosen more wisely. I'm a surgeon; my patients don't generally answer back.'

'Then I'm sure it'll be a learning exercise for you.' Andrea doubted it would be. Cal was so easy to talk to.

He frowned suddenly. 'I know my limitations. Ask Joe...'

That sounded suspiciously like a warning. One that was aimed at her. 'What if I ask you?'

His brow furrowed. Cal was clearly thinking carefully about his answer.

'I'd say I was a control freak. Uncompromising, when I'm not being inflexible.'

It *was* a warning. One that Andrea didn't understand, because it didn't sound like Cal at all. She shivered, wondering why he should think that of himself. And why he should be so keen to tell her about it.

'Just do it, Cal. I'll be back in a minute.'

He nodded quietly, turning towards the girls. Sylvia and Maria made room for him at Giulia's bedside and suddenly he was all charm again, smiling at Giulia and resuming his attempts at communication with a few words in halting Italian, supplemented by gestures and laughter.

Maybe she should take him at his word. Maybe she should stop thinking of him as the one person who might pull her back from her past, and allow her to look forward again. Or maybe she was already in too deep to take heed of any of Cal's warnings.

Cal wasn't sure what this was. In less than three days, he'd found himself caring about Andrea. As a friend, maybe. Perhaps as someone who seemed wounded, and who was crying out for a little honesty. Anything more was going somewhere he couldn't bring himself to think about.

But staying on, instead of leaving to go back to the hotel alone, was for Giulia's benefit. A sign that whatever she'd said to him, when she'd hung onto his hand, tears rolling down her cheeks, was okay. If Giulia had needed a safe place to express her fears, before she could begin the long process of letting go of them, then maybe that was what Andrea needed too.

But Cal knew that he wasn't the one. She should talk to a professional, or to Maggie, the friend she'd known since she was a child. Not him, because he couldn't maintain his distance from Andrea, however hard he tried. And Mary had already told him that he was bad news for any woman to become involved with.

They left Giulia, drowsy and ready to sleep, all squeezing into a taxi parked outside the hospital. Sylvia and Maria met their friends at the railway terminus, leaving Cal and Andrea on the platform, waiting for the train to return back down the mountain again.

'Is it just me?' Cal watched the girls walk away. 'I want to give them a good talking-to about staying safe this evening. Not talking to strangers and getting back to the hotel before midnight.'

Andrea looked up at him. 'No, it's not just you. But they're eighteen, and they're perfectly sensible. They'll be fine, and anyway the last train leaves at eleven o'clock.'

'Do they know that?'

'Yes, of course they do. When I was eighteen I was...' She pressed her lips together suddenly.

'When you were eighteen you were what? Come on, you can't just stop there.'

'When I was eighteen, I was on my way to medical school, living on my own for the first time, getting to know new people and learning new things. What about you?'

'I was...probably doing much the same thing.'

'Probably? Don't you remember? I was so thrilled with it all. My dad took me to the bookshop, and we bought all of the books I'd need for my first term. Along with a few extra that he reckoned would come in handy. He's a doctor too.'

'So he and your mother were all for you going to medical school?' Cal wondered what that might be like. Two parents who agreed on something.

'Yes. Dad knew how hard the studying would be, but I could always go to him if I needed help with something. Mum was really pleased too.' Andrea pursed her lips. 'What about your parents?'

She seemed to know already that his experience had been different. It felt as if Andrea knew everything about him, without having to be told. 'My parents were...well, my father wasn't around when I left home for university. He travelled with his job a great deal.'

'What did he do?'

'He still does it, even though he should be thinking about retiring soon. I'm not sure he ever will, though. He's a news photographer—did you see the photos of the recent typhoon in Indonesia?'

Andrea's eyes widened. 'Your father's Terry Lewis? Yes, I saw the photos; they were incredible. Although, I wondered how anyone could manage to get so close...'

'Yeah, that was my first thought too. I've stopped worrying about him, because he'll never change. He always comes back in one piece, and before long he goes away again.' Cal could hear the bitterness in his voice.

'That must be very hard for your mother.'

'She doesn't read the news. Doesn't ever look at the pictures. He and Mum divorced when I was ten. She couldn't cope with him never being there. Or worrying about what he was up to.'

Andrea nodded. The wind whipped along the station platform, bringing with it flurries of snow, and she shivered, stamping her feet. Cal tucked his hand in the crook of her arm, guiding her towards the waiting room, and she walked over to the small heater in the corner.

'That's better.' She stripped off her gloves, holding her hands out to the warmth. 'So your parents didn't approve of you going to medical school, then?'

'It's not that they didn't approve. It just wasn't what either of them had decided I should be doing with my life. Mum wanted me to do something that guaranteed my staying in one place and settling down. My father wanted similar guarantees that I'd be travelling the world, the way he does.'

'That's what you do, isn't it?'

'Not quite in the way he wanted me to. I travel to help set up medical facilities in the places that need them most. He travels for kicks, goes to the most dangerous places he can find. He doesn't think that's the same.'

'And what about your mother?'

This had already gone further than Cal had meant it to, but he didn't want to turn back, now. 'My mother lives with it. She knows I don't take the kinds of risks that my father does, but she still asks me whether I'm any nearer to settling down whenever she sees me.'

Andrea's fingers curled, as if she were trying to get hold of something. Trying to think it all through. That was what Cal had been doing for most of his life, and he could have told her that it was an insoluble conundrum.

'I suppose…it must be hard, finding your own space when they both had such different ambitions for you.'

That was just how he'd felt when he was eighteen. Suffocated by his parents' ambitions. 'Yeah. It was. It took the gloss off things, knowing that there was never anything I could do that would make them both proud of me.'

'Is that what you meant when you said you were inflexible? It strikes me that everyone should be a little inflexible when it comes to fulfilling what they want to do with their lives. You should be proud of yourself.'

The look in her eyes did make Cal feel proud—that he could engender such warmth, such compassion.

'It is what it is. My job... I feel that's what I'm meant to be doing.' Cal held his shaking hands out to the warmth of the heater. It suddenly meant a great deal, more than he'd bargained for, that someone understood. It meant a great deal more that it wasn't just any old someone, but that Andrea understood.

'That's nice. It's a good thing.' Andrea seemed lost in her thoughts again. Cal wondered what she had been meant to do, feeling sure that, whatever it was, it wasn't to be a hotel doctor at a mountain resort. She'd seemed to thrive on her work today, but it was just one day, in a whole procession of days that brought the same minor injuries and illnesses, which in truth could have been treated by any competent year one medical student.

The train drew into the station, and people spilled out of it, ready for their evening out. Andrea suddenly caught his hand, hurrying out of the waiting room.

'Quick...' She was weaving through the crowd, towards the back of the train, right at the other end of the platform. When she got to the last carriage, they jumped inside, just as the doors were closing.

'This is the carriage that suits you?' It was good to forget about everything that the past held, and just run towards something. Cal wondered if Andrea had some aim in mind, or whether she'd just wanted to run.

'Yes, this is the one. It's my favourite part of the train.' The carriage was deserted, most people wanting to go out at this time, rather than back to the hotel. She led him to the end, pulling back the sliding glass doors and entering a domed glass section.

He already knew that the views were spectacular, but as the train pulled away from the station he realised that being surrounded entirely by glass was a different experience entirely. Cal took hold of the handrail to steady himself, feeling almost as if he were suspended in mid-air as the funicular climbed away from the town, and up into the mountains.

It was breathtaking. The snow-covered peaks sparkled in the setting sun, a clear sky above their heads. Beneath them, the lights of the village were drawing further and further away. It felt almost as if they were flying.

'What do you think?'

Cal smiled. 'You chose well. This is definitely the best carriage.'

The train lurched slightly, and he reached out to steady her. She turned, looking up at him, and Cal couldn't draw away.

'This inflexible, uncompromising control-freakery of yours…'

So she'd taken note of what he'd said. It was almost a disappointment. But Cal couldn't help the sizzling tension that flashed between them, and it had seemed only fair to give her a reason to ignore it.

'You don't believe me?' Mary hadn't believed him, and that had caused all kinds of pain…for both of them.

'I believe you. I'm just wondering if you're as good at it as you make out.'

There was no answer to that. Suddenly the world seemed to be turning around them both in a giddying whirlpool. Here, at the centre, was the only thing that mattered.

And here he could entertain the thought that Andrea might be right. That he could change, and that she could change and… Suddenly she moved against him, standing on her toes and planting a kiss on his cheek.

'What…?' He didn't dare ask what she was doing.

'You see, if you really were in control, I wouldn't have been able to surprise you like that.'

Was that a challenge? Some kind of battle of wills? He wasn't in control and they both knew it. Maybe Andrea wanted him to say it.

He drew back a little, gazing into her eyes. Such gorgeous eyes, that set the ever-changing beauty of the mountains to shame. Touching her cheek with his fingertips was like feeling the warmth of a summer's day trickling through his senses.

'Maybe I've just met my match…'

'Maybe you have.'

She brushed a kiss against his lips. When Cal returned it, she smiled up at him.

He couldn't resist kissing her again, and this time she responded more urgently. As if this one moment were everything, and she was going to wring every last drop of its potential from it.

It *was* everything. It had to be, because it couldn't be repeated. The thought only made Cal more determined, desperately seeking everything that he knew wouldn't happen again. He felt her shift in his arms, clinging to him tightly. The feeling was electrifying.

'This isn't what we agreed…' He had to stop this. 'We can pretend all we like, but neither of us is in the right place for a relationship.'

'I know.' Her eyes seemed almost luminous in the light of a brilliant sunset. 'Maybe we could pretend just a little more.'

He could keep this pretence up for a very long time. When she kissed him again, it was just as wonderful as the first touch of her lips—more so, because he was already under her spell. Already bound to her in a way that defied logic.

'I'd say that was pretty near perfect.'

Cal raised his eyebrows. 'Pretty near? What's your definition of perfect?'

'Trying it one more time...'

CHAPTER FIVE

WHAT ON EARTH had she been thinking? Ah, yes. That was right. She *hadn't* been thinking.

But Andrea hadn't been able to resist it. He seemed somehow as broken as she was, and she'd wanted to push him the way he'd pushed her. To make him see that his future didn't need to be defined by his past, in the same way that his strength had made her believe that maybe, one day, she'd spread her wings and fly again.

And…she'd just wanted to kiss him. To see whether it would be as perfect as she'd imagined. And he'd gone and surprised her, by making it so much more than she could ever have dreamed.

It had been rash, and exciting, and Cal probably was a bit of a control freak after all. But in the nicest way possible because he still made her feel as if she were the most beautiful woman alive.

But it *was* just an interlude. As they drew into the hotel terminus, the tender regret in his face told her that Cal wasn't taking this any further. Maybe he was right. He'd struggled so hard to stand in his own space, and he needed someone who could stand with him. Being a part of Cal's life would mean stepping out of her own comfort zone, her happy place where she didn't have to think about letting down someone she loved, ever again. If she really cared about him, she would let him go.

They stepped off the train, and the doors slid closed behind them. Andrea was wondering just how much of a goodbye this was when he held out his arm, a wry smile on his face.

'You're still speaking to me, then?' She slipped her hand into the crook of his elbow.

He shot her a questioning look. 'Always. I'm always speaking to you, Andrea.'

That was the nice thing about Cal. He said what was on his mind, and expected her to do the same.

'That's good. I'm glad about that.'

He nodded. 'What happens on the train, stays on the train?'

If that was the case, she could spend the whole of the next week riding up and down on the funicular railway. Andrea resisted the temptation to suggest it. They had a wedding to organise.

'Yes. As long as we can still be friends.'

'I'd like that very much.'

They walked together into the hotel lobby. It felt wrong to leave him here when the night could hold so much more for them, but it was the only right thing to do.

'I promised to ring Giulia's parents when I got back, to let them know how she is. They'll be here in the morning...'

Cal nodded. 'That's good. Will you be free later on, to go through some of the arrangements for the wedding?'

'I was hoping you might say that. Yes, after my morning surgery?'

'I'll meet you then.'

Cal hesitated, smiling suddenly. 'I think too much of you to kiss you goodnight. It doesn't mean I don't want to.'

He turned, walking away without looking back, as if he knew that Andrea was watching him go. He was a lot braver than she was. A lot stronger. And he was willing to give up the idea of a brief affair, in order to be her friend. There was something chivalrous about that, and the thought warmed her as she walked back up to her apartment alone.

Andrea found Cal waiting for her after her morning surgery the following day with a long list of questions. What would happen if someone was taken ill at the wedding? Did the translator, required at all Italian weddings, need to be licensed, or would someone who spoke both Italian and English do? Could the three other bridesmaids, ranging in age from six to ten, be persuaded not to fidget during the ceremony?

'I'm not entirely sure that's going to be possible.' The earnest look on his face made Andrea smile. 'Anyway, fidgeting and pulling faces is half the charm of it. I'll be stopping them from doing anything really disruptive.'

'Okay.' He seemed to be mentally scanning the long list of disruptive things that little girls could do. 'I'll leave the exact definition of disruptive for you to work out. What about the venue?'

'You haven't seen it?'

He shook his head. 'Not yet. Just your photographs.'

Cal really was leaving nothing to chance. Andrea led him to the hall at the back of the building, unlocking the double doors with the key card that hung around her neck.

'So wheelchair access isn't going to be a problem.' He stepped inside, looking around.

The large empty space had been designed to take advantage of its surroundings. The floor-to-ceiling windows and a domed glass roof made it seem as if they could almost touch the gentle slope that lay between them and the mountains.

'Spectacular.' Cal walked to the centre of the space. 'You're going to decorate in here?'

'I suggested that Maggie kept it simple, with just some flowers along the aisle we'll create between the seating and two large arrangements at the front. I'm not entirely sure that anything we can contrive will compete with this. There are floodlights outside that make the most of the scenery after dark.' She gestured towards the windows.

Cal nodded his approval. 'And then we all go through to the reception.'

'Yes, there's a lobby at the other end of this space, which leads straight through to the large ballroom, where there will be a sit-down meal and then dancing later on. This space will be cleared and Maggie and Joe will come back in here to cut the cake around about sunset, so we'd better hope it's a good one on the day...' A lump formed in her throat, at the thought of the use that she and Cal had made of yesterday's sunset.

She saw a knowing glimmer in Cal's eyes. He felt it too. However hard they both tried to deny it, Maggie had been right. There was something between her and Cal that couldn't be quantified but was as solid and real as the mountains that surrounded them.

'That sounds very romantic.' He was clearly making an effort to keep from smiling. 'You've thought of everything.'

'The hotel hosts weddings on a regular basis so I've had the opportunity to see what other people have done, and learn from it.'

'Now that you mention learning from experience, I've been thinking about all you've done here, at the hotel's medical suite. I'd really like to take a look around. Professional interest...'

That was a little more daunting than wedding arrangements. Andrea didn't talk about what had happened before she came here, but she'd used the experience she'd gained, working quietly to make small changes, which all added up to big ones. The medical centre was working smoothly and efficiently now, and no one even noticed the lack of fuss over things that had once been dramas.

Of course, Cal had noticed. It was part of his job. And it was perfectly natural that he should take an interest.

'Of course. I'll show you around some time.'

'How about now? I think we're just about done here, aren't we?'

He wasn't going to let her off the hook. That was a challenge, because she knew that Cal would question her, and he'd already shown that he took nothing for granted. But her heart was beating a little faster at the opportunity to show someone who really knew all of the issues involved in what she'd done here.

He followed her to the medical centre, and she opened the door.

'Waiting room.'

Cal was grinning as he looked around the bright comfortable space.

'Very nice. Did you make any changes here?'

Andrea rolled her eyes. He knew as well as she did

that every part of the doctor-patient process had to be thought through.

'Actually, I did. The old doctor used to have a drop-in area here, where people could get leaflets and over-the-counter medicines and dressings. It was convenient and very popular—you'd be surprised how many people would rather treat themselves than have a doctor disrupt their holiday by telling them they're ill. So now every-one has to at least see me or Tomas, and we dispense the medicines free.'

Cal nodded. 'I imagine that's a particular issue with some of the hardcore skiers.'

'Yes. I had a guy who sauntered in the other week, five minutes before the end of my surgery, wondering if I had a couple of paracetamol to spare. It turned out he had a fractured wrist but he wasn't going to let a little thing like that keep him from the slopes.'

'I wouldn't think he was too happy about you send-ing him down to the hospital.'

'I dealt with it here. And he actually didn't mind all that much; it's sometimes just a matter of saving peo-ple's pride. He was here with his mates, and he didn't want to be the one to say that he couldn't do anything, so I said it for him.'

'You can deal with fractures here?'

'Simple ones, yes. We have X-ray facilities, which were never used before I got here... You want to see?' Andrea was beginning to feel that she wanted Cal's as-sessing eye to see what she'd done here. His approval was addictive, and she was beginning to crave it.

'Yes, very much...'

Andrea didn't make a big thing of it, but the medical centre here was well organised and able to deal with a wide range of medical situations. She'd anticipated various different scenarios, working out the best way to deal with each of them. He was very well aware that this type of forward planning took experience.

'You've obviously done this kind of thing before.'

'Worked at a ski resort? No, this is my first time.' She deliberately ducked the question.

Cal wished he could show her that he wasn't fooled by this. Not just because he wanted to know all about Andrea, but because it felt as if there was something there that was just bursting to get out—a committed, talented doctor, who knew exactly how to manage a medical project on her own, and who had the ability to take any situation and make it better. But he'd already gone too far down that route, and Andrea had as much as told him to mind his own business.

'Your job must involve a great deal of contingency planning.' She switched the subject adroitly onto him.

'Yes, it does. A lot of the places I visit have a great deal of potential, and it's just a matter of providing a few things that will help it come to fruition. They tell me what they need, and I do my best to provide it.'

'Not the other way round?' From the smile she gave him, Andrea already knew the answer she wanted to hear.

'No. Projects that we help with are led by local communities and experts. We listen and discuss, and offer what resources we can. That might be money, or it might be training or scholarships. In my experience it's very rarely telling someone what I think they need.'

She nodded. Right answer. 'And your surgical skills?'

'I've learned a lot more than I've been able to teach. I may be able to help with the more complex surgical procedures and techniques, made possible by technology that's hard to obtain in developing countries, but I'm constantly surprised by how much is possible with so little.'

Right answer again. Cal's suspicions were fast solidifying into certainty. Andrea had once worked on projects far beyond the scope of her work here. Something bad had happened, and she'd been hurt. She'd found her 'happy place' here, but she couldn't quite leave behind the impulse to make a difference.

And maybe that was his way in. 'I've got some photos. Rather a lot of them, actually.'

'Oh! On there?' She pointed to the tablet he was holding.

'Yes. Would you like a bite to eat?'

'That sounds good. If you have the time...'

He had nothing else to do. These two weeks had been earmarked for Maggie and Joe, and now they were for Andrea too.

'How about pizza?'

Everyone seemed to know Andrea. As she walked past the tables in the pizzeria, there were flashed smiles and greetings from both holidaymakers and staff. But she didn't appear to have any real friends. She was clearly popular amongst the staff, but not really one of them. And the ever-changing tide of hotel guests meant that they were never any more than just passing acquaintances.

She found a table by the window and sat down. Cal decided to try something. His photographs were ordered by country, and he slid the tablet across the table towards her, allowing Andrea to choose which she looked at first. Maybe that would tell him where she'd been.

India. She flipped through the photographs, asking questions and stopping to study some carefully. It wasn't India.

South America. Andrea spent a little more time over his photographs from Peru, but that was just because this batch included some he'd taken of one of the mobile operating theatres that the clinic sponsored. It was no particular surprise that Andrea wanted to know more about that. So, it wasn't South America.

Then their pizzas arrived. She laid his tablet aside, and they both started to eat.

'Your photos are amazing. You have a good eye.'

'My father taught me. He always says that photography is a dialogue.'

Andrea shot him a mystified look. 'That sounds pretty deep to me.'

'Yeah, it does to most people.' Most people didn't admit it and just nodded sagely, but Andrea's enquiring mind wouldn't let it go. 'He means that photography is all about how you interact with what's around you. What you pick out as important and how you choose to show it.'

'Bit difficult to interact with a tornado, I'd say.' Andrea smirked at him.

No one had ever really questioned that because Terry Lewis was acclaimed as one of the best photographers of his generation. No one but Andrea, who weighed everything up, and came to her own conclusions.

'I think it's a conversation with himself. He's drawn to the excitement; he feels most alive when he's facing something with such raw power.'

Andrea turned the corners of her mouth down, but said nothing. It came as a relief that she didn't try to convince him that the quality of his father's photographs justified everything, because she knew as well as he did that it didn't. They were both doctors, and their challenges were in putting pieces back together again, not tearing them apart.

She abandoned her knife and fork, picking up a slice of her pizza so she could eat and flip through the photographs at the same time. The ones of New Guinea prompted questions about the particular challenges that the region faced, and those of Malaysia about the children's hospital he'd visited. Unless there was some sign of recognition that he'd missed, the world of possibilities was beginning to shrink.

'Oh! These are wonderful.' She abandoned the last slice of pizza so that she could pay full attention to the photographs in front of her. If photography *was* a dialogue, then the emotion in her eyes said everything.

Africa. It was Africa.

There was no need to ask, and maybe Andrea would have evaded his question anyway or told him to mind his own business. He watched as she flipped slowly through the images, returning the smiles of the hospital staff and patients he'd photographed. Then she put the tablet aside, decisively switching it off.

'Tell me you've brought your camera with you.' Cal had seen a flicker of regret when Andrea put the tablet to one side, but now she was smiling at him.

'Yeah. I've been taking a few shots. When no one's looking.'

'They're the best kind.' She leaned conspiratorially across the table towards him. 'And speaking of photographs, I've been putting off doing Joe and Maggie's album for too long now. Have you sorted out the ones you have of Joe yet?'

'No, not yet. I've been wondering how embarrassing I can go...'

She grinned naughtily. 'I'd say somewhere between uncomfortable and completely mortifying would be about right.'

'Okay. I'll get right on it. What are you up to tomorrow? I need to take a look at the venues you suggested for Joe's stag, but I should be back in the evening. I really should have dinner with Maggie and Joe tonight; I've hardly seen them since we arrived.'

'Tomorrow's good. I can come along with you in the afternoon if you'd like. I'll ask Tomas if he'll fill in for me at the surgery. I'm due some time off, and he's happy to do it while I concentrate on the wedding.'

'Sounds great. I'll come and find you after your morning surgery, and maybe we can get some lunch in the village.'

She nodded, inspecting the discarded slice of pizza on her plate. 'I think that's cold, now. Shall we have some dessert?'

'I'll just have coffee. But don't let me stop you.' Cal handed her the menu, and she started to peruse it, pressing her lips together as if this was a real treat and she should choose carefully.

As beautiful as she was, however much joy she took from little things, it still felt as if there was something missing. Some piece of her that she'd deliberately pushed aside in exchange for a fragile peace of mind. He knew now that Africa had once been her dream and she never talked about it.

Cal dismissed the thought. Maybe it was better to forget all about it and concentrate on the wedding. But regardless of whether he was her friend, or her lover, he owed Andrea more than that now. And he was determined to pay that debt.

CHAPTER SIX

THE NEXT DAY was bright and clear, a cold wind blowing in from the mountains. Andrea stumbled out of bed, still bleary eyed from a dream that found her shivering in Cal's arms, sheltering from a blast of freezing air. She'd woken to find that the duvet had slipped halfway off the bed during the night. That accounted for the cold part of the dream, but not for the warmth of his touch.

She should never have kissed him. She'd given in to temptation and the exhilaration of the moment, but this was the second night now that she'd dreamed about him. And the second morning that she'd woken with the feeling that after everything they'd done in those dreams, she couldn't look him in the eye.

A shower and a glance at her wedding folder over breakfast would handle it. Focus on what needed to be done.

The morning's list of patients included a strained back and two upset stomachs, along with the usual cuts and bruises. Somehow it didn't seem enough. Those photographs of Cal's had awoken a longing that she'd thought she'd managed to put behind her. It was yet another thing that she needed to ignore if she was going to get through the run-up to the wedding in one piece.

She got to the reception area bang on twelve, but he

was already waiting for her, sitting in one of the deep armchairs and reading the paper. When he saw her, he refolded the paper, putting it back into the rack, and grabbed his coat and scarf.

'It looks cold out there.' He was dressed for it, wearing a thick sweater that emphasised the breadth of his shoulders. She allowed herself to watch as he pulled on his coat, because watching Cal do pretty much anything was a pleasure.

The manager interrupted her reverie, and Andrea swallowed down the impulse to tell her that she was busy and to go away.

'Andrea, we've got a situation.'

That was hotel-speak for something bad happening. 'What's the matter, Gina?'

'We have a missing child. His name's Matthew, he's ten years old, and the last time his parents saw him was half an hour ago. We're making a thorough search of the building and the outdoor teams are setting off.'

Andrea nodded. She'd helped write and implement the search procedures, and she knew it was unlikely that an in-house search would have missed the boy. She held the current record for being able to evade a co-ordinated search drill and it stood at twenty-four minutes.

'Does anyone know where he might have gone?'

'We fear he may be outside. His parents decided not to go out skiing because of the cold and apparently he was disappointed. And his coat is gone.'

That was one layer of warmth at least. But a ten-year-old, alone in the snow, in these wind-chill conditions, would get cold very fast.

'I've paged Tomas, as he's on duty this afternoon. But we can do with all the help we can get.' Gina knew already that Andrea wouldn't be going anywhere when there was a missing child that needed to be found.

'Of course.' Andrea turned to find Cal and bumped straight into him. He'd been standing right behind her, listening to what Gina had been saying.

'I'll help.' Clearly it wasn't necessary for Andrea to apologise to him about cancelling their afternoon. Cal wasn't going anywhere either.

Gina turned to him, smiling. 'Thank you, but our staff have everything under control. We're advising all guests—'

'I'm a doctor. I've worked with search and rescue teams before.' Cal clearly wasn't going to take no for an answer.

Gina's smile turned from placatory to businesslike. 'In that case, thank you. Andrea will tell you where you're needed.'

The rescue plan stated that Andrea and Tomas would stay in the medical centre, so that they could be summoned quickly if they were needed. But a lost child required that as many people as possible should be out searching. If she was with Cal, then Andrea could risk expanding her role a little...

'I think the best thing is for Tomas to stay in the medical centre, so he's there to receive the boy when he's found. Cal and I will go outside to see if we can help the search teams there. You're co-ordinating, Gina?'

'Yes. You have your phone?' Gina would send text updates to all of the team leaders' phones. If the initial search proved fruitless, the Search and Rescue helicopters would be scrambled.

Andrea nodded, turning to Cal. 'We'll get going, then.'

The organisation was impressive. Ski lessons and other activities had quickly been called to a halt, and some of the guests were filing back towards the hotel, while others had volunteered to join the search teams, which were already beginning to spread out across pre-defined areas. Cal could see skidoos further out, making for high points and covering the ever-widening distance that a ten-year-old might have travelled.

Speed was of the essence, and every moment that Andrea had managed to shave from the staff's response times was another moment when the boy could be found safe and well.

Andrea stopped to speak to one of the hotel staff who was wearing a hi-vis jacket, and seemed to be co-ordinating the outdoor search teams. He handed her one of the small backpacks that lay ready at his feet, and Cal took it from her before she could shoulder it herself.

'He has a red jacket. We'll go up to the ridge, over there.' Andrea indicated a low ridge that ran to one side of one of the nursery slopes.

'Okay. It looks like a pretty stiff climb. Do you think he'll have made it up there?'

'It's possible; there's a way around the ridge from the hotel, which is a flatter walk. Or he might have climbed. There are other teams covering the more likely places, and from up there we'll get a bird's eye view.'

They set off at a brisk pace and as they reached the untrodden snow, Cal looked for footprints or any other signs that the boy had been this way. As the incline became steeper, he saw that Andrea was holding her left arm a little stiffly and decided to say nothing. Andrea probably wouldn't thank him for it, and it might just be an instinctive protectiveness of what she knew was a weakness. He'd deal with it if she seemed to be in any difficulty.

'This kind of thing happens a lot, then?' Perhaps he should revise his opinion of Andrea's job.

'We don't usually get one incident like this in a week, let alone two.' Andrea stopped to catch her breath. 'We have our share of lost kids, but generally by the time we've done a search inside they're found. And avalanches aren't that unusual anywhere in the Alps, but we patrol regularly and most people obey the warning flags.'

'So this is unusual.' Cal was scanning the ridge, looking for any sign of the boy.

'Very. You chose the wrong week if you were expecting a holiday.'

Her phone beeped and she pulled it from her pocket, reading the text that had just been received. 'They've finished the search inside the hotel. They're doing a second sweep, but I doubt they've missed him.'

'So he's probably out here somewhere.'

'Yep. And the sooner we find him, the better.' Andrea started walking again. It was hard going. The snow was deep in places and the wind seemed to be getting stronger, stinging his face. But Andrea's quiet determination told Cal that she wouldn't be stopping until the boy was found, however long that took.

When they reached the top of the ridge, Andrea dropped to her knees in the snow. This time Cal asked.

'Okay?' He tried to make the question sound casual.

'Yeah. That got my heart pumping...'

His too. Cal shot her a grin, and slipped the backpack from his shoulders, inspecting its contents. Basic medical supplies, distress flags and flares, a pair of binoculars... He took the binoculars out, scanning in a slow, three-hundred-and-sixty-degree arc.

'Anything?'

'No...' A movement caught his eye and Cal swung back to locate it. 'Over there. I'm not sure...'

As he handed her the binoculars, he saw a flash of red. Andrea followed the direction of his pointing finger and let out a cry.

'Yes. It's him. I can see him moving.'

That was something. Andrea pulled her phone from her pocket, stripping off her gloves and hitting autodial.

'Gina, we're at the top of the ridge. We can see him on the far side... Yeah, the snow ambulance is going to have to come round... Great, thanks.'

She ended the call, putting her phone back into her pocket. Cal had been surveying the steep drop on the other side of the ridge. Andrea was right in saying that the snow ambulance couldn't make it over the top of the ridge, but the flatter route would take longer. They needed to get to the boy as fast as they could.

A man could make it down there. Maybe... He took a moment to gauge the angle of the incline, reckoning that if he lost his footing at least the snow would break his fall.

'They're sending the snow ambulance now. I need you to stay here and guide it to Matthew; they might not be able to see him...'

'Where are you going?'

'I'm going to try to get to him.' Andrea started to survey the steep drop with the binoculars.

What? Not in a million years. Not even if her shoulder had been in perfect condition.

A bright, hard protectiveness flared in Cal's chest.

He wasn't going to argue with her. There wasn't any point, because there was no way that he'd let Andrea go down there. She was still looking through the binoculars and never even noticed him bending to take the flares from the backpack and leaving them in the snow at her feet. Then he shouldered the backpack, took one deep breath to steady himself and started to slide down towards the boy.

No! Cal!

The shock was almost as if she'd been punched in the chest. Cal was making his way down the steep incline, his stance almost that of a skier, leaning into the slope with his arms held out to keep his balance. She had no choice but to stay here now. She needed to use the flares he'd left behind to help to guide the snow ambulance.

Tears of helpless rage began to form in Andrea's eyes. She'd lost Judd. She'd watched him die, unable to save him. She couldn't lose Cal. Fixing her gaze on him, as if somehow that might improve his balance, she watched his progress.

Just as she thought he was going to make it, he fell, tumbling down the last ten feet of the drop. Andrea let out a howl of anguish, and then he moved. He got to his feet, brushing himself off, and then… *Then* he had the audacity to wave at her.

Fine. She wasn't waving back. She watched as Cal walked towards the tiny figure in the snow. There seemed to be hardly any reaction—Matthew must already be suffering from the effects of the cold. Cal bent down in front of him, taking the thermal blanket from the backpack and wrapping it around him. He picked Matthew up, carrying him to the meagre shelter of a rocky outcrop.

They were both safe, she had to concentrate on that. Andrea jumped as her phone rang. She had to blow on her fingers to warm them before the touch screen would register.

'I've got him. He's a little drowsy, but he's lucid. His feet are wet, and he has no gloves, but his body seems warm. Any idea when the snow ambulance will be here?'

'It shouldn't be any more than ten minutes.' Andrea closed her eyes, counting to ten. She'd give Cal a piece of her mind later.

'Great, thanks.'

Andrea ended the call, not trusting herself to say any more. She called Gina, relaying the boy's status, and then trained the binoculars on the path that she knew the snow ambulance would be taking. When she saw it, she let off the flare. Cal would see it too, and know that help was almost there.

She saw Cal make his way towards the vehicle as it drew up next to him. He could start to warm Matthew up in the ambulance, and Tomas would be waiting in the medical centre, ready to shepherd them inside and take over his treatment.

She started to trudge back down the slope. Cal was all right; he'd taken a tumble but he'd got back up again. She shouldn't care so much that it was him who'd taken the risk of sliding down to the boy, instead of her. But she did.

Andrea was back in time to see the ambulance draw up, and Cal carry the boy into the medical centre. He handed him over to Tomas, just as a woman burst through the door from the waiting room, crying hysterically.

'You're the doctor...?' She caught hold of Andrea's arm. 'I'm Matthew's mother. Please, is he all right?'

'I'm going to examine him now.' Andrea tried to

break free, but Matthew's mother was holding her tight and a man, tight-lipped and white-faced with worry, was blocking Andrea's path through to the treatment room.

Then, suddenly all the obstacles melted away. Cal had freed Andrea, and managed to manoeuvre himself in between her and the couple, declaring himself to be a doctor, and able to tell them what was going on. It was best if they all waited together and gave Andrea a chance to examine Matthew properly.

It was the right thing to do. Normally any child would benefit from having their mother present during an examination, but Matthew's mother's tears would only distress him further. And Cal's quiet reassurances seemed to be calming both of Matthew's parents. Andrea shot them a smile, before hurrying after Tomas into the treatment room.

Cal had already stripped off Matthew's shoes and jeans, wrapping his legs in another blanket from the ambulance to keep him warm. Andrea examined his fingers and toes carefully, while Tomas turned the warm-air blowers on to warm him gently. His hands and feet were cold, and very red, but there was no sign of frostbite.

'Keep monitoring him, Tomas. I'll be out in the waiting room if you need me.' Andrea was pleased with what she saw, and it was time to go and see how Cal was doing with the boy's parents.

Matthew's mother was much calmer now, her husband sitting with his arm around her. Both were listening as Cal spoke quietly to them, his words inaudible, but his manner calm and reassuring.

He was so good at defusing situations, finding a way through with the minimum of fuss. Even Andrea felt the warmth of the atmosphere here in the waiting room, as she sat down next to him.

'I've examined Matthew and he's very cold, but I don't see any signs of frostbite. He has what we call frostnip, which is much less serious, and we can deal with that easily now that we have him in the warm.'

'May I see him?' Matthew's mother glanced at Cal and he smiled. He must have already told her that the best thing she could do for her son was to be calm.

'Of course. He's a little bit drowsy but that's to be expected. He's complaining that his hands are cold as well, but don't let that worry you. Feeling cold is a sign that there's no permanent damage.'

Matthew's father nodded. 'Cal said you'd be warming him up slowly.'

'Yes, that's right. It may take a little while, but you can sit with him. You might like to bring a few books or toys down, so that you can keep him amused when he starts to feel a bit better.'

'Thank you.' Matthew's mother turned, clasping Cal's hand between hers. 'And you too, Doctor. Thank you.'

Andrea ushered Matthew's parents into the treatment room, where Tomas had him tucked up under a blanket, his hands and feet protruding so that they'd warm gradually. She pulled a chair up, beside the couch, and Matthew's mother sat down, smiling at her son. Signalling to Tomas to stay put, she walked back out into the waiting room.

'He's okay?' Cal turned to her.

'Yes. We got to him in time.' Andrea pressed her lips together. She'd decided that she wouldn't mention Cal's precipitous slide down the slope.

'Good.'

She would have left it at that but Cal was watching her thoughtfully, the look on his face making it very clear he wasn't going to let things rest. She didn't want to let things rest either. Andrea took a moment to choose her words carefully.

'I wish you'd said what you were going to do. Before you went down that slope.'

'You were thinking that you wanted to discuss it?'

'In these situations it's always a good thing.' Andrea tried to keep the observation as neutral as possible.

'Yes, it is. And considering the impressive organisation that you've put in place for emergencies, I was a little surprised that you didn't discuss who was best placed to tackle that slope with me.'

Andrea frowned. It was difficult to work out whether that was a compliment or an insult. Or whether it was just the truth, which was rather more challenging at the moment.

'*I'm* extremely surprised that you didn't discuss it with *me*.' Andrea pressed her lips together. This was turning into one of those petty tit-for-tat arguments that generally didn't get anyone anywhere. But she was so cross with Cal…

'Would it have made any difference if I had?'

Andrea puffed out a breath. Of course it wouldn't. She'd decided to go herself, and nothing that Cal could have said would have changed her mind.

'Cal, I know you've got a lot of experience. But it may have slipped your mind that I'm actually on the payroll here as the doctor in charge.'

'Pulling rank on me isn't going to change the facts, Andrea. If you'd taken a fall like the one I did, I'd probably have you in the other treatment room practising my reduction technique on your shoulder.' Cal was obviously getting irritated too.

She couldn't help that. This couldn't go unanswered.

'I've had the surgery, Cal. My shoulder might hurt at times, but it's probably no more likely to dislocate than yours. And if you want to play doctors, let's do that, shall we? You're cold, you need to warm up a bit.'

Even though his manner had been one of relaxed well-being with Matthew's mother, he *was* shivering now. No wonder, he'd ripped his over-trousers in the fall, and his jeans were wet. And Andrea had noticed that he'd left his coat in the ambulance, so he must have taken it off and tucked it over Matthew to provide another layer of warmth.

'I'm fine.' He pressed his lips together. It was a bit late now to decide he didn't want to talk about it.

'No, you're not, Cal. Will you please go and warm up and let me get on with my job?' At least he could negotiate whatever risks that the journey back to his room presented without Andrea having to stand and watch him.

He gave her a long, searching look. If he thought that would give her time to change her mind, then he could think again. As she'd watched him go down that slope, the truth had slapped her in the face. She cared too much about Cal. And now she felt ashamed that she'd reacted the way she had. This all had to stop.

'Okay. I dare say you'll be busy with Matthew for a while, but I'll see you later?' His voice had taken on those warm honey tones again, and only his eyes flashed a message of concern.

Already her resolve to keep him at a distance was

weakening. Andrea got to her feet, and opened the door that led out of the medical suite. 'Yeah. Maybe. I'll see how things go.'

Cal went to his room. Andrea was the doctor here, and she had every right to order him out of her surgery. To be fair, she hadn't actually ordered him out, it just felt as if she had.

He stripped off his clothes. He *was* cold, and red patches on his legs where his jeans had been wet were beginning to tingle painfully. That was all to the good; it showed he was beginning to warm up again and hadn't done himself any damage. He hadn't even noticed that he was cold before, he'd been so focussed on looking after Matthew and then talking with the parents.

But Andrea's cool reaction afterwards had frozen him to the bone. All of the things he'd wondered about were spinning in his head, along with the knowledge that he too could have handled things a little better. He pulled on a pair of warm sweatpants, and a T-shirt, adding a sweater for good measure. The thought that the bright heat that flashed between him and Andrea was probably now gone for good was the most chilling thing of all.

He switched on the television, flinging himself down onto the bed and flipping through the channels until he came to one in English. He had no right to push Andrea, trying to make her give more than she was ready to. She'd come to terms with whatever kept her here in her own time. He might be a lost cause, but he couldn't believe the same applied to her.

A knock sounded on the door. When he opened it, she was there, as if all his fantasies had fleshed out and turned into reality. She was holding a printer, a packet of paper balanced precariously on top of it.

'Are you all right?' The question blurted from her lips.

'Yes, I'm fine. You were right, I did need to warm up a bit. Let me take that.' Somehow he managed to relieve her of the printer and paper without touching her.

'Thanks. Look, I'm sorry, Cal. The last few days have been a bit stressful.' She rubbed at her face with her sleeve.

'Forget it. There's nothing to be sorry for. How's Matthew?'

'He's fine. Tomas is looking after him for a minute but I need to get straight back to him.'

Cal imagined that Tomas could manage perfectly well for more than a minute. But he'd already decided not to push Andrea so much. Cal nodded at the printer.

'What's this for?'

'I was wondering if you could print out the photographs you have of Joe. The printer's set up to work on the hotel's Wi-Fi, and I've brought some spare ink cartridges.' She fished in her pocket, bringing out a couple of small boxes.

'No problem. I'll get it done.' That was an unequivocal message. He wouldn't be seeing her again this evening.

Andrea was obviously battling to keep something under wraps, and it was clear he wasn't helping at the moment. Perhaps she'd decided she needed the evening off from him…

'I'll see you tomorrow, then.' Cal turned, dumping the printer onto the bed, and then took the ink cartridges from her hand. This time his fingers brushed her palm.

It felt as if a moment's warmth had flashed between them, and then it was gone.

'Yeah. Tomorrow. Um... I should be going. Things to do...' She was edging away from him now.

Suddenly, Cal needed to put things straight between them. He reached forward, taking her by the shoulders, and Andrea stared dumbly up at him.

'Look, Andrea, I know you're under stress at the moment, and I'm sure I haven't made things any better. I'm sorry for that...'

'It's nothing.' Her chin jutted out defensively. 'Everything will be fine for the wedding.'

He wasn't talking about the wedding. He was talking about the one person that he wanted... *needed* to be happy. None of his careful resolve not to get too involved with her would be worth anything if Andrea wasn't happy.

But it all came back to the fact that he felt she needed to talk, and she didn't want to. What made him think he knew any better than Andrea? It might feel like a lifetime, but he'd only known her a few days.

His hands dropped to his sides, and he nodded. 'I know it will. Forget I said anything.'

The look she gave him set him on fire. Vulnerable, and yet with the strength that came from suffering.

'I appreciate your concern, Cal. But I have to go now.'

'I know. Go.' Cal watched her as she hurried away along the corridor, walking so fast that it looked as if she was going to break into a run any moment.

He went back into his room and closed the door. Leaning back against it, he shut his eyes, murmuring the words he'd really wanted to say to Andrea's face.

Will you please just talk it out with someone, Andrea?

CHAPTER SEVEN

CAL SPENT THE EVENING, and the better part of the following morning hiding out in his room. Just as he was considering ordering brunch, a tap sounded at his door. He'd chased away the friendly cleaning woman who'd knocked earlier, preferring to make his own bed than to risk her vacuuming up the photographs he had laid out on the floor, but he wondered if maybe she was giving him a second try.

'Thanks but...' Cal opened the door, the words drying in his throat. It was Andrea.

She looked bright and just as beautiful as ever in jeans and a patterned sweater. And she was holding a tray.

'I bought you apology hot chocolate.' She nodded down towards two cups, filled to the brim. 'With mortification sprinkles, and embarrassment toasties.'

Suddenly, he was perfectly happy. '*Mortification* sprinkles? How did you know they're my favourite?' Cal stood back from the door. The egg and bacon toasties looked pretty good, as well.

'It was just a wild guess.' She grinned suddenly, stepping into the room. She brought with her the smell of food—making Cal realise just how hungry he was—and a shaft of pure sunshine.

There was nowhere to put the tray since all the available surfaces had been used for the printer and the photographs last night, before Cal had resorted to the floor this morning. Cal took it from her and put it down on the bed, pleased to see that she felt comfortable enough to sit down next to it. He followed suit, taking a seat on the other side of the tray, careful not to tip its contents to one side.

'Look…' They both spoke together, falling silent to let the other one go first. Cal would have listened to anything that Andrea had to say to him, but he needed to say this right now, before she started to apologise again.

'Andrea, you have nothing to apologise for or to feel embarrassed about. This is my fault. I knew that there was something you didn't talk about and I went ahead and pushed you anyway. I'm sorry, and I won't do it again.'

He might have said more. He could have admitted to his reason for pushing her, but Cal wasn't ready to tell her how much she fascinated him, and he doubted there would ever be a time when he would be. But he could make his peace with her. That was important to him beyond the need to work together on the wedding arrangements.

Warmth ignited in her eyes. Cal's one apology was enough to satisfy her, while she just couldn't stop apologising for something that wasn't her fault.

'I shouldn't have—'

'Stop, Andrea. Just stop. You have every right to tell me to back off. Much more explicitly than you did. Let's put an end to this, shall we?'

She nodded, wordlessly. Cal picked up one of the

cups from the tray and took a sip from it. 'This is really nice.'

'It's Craig's secret recipe. Our pastry cook. I did a deal with him for it...'

Who wouldn't share their secrets with Andrea? Her practical good sense, her kindness and that edge of fragile vulnerability made it obvious that she'd seen more than she said, and that she could understand anything. She understood Cal well enough already.

'His wife's pregnant. She's Italian and he's from London; he can get by in Italian but he couldn't understand all the leaflets she'd been given. I translated them for him.' Andrea smiled. 'And gave him a bit of advice about not being quite so worried about her.'

'You would have done that anyway, wouldn't you?' Cal took another sip. 'I think you got the better deal.'

'Yes, so do I.'

Cal picked up one of the toasted sandwiches, removing the cocktail stick that bound it all together and taking a bite. He nodded his approval, still chewing, and Andrea finally started to relax, taking a sip of her own drink.

'You've been busy.' She looked at the photographs scattered around the room.

'I printed out everything I thought would do. Seems I have more than I realised.'

'I have too. Perhaps an album isn't really the thing. I could ask the manager if she'll lend me some of the display boards the hotel has for conferences, and use those. She has some full-height ones that are really attractive and they wouldn't be out of place at the reception. Maybe decorate them with some flowers...'

'Sounds great. Much better. What about printing some of the photos a little larger?'

'Yes, that's good.'

He was still curious, but Cal had learned his lesson, and he knew if he pushed Andrea she was going to retreat again. He'd deserve every ounce of silence and every blank look that she could give him. He collected the photographs up from the floor, placing the pile down next to her, so she could look through them while she was eating.

She started to separate them out, picking the best ones to use. When she came to the one that Cal had pondered over the most, she stopped.

'This is...amazing.'

'I'm not sure Maggie will want it in there.' It was one of his favourite photographs of Joe and Maggie but maybe her wedding wasn't the time to remind her of that point in her life.

Andrea thought for a moment, staring at the photograph. 'I think she will. This is what their marriage vows are all about, isn't it? In sickness and in health.'

The photograph showed exactly that. Maggie's face was pale, with dark rings under her eyes, and her head was swathed in a scarf to hide her rapidly thinning hair. But Joe was looking at her as if she was the most beautiful woman in the world. The only one he loved, whatever happened.

'I'll leave that to you. You know her best.' Cal picked up the tray, moving it to a side table, and when he sat back down, Andrea put the photograph onto the 'definite' pile.

'I know she'll want me to include it. She used to tell me that one of the things she loved the most about Joe was that he never stopped looking at her like this, even on her worst days.'

She picked up the next photograph, squinting at it.

Then she sighed, her hand dropping to her lap. However much they both tried, it was obvious that hot chocolate and old photographs weren't enough to divert their thoughts.

'Cal, you're right. I want to talk, I just…can't.'

He took a deep breath. Whatever he said next would be crucial.

'Maybe…do things one step at a time. If you don't feel comfortable talking to a friend, then maybe set up an appointment with a professional. A good counsellor will help you get to the point where you feel you can talk in a safe environment.'

She nodded, staring at her fingers, twined impossibly together now. 'Not you?'

'I've lost the right to expect that of you. I gave it away when I pushed you.' Cal felt the corners of his mouth turning down in regret. If he'd only been less sure of himself, and more sure of Andrea.

'You saw…' Suddenly she looked up at him. The distress in her face was enough to make any heart break. 'You saw it, Cal. Maybe the thing I really needed was for someone else to see what I've been trying to ignore.'

He couldn't think of anything to say. He was sure that whatever he *did* say should leave Andrea plenty of space to do whatever she needed to do.

'Will you do something for me? If there's anything you ever need or want… It doesn't matter what it is, just wanting it is enough.'

He expected her to give one of those little nods, that was all they ever needed to signify that they thought the same way on something. But Andrea was studying her hands again.

'You know about Africa, right?'

'I know…that the photographs meant something to you.'

She nodded. 'My dad worked there for a while when I was little. I loved it, and when I graduated from medical school I wanted to go back because it seemed that there was something I could do there. It took a couple of years before I had the right experience…'

This only gave him more questions. But now wasn't the time for Cal to ask; he should be grateful that she was even still speaking to him, let alone saying this much. He should just stay quiet and let her say whatever she wanted to say.

'You know how it is. It can be heartbreaking and challenging, but ultimately you get more out of it than the people you're supposed to be helping.'

'What were you doing out there?'

'You know how it is. Where there's a need, you do whatever has to be done, and I was involved with all kinds of medical care. But my speciality was working with people with disabilities. Helping to provide a framework that would give them opportunities.'

Cal nodded. People like Andrea were much needed everywhere in the world.

'How long were you there?'

'Three years. It was hard, but I loved my work. And I fell in love as well.'

Lucky man. Cal took the thought back immediately, because Andrea had already told him that it had ended badly. Anyone who could love Andrea and make her happy deserved his respect.

'Who…?'

'Judd was a paramedic. He took me under his wing when I first arrived and taught me the ropes. We did a lot of outreach work together, travelling to the more remote places.'

'It's good work.' Cal knew that getting the right people to the right places was half the battle. People living in isolated communities often had to travel many miles to get medical help.

'I thought so. I *think* so...' Andrea hadn't lost the commitment that had made her want to help. She'd lost something else though, and Cal knew that whatever was coming next wouldn't be good.

'We were on our way back from a trip. Judd was driving and we were talking about our leave, back in the UK. All the things we were going to do, the people we'd see. I was so looking forward to introducing him to my parents; Dad would have loved him...' Andrea fell silent for a moment. As if this was a last happy memory and she wanted to keep hold of it for a little while longer.

'The truck hit a pothole. We went off the road, and down a ravine. There had been a lot of rain that spring, and the river had almost burst its banks.'

Andrea was shaking, looking down at her hands, and he reached out, touching her arm just to let her know that he was there. She leaned against him, and he put his arm around her shoulders.

'I don't know how I got Judd out of the truck. I remember the cabin filling with water, and...he was barely conscious. I'd dislocated my shoulder, and it was the most I could do just to get him to the river bank.'

'I wouldn't fancy my chances in those circumstances.' It must have been an almost superhuman effort for Andrea, hampered by a useless arm and blinding pain.

'There was no one to help us. By some miracle my phone worked, and I called our central clinic. But he was too badly injured. He died before they could reach us, and all I could do was hold him.'

'Andrea… I'm so sorry.' There was nothing more he could say. But he could hold her in his arms, and she snuggled against him, seeming to derive some comfort from that.

'Is that why you didn't want me to go down to Matthew, yesterday?' He put his own pride aside, allowing that Andrea might have felt as protective of him as he had of her.

'It was…stupid…'

'It was incredibly brave, Andrea. Most people would have just baulked at it.'

She moved against him, giving a little shrug. But he could tell that his words had pleased her.

'I came home to London, and I was in hospital for a while, and then went to Mum and Dad's in Oxfordshire to recuperate. Maggie was great; I don't think I could have got through it without her.'

'You didn't talk to her about it?'

'I did, and she never minded; she always listened. I suppose I just wanted to get back to something that approached normality and reckoned that I'd said enough. I felt I ought to be moving on.' Andrea gave a little shrug.

'So you made it happen. I can understand that.'

'Yeah. Maggie told me to take things slowly, but I knew better. I'm a doctor, and I should have known how to deal with it but…'

Cal chuckled. 'Doctor heal thyself, you mean? If you've worked out how to do *that*, you'll be the first. We're only human.'

She looked up at him, her face stained with tears. 'Nice to know. I always thought I was indestructible.'

'I reckon I'm indestructible too. But don't tell anyone.' There was more. Maybe Andrea would tell him and maybe not. He would just hold her, and let her make her own decision about that.

'That's the thing, though. I could handle losing Judd. Not easily, but grief's a process and I knew I had to go through it and come out the other side. Somehow, I couldn't bring myself to go back to work, though.'

'From what I've seen of your shoulder, you must have had a fair bit of healing to do there, as well.'

'I did, but that wasn't it. You know how it is when you can't save someone, Cal, but as doctors we have to move on. I couldn't save him. I tried…'

He saw it all, now. The man she loved had died in her arms, and Andrea had been able to do nothing to stop it. It was enough to shatter anyone's confidence.

'You lost your trust in yourself?' He ventured the obvious conclusion.

'Yes. I tried going back to work, but I just froze whenever I had to deal with something on my own. I was more of a liability than anything else. I decided to go away for a while, and found myself here…not here at this hotel, but in a little boarding house in the village. I heard they needed a new doctor, and came up to find out a bit more.'

'And this was something you could deal with?'

A smile spread across her face. 'You're never alone in a hotel, Cal. Twenty-four-hour everything, including medical staff. Tomas and I cover for each other, there's always a nurse on duty, and there are a dozen people who are trained to deal with medical emergencies on the slopes.'

'And you've made sure that everyone rehearses every possible emergency scenario.'

'Yes. The manager wanted someone who'd take the

initiative and do that, and I was very motivated in that
direction too. I found some peace here. There's something reassuring about waking up and seeing the mountains, still there, every morning.'

'It's a good place, Andrea.' He should never have
tried to make Andrea see beyond her life here. Not
without knowing what she'd been through.

'It is. But it's not enough for me any more. It hasn't
been for some time, but... I don't know how to live and
work anywhere else any more.'

Cal hugged her. She clung to him, no longer crying.
It was as if their conversation had given her some peace
as well, although he had no right to hope that it might.

'You could take your time. Your job doesn't always
have to define you.'

Andrea drew back from him, looking him steadily
in the eye. Then suddenly she smiled. 'Could you just
say that again, please? I want to appreciate just how bizarre it sounds, coming from you.'

Cal chuckled, holding up his hands. 'Yeah. Okay, I
suppose I haven't exactly lived out that principle.'

'Not entirely. Although I can see why it's important
to you to hang onto your professional ambitions. You
had to battle so hard to do what you wanted to do.'

He flopped onto his back on the bed, covering his
eyes with his hands. 'I'm really that transparent?'

'More translucent, I'd say. The lights are obviously
on in there, but I'm never quite sure what you'll do next.'

'That's good. I'm not sure what I'll do next, either.'

'Your job? Or the wedding?' She lay down next to
him, curling her legs up onto the bed, and propping
herself up on her elbow.

'Is this your way of telling me to stop now, because

you're done talking? I've learned my lesson, and you can just say it.'

'Stop, then. I'm not really done, I know that, but I'm done for now.'

'And you're okay?' That was the only thing that really mattered to Cal.

'Yes, I'm okay. There's always a light at the end of the tunnel.'

Cal would agree with that, if only he could find where his tunnel was. If he'd been instrumental in helping Andrea find hers, then that was everything he could wish for.

'That sounds like something Maggie would say.'

'She's mentioned it.' Andrea gave a little laugh. 'Once or twice.'

Maggie's matchmaking didn't seem so frivolous now. She was trying to encourage her friend to move on. She might have chosen the wrong man for Andrea to move on with, but Cal could respect the reasoning behind it all.

'So. Cal...'

'Yes?' He had the feeling that something of some import was coming.

'What are you not sure about?'

He'd told no one about this, not even Joe. But Andrea had trusted him...

'It's just my job. I'm not sure whether I should move on or not.'

'You're thinking of leaving your job? I thought you loved it.'

'I do. The board's offered me a new position, as director, and I'm not sure whether to take it or not.'

'Why wouldn't you? Does the promotion mean you'll have less contact with patients?'

'I'd still be operating, and caring for my own patients, but I wouldn't be travelling so much; I'd need to be in London to keep an eye on things there.'

'And the travel means that much to you?'

Now that she mentioned it, he realised it really didn't, and that he couldn't pin down why he felt so uneasy about taking the job.

'Travel is… really just a way of being somewhere I can make a difference. As the London Director, I'd have the opportunity to make an even greater difference than I do now.'

She pressed her lips together, laying her hand on his chest. Cal wondered if she could feel his heart beat, and whether she knew that right now his heart was beating just for her.

'I guess that for someone who's always prided themselves on making their own decisions, it's difficult to consider something that someone else has suggested.'

Cal turned the idea over in his head. Suddenly his own reticence in taking up what was a once-in-a-lifetime opportunity made a bit of sense.

'Is that a nice way of saying that I'd rather be in control and to have applied for the job myself?'

'If you like. Why don't you imagine that you had, and see how you feel about it then?'

Cal rolled over onto his side, to face her. 'You may have a point. But I don't need to make that decision right now, which means that we can concentrate on photographs for today.'

'Is that your way of telling me that you want to stop now?' She gave him a quizzical look.

'Yeah.' He grinned at her. 'I appreciated the conversation, though.'

'Me too. And now we've got a wedding to arrange.'

CHAPTER EIGHT

THEY'D WAITED UNTIL Maggie and Joe were off skiing for the afternoon and then Cal had helped Andrea carry the boards upstairs. They were a bit more difficult to hide than an album, and, since Maggie was in and out of Andrea's apartment all the time, he'd offered his room.

By the time Andrea had finished her afternoon surgery, Cal had set up the boards. Closeted in his room, sorting through old photographs, was a treat. Andrea had laughed over the photos of Cal and Joe when they were at medical school together, and Cal had insisted that the picture of Maggie and Andrea, aged ten and dressed up for their school's Halloween party, should go into the 'definites' pile.

'No! Not that one!' Andrea snatched the photograph from his hand. 'Goodness only knows what I was thinking.'

'I think you look adorable.' Cal chuckled. 'Sweet sixteen.'

'Even then I should have known better than to wear a neckline like that. I thought it was sophisticated.'

'It's a nice one of Maggie...' Cal gave her a cajoling smile that was immensely difficult to resist.

'There's another one here of her. On her own.' Andrea shuffled through the pile and found it. 'That's much better.'

'Whatever you say. Are you hungry? Since we seem to be on a roll with this, maybe we should get room service?'

Maggie would *love* that if she found out. She would add Cal and Andrea together, multiply them by room service, and total it all up to an I-told-you-so. But Andrea didn't care. It had been a long time since she'd been able to mess around with someone the way she and Cal did. A long time since she'd talked to someone who seemed to understand so completely. Something *had* happened between them. It *was* happening. Just because she had no name for it, didn't mean it wasn't real.

Andrea found the room-service menu hidden under a pile of printer paper. 'What do you fancy?'

He craned his neck to read over her shoulder. Since this morning he'd seemed less reticent in allowing himself to be close to her, and it was an entirely delicious evolution in their relationship.

'Um... I don't know. What's good?'

'I can phone down to the kitchen and get them to send the dish of the day up? That's always nice.'

'Perfect. Half-bottle of wine?'

She probably shouldn't. Andrea needed all the inhibitions she could muster at the moment. But she'd told him her most closely guarded secret already. What did she have left to lose?

'Sounds good. I'll get them to choose something...'

The boards were ready. They were decorated with paper flowers, which matched the colour scheme that Maggie had chosen for the real flowers, and there was a pad of sticky hearts, where the guests could write their own special messages for Maggie and Joe. Andrea and Cal had got together at the end of each day and ticked off the things they'd sorted, reviewing what still needed to be done.

Somehow, and Cal wasn't entirely sure how, they'd made it through the first difficult days here in Italy. The calm after the storm seemed particularly welcome to him, because Andrea seemed happier and more beautiful than ever.

He woke early, on a fine bright day. Stretching lazily in bed reminded him that he'd let his morning exercise regime slip, and he decided that the gym and a few laps in the hotel pool would be in order.

Few people rose at seven o'clock on a Sunday morning when they were on holiday, and he had the gym to himself. Almost... In one corner he could see Andrea, clad in a pair of figure-hugging leggings and a sleeveless vest.

'Morning.' She was concentrating on adjusting one of the machines, and didn't notice his approach.

'Oh, hello. You're up early.' She gave a little frown. 'Not worried about the wedding, are you?'

'No. That all seems to be going quite spectacularly well.'

She laughed. 'Shh. You'll spoil it.'

This suited her. Getting back into a routine and feeling that she was in control of her life. Cal's own routine often amounted to little more than taking each day as it came, assessing which need was the more urgent and hoping that the others would be able to wait.

'I'm over there.' He grinned, pointing to one of the machines in the far corner.

Andrea turned to look. 'Ah, yes. That one's got a rather nice view.'

That wasn't the reason. Working up a sweat with Andrea seemed like a fine start to the morning, but he didn't want to spoil things. They'd been getting on so well in the last few days.

'I don't suppose you could...' She called after him and Cal turned quickly. Yes. Whatever it was she wanted him to do, the view would be a lot better if Andrea was somewhere in his line of sight.

'I can't get the latch on this machine.'

He walked over and examined the adjustment lever. It wouldn't move and he applied a bit more pressure. 'Looks as if it's stuck. It doesn't want to budge.'

She puffed out an exasperated breath. Obviously she'd been trying to set the machine to offer the least resistance, presumably to accommodate her injured shoulder.

'I'll just have to try something else, then.'

Cal hesitated. It was good to see that Andrea *was* exercising, and maybe he should leave her to it. But in the last few days, she'd stopped trying to hide the effects of her injury, flexing her shoulder whenever it hurt instead of holding her arm stiffly at her side. That alone must have made a big difference.

'You're doing mild resistance exercises?' They were pretty standard for the kind of shoulder injury that Andrea was recovering from. 'Want to try them together?'

'Yes. Thanks.'

Cal swung his leg over the long bench, sitting down. He could gauge the strength of Andrea's shoulder much better than any machine could, and provide exactly the right amount of resistance. She sat down opposite him, astride the bench.

'All right. A little closer. Keep your back straight.'

She moved until her knees were almost touching his.

Cal held up his right arm. 'Let's try with your good arm first, so I can see how much strength you have there.'

Andrea grinned. 'You're doing this properly, then.'

There actually wasn't much choice. If she was going to be this close then he needed to have something to concentrate on, other than the blue-grey colour of her eyes. They fascinated him endlessly, changing in response to the light.

'Am I interfering?'

'No, that's okay. I'd like a bit of feedback, I don't get to the physiotherapist as often as I probably should. One of the penalties of being up here.'

She pressed her palm against his, pushing against it. She was strong, but Cal could see that she wasn't really trying.

'You can do better than that.'

Suddenly the pressure increased. This was turning into a real contest. Cal had positioned his own arm at an awkward angle, so that Andrea's would be in exactly the correct position, and he was beginning to feel the strain.

'Uh. That's enough.' He gave in before she did.

'Sorry... Did I push too hard?' The innocent smile on her lips told Cal that she was enjoying the competitive side of this exercise.

'No. I'm just fine.' Cal rubbed his shoulder, grinning at her. He rather liked this new side to their dynamic, where Andrea was pushing to test her strength against his, rather than pushing him away.

'I wouldn't want to hurt you.'

'You won't. Let's try the other arm, shall we?'

Her other arm was much weaker. Cal could hold his hand in place easily and Andrea was clearly pushing as hard as she could.

'All right. Keep your body straight, the force should

be coming from here…' He indicated which muscles she should be using on his own shoulder.

She nodded, trying again. Better posture this time, but less force.

'You haven't been doing these for a while, have you?' He ventured the observation. It was obvious that Andrea had abandoned her exercises for more than just a couple of weeks.

She wrinkled her nose. 'No, I haven't. Would being busy be a good excuse?'

'No, not really.'

'I thought not. I wouldn't take it as one either. How about just not wanting to think about it?'

'Yeah, that'll do.' It was common enough, and in Andrea's situation more than understandable. Her shoulder was strong enough to perform all the everyday tasks she needed to do, probably even for light exercise and sport. But she was continually compensating, and that might well set up long-term problems.

She knew all that. He didn't need to explain, just to stick with her and show her, if he could, that a full recovery was possible. She'd been working at half throttle for a while now and he could see that it was beginning to frustrate her.

'Let's try again. Ten reps will be enough for starters.'

They went through the whole range of exercises and Cal slowly began to push her. Andrea pushed back, harder sometimes than she should, but when he called a halt she stopped. Helping her achieve something had taken over from the physical frisson of contact, and it was a deeper kind of thrill.

'Last one. We need to get this exactly right.' He sat back down on the bench. 'How do you do with backward movement?'

'Not all that well.' She turned the corners of her mouth down. 'That's the most difficult.'

'You want to give it a go?'

Of course she did. *Difficult* was like a red rag to a bull with Andrea. She had the kind of drive that would scatter every obstacle from her path, if only she could bring herself to use it.

She sat astride the bench, pushing herself back until her shoulders almost touched his chest. Cal swallowed hard, trying not to think about it. So far, Andrea's backward movements were just fine...

'Shoulders back.' He rapped out the instruction a little harshly, instinctively obeying it himself. He held out his hands, touching her elbows lightly with his palms.

'Uh. That's no good, is it?' Her right shoulder was noticeably weak and stiff.

'It could be better. You can improve it a lot if you keep working, though.' There was no point in telling her that it wasn't so bad. Andrea knew as well as he did that the shoulder needed some work.

Her body was warm against his. It was hard to remain unresponsive to her scent, and the feel of her so close. Cal closed his eyes and thought of...the wedding.

'Try again. Ten very gentle reps.' Andrea started to push against the pressure of his hand. 'I'm going to have to check out the venues for the stag night. Interested?'

'I can come with you on Tuesday. I'll be going down to the airport to meet some of the wedding guests, and I can put them on the hotel's minibus and meet you in the village afterwards. I'll leave Maggie and Joe to greet them at the hotel.'

'Yeah? Thanks, that would be good.' He could feel the pressure of Andrea's arm begin to falter against his hand. 'That's enough. Rest. You don't want to do too much today; we're skiing tomorrow.'

'Yes, I don't want to miss that. Although I may not be able to keep up with you guys.' It had been decided that tomorrow they'd all take a day off and go skiing together.

'I'm sure you won't have much trouble. Living here gives you much more opportunity to practise.'

'Ah, yes. My wonderful technique makes up for a lot.' Andrea chuckled. 'I can manage another ten.'

'Okay. Don't push it. Five for starters.'

He was pushing things to the very limit, wanting more of this warmth, more of the relaxed jokes and the underlying competitiveness that added a little spice to it all.

She managed five reps and then stopped. She turned suddenly to give him a smile.

'I think I'm done, now. Thanks, Cal. I don't suppose you could fly in every other morning, for the next six weeks, could you?' Andrea clearly knew that was impossible, but suddenly it didn't seem like such a bad idea.

'You don't need me. You know what to do, it's just a matter of keeping it a part of your routine.' This was what he told all his patients. Their recovery was as much in their hands as it was in his. It was usually an affirmation, a way of giving someone back control of their own body after they'd experienced surgery.

Now it was loss. Not just yet, though...

'What do you say we do this every other morning, until the end of the week? You'll start to see some difference, even after that. And I could do with a few sessions here in the gym.'

'Really?' She unashamedly looked him up and down,

and Cal felt a tingle follow the path of her gaze. 'You look like you're in pretty good shape to me.'

He *had* to move now. Cal got up, leaving her sitting on the bench. He was pretty sure that her gaze was still on him, and he resisted the temptation to throw back his shoulders and beat his chest in a primitive response.

'We'll ski tomorrow, and then if your shoulder's okay we'll try a short session on Tuesday morning. I'll come along to the airport if you like and we can go on to the village together.'

Andrea gave that sudden, gleaming smile of hers. 'Are you sure? I imagine you just *love* airports; you must see enough of them.'

'Yeah, I do. They're not so bad. The airport's always the start of something new.'

'Ah, well, in that case you can definitely come. First round's on me when we get to the village.'

'You're on. What are you doing today?'

'Consulting my list. Checking it twice...'

Cal chuckled. 'I'll catch up with you, then, when I've finished here. We can check both our lists together.'

CHAPTER NINE

IT WAS NICE having Cal around. He'd helped her take those first tentative steps yesterday morning, which marked her commitment to making a full recovery from her operation, instead of one that was just good enough. Afterwards, he hadn't minded wrapping little treats and gifts for the wedding while Andrea caught up with her emails.

The more normal routine of bumps, bruises, strains and the odd cut had reasserted itself in the medical suite. Tomas was managing perfectly well without her so Andrea could get on with her preparations for the wedding.

Monday dawned bright and clear, a perfect day for skiing. Andrea sat at her dressing table, carefully smoothing oil onto her scars.

She hadn't done that in a while, either. Sometimes the operation scar pulled a little and she'd started to just ignore it, along with the other jagged scar from the accident. But now she felt a little more conscious of them both. She just hadn't looked before, hadn't considered the possibility that the appearance of her scars could be improved. Why bother, when everything else was in ruins around her? Now, the possibility of something more shone brightly in the distance. A long way away, still, but it was there.

'We're not going to mention the W-E-D-D-I-N-G, today,' Maggie announced when the four of them were assembled in the reception area at the hotel. 'We're taking a break.'

Joe pulled a face of mock despair. 'You want a break already? We're not even married yet.'

'Not from you.' Maggie planted a kiss on his cheek. 'From everything else. Andrea and I have been working really hard to get everything organised. There's so much to think about.'

'Fair enough. I'm sure we've been doing a lot too, eh, Cal?'

Cal scratched his nose, grinning. 'Choosing the waistcoats was a tough one.'

'Yeah. Yeah, that was particularly gruelling.'

They might joke about it, but Cal had been there for her, just as much as Joe had been there for Maggie. And maybe it would be good to take a break from talking about the wedding, just for today.

They'd decided on a one-day ski tour, which would take them on an easy route up into the mountains, and then back down again at sunset. The group of ten was led by Francine and Bruno, who set off at the head of the party.

Out here in the mountains was the perfect place to forget about everything. The pace was brisk enough to keep everyone occupied, but there was time to stop and catch their breath, and to appreciate the snowscape around them.

'How are you doing?' Cal too seemed to have left his worries back at the hotel. A warm beanie and wrap-around reflective sunglasses, along with the fact that he hadn't shaved this morning, gave him a relaxed air.

'Fine.' Andrea knew the real intent of his question.

'My shoulder didn't hurt this morning, but I've put a support on, just as a precaution.'

They trekked together silently, up a long, steep slope. At the top, Francine called a halt for everyone to rest and admire the view.

'It's difficult, isn't it? Now that Maggie's put an embargo on mentioning the you-know-what, it's all I can think about.'

'What, out here? Cal, look around you.'

'Yeah, I know.' He laughed, propping his sunglasses on the rim of his hat. 'It's beautiful.'

He swung round, his gaze finding hers, just for a moment, but there was no question about his intended meaning. She was beautiful, too. Even after all she'd shown him of the uglier side of her life, he thought her beautiful.

'Cal, I've been thinking...and I want to apologise.'

'Again? What have you done this time?'

'I didn't make things very easy for you when you arrived. You were only trying to help.'

He grinned. 'I like a challenge.'

'Don't, Cal... I know I behaved badly.' The thought had been preying on Andrea's mind for days.

'You were protecting yourself. And I didn't respect that.' He turned the corners of his mouth down. 'You really don't have anything to apologise for.'

'Perhaps I should think a bit more carefully about who I choose to protect myself from.' The look in his eyes told Andrea that she'd been right in feeling that this was a sore spot for Cal. He really didn't like the thought that Andrea had been protecting herself from him, and when she thought about it, Andrea didn't much like it either.

'I'll leave you to make those decisions. And in the

meantime, I'm going to take a leaf out of Maggie's book and ban a word. Today isn't a day to be S-O-R-R-Y about anything.'

It wasn't. Cal stayed by her side as they trekked further into the mountains, making tracks in the fresh snow. It was enough that he was there. Everything was all right between them, and the silence warmed her.

Bruno had gone on ahead, and by the time they reached the log cabin he'd lit the wood-burning stove. Thick soup was bubbling in a pan, and the cabin was warming up.

Joe and Cal were arguing amicably about something and Maggie slipped her arm around Andrea's. 'I can see why you love it here. It's so…fresh. Clean. It's a good place for new starts.'

Maggie had made a new start. She was putting the cancer behind her, along with all the pain and worry it had brought. She and Joe were solid, and all they'd been through together had only brought them closer.

'It's a great place for new starts. Perfect for a…' Andrea stopped herself before she said it. 'A *you-know-what*.'

Maggie chuckled. 'Glad you're keeping to the rules. Yes, I'm glad we decided on here. Not least because you're here and we can spend some time together. I miss you.'

'I'll be back. I'm not sure when…'

'I know. That's okay. In the meantime, I can still miss you, can't I?' Maggie grinned at her friend.

It was on the tip of Andrea's tongue, but she didn't say it. She was beginning to think she might leave here sooner than Maggie thought, but she wasn't quite ready to make any firm decisions yet. It was as Cal had said.

Building new muscle took time, and that applied to emotional muscle as well.

'Yes, you can miss me. I miss you too.'

They spent an hour at the cabin, leaving it spick and span for the next group who would be arriving. Francine pulled a large block of chocolate from her pack, leaving it by the stove to replace the one that had been opened and shared around amongst the party.

It was all perfectly timed. The sun was going down as they reached a high ridge above the hotel and they stopped to take it all in. Golden light bathed the mountain tops, as the valleys became dark with shadow. Maggie flung her arms around Joe's neck, kissing him.

'There's one for the board.' Cal had taken his camera from the pouch inside his jacket and he showed Andrea the small display screen at the back. He'd caught their friends in an embrace, silhouetted against the sunset.

'That's gorgeous. Does that mean we can take down the one of Maggie and me having a water fight, and replace it with this?' Two little girls, both soaked to the skin and still trying to get each other even wetter than they already were.

'No. I particularly like that one; something else is going to have to go.' Cal put his camera back into the pouch. He didn't take many photographs, nor did he walk around with his camera in his hand all the time. But from time to time, he'd see something that he knew would make a good photograph and take the shot.

'You're not going to take any more?'

Cal shook his head. 'That was the one I wanted. I'd prefer to just enjoy this first hand.'

He put his arm around her shoulders. The way a good friend might do. Cal wasn't a good friend or a lover—they hadn't known each other long enough for either—but it felt right somehow. As if that was where she belonged.

'Maggie's watching...'

He chuckled. 'Fair enough. Is she taking photographs?'

'No. She isn't as bold as we are.'

He was very close. Andrea could almost feel Maggie's gaze boring into the back of her head, but her friend was too far away to see exactly what was happening between her and Cal. And Joe would surely keep her from borrowing Francine's binoculars...

Somehow it didn't seem right. Cal's kisses were wonderful, but it was the bond of honesty that had been formed between them that made them so special. And kissing out here, in front of everyone, wouldn't be honest because they'd both decided that they couldn't contemplate a relationship.

His gaze held hers for several heartbeats. The span of a kiss, and then another. Then they turned together towards the sunset.

As the sun disappeared behind the mountains, a spark in the half-light drew Cal's attention. 'What's Bruno doing?'

'Wait and see. They always do this...' One of the other instructors from the hotel had come up to meet them, carrying four long torches, which Bruno had staked into the snow. When he lit them, flames jumped high into the air.

Francine took two of them, and Bruno the other two. They looked at each other nodding a countdown, and at the same moment they both launched themselves onto the slope.

It was a complex fire dance that never failed to thrill

Andrea. The instructors all prided themselves on it and practised regularly, but all the artifice of balance and co-ordination was subsumed in the magic of trails of fire that wound their way down in the darkness. She took Cal's arm and snuggled against him. He was the only person she wanted to share this with.

Francine and Bruno reached the bottom and everyone cheered and applauded. The third instructor was giving out electric torches so the trekkers could hold them up as they descended, and at the bottom of the slope Bruno threw one of his flaming torches theatrically in the air, spinning it like a Catherine wheel.

'Andrea… Andrea!' Maggie and Joe were making their way towards her, Maggie waving excitedly.

'Wasn't that wonderful? Do you think… I don't want to impose but…might they do that for the wedding?'

'Don't mention the wedding!' Both she and Cal chorused the words, and Joe laughed.

'But this is different! Would it be out of order if you just asked…?'

'I promise I'll ask them, but I can't promise a yes.'

Andrea saw Cal's lips twitch before he straightened his face. He'd read the wedding folder, including the part she hadn't shown Maggie. When Andrea had mentioned the possibility to Francine, she'd told her that the instructors would have been insulted *not* to be asked. Eight of them were already practising a new descent formation, which would take place at sunset when Maggie and Joe were cutting the cake, and Francine had promised Andrea that it would be spectacular.

'Thank you.' Maggie seemed content with Andrea's diffident reply. 'I'm sure they might be busy or something. It's terribly short notice but it would be lovely.'

Cal stepped in, relieving Andrea of the temptation to

tell her friend everything. He took Maggie's arm, and began to walk towards the instructor who was giving out the torches. 'If they can't do it, I'll do it myself for you, Maggie. Naked. With a rose between my teeth.'

The joke had the desired effect. Maggie screamed with laughter, digging her elbow into Cal's ribs, and Joe made a comment about wanting to see that.

'So I'll cancel with Francine, then.' She murmured the words as they joined the line of skiers making their way downhill. 'What colour rose would you like me to get you?'

Cal chuckled. 'Better get blue. It'll match my fingers.'

Their second morning in the gym together left Cal quietly satisfied. It was too soon for Maggie's shoulder to show any improvement, but she was more focussed. He had always felt that the continuation of therapeutic exercise was a matter of self-care and getting into the right head space, and Andrea was more careful about getting her posture exactly right today.

The hotel's minibus was waiting for them in the village for the journey to the airport to pick up the wedding guests who were arriving on the noon flight. As they waited at the gates, Andrea was getting more and more excited.

'How long is it since you've seen your parents?'

'Three months. I stayed with them for a couple of weeks before the season got started, and we video conference once a week, but it's not the same.'

The passengers began to file through the gates, and Andrea waved whenever she recognised someone. Cal accompanied the first arrivals over to the luggage carousel, helping them lift their suitcases off, while

Andrea greeted the next group and pointed them in his direction.

Then he heard her calling out. A couple in their fifties were walking towards her, smiling.

'Mum! Dad!' Andrea hugged her mother and then her father. Turning, she beckoned Cal over.

'This is Cal, Joe's best man. Cal, this is my mum, Linda, and my dad, George.'

Cal shook Linda's hand, feeling it cool in his. She was a slight woman and seemed tired from the trip, her dark eyes a little faraway in their gaze. George's grip was firm and assured and his smile was broader. He had white curls and blue-grey eyes that were a lot like Andrea's.

'Cal. Andrea's told me that you're a doctor, as well.'

'Yes.' The thought that some of Andrea's precious video-conferencing time had been spent talking about him was gratifying. 'You've worked in Africa, I hear.'

'That was a long time ago. I'd like to sit down with you, though, and hear about your travels. Andrea says that you're involved with setting up medical facilities all over the world. I'd be interested to hear what's changed since I worked abroad. Lin—?' George broke off suddenly, looking round at his wife.

Linda swayed slightly, and then her legs seemed to just crumple under her. Cal had to move fast to catch her before she hit the floor. She was dead weight in his arms, and he picked her up, carrying her over to a line of seats.

George was at his side, helping him to lay Linda down and rolling up his jacket to put under her head. But when Cal looked quickly over his shoulder, Andrea was standing stock-still.

All the colour had drained out of her face, and she

was trembling, seeming not to notice the people hurrying back and forth around her.

'George…' He heard Linda's voice and focussed his attention back on her, silently willing Andrea to come to her senses. He knew why this must be such a shock to her, but she'd come so far in the past week. If she froze now, it would be yet another knock to her confidence.

There was nothing he could do about that now. George was kneeling beside his wife and he shouldn't be left to deal with her alone.

'Just lie still for a minute, Lin.'

'I'm all right.' Linda tried to sit up, and George gently stopped her. 'I think I must have fainted…'

George smiled at his wife, the same warmth registering in his eyes that Cal had seen in Andrea's. 'Stay there for a minute, love. I just want to make sure you're all right.'

'But, George—'

'Do as Dad says, Mum.' Andrea's voice sounded clear and firm behind him. Cal got out of the way, allowing her to bend down beside her mother.

Andrea reached forward, placing her hand on her mother's forehead. 'You've not got a fever. Any headaches?'

George got to his feet, standing next to Cal, his gaze flipping from his wife to his daughter. 'We'll let Andrea see to her mother.'

Cal nodded. Both men were of the same mind, that Andrea needed to be the one to do this. She was asking all the right questions, doing all the right things. Cal wondered if George was ticking off each possibility in his mind, the same way he was.

Finally, Andrea helped her mother to sit up, turning to face them. 'She's all right. She just fainted.'

'I told you so, dear.' Some colour was beginning to return to Linda's cheeks. 'We should have had breakfast before we came out.'

The other wedding guests were standing in a small knot beside the luggage carousel. An elderly woman in a bright purple windcheater stepped forward, jabbing her finger at his arm. Cal had been told that this was Aunt Mae, but, since everyone seemed to call her that, it wasn't entirely clear whose aunt she was.

'Is she all right?'

'She fainted, Aunt Mae. Have you got any water in your handbag, please?' Andrea answered for him.

The question seemed an odd one, but Aunt Mae began to rummage in her flight bag, producing a bottle of water and a plastic cup. Andrea collected them, sitting back down beside her mother and pouring the water for her.

'I've got a sandwich as well.'

'No, thanks, Aunt Mae, I'm feeling better now.' Linda smiled at her. 'Thanks for the water.'

'You should have something to eat.' Aunt Mae wasn't going to take no for an answer. 'Ham and tomato.'

Linda gave in to the inevitable. 'Maybe just a bite, then. If you could break a little piece off...'

'That's all right.' Mae produced a film-wrapped sandwich from her bag, handing it to Andrea. 'I've got another one. Eating something will make you feel better.'

Andrea accepted the sandwich, moving her father's jacket so that Aunt Mae could come and sit down next to Linda. As George shrugged the coat back on, he turned to Cal.

'Three doctors in attendance, and it turns out that Aunt Mae's got the remedy in her handbag. Typical, eh?'

Cal laughed, nodding in agreement. He was so proud of Andrea. Anyone would have forgiven her for panicking when she saw her mother taken ill so unexpectedly. She'd needed a moment, but she'd pulled herself together and come to help. He could see the pride in George's eyes too as he looked at his daughter.

He wished he could stay but the other guests were still standing by the carousel, not sure what to do next. He walked over to them, assuring everyone that Linda was quite all right, and shepherding them out of the airport and into the waiting minibus.

When he returned, George was retrieving his and Linda's suitcases from the luggage carousel. Andrea walked to the minibus with her mother, helping her in, while Cal and the driver finished loading up the boot.

As he got into the bus, Andrea caught his arm. 'I'm sorry, Cal. I don't think I can make tonight...'

'That's okay. I'm going to come back to the hotel as well.' He wanted to be there for Andrea, if she needed to talk.

'Thanks.' She shot him a glistening smile and Cal went to sit down next to Aunt Mae, who was busy handing round a packet of extra-strong peppermints.

Cal was right where she'd expected him to be, sitting in one of the armchairs in the reception area with a cup of hot chocolate and an English newspaper. He liked busy places, and seemed to be able to concentrate even though people were moving back and forth all around him. Andrea sat down in the chair opposite his.

'Hey. How's your mum?' He looked up from the paper, putting it aside.

'She's fine. Dad and I have been through the entire

medical dictionary together, and our joint medical opinion is that she fainted.'

Cal chuckled. 'Must be challenging having a husband and a daughter who are doctors.'

'Must be. My brother's a doctor as well.'

He winced. 'No wonder she prefers to listen to Aunt Mae. Whose aunt is she, by the way?'

'No one's, actually. She's Maggie's mother's next-door neighbour, and Maggie and I have known her since we were kids. She used to ask us to tea and we'd have soda water in china cups and little cakes. We thought we were very grown up.'

'And she always has a sandwich in her handbag?'

'Always. She takes a bottle of water and a sandwich with her when she goes shopping, and sits down and has them in the library. You're not supposed to eat in there, but they all know her and turn a blind eye.'

'She's great. She was telling me all about ancient Sami warriors from northern Finland on the minibus. Apparently the women used to fight with bows and arrows on skis.'

'She's a mine of information; her house is full of books. When I went to medical school, she gave me a twenty-pound note in an envelope, and told me to spend it on going out and having fun. She said I was going to be a fine doctor, like my dad...' Andrea felt her lip quiver. Aunt Mae had made a big mistake on that score.

'You *are* a fine doctor.' Cal was looking at her steadily.

'I froze, Cal.' He'd seen her do it and it was impossible for him to deny it.

'I know. And then you pulled yourself together and made sure that she was all right.'

'It wasn't too difficult. Even Aunt Mae knew that

she'd only fainted.' Andrea heaved a sigh. It was okay. She knew her limitations. She'd just dared to think that one day she might break through those barriers.

'Andrea, there's a reason why I wouldn't operate on a member of my family. It's because I'm too personally involved with them. Are you telling me you should feel nothing when your own mother collapses?'

Andrea shrugged. 'No, I suppose not.'

'You had every reason to freeze after what you've been through. What matters is that you helped her. She could have been really ill and you had no way of knowing that. But I saw you check her over and you did it thoroughly without worrying her. You are a *very* fine doctor.'

Andrea's head was reeling. Cal was asking her to believe in herself. And somehow that suddenly wasn't so hard, because *he* believed in her.

'In that case...thank you.'

He gave her a quizzical look. 'Is that all you have to say?'

'Yes. I think it is. Thank you, Cal.'

He smiled. 'Seems I'm more persuasive than I thought.'

'Seems you are.' Andrea looked at her watch. 'Do you still want to go down to the village? We've got enough time to look at the places on my list if we're quick.'

He shook his head. 'No. I think I'd rather stay here and have an early night.'

That sounded as if it was for her benefit. Andrea felt as if she could do with an early night, and probably looked that way too.

'But we won't have another chance. Maggie and Joc's parents are flying in tomorrow morning, and then there's the rehearsal in the afternoon, and we'll all be having dinner together afterwards. Then on Thursday it's the stag and hen nights.'

'You choose a place. You've already made the list, you may as well. Where would you go?'

'But it's a stag night. I've never been on one of those before.'

He rolled his eyes. 'Andrea, if I was taken ill, there's no one I'd rather have around than you. If I can trust you with that, then I'm sure I can trust you to choose a good place for Joe's stag night.'

There was a note of exasperation in his tone. And Cal always told the truth, particularly when he was exasperated. The thought that he really did trust her lifted some of the weight that had been pressing on Andrea's chest for the last couple of hours.

'Okay. There's a little family-run place about five minutes' walk from the funicular railway. They do great food, good beer, and it's a really relaxed atmosphere. Later on in the evening there's music and lots of singing. How does that sound?'

He gave her a delicious smile. 'It sounds perfect. Sorted.'

CHAPTER TEN

EVERYONE HAD ARRIVED SAFELY, the rehearsal had been relaxed, and now the stag night had gone smoothly. Cal had counted everyone onto the funicular railway and then back off again. He and Joe had agreed that it was one of the better stag parties they'd attended, before Joe went to find Maggie. Cal should go and get a good night's sleep now, but there was one thing he had to do before he turned in.

As he said his farewells to everyone, shaking their hands and wishing them a good night, he saw Joe walk back towards the lift with Maggie. They were laughing together, Joe's arm around Maggie's shoulders. Maggie's choice of wardrobe—a pair of sheepskin boots teamed up with a towelling robe—was a bit of a give-away for where he might find Andrea.

He walked through the bar and out onto the wide veranda. At the far end, the hot tub was surrounded by light and shadow, and as he approached it he could see a figure resting against one corner of the large hexagonal tub, luxuriating in the bubbles.

'Hey there.' Andrea saw him coming and gave him a wave. 'How did it go?'

'Good. The bar was great, and everyone's in one piece. Yours?'

'We had a lovely time. Maggie's just left with Joe.' Andrea half swam towards him, holding her cocktail glass up above the bubbles, but it slipped out of her hand. 'Oops.'

Cal squatted on his heels, chuckling. Andrea was watching the glass bob up and down on the surface of the water, and he pulled up his sleeve, retrieving it.

'So how drunk are you?'

She raised her eyebrows. 'Not even slightly. I've been on virgin cocktails all night. I wanted to make sure everything went well.'

'Me too. Only it was non-alcoholic beer.'

She quirked her mouth down. 'Too bad. So you're not even a little bit tipsy?'

Andrea gave all the appearance of being a little tipsy herself. Maybe it was the stars above their heads, relief that the evening had gone well, or maybe just relaxing with her friends had that heady, bright-eyed effect on her.

'Now that it's all over, and we don't have to worry about anyone else, would you like a drink?'

'Only if you join me. It's wonderful in here.'

Too much temptation. Far too much. And Cal was only human...

He hurried up to his room, changing into his bathing trunks. He wrapped one of the warm towelling bathrobes that the hotel supplied around him, and made a detour to the bar on the way back.

'Ooh! Champagne.' She grinned at him as he traversed the heated tiles that led to the tub. Cal propped the bottle in the snow, shivering in the night air as he hurriedly took off his robe and got into the tub.

'Ahh. This is very relaxing.' The warm bubbles against his skin almost took him by surprise. His eyes were telling him that they were surrounded by snow, but the rest of his senses were registering a delicious heat. Made no less delicious by the fact that he was sharing a tub with Andrea.

'Isn't it? I could almost *be* drunk.'

But she wasn't. Andrea was just relaxed and happy, and seeing her like this made Cal's own head swim a little.

He reached out of the tub, pouring two glasses of champagne and handing one to her. 'What shall we drink to?'

'A successful night. Joe and Maggie tucked up safe and sound together.'

'Sounds good to me. Joe and Maggie.'

He tipped his glass against hers. He was caught in her gaze, and the first sip of champagne seemed to go right to his head. He drifted over to the other side of the tub, in an effort to gather his senses, but Andrea was entrancing, tonight.

It wasn't just the stars above their heads or the champagne. Her curls were caught up at the back of her head, and her neck formed a perfect curve that he could contemplate all night. Her cheeks were pink, and beneath the bubbles he could catch a tantalising glimpse of slim legs.

'So. Give me all the gossip, then. Did Joe's uncle Pete have one too many?'

'He was heading that way. I ordered him a few rounds of non-alcoholic beer, and he never knew the difference.'

'Good thinking. Maggie was a little worried he might get out of order and spoil the evening.'

'He was fine. Going somewhere where we could have something to eat made a big difference. Joe's little brother took a shine to one of the girls on the next table to us, and spent most of the evening chatting to her.'

'Fabulous. Did he get her number?'

'After a fashion. He wrote it on his hand, but it's probably worn off by now. She said she wanted to give him a call so I texted her his number.'

'Nice. You're *really* good at this. What about Joe's grandfather? Did he stay the course?'

'You're joking, right? Grandpa Dave had more stamina than all of us. He wanted to go on somewhere else but I managed to persuade him to get the last train back with us. He told me that young people these days don't know how to have a good time.'

'Mm. He might be right. Maggie's grandmother wanted to know when the male strippers were going to turn up, and she was very disappointed when I told her that Maggie would have been completely mortified at the thought, and I hadn't booked any.' Andrea grinned at him. 'So were you a bit rowdy?'

'It was a stag night. Of course we were rowdy.'

Andrea nodded in approval. 'Yes, so were we. I feel so much better about the wedding now. I really needed a good night out.'

She held her glass out and Cal took it, refilling it along with his. It had been a good evening but *this* was the best part. It felt like coming home and finding Andrea there waiting for him—having a drink together, taking the time to relax and talk about the day.

And then what? Just appreciating the silence as they were now? Warm in the knowledge that the person he was with was his soulmate, and that they could face whatever the morning threw at them together?

Maybe reaching for her in the night. Cal adjusted the emphasis. *Definitely* reaching for her in the night.

Knowing that she would want him as much as he wanted her.

Falling in love with her seemed only a whisper away tonight, but it still wasn't enough. Cal had struggled so hard to walk his own path in life that he couldn't imagine sharing it with someone else. Joe and Maggie seemed to do it effortlessly, merging their hopes and dreams into one. But Cal wasn't sure that he'd ever have whatever it was that allowed them to do that.

'It's getting late.' Something in Andrea's eyes told him that she didn't want the evening to end, either.

'Yeah. I guess we should both go and get some sleep. Busy day tomorrow.' His regret must have shown in his face, because she smiled and gave a little nod.

Cal got out of the pool, feeling the tang of cold air on his skin. Wrapping himself quickly in his robe, he picked Andrea's up and held it open for her. She climbed out of the tub, slipping her arms into the sleeves and knotting the robe tightly around her waist.

'Thank you.' She smiled up at him. 'Best part of my evening.'

'Mine too.' He picked up the bottle of champagne. 'You want to take this with you?'

She thought about it and then shook her head. 'Thanks, but no. There's a little too much there for me, and I wouldn't want to waste it.'

Nothing was wasted on Andrea. If she'd taken just one sip then the whole bottle would have been worth it.

'Put it in the fridge, with a spoon in the top. That's supposed to keep it fresh, isn't it?'

'Mmm. Never sure if that really works or not. They've got some champagne stoppers behind the bar for just this situation. Let's go and see whether *they* work.'

Cal was beginning to feel the cool of the air on his

skin now, and he hurried her inside. His last vision of Andrea was of seeing her walk away from him, swathed in a white towelling robe, a half-bottle of champagne dangling from her hand.

And it took all his strength of will not to follow her.

Andrea woke with one thought crisp and clear in her mind.

Cal.

He was just as beautiful as she'd imagined he would be. Strong shoulders, and the kind of chest that was just made to run your fingers across. The steam rising from the water had liquefied on his skin and in his hair, making him look even more delicious. And the best thing about him was that Andrea was sure that Cal knew exactly how to use those slim hips and sensitive fingers, that he was a man who would make love with his head and his heart, and that both of those could be tender and commanding in exactly the right measure.

Maggie had been right. Cal *was* a great guy, and he *was* just what she needed. Andrea sat bolt upright in bed. Maggie. Joe. The Wedding! How could she have forgotten?

Cal, that was how. He could drive every other thought from her head with just a smile. Last night had been perfect and the best part of it had been him.

But now she had things to do. Lots of them. Andrea got out of bed, heading purposefully for the shower.

'Cal, I don't suppose you could help Maggie's grandmother, could you? She's lost one of her hearing aids...' Andrea's morning had been spent facing a thousand last-minute catastrophes, and she'd somehow managed to find a solution for all of them. Now she was busy with the flowers for the room where the reception would be held.

'Yeah, sure. Where is she?'

'Um…not quite sure. Looking for her hearing aid, I think…' Andrea looked around for the florist but she seemed to have disappeared as well.

'Okay. If she's found the hearing aid, does that mean she's lost now?'

Suddenly today didn't seem quite so much of an uphill battle. Cal's dry humour always made things less daunting.

'Yes, I suppose it does.'

'Okay, just so I know. I'll make sure that Maggie's grandmother is in the same place as both of her hearing aids, and that we know where that is.'

Andrea laughed, feeling the tension in her chest ease. 'That would be great. Thanks.'

Her phone buzzed and she took it out of her pocket. 'Oh, no! Why didn't Craig call Tomas? He's on duty today.'

'What's the matter?'

'One of the cooks has fallen down the stairs. They don't think he's hurt but they want me to go down there.'

'I can do that if you like.'

'Would you? I know it's a bit much to ask, but I really need to find the florist.'

'You get on. Consider the cook and Maggie's grandmother sorted.'

He made everything so much easier. Andrea leaned towards him, kissing him on the cheek. 'Thank you so much, Cal.'

She felt the light brush of his fingers on her waist before she stepped back again. How so little could make her feel so much was a mystery—one of those fabulous, enchanting mysteries that could keep you guessing for hours. Now that she'd seen him without most of his clothes, his touch was even more potent.

'My pleasure.' He made that sound as if it referred to the kiss.

'Oh, you know how to get downstairs to the kitchen? Go into the restaurant and tell them you're the doctor, and you need to see Craig.'

'Gotcha.' He turned, and Andrea watched as he walked away.

One more moment of calm, still pleasure. Then Andrea turned her attention back to the flowers.

The strap had been glued back onto the youngest bridesmaid's sandal. Maggie's grandmother had thanked her for sending that nice young man to help her with her hearing aids. Cal had texted to say that the cook was all right, and Andrea had shown Joe's little brother how to knot a bow tie.

Maggie had seemed to float through it all. Her dress was fine, she could find the diamond earrings that her parents had given her, and she hadn't fallen prey to a plague of spots. Andrea had taken the half-bottle of champagne, along with two glasses, to Maggie's room.

'Ooh, champagne!' Maggie took a sip. 'It's the good stuff as well. Where did you get that from?'

'It was left over from last night.' Maggie would have been delighted to hear that she and Cal had been sharing it, but that was something that Andrea wanted to keep for herself. She tipped her glass against Maggie's.

'I'd like to propose a toast. Maggie, you're the most beautiful, lowest-maintenance bride I've ever seen. It's a real honour to be your bridesmaid.'

Maggie flung her arms around Andrea, almost spilling champagne down the back of her neck. 'You've done so much for me, Andrea. Where would I be without you?'

Andrea laughed. 'Maybe the same place I'd be without you. I suppose at least we'd be together.'

'Mmm. Together always. That's nice.' Maggie took another swallow of champagne. 'Now, why don't you sit down for a moment? I'll go and fetch your dress for tonight's dinner, and press it for you.'

'No! You're not supposed to be doing that.'

'Don't be silly. You've been running around after everyone else, can't I do something for you?'

'The only thing that you can do for me is to enjoy your wedding day. Anyway, I wouldn't mind half an hour to myself, just to get ready.'

Maggie nodded. 'Okay. I'll see you downstairs, then.'

It took Andrea three quarters of an hour to get ready, most of which was spent luxuriating in a hot shower. It had been a busy day, but everything was done now. The wedding would go off without a hitch tomorrow.

By the time she arrived in the main restaurant, everyone was seated and the waiters were dispensing drinks. She looked around for Cal, but couldn't see him. How could a room full of friends and family seem empty without him?

As she opened her bag to take out her phone, she felt it vibrate. He must be on his way... Andrea opened his text.

Wedding emergency!

Andrea frowned. There was just enough information to send a tingle of alarm down her spine and not enough to reassure.

But it's okay. We can fix things.

Right. Now she was really worried. Her phone buzzed again as the next instalment of his text arrived.

Don't tell Maggie or Joe.

Maggie and Joe were sitting together and someone had proposed a toast. The clinking of glasses and a round of applause drowned out Andrea's exasperated words.

'You didn't need to tell me that, Cal.'

She started to type a return text but her phone buzzed again.

Get away when you can and meet me in the kitchen. Everything's going to be fine.

Going over to the table and sitting down until she could think of a reason to tear herself away wasn't going to work. Andrea walked over to Maggie, who turned and pulled the empty seat next to her back from the table.

'At last! Where were you?' Maggie's face was shining.

'I had a long, hot shower. And… I'm sorry, I've been called away. Nothing major, I won't be more than a few minutes…'

'That's okay. A doctor's work is never done, eh?'

'Um…no.' Maggie had provided her with as good an excuse as any. 'I'll be as quick as I can.'

'We'll save some champagne for you.' Joe leaned over, smiling.

'Great, thanks. I'll be back in two ticks.'

Andrea hurried down to the kitchen. They were busy with the meal for tonight, and she couldn't see Cal amongst the to and fro. But he'd obviously been watching for her, and after a few moments she saw him striding towards her.

'I didn't mean for you to come straight away...'

'Cal, what is there about "wedding emergency" that doesn't imply urgency?'

He frowned. 'Yes, I suppose that was a little over the top. I just meant for you to come as soon as you could.'

It wasn't like Cal to panic over anything. 'Cal, you're really worrying me now. Just get it over with and tell me what's wrong.'

He wordlessly took her hand, leading her over to the large larder at the far end of the kitchen. Craig, the pastry chef, was hovering by the door, and Cal led the way inside.

'We can fix this. I have a plan...' He seemed intent on giving her the good news first, when Andrea was only really interested in the bad news. She could deal with that, whatever it was.

Or...maybe not.

'Cal! What happened?' Maggie's beautiful wedding cake was lying on the long bench that ran along one wall. In about a million pieces.

'The guy who fell down the stairs...he was carrying the wedding cake.'

'What? What was he doing carrying the wedding cake around? He's all right though, isn't he?'

'Yes, he's fine. He might have a couple of bruises. Craig told him to take it upstairs so they could check what it looked like in situ.'

Andrea rolled her eyes. 'Couldn't they just have imagined what it would look like?'

Cal shrugged. 'We can't blame the kitchen staff. We did make a bit of a thing about checking that everything was going to be perfect.'

'Oh, so it's *my* fault, is it?' After she had navigated so many small problems today, this unexpected disaster was threatening to overwhelm Andrea.

'No, I didn't mean it like that. It's no one's fault, it was an accident, and, to be honest, I'd rather see the cake in pieces than the cook.'

'You're right. Of course you are.' Andrea pressed her hand against her chest in an attempt to slow her racing heart. 'I'm going to take a breath...'

'That sounds like a good idea. I think I'll join you.' Cal made a visible effort to steady himself. 'Why are we panicking so much? If my hand shook like this in the operating theatre, I'd be out of a job.'

'You know what to do in the operating theatre. How many culinary disasters have you dealt with lately?'

'You've got a point. Perhaps we should pretend we're doing an emergency appendectomy...'

'Whatever works, Cal. What are we going to do?'

'I have a plan. I told Craig that we'd need a new cake, three actually, as there are three tiers, and they're already in the oven. He's done three different kinds: carrot cake for the bottom layer, then chocolate, then red velvet for the top tier.'

'Oh. That sounds rather nice. Red velvet, you say?'

'Yeah. Don't imagine that just because I'm passing on the message it means I know what a red velvet cake is.'

'It's a bit like devil's food cake, only it has cocoa instead of chocolate.'

Cal grinned. 'There. I thought you'd know more about cake than I do. Anyway, Craig says they'll be fine for tomorrow. He's going to put them in the large chiller cabinet to cool, and make a white buttercream icing...'

Andrea nodded. 'That's right. We won't have time for marzipan and royal icing.'

'Yes he mentioned that, too. It'll all be ready by to-morrow.'

'Are you sure?' Cal's optimism was heartening, but Andrea wasn't sure whether it was based on hard facts. 'It'll take most of the night to decorate it, and we can't ask Craig to stay here. His wife's about to have a baby.'

'Yeah, he did offer; he's feeling pretty guilty about the accident with the first cake. But I told him he should go home and that I'd do it. So...well, he's teaching me how to make icing-sugar roses.'

What? Now wasn't the time to mention that Craig made it look easy because he'd had years of practice.

'Okay... Well...that'll be okay.' Andrea searched her mind for something positive and encouraging to say. 'You're a surgeon, so you must be good with a knife.'

'A scalpel, actually...' He shot her an unconvinced look.

'Use a scalpel, then. There's a whole box of them up in the medical suite. Imagine... I don't know, imagine you're doing sutures.'

'Operation Cake, then.'

'Yes. Operation Cake.' Andrea caught sight of something in the ruins of the old cake. She picked it up, wiping it off. 'Look, the little statuette of the bride and groom is okay. We've still got that.'

Suddenly he caught her hand, pressing her fingers to his lips. That, more than anything else, made the panic subside. 'You think it'll work, then.'

'Yes, of course it'll work. We don't have any choice,

do we? I'm not going to be the one to tell Maggie that she can't have a cake on her wedding day.'

'No. Me neither.'

'I'd better go back to the dinner. Maggie will get suspicious and come to find us if we're both AWOL. I'll come back here as soon as I can slip away and give you a hand.'

Cal shook his head. 'You'll be up all night. You've been working hard all day.'

'So have you. And it won't be the first time I've pulled an all-nighter. We can do this, Cal.'

He nodded quietly. The calm, cool-headed doctor was back. 'Okay. Thanks. I'll see you later, then. Even if you can just stay for an hour or so, that would be fantastic.'

Andrea put the little bride and groom statuette into his hand. She really wanted to stay here now, with Cal, but she had to cover for him at the dinner.

'I forgot the most important thing...' Andrea heard his voice behind her as she was turning to go.

'Yes?'

'You look beautiful tonight.'

CHAPTER ELEVEN

THE DINNER WAS AGONY. Despite her reassurances to Cal, Andrea was swallowing down her panic. Less than eighteen hours until the wedding and they had no cake.

Somehow, she got through the dinner. She told Maggie and Joe that Cal was arranging a last-minute surprise for the bridesmaids, which was close enough to the truth. This particular bridesmaid was going to be completely gobsmacked if they managed to produce something that even approximated a wedding cake, let alone compared with the beautiful cake that Maggie had chosen.

She took her leave as soon as she could. Then Andrea hurried back to her apartment, changing into a T-shirt and jeans and using the back stairs to go down to the kitchen so she wouldn't be seen.

Washing up was under way and the gleaming kitchen was being restored to its usual order for the morning. Cal was in one corner, wearing a borrowed chef's jacket and apron. Hopefully the cake was on course to be as delicious as he looked.

'Hey.' He gave her a smile. 'I didn't expect you so soon.'

'How's it going?' Andrea craned her head around him and saw a white sugar rose, placed carefully at the far end of his work station. 'That's the one Craig gave you as an example?'

'It's my first try...well, it's the fourth try, but this is the first one I didn't throw away. What do you think?' He surveyed the rose with a critical eye.

'You did that? It's brilliant, Cal.'

'Just another dozen to go, then.' He pointed at a sketch, tacked up on the tiled splashback. 'This is what we're aiming for.'

It was ambitious. A three-tiered cake, with a spray of leaves and roses snaking from top to bottom. There were butterflies amongst the leaves, and tiny roses around the statuette of the bride and groom.

'We're doing *that*? Isn't it a bit ambitious?'

'Craig showed me a few tricks for making the roses. They'll cover up the imperfections in the icing—that's the most difficult part to get right. He's left a list of all the things we need to do, and a diagram of where the support dowels go. That part actually looks quite easy...'

'You can do that, then. What can I do to help?'

Cal grinned. 'He left a jacket and apron for you. The cakes should be cool now so they need to be iced. There's a butterfly cutter just there, or I'll show you how to do the roses.'

'You stick with the roses; it looks as if you've mastered them now. I'll ice the cakes, shall I? I've plastered an old fireplace before...'

'Great. You have all the skills you need, then.' Cal's smile was enough to supply Andrea with the confidence she needed. 'Craig's left about a tonne of icing in those bowls over there, so we've got plenty to work with. I asked him to do some extra in case of mistakes.'

It looked as if Craig had anticipated more than a few

mistakes. There was enough icing here to cover the whole ballroom. But now wasn't the time to be thinking about what could go wrong. Andrea fixed her gaze onto the sketch. If this went right, it would be beautiful.

Andrea picked up the apron, looping it over her head. 'Let's get started, then.'

Two o'clock in the morning. It was usually the lowest point in any long night, but Cal's presence had kept Andrea going. Always positive, always supportive. There was a line of roses now, of various different sizes, and he'd applied a dark pink blush to the pale pink ones. The icing on the cakes wasn't perfectly smooth but it would do, and Cal had carefully sunk the supporting dowels into the cakes and stacked them. Andrea's icing-sugar butterflies had turned out to be better than she expected and Cal had brought them to life with a few adept strokes of a fine brush, coated with food dye. Andrea stood back to survey their handiwork.

'You know, if ever we can't find work as doctors, speciality cakes might be an option.'

Cal chuckled, straightening his back and stretching. 'We could. Although this is surprisingly nerve-racking. I don't know how Craig stands the strain.'

'It's all a matter of what you know, isn't it?' Andrea suspected that Cal had put his surgical skills to use tonight: the care and the concentration; the exact precision of his work; his steady hand.

Cal nodded. 'I think that's it now. Just one more thing before we can start putting the roses onto the cake.'

'What's that?'

'The last one. We'll make it together.'

But...he was so good at them. And it would be

quicker if Cal did it himself. But he seemed determined that she should help.

'Yes. I'd really like that.'

She rolled out the icing, and Cal cut each layer of petals carefully to shape. Then it was a matter of teasing out the edges of each layer, so they would look like the delicate folds of a petal.

'Ah. No, that's no good.' Andrea discarded the rather odd-looking rose.

'Try again. Like this.' Cal cut another layer, nudging her fingers into just the right place as she made the tiny centre. 'Now you curl the petals out, thinning the edges. And you build up your rose from there.'

He was so close. So careful and precise. He guided her shaking fingers, his thumb pressing on hers to flatten the edges of each petal. Perfectly in unison, making something wonderful together.

'That's it. Beautiful.' His voice sounded quietly in her ear. 'Now we sign our work.'

He dipped the brush into the food dye, carefully inscribing a small 'C' on the back of the rose where it couldn't be seen. Then he handed Andrea the brush, and she made a wobbly 'A', right next to it.

'Cal...' Andrea set the rose down, turning to wrap her arms around him.

'Never thought we'd get this far?' He returned the hug.

'No.' She laid her head against his chest. The kitchen was still warm but nothing like as hot as it had been in the aftermath of the evening's cooking. His warmth seeped through her, making her feel strong and confident enough to finish what they'd started, and place the roses and butterflies on the cake according to the sketch.

'Me neither. But we're nearly there now...' He was gazing down at her. Nearly there suddenly seemed tantalisingly far away. Andrea stood on her toes, planting a kiss onto his jaw.

There was that sharp sigh that told her he wanted just the same as she did. And then his mouth on hers, soft as the touch of rose petals. Demanding, in the way that Cal did so well. She could feel her whole body responding to the kiss, her legs beginning to shake...

But he was there. Strong and solid. Holding her in his arms as if she was the most precious thing in the world. Kissing her as if that was the most beautiful thing in the world. Having to let him go was so very unfair.

And so very necessary. Amongst other things, they had a cake to finish.

'We'll be here when the morning shift comes in to make breakfast at this rate.' It was Cal who broke the spell.

'Yes. Better get on...'

It was gone three o'clock but the cake was done. Cal carried it to the store room, giving it one last look before he covered it carefully. He couldn't believe they'd actually managed to produce something that looked vaguely like the sketch Craig had given him. They took off their aprons, making for the stairs together.

'I think I've got my second wind. I'm starting to feel wide awake.' Andrea smiled up at him when they reached the door of her apartment.

'Yes, me too. Must be relief. I didn't think we'd do as well as we have.'

'No, me neither. Would you like to come in for some hot chocolate?'

The hot chocolate he could take or leave. Another ten

minutes with Andrea, before he went alone to his bed, seemed absolutely necessary. 'Yes. Thanks.'

When he sat down on the long, comfortable sofa, Cal realised his back was aching from bending over the countertop. Andrea disappeared into the kitchen, coming back with two steaming cups of chocolate. She sat down next to him.

This companionable silence was nice—warm and comfortable, and spiced with the knowledge that they'd taken on something that had seemed impossible, and somehow managed it. Andrea snuggled against him, and he felt his eyelids begin to droop...

Cal was warm and comfortable. It must be a dream because he could feel the soft weight of a woman, half on top of him. He knew it must be Andrea because she smelled of icing-sugar roses.

Cal's eyes snapped open. Andrea. Her sofa. Her apartment. In a moment of sudden panic, he tried to piece together their progress here, but he could only get as far as two cups of hot chocolate. Then he realised he was fully dressed and so was she.

They'd both been tired last night. He'd probably kicked off his shoes while still dreaming, and one or other of them had pulled the throw from the back of the sofa across them. But now he was awake and able to appreciate every breath she took—and each one of the moments that he could hold her sleeping body.

It was overwhelming. Cal wondered if it could have been any more perfect if they *had* made love last night.

Andrea moved slightly, and he saw her hand move towards her face, as if to brush the sleep from her eyes. She was awake too. But he lay still, savouring these last moments of being able to hold her.

Then an alarm sounded in the bedroom. Andrea shifted, disentangling herself from his arms.

'You're awake, then.' She made no pretence of having been woken by the alarm.

'Yes. You too...'

She wasn't going to ask, and neither was he. Admitting that they'd both lain in each other's arms, not wanting to move, was a step too far for both of them. He swung his legs off the sofa, taking her with him as he sat up.

She scrubbed her hands across her head, obviously trying to tame her curls. He liked them just the way they were, along with the pinkness of her cheeks, and her sleepy eyes.

'I didn't realise I was so tired. I must have just sat down and fallen asleep.'

'Same here.' Cal didn't really want to talk about it. He didn't want to make excuses or pretend that nothing had happened. Something *had* happened, and this morning he felt so close to her. He didn't want to lose that feeling.

But it was slowly ebbing away anyway. Andrea walked into the bedroom to switch off the alarm, and then collected the untouched cups of chocolate.

'We're going to have to show Maggie the cake.' She plumped herself down in one of the easy chairs opposite him. So far away now.

'Yes. Probably best to get it over with as soon as possible. If she's really disappointed then you and Joe will have a chance to talk her round.'

'Don't think like that, Cal. I know it's not what she chose, but it's lovely. I'll have a shower then I'll go and get her; she'll be up by now. Meet you down in the kitchen in fifteen minutes?'

Cal made it down to the kitchen in ten. When he got there, Craig was in the store room, surveying the cake.

'What do you think? The icing looks great, doesn't it? Andrea did a good job with that.' Cal stared at it. In the cold light of day, he could see a couple of places where the rose petals weren't exactly right.

'Good effort, both of you. *Really* good effort.' Craig nodded his approval. 'I probably couldn't have done better myself.'

That was real praise. Cal felt the nagging worry lift slightly.

'Thanks. How's your wife?'

'Oh... We're still waiting. She woke me up last night saying that she thought the baby might be coming, but it turned out to be...what do you call it?'

'Braxton Hicks? They usually stop if you change position, or move around a bit.'

'That's right. Braxton Hicks.' Craig wiped his hand across his face. 'The waiting's driving me crazy.'

'Babies have a habit of coming only when *they're* ready.'

Craig laughed. 'She's working to her own timetable all right. She's a strong little lass; I feel her kick sometimes when the wife's lying next to me in bed.'

A sudden burst of longing filled Cal's chest and he swallowed hard. 'That's good. It sounds as if everything's going as it should.'

'Yeah, yeah. The midwife's really pleased...' Craig broke off, looking through the open door. 'Here they are...'

Andrea was leading Joe and Maggie across the kitchen towards them. Cal stepped out of the store room, and Craig closed the door behind them.

'What are we all doing down here? We've already

tasted everything on the menu...' Maggie was glowing. Andrea was hiding it well, but, despite her earlier reassurances, Cal could see something akin to terror in her eyes.

'There was a problem with the cake, Maggie. We've made you another one.' Andrea had obviously decided that it was necessary to give the bad news first, but that she should follow it up as quickly as possible with the good news.

But Maggie heard only the bad news. Her hand flew to her mouth and her eyes filled with tears.

'My cake? No!'

'It's all right, Maggie—' Andrea was almost pleading with her friend.

'Yes. Yes, it's all right.' Maggie turned to Joe, flinging her arms around him. 'We don't need cake, do we, Joe? We have each other...'

Joe was smiling. 'Seems we have cake as well. Didn't you hear Andrea say that they've made us another one?'

Maggie looked around the kitchen wildly. Andrea seemed paralysed with a mixture of hope and dread, and Cal decided he'd better do something. He opened the door of the store room, leading Maggie inside.

She stared at the cake. Everyone seemed to be holding their breath.

'You made a cake... For us... It's *beautiful*. Look, Joe. Better than the other one.' Maggie flung her arms around Cal, almost knocking him over, and then hugged Andrea.

'You're so clever. I didn't know you could make icing-sugar roses.'

Andrea finally smiled. 'I can't. I just did the icing. Craig baked the cake and made the icing, and Cal did the roses.'

'Cal! You're such a dark horse. Who'd have thought you could make roses? And, Craig, thank you so much.' A thought occurred to Maggie. 'So what happened to the other one?'

'One of the cooks fell down the stairs. He was carrying the cake.' Andrea volunteered the information.

'Oh! I hope he's all right?'

'Yes, he's fine. When Cal showed me what was left of the cake, it looked as if it had broken his fall.'

'That's just as well. I wouldn't have wanted him to be hurt and we couldn't wish for anything better than this, could we, Joe? Our friends making us this gorgeous cake.'

'No, we couldn't. Thank you both. And you, Craig.' Joe shook Craig's hand and then put his arm around Maggie. 'Is it okay with you if we go and get married now?'

CHAPTER TWELVE

IT WAS A beautiful ceremony. The huge auditorium had been cleared and decked with flowers, and Maggie and Joe both shone with happiness as they said their vows. Everyone's eyes were on the bride...except for Cal's. It was every bridesmaid's intention not to outshine the bride, but, in his eyes, Andrea just couldn't help it.

It was artifice of the very best kind. Andrea looked as if a passing cherub had sprinkled pearls into her hair, while another had wound soft tendrils of dusty pink satin around her body. Simple and yet immaculate, perfect in every way. He could have rested his gaze on the curve of her neck for hours.

She presided quietly over everything, giving a nudge here and a push there to smooth Maggie's path through the day. The three younger bridesmaids, wearing white lace dresses with pink sashes that matched Andrea's dress, were exactly where they should be without any apparent effort on Andrea's part. The guests moved into the ballroom, and the food was served. When the time came to make his speech, Andrea leaned towards him, her smile propelling him to his feet.

And then the moment he'd been waiting for. The toasts had been made, the tables cleared away. Maggie floated across the dance floor in Joe's arms, and even then Cal could only see Andrea.

'What's next?' He leaned over, whispering the words. They both knew exactly what came next.

'Oh… I'm not sure. Something to do with the best man, I think.'

'There's something I've forgotten?' Fat chance. Cal had been thinking about this all day.

'I can't for the life of me think what it is…' She gasped as he swung her onto the dance floor.

Two bodies moving in exact rhythm. There was nothing else, just the two of them, alone on a dance floor that was already full of other couples. She melted into his arms, finally letting go of the quiet watchfulness that had guided the day this far.

'You've done a wonderful job, Andrea. It's been a day to remember.'

'I couldn't have done it without you. Thank you, Cal.'

'I just followed the instructions in the folder.' He smiled down at her. 'You're the one who wrote them.'

She was silent for a moment, her cheek resting lightly against his chest. Cal wondered if silence would ever be the same again, when soon it would just be silence, without Andrea to share it. Without her to fill it with the sweetest things.

'I don't mean just the wedding. I'm not sure I could have done any of the last two weeks without you. I feel…different. Freer than I was.'

He felt different too. Cal allowed himself to wonder if that might be enough. If somehow they'd both managed to change and become entirely different people. The kinds of people who didn't have to part in a few days.

Even now, he couldn't see it. When Andrea was in

his arms, almost anything seemed possible, but not the thing he really wanted.

'I'm glad.' It meant more to Cal than a wedding, more than anything they'd encountered in the last two weeks. One day, Andrea would be free of the ghosts that haunted her. Maybe not any time soon, but she'd taken the first step—wanting to be free instead of accepting that she never would be.

Time would tell. But time wasn't something they had at their disposal. Cal had to let go of her.

Not yet, though. Not while the music was still playing and he could hold her in his arms. Cal spread his fingers across her back, trying to take in every part of the sensation of having her close.

She wanted to keep Cal for herself, but that would be greedy, and the wedding folder itinerary dictated that he dance with a whole string of other people. Aunt Mae took her turn, looking gorgeous in a sequinned dress, and surprisingly light on her feet when she got onto the dance floor.

When it was time to cut the cake, Joe gave a little speech, just in case no one had heard about the catastrophe with the original cake yet. Then Maggie squealed with delight as skiers with flaming torches traversed the slopes outside in a complicated fire dance, which ended with torches being stuck into the snow outside in the shape of a heart.

Craig handed Joe a shining silver knife, and he and Maggie made the first cut, then insisted on Andrea and Cal making the second. She felt his fingers curl around hers, and the applause was just as enthusiastic as it had been for Joe and Maggie.

Despite Craig's insistence that Maggie leave all this

to him, she made sure that a large piece was wrapped carefully for Craig to take home to his wife. And somehow, the rose that bore their initials found its way onto Andrea's plate.

'I can't bring myself to eat it.' She pulled a face. She couldn't bring herself not to eat it either, because she couldn't keep it. It would crack and fade, and become a worn-out memory of something that should stay fresh for ever.

'It was made to be enjoyed.'

That was always Cal's response. Live for the here and now, not the past and maybe not the future. Andrea broke off a couple of the petals, putting them onto his plate.

'Will you help me with it, then?'

Their rose. Eaten together at the wedding that they had helped to create. It seemed to seal an unspoken promise between them, just as much as the spoken promises that Joe and Maggie had made.

Suddenly, it was a little too much to bear. Andrea turned away from him, finding that one of the bridesmaids was about to smear chocolate cake all over her dress, and that the little girl's face required a quick wipe with a paper napkin. When she glanced at Cal again, he was eating the sugar petals, his gaze still fixed on her.

Something had to be done about this. She had to make a decision, one way or the other, and stick by it.

The world wouldn't stop changing just because she wanted it to.

It was time to reach out and take it by the scruff of the neck.

Andrea heaved a sigh of relief as Joe and Maggie left the reception, bound for their suite. The party was beginning to break up, and if any stragglers decided they wanted to make a night of it, the hotel staff would deal with that. She took a deep breath and walked over to where Cal was standing. He still looked as handsome as he had this morning and just as immaculate, seemingly untouched by the rigours of avoiding champagne spills on his jacket, icing sugar on his tie, and the creasing effect that an evening's dancing could have on a shirt.

First step: get him alone.

'Would you like a nightcap? Hot chocolate instead of champagne? I promise to stay awake this time.'

He nodded. 'I could definitely sit down and relax for a moment. Chocolate would be nice, too.'

Second step: back to her apartment and kick off her shoes.

That was a relief. Andrea padded into the kitchen to make the hot chocolate, and Cal took off his jacket and loosened his tie, lowering himself onto the sofa.

He looked even more delicious now. That, and the knowledge that Cal would never hurt her, made the third step laughably easy.

'A lot's happened in the last two weeks...' Andrea sat next to him on the sofa, taking a sip of her chocolate.

'Yeah. It's been...' He twisted his mouth in a wry smile. 'I wouldn't exactly say it's all been fun. But it's been good. And a lot more than just special.'

So he felt the way she did. If she'd stopped to think for a moment she would have known that already. She also knew that Cal would never ask. He'd made an agreement with her and he would respect that, however much they both wanted to change it now.

'I want you to stay tonight.' Six words. So very quick and easy to say, but once they were out she couldn't take them back. There was no uncertainty, no ambiguity to hide behind.

His face hardened suddenly. 'I...can't, Andrea. It's not that I don't want to, but you said it yourself. You don't need anyone in your life, right now.'

He was hiding something. She'd been honest with him, and if he could give her nothing else then he could return that favour.

'You're telling me what I need? If I didn't know you better, I'd say that was a little arrogant.'

He held up his hands in a gesture of surrender. 'No. I'm sorry, I didn't mean it that way. But I'm going home in two days and...we have very different lives. I can't just take what I want and then leave you behind. We both know that's what will happen. I'm the kind of person who thinks twice about taking a job I really want just because it wasn't my idea.'

She'd thought about that. And she was okay with it.

'So what's wrong with knowing it, and accepting it? Taking what we're both able to take?'

For a moment she thought he was going to forget all about his reservations and kiss her. If he did, she knew there would be no going back this time. But then the bright possibilities of a whole night spent together faded from his eyes.

'I'm not...' He shook his head. Leaning forward, and planting his elbows on his knees, he seemed to be studying the pattern on the carpet.

Andrea laid her hand on his shoulder. Whatever this was, she was here for him, the way he'd been there for her. But as soon as she touched him he flinched, and she snatched her hand away again.

'Andrea, I'm sorry...' He turned, catching her hand in his. 'I didn't mean...'

'What *do* you mean, Cal?' she chided him gently. 'Come on. Out with it.'

One side of his lip curled suddenly, in a lopsided smile. 'I guess I deserve that.'

'You absolutely do.'

He let out a sigh, leaning back against the sofa cushions. Now the ceiling seemed to be the object of his full attention. Andrea waited.

'It took me a long time to achieve my ambitions. Even longer to come to terms with it and feel comfortable with what I wanted out of life.'

'I know.' Andrea wasn't sure what that had to do with anything at the moment.

'You're not ready to change either, are you?'

'No, but... Look, we made an agreement that we weren't going to get involved, Cal. We can keep to that, can't we?'

'And what happens if we can't?'

Andrea swallowed hard. She'd been trying not to think about that. Today had spun a magical web around them, but she could feel its tendrils loosening now. She reached for his hand before the spell was completely broken, and even now his fingers curled around hers in the instinctive reaction that happened between them every time.

'I hurt someone, Andrea. Badly.'

'What?' The idea that Cal would knowingly hurt anyone was ridiculous. But he was only human, and who could truthfully say that they'd never—even unwittingly—hurt someone?

'I was reckless, believing I could have things all my own way, and that the usual rules didn't apply to me. Mary's a good person, and she was a good friend. I told myself that it was possible to have a relationship with her, without letting it touch any other part of my life.'

'Did she know that was what you wanted?'

'It was her idea. Mary had the same kind of work commitments I did; she was a civil rights lawyer and she cared about the people who came to her for help. She worked hard and we both thought that a no-strings affair between friends would suit us.'

Something cold began to form in the pit of Andrea's stomach. That was pretty much what she'd suggested to Cal.

'She fell in love. Mary had that option—she could compromise and let her work fit around the rest of her life for a while. I couldn't even contemplate it, and that's what hurt her the most.'

'This isn't the same, Cal.' She spoke without thinking, talking from the part of her that wanted him more than anything else.

He stared at her for a moment, and then shook his head. 'Your place is here, Andrea. Mine isn't. It's my heart and yours we're talking about, not a cake. If they break, we can't just whip another one up by the morning.'

Suddenly she was angry. Angry at all the things that had pulled them together, and all the things that kept them apart. Angry with Cal, because she suspected he was right, that they couldn't just walk away from each other after spending a night together.

'They don't *have* to break...'

He studied her face. 'Don't tell me you can do this, Andrea. I can't and I know you can't either.'

'I guess you should leave, then.' Her words came out cross and hurt instead of understanding and regretful, and when he got to his feet, catching up his jacket, she didn't stop him. There wasn't any point in stopping him, because he really did need to go before something persuaded him to forget about that wretched honourable streak of his.

The latch on the door locked shut with a click. That was okay, because it meant he wouldn't be coming back. And if she had to be alone tonight, crying bitter tears into her pillow, then she might as well get on with it. Bring it on.

CHAPTER THIRTEEN

THE RESTAURANT, THE breakfast bar, and the covered veranda, where space heaters made it warm enough to sit and drink piping hot coffee, were still deserted. No one was up and about yet, and it looked as if most of the wedding guests had decided that brunch was a better option than breakfast.

Maggie had knocked on the door of Andrea's apartment this morning, asking if she wanted to come for coffee with her. Joe had gone out for a walk with his grandfather, who was anxious to impart the secret of a long and happy marriage.

'I suppose if anyone's going to know it would be Joe's grandpa. His grandparents have been married for nearly sixty years, without so much as a cross word.'

'Really? Isn't that a little bit boring?' Andrea wasn't in the mood to hear about domestic harmony this morning. Last night had been full of every kind of regret imaginable.

Maggie chuckled dryly. 'I don't think it's actually true. Joe's mum told me they've definitely been known to argue. They just keep it between themselves and work things out together.'

'Not such a bad approach.' Andrea should take a leaf from their book. She'd already decided to keep what had happened between her and Cal to herself. It would be a shame to cast any shadow over Maggie's obvious happiness, however much Andrea needed her friend right now.

'Yes, it sounds good to me too. Although Grandpa Dave's a bit late with the advice on how Joe can make me happy, because he's already done that. I think he just wants to go for a walk with Joe; they've always been close.'

'So…where shall we go?'

Maggie surveyed the display of food on the counter of the breakfast bar. 'Are you hungry? Joe and I already ate so I just want coffee.'

'That's all I want.' Andrea didn't even want to think about food at the moment.

'How about the veranda, then? Unless it's too cold for you?'

'No, it's fine.' Andrea had woken in the night, shivering, unable to get warm, even though she'd gone and sat in front of the fire in the sitting room. The crisp cold of the morning was nothing compared to the icy fingers of regret over things she ought to be able to change, but couldn't. And they'd be less likely to run into Cal on the veranda.

They sat down, arranging rugs over their legs. The waiter brought mugs of coffee and Maggie let out a contented sigh. 'It's so beautiful here. And you… You've done so much, Andrea. Thank you.'

'I've enjoyed it too. It's been a wonderful time.' That at least was true. It was over now, but it had been wonderful.

'Andrea?' Maggie set her mug down, grabbing Andrea's hand. It was only then that Andrea realised her eyes were full of tears. 'What's the matter, honey?'

'Nothing… I mean…' Andrea wiped the tears away with the sleeve of her sweater. 'It's just been so great to have you here. I'll miss you.'

'Are you sure that's all it is?' Maggie squeezed her hand. 'Did anything happen?'

Did anything happen with Cal? That was what Maggie meant; she wasn't blind. It was impossible to miss the chemistry between her and Cal.

'Nothing happened. And everything's fine, truly. I'm just a little tired.'

'Because you and Cal stayed up so late, making our cake.' Maggie smiled at her, leaning over for a hug. 'You're the best friend that anyone could have, Andrea.'

Maggie and Joe were leaving this afternoon for a week in the sunshine. Just six hours, and then Andrea could drop all the pretence and go and lock herself away in her apartment, until Cal left the hotel.

But there were still the goodbyes to get through. It was impossible that she shouldn't be there to wave her friends off, and if she knew Cal at all then he'd be thinking the same. At least she could position herself on the opposite side of the gaggle of friends and family, while Maggie and Joe worked their way round, kissing cheeks and shaking hands.

'We have to have a photo…' Maggie's mother had brought her camera with her. 'Andrea, go and stand next to Joe. And where's Cal?'

She could see the tension in Cal's face when he stepped forward. He took his place by Maggie's side, smiling for the camera. Andrea wondered if her own smile looked as pasted on as his did, but no one seemed to notice. Maggie's mother fiddled with her camera, taking photograph after photograph.

'That'll be enough, Mum, surely.' Maggie stepped forward, grinning, and took the camera from her mother. 'What about one with just Andrea and Cal?'

The relief at the ordeal almost being over was tempered by the knowledge that the worst was still to come. Joe ducked out from between them, and she felt Cal put his arm around her.

He could hardly touch her. Cal was doing all the right things, standing next to her and smiling for the camera, but his hand wasn't so much on her shoulder as hovering a millimetre above it. Andrea smiled, unable to move under the weight of numb misery.

As soon as Maggie had taken the photograph, he was gone. Maybe he had nothing to say to her, or maybe he too was taking Grandpa Dave's approach and keeping their argument between themselves alone. Andrea silently sent up a sigh of relief as Maggie and Joe climbed onto the train, waving.

She could see Cal waving too, but as soon as the train drew away, he turned to Grandpa Dave. As the two walked away together, Grandpa Dave seemed to be giving Cal the benefit of his experience on something or other and Cal was nodding gravely.

That was it, then. After all the excitement and the hubbub, the only thing that remained was for everyone to go home. Then, finally, Andrea could grieve, for the loss of the future that had seemed to open up before her and which she'd been too afraid to grab hold of.

Cal had done everything that was expected of him. He'd spent the night trying to get a few hours' sleep, but it had slipped through his fingers, as if it were playing a game of tag with him. Then he'd downed three cups of coffee, which had only served to leave him feeling like an overstretched piece of piano wire, before turning his mind to tackling the day.

He doggedly made the rounds of all the hotel staff who'd helped with the wedding, thanking each one personally. Somehow he managed to avoid Andrea, and he couldn't help wondering if it was because she was also avoiding him.

When the time came to see Maggie and Joe off, she couldn't even meet his gaze. Last night hadn't been an aberration or a misunderstanding between friends. It had shown them both that they could never be together.

A call to the airline secured a ticket home for this evening in exchange for the one he'd booked in two days' time. Cal packed his bags, walking down to the railway terminus. As the train drew into the station, the impulse to run back and try and make things right with Andrea seized him.

But things *were* right. He should never have allowed their relationship to go as far as it had, and he had no excuse other than having been dazzled by her. Andrea had found peace here, and if he loved her at all, then he should leave.

He picked up his bags and stepped into the carriage of the funicular train. As it drew away from the lights of the hotel, he didn't allow himself to look back.

Four days. It had been four days since Cal had left without a word. Andrea had been angry with him, and then angry at herself. Now she just felt numb.

But she had to keep going. She kept on smiling for the family and friends who were still at the hotel for a few days' holiday after the wedding. And kept on crying when she was alone.

She was woken by the doorbell. Sleeping late wasn't

her usual habit—the mornings were far too crisp and beautiful for that—but she was exhausted from nights of staring at the ceiling, wondering how she'd managed to be so stupid as to lose Cal. He'd *told* her how he felt. They'd agreed that they wouldn't act on their feelings. She could have waved him off, knowing he'd be a friend she could contact any time she liked, but she'd destroyed all of that.

Aunt Mae was standing at the door of her apartment. She wore one of the hotel's Ski Mavericks bright pink sweatshirts over immaculate cream trousers and a polo neck.

'Aunt Mae. Come in.' Andrea wondered for a moment if she was still dreaming, and decided she wasn't. She'd arranged for Francine to take Aunt Mae for a ride on the slopes on one of the skidoos; Aunt Mae had obviously enjoyed herself and wanted a souvenir of the trip.

'You look as if you need something to start your day.' Aunt Mae walked determinedly into the small sitting room and sat down.

'Uh. Yes. I'm just going to make coffee. Would you like some?'

A visit from Aunt Mae always required that cups and saucers be used. Andrea combed her hair in the kitchen while she was waiting for the coffee to brew, and when she returned to the sitting room she found Aunt Mae emptying the contents of her handbag onto the coffee table, presumably looking for a sandwich.

'Would you like some toast?' Andrea set the cups down.

'No, I had breakfast some time ago. Don't let me stop you though, dear.'

'That's okay. I'm not hungry.' The bread in the kitchen was stale anyway.

Aunt Mae found what she was looking for and started
to tip everything else back into her handbag. Andrea
focussed on a small bottle of whisky, which must have
come from the minibar in Aunt Mae's room.

'It's a bit early, isn't it?'

'Needs must, dear.' Aunt Mae opened the bottle, tipping a measure into both cups.

Andrea shrugged. 'Okay.' She obediently took a sip
of her coffee, blinking from the taste of caffeine with
alcohol. Maybe one sip was enough for courtesy's sake.

'Cal's very handsome, isn't he? He's got that sparkle
I like in a man.'

So *this* was what Mae was here for. Not much got
past her, and she must have seen what Andrea had been
trying so hard to conceal. She'd obviously decided that
Andrea needed a pick-me-up and that fortifying her
coffee at ten-thirty in the morning was going to do
the trick.

'Yes, he has. It's okay, Aunt Mae. I'm not going to
fall to pieces.'

Aunt Mae reached into the neck of her sweatshirt,
pulling out the old-fashioned locket that she always
wore, and lifting the chain over her white, perfectly
coiffed curls. 'I don't think I've ever shown you this,
have I?'

'No, you haven't.' The locket was heavy in Andrea's
hand. 'May I look inside?'

Aunt Mae nodded, and Andrea opened the locket.
On one side was the picture of a young man in an army
cap. On the other, an older man with a jovial smile.

'My two husbands.'

What? 'I didn't know you were married, Aunt Mae.'

'I haven't always been eighty, dear. I married Ted,
the one on the right, when I was eighteen, just before

he went away to do his National Service. He was killed, making me a widow at nineteen.'

Andrea caught her breath. Suddenly her own troubles seemed very small. 'I'm so sorry, Aunt Mae.'

'It was a long time ago, dear, and, as you know, time heals. I married my second husband, Harry, ten years later. We had twenty good years together, before he died of a heart attack.'

Andrea stared at Aunt Mae dumbly. Aunt Mae never failed to surprise, but she was pulling out all the stops this morning.

'It's… Aunt Mae, I never knew…' Andrea moved over to the sofa, giving Aunt Mae a hug.

'It's all right, dear. I loved them both and I'm thankful for every moment I had with each of them.' Aunt Mae extricated herself from Andrea's embrace. 'Harry was a tiger between the sheets, you know.'

'Aunt Mae!'

'You think you invented sex? You're not twelve years old any more, dear, and I assume you have a good idea about what I mean. Cal has that same something about him as my Harry did.'

Okay. Andrea definitely needed a drink now. She took a gulp of her coffee, blinking as it hit the back of her throat.

'We…um. We didn't ever get that far.'

Aunt Mae shot her a derisive look. 'In those days we didn't live together before we got married. But I knew exactly what to expect with my Harry, and he didn't disappoint.'

Andrea picked up the locket from the coffee table, gently fixing the chain back around Aunt Mae's neck. The worn engraving glinted in the sunlight, a testament to memories that had become mellow with age.

'Whisky at ten-thirty in the morning, and telling me you had two husbands. This isn't just a social call, is it, Aunt Mae? What is it you came to say?'

'I've had a good life, and I don't regret anything that I did. A few things that I didn't do, maybe...' Aunt Mae took a sip of her coffee, pausing as if to make a list in her head of the things she hadn't done. Clearly that wasn't relevant to her point.

'Live your life, Andrea. Take it from me: if you don't try for what you want you'll always regret it.'

'But... It's complicated. He doesn't want me...'

Aunt Mae snorted in disbelief. 'It's always complicated. In my experience, men are full of complications of one kind or the other. But they don't dance that way with women they don't want.'

Andrea felt a tear form at the corner of her eye. Aunt Mae had voiced the feeling that had been growing over the last few days, and suddenly it didn't seem so outrageous after all.

'Thank you...' She hugged Aunt Mae again, feeling the tears begin to flow down her cheeks. 'Thank you for...everything.'

'My pleasure, dear. There isn't much point in being this old if you can't dispense a little wisdom from time to time. Now, drink your coffee and go and get dressed. There's a little errand I want you to run for me.'

'What is it?' Andrea grinned, wiping her eyes. 'If you don't ask, then you don't get.'

'I'm glad you've been listening. Those torch processions they do at dusk...' Aunt Mae patted the design on her Ski Mavericks sweatshirt.

Andrea nodded. 'You want to be a part of one?'

'They *do* look rather exciting.'

'Consider it done. I'll come with you and take some

pictures, shall I?' Andrea was sure that Francine and Bruno would be eager to make the occasion special, and that her parents would be there too, ready to celebrate Aunt Mae's intrepid zest for life when she reached the bottom of the slope.

Aunt Mae clapped her hands together. 'That would be lovely, thank you. Something to show everyone at the library, when I get home…'

'So how's married life, then?' Cal put two pints of best bitter down onto the table in the cosy 'snug' bar of Joe's local pub.

'Good. I'd recommend it.' Joe picked up his glass. 'Cheers.'

It was good to see Joe so happy. It took some of the edge off Cal's own unhappiness, making him feel that the world hadn't completely faded into grey.

'How are things with you? You said you'd taken the job you were offered?'

Cal nodded. 'The board of directors offered me a great deal. We agreed that I'll be a relatively free agent for the next couple of months, working with the other directors to create new strategies for innovation. Then I'll take up my new role as London Director and start implementing some of those strategies.'

'Sounds great. You got over whatever it was that was giving you the heebie-jeebies about it?'

A vision of Andrea's smile formed in Cal's imagination. She'd been following him for a while now—all the way back from Italy, in fact. Cal sent a silent thank-you to her and hoped that whatever she was doing this evening brought her happiness. It was the only thing that justified the pain that, for the last two weeks, had sometimes seemed to be tearing his heart from his chest.

'Yeah. I took some good advice.'

Joe raised his eyebrows. 'That's new. Since when did you listen to anything anyone else had to say about your career?'

Since Andrea. It was as if everything had stopped when he'd met her, and then started anew.

'People change.'

'Yeah. I wouldn't disagree with you there.' Joe reached forward, picking up his beer. 'I just didn't think I'd ever hear *you* say it.'

Cal shrugged. 'Like I say, people change.'

Joe narrowed his eyes. 'Am I missing something? You could sound a lot more enthusiastic about this.'

His friend hadn't missed anything. It was hard to keep up a positive façade when he felt his heart was breaking—a slow-motion disintegration that robbed Cal daily of even the smallest pleasures.

'You remember when you told me that you'd met the woman you wanted to marry?' Cal took a sip of his beer, the taste sour in his mouth.

'Of course I do…' Understanding dawned in Joe's face. 'Ah. Andrea.'

'Was it *that* obvious?'

'Put it like this: I haven't witnessed that much chemistry since I was at school, doing my science A levels. You've told her?'

Cal shook his head. 'You know as well as I do that Andrea's vulnerable. She has her own comfort zone and she's happy there. She doesn't need me crashing into her life.'

Joe thought for a moment. 'You're sure about that? A good friend once told me that if I loved Maggie, then I shouldn't let her go so easily.'

'That's different. You're not an uncompromising control freak.'

'She said *that* about you?' Joe raised his eyebrows.

'No, actually. She doesn't know me quite as well as you do. You've said it a few times.'

'Only in jest...' Joe shrugged, but he knew it was true, just as well as Cal did.

Somehow, though, Andrea was still here: sitting at his elbow, telling him that he could change; believing in him the way he believed in her. The distant possibility that maybe one day they could both change, and that they'd be together, was all that kept him going at the moment.

'Look, Cal. I know this is hard, but... If you really love her, isn't it better to face the obstacles together?'

Cal shook his head. 'You and Maggie are different. You weren't the obstacle, were you?'

Joe grumbled into his beer, but he couldn't disagree. Cal didn't want to talk about it any more, and he walked over to the deep window ledge, sorting out the chess men from the pile of different board games, and setting them out on the chequered table between him and Joe.

The black-hearted king, who loved a glimmering white queen. Cal's very nature made it impossible. But some impossible things were just harder and took longer. He had nothing left but a distant, unreachable hope and, despite everything his head was telling him, his instinct was to cling to it.

Joe rubbed his hands together, flexing his fingers in preparation for the battle ahead.

CHAPTER FOURTEEN

One week later

'ANDREA…?' FOR ONE split second Cal looked as if he'd seen a ghost. But he'd always been able to think on his feet. 'It's nice to see you.'

'It's good to see you too, Cal.'

He stepped back from the doorway, beckoning her inside. 'You're in London to see Maggie and Joe?'

'No, I flew in this morning. I'm on my way up to Oxford. I thought I'd surprise my mum and dad with a visit. Maybe drop in on Aunt Mae.'

The excuse seemed thin at best but Cal accepted it without a murmur. He was a perfect facsimile of someone who'd opened the door and found an old friend standing on his front step. Andrea saw straight through him.

'I was just about to make some tea…' He hadn't offered to take her coat and Andrea assumed he was hoping she wouldn't stay long enough for tea.

'Tea would be really nice. Thank you.'

He nodded, leading her to the back of the hallway and into the kitchen. Andrea bit back the urge to shake him. Surely he couldn't keep this up for much longer.

He was smiling, but the dark rings under his eyes told a different story.

'I'm beginning to wonder whether I've done the right thing.'

He flipped the kettle on, feigning a questioning look. 'How so?'

'Because the Cal Lewis I know is a darn sight more honest than this.'

He was doing exactly what she'd been doing for the last three weeks. Pasting on a smile and pretending that nothing had happened, even though she knew that she'd always regret losing Cal.

He was suddenly still, staring at her silently. Andrea could almost hear her own heart beating furiously in her chest. If he didn't say something…anything…she was going to lose it and burst into tears. That, or threaten him with one of those fancy frying pans that hung over the large, gleaming hob.

'What are you doing here, Andrea?' There was a look of such anguish in his eyes that she forgave him everything.

'I came to talk to you, Cal. I *need* to talk to you.'

He shook his head, slowly. 'Is there anything left to say, Andrea? We can't do this.'

That was all part of the problem—this fantasy that they hadn't gone all the way and that it was possible to draw back without any loss. Somehow, in the space of two weeks, they'd got in so deep that the only way out was to work their way through to the other side.

And then…she had to convince Cal that she didn't *want* out. And find out whether he felt the same.

She walked across the kitchen to where he was standing. Facing him down. There was nowhere for him to go; his back was already against the sleek grey counter top.

He could smile. He could pretend he felt nothing, but his body told the truth. Cal couldn't control the sudden dilation of his eyes, the pulse that beat wildly at the side of his neck. They were both doctors, trained to see these things, and he could probably see it in her too. The way her whole body was screaming for him even though they weren't touching.

'How does this make you feel, Cal?' She held his gaze steadily, knowing he was helpless to tear himself away.

'It makes me feel…too many things.'

'Me too.'

He reached out, his fingers following the curve of her cheek. Cal didn't even touch her, but she could feel her skin begin to heat.

'I can't deny what we have, Andrea. That's the reason I left, because I can't resist it.'

She nodded. Now that he was being honest, she should be too.

'I let you leave because I was angry with you. And then I missed you, and then, when I got my head straight and thought about things a little more, I was angry with myself. Then I just missed you again.'

He smiled suddenly. Not the controlled smile he'd been wearing before, but something that came from deep inside. Seeing it again made Andrea tremble.

'I guess it's a pretty standard process.' The kettle began to boil and switched itself off with a snap. He didn't even look at it, but shot her an apologetic look. 'Tea…?'

'Yes.' Andrea needed to break the tension too. Her

head was beginning to swim, and her knees were starting to shake. She nodded, moving away from him.

But they'd broken through. No more pretending that
this wasn't happening, and no more hiding from it. As
with everything else, it had taken far less time than Andrea could have imagined.

She watched him as he made the tea. He seemed to
feel her gaze, turning to smile at her. Then, picking up
the cups, he walked through to a large sitting room,
perching them on the end of a large coffee table that
was stacked with books and papers.

'I interrupted you. You're working.' Cal had obviously been using his Saturday morning to catch up on
some paperwork.

He eyed the pile thoughtfully. Then, suddenly, in a
broad sweep of movement that took her breath away,
he cleared it all to one side, tipping it onto the floor.

'Not any more.'

It was the only thing he could think of in the heart-
stopping moment he'd seen Andrea on his doorstep.
Act normal, and pretend he'd bumped into an old friend
with whom he'd shared a few might-haves. But he'd
seen the look in Andrea's eyes right from the start, and
it was impossible to keep the sham up.

She had his full attention. He'd tried filling his
thoughts with as many other things as he could, and
all that had done was exhaust him. Andrea had always
had his full attention, from the very first moment he'd
seen her.

Andrea sat at one end of the sofa and Cal sat at the
other. Now that she was a little further away from him,
he could at least think of something other than the mad-

ness of having her close. The madness of wanting her close, maybe...

'Andrea, this thing we have...' He wasn't explaining himself very well but she nodded in understanding. 'It'll destroy us both if we let it.'

'How so?'

So she wanted him to say it. Out loud. At this moment he'd do anything she asked.

'You've made a life for yourself again, and found a place where you can heal. I want to tell you that I can give you everything you need to heal, but... I can try my best, but if that's not good enough...' It would break both their hearts. His didn't matter, but Andrea's was precious beyond measure.

Her eyes softened, and the pain of knowing that he would lose her all over again was almost unbearable.

'Cal, I know you don't want to hurt me. I came here to tell you that you can't. I told you that the mountains were my happy place, and they were. But you've helped me move on from that. My happy place is with you.'

He still couldn't believe it. Didn't dare believe it. The stakes were too high.

'You can't know that, Andrea. We were together for two weeks, and we never even...' He couldn't say it. But she held his gaze, even if her cheeks were beginning to flush.

'We never even slept together?'

'No.' Only in his head, and quite obviously in hers too. 'We hardly know each other.'

'I know everything I need to know about you, Cal. You're the man I've been looking for, and I love you. Everything else is just...' she waved her hand dismissively '...details.'

'I wouldn't have called it *just details*.' He grinned at her. Andrea was smiling too.

'Attention to detail is always a good thing.'

'Yes, it is. Always.'

She loved him. Cal couldn't tear his thoughts away from that particular detail, because he loved Andrea too. Completely and unreservedly.

Suddenly, he knew. Cal could do anything if Andrea was by his side, guiding him. The one piece of the puzzle that held all of the answers was sitting here beside him. Andrea had given him another chance, and he couldn't let it go.

'I think...' She took an unsteady breath. 'We probably need some time to think about this.'

'You mean *I* do?' Cal had spent far too much time thinking about this, and the answer was clear. He knew now exactly what he'd be doing with the rest of his life.

'I have rather sprung this on you.'

He reached for her, taking her hands between his. 'Andrea, I love you. If you know an answer to this, a way we can be together...please tell me.'

She flushed, suddenly. 'I don't have all the answers. But I trust you and I think that if you trust me back then there's nothing we can't do together.'

'I trust you enough to believe you. Do you trust me enough to allow me to kiss you?'

Her eyes darkened in delicious welcome. 'Yes.'

They'd stayed in the moment for a long time, exploring every facet of it, sharing each beat of their hearts. When Cal took her in his arms, carrying her into the bedroom, the next moment began to unfold before her.

He was tender, and yet passionate. He undressed

her slowly, not allowing her to lose sight of the bright promise of what was to come.

'Cal, I...' As he slipped her blouse off, his kisses moving from her neck to her shoulder, she felt suddenly embarrassed and clung to him for comfort.

'Tell me.' He folded her in his arms.

She'd never minded her scars. Most had faded, and were almost invisible now, but the two on her shoulder were still evident and always would be. And suddenly they seemed to matter, because Cal was so perfect. So flawless.

'My shoulder is... I never really looked at it before and it didn't seem to matter. Now I don't think it looks so nice.' Perhaps he could concentrate on kissing the other one.

He sat down on the bed, taking her in his lap. 'You're the most beautiful woman I've ever seen, Andrea. I could tell you that the scars don't matter, but they do. They matter because every part of you matters. I want to be here for you as you reclaim yourself.'

He understood. Now everything seemed to matter just that bit more, because she'd started to care again. But Cal wouldn't let her down. He'd be there to help her recover every part of her life.

She kissed him, cradling his face in her hands. Passion didn't lie and she knew he found her beautiful.

'You'll be here with me?' He asked.

'Always. I won't let you get away with anything, Cal. We'll bend together...'

He smiled. 'I can't think of anything I want more. Bending with you in a warm breeze and building our future. I love you, Andrea.'

She kissed him, whispering her agreement against his cheek. She wanted everything that Cal's love could give her. They took their pleasure slowly, exploring every part of each other's bodies, until finally they could take no more. Cal tipped her onto her back, holding her tight as she wrapped her legs around his waist.

There was a moment of sweet, still silence. Then he whispered her name as he slowly pushed inside her, and she felt her own body welcoming his in a yearning embrace.

He was still again, kissing her tenderly. Telling her how much he'd wanted this, and that he'd loved her from the first moment he saw her.

And then the passion began to rise between them. There was no hesitation, and no uncertainty. No limits.

She was home. Finally home.

Andrea lay tangled in his arms as the first light of morning slanted through the window.

'One thing I didn't know about you...' She caressed his cheek and his eyes opened.

'Hmm? What's that?'

'All those fantasies. They weren't as good as the real thing.'

Cal grinned sleepily. 'You had fantasies? That's nice. I think I'll be fantasising about you fantasising about me.'

'All the time.' There wasn't a single thing she couldn't tell him, and nothing she couldn't ask, either. 'What about you?'

'Just the one. It started about ten seconds after I met you. And lasted until yesterday morning. Then you made it all real.' He gave her a broad, contented smile. 'Several times.' He chuckled. 'Reality's good. I can take a great deal more of it.'

'Just as well that I happen to be free, then.'

He stretched luxuriously, propping himself up on one elbow. 'Italy or London. What do you think?'

Andrea had already made up her mind. 'London. Definitely.'

'You're sure? I was thinking how much I liked the mountains.'

'Your job's here, Cal.'

'Everything's up for grabs, Andrea. Everything apart from us being together, that is.' He grinned at her.

Cal would have left his job behind, everything he'd built, to be with her. And Andrea knew he'd do it without looking back; he'd made it clear that his happy place was with her, just as hers was with him.

'The Alps will always be there for us whenever we want, Cal. But I want to come back home and live in London. I've been away too long already, and there's a lot I still want to do.'

'If that's what you really want—'

Andrea silenced him with a kiss. That settled the question.

'All right. I hear you. London it is. I do have one condition, though.'

'What's that?'

'I told the board of directors at the clinic that I'd take the job they were offering. It means working from home for a few months, and that's an opportunity to come out to Italy with you for a while. We won't rush back, we'll take our time over it.'

'But, Cal...you know I believe in the work you do. It's important. If you need to be here in London I'll join you as soon as I can...'

He put his finger lightly on her lips. 'We belong together and it only takes a little flexibility to make that happen. I'll be needing to talk to a lot of people, based in various different places, and I can do that from Italy just as well as I can from here.'

'You're sure?'

'I'll need your support, and I'll be asking you for some ideas, too. You have experience of overhauling systems so that everything's working in the best way possible.'

'You have my support, always.' She reached up, winding her arms around his neck. 'Now that we know where we're going to live, and what you're going to do, the only thing left is for us to find something for me to do. We can think about that later, though...'

'Yeah? What do you have in mind in the meantime?' Cal grinned. His body was already responding to the pressure of hers as she pulled him close.

'I'm overhauling our own personal system. Establishing a precedent for lazy Sunday mornings in bed.'

'That sounds like an interesting concept. I think we should explore it a little more fully...'

It had been the best weekend of his life. He'd taken Andrea to the airport early on Monday morning, promising that he'd be in Italy on Friday evening. Then he'd gone into work, and outlined his plans to the other directors, who had given him their full support.

Everything was coming together. Andrea had called him, saying she'd given in her notice at the hotel, and told them she'd stay on for a couple of months to ensure a smooth handover. That evening he'd called Joe.

'Joe, I want to ask a favour.'

'Sure.'

'You know I told you that I'd met the woman I want to marry...'

'Yeah?' A note of caution sounded in Joe's voice.

'Well, it appears that Andrea's crazy enough to want to spend some time with me. I need your help with something.'

Joe's delighted chuckle sounded in his ear. 'What do you need, mate?'

She was waiting on the platform as the funicular drew into the hotel terminus. Cal waited impatiently for the doors to open, and as soon as they did Andrea flung herself into his arms, almost squashing the roses he'd bought for her.

It felt like an age since he'd touched her. He told her how much he'd missed her and she whispered that they'd make up for that tonight. But first they'd eat; he must be famished.

They had dinner in the restaurant, at Andrea's favourite table, the one by the window.

'You'll miss this, when we're back in London.' Cal looked out at the dark shapes of the mountains, under a sky bright with stars.

'A little. Maybe…' Andrea shrugged.

'It's okay. You can miss it more than a little.' They'd already talked about this. Cal had made sure that Andrea had really thought about her decision to move to London, and that it was what she really wanted. He trusted her, and knew that Andrea trusted him. That silenced whatever fears either of them might have.

She nodded. 'It's going to be difficult to leave. But it's time for me to move on; I want to come home.'

'We won't be doing that until you've finished up here. When I spoke to the board, they were more than happy to give me as much time as I need. I'll have plenty to keep me occupied here.'

'You're sure they're okay with that? This is an important opportunity for you, Cal.'

'I promised I'd be there for you, and I will.' Cal knew this wasn't easy for Andrea, and he wanted to make the transition as painless as possible for her.

'Thank you. I'm feeling better about it already.'

'Shall we take a stroll on the veranda? It's a beautiful evening.'

She nodded. 'Yes, that would be nice. Kissing you by the light of the moon.'

Cal went to fetch their coats, speaking to the waiter on the way back. When they sauntered out onto the deserted veranda, he could see the small table being prepared for them at the other end.

By the time they reached it the waiters had gone. Cal picked up the champagne bottle from the ice bucket, showing her the label.

'*Very* nice.' She nodded her approval.

'Joe suggested this vintage.'

'Ah. I see. So while Maggie and I have been getting excited about living in the same city, you and Joe have been discussing vintages, have you?'

They both jumped as the champagne cork popped, and Cal filled the two glasses that were standing ready. He'd meant to do this later on in the evening but he couldn't wait. Why wait, when they already had everything they needed?

'This was all my idea...' He fell to one knee, feeling in his pocket for the ring. Andrea almost dropped her champagne glass in astonishment, and he took it from her hand.

'We've made our commitment already. I'm never going back on that, and I want you to marry me, Andrea.'

'Yes. I want you to marry me too. I mean... I want to

marry you back…' She was stammering now, her eyes full of tears. Cal caught her hand, bringing it to his lips, before he took the ring from his pocket.

'Cal…!'

'You're sure?'

'Yes! I'm sure.' She watched as he slid the ring onto her finger. 'It's so beautiful, Cal.'

'I knew this was yours the moment I saw it. You really like it?' Two diamonds, mounted together in a twined knot of gold. Inseparable, the way he and Andrea were.

'I love it. Thank you, Cal…' She pulled him to his feet, and Cal allowed himself the ultimate pleasure. He kissed the woman that he was going to marry.

EPILOGUE

A PAIR OF PEACOCKS strutted across the grass outside the large conservatory. Even the smallest details seemed to be conspiring to make Cal and Andrea's wedding day perfect.

The venue had needed almost no decoration because it was already stunning. The central paved area of the conservatory, which was now filled with chairs for the wedding ceremony, was surrounded by plants and greenery of all kinds. Orchids hung from the Victorian cast-iron framework that arched over their heads and Cal had even found a small area where medicinal plants were grown. He and Joe had joked that they might come in handy if anyone was taken ill.

On the other side of the grassed area was an old orangery, which was perfect for the reception. And on a day like today, the guests could join the peacocks outside in the warm sunshine.

Aunt Mae was sitting with Andrea's mother, dressed in fuchsia-pink with a large hat. Cal sat next to his best man, waiting for Andrea to arrive.

Joe patted the pocket of his waistcoat. 'I've got the rings.'

'Great. Thanks.'

'Everything's going to be fine, you know.' Joe reminded him of that fact for the umpteenth time.

'Yeah. Nothing to worry about.'

Joe sighed. 'Can't you just pretend to be a little nervous? I've read the book, and there's a whole chapter on ways that the best man can calm the groom's nerves.'

'Really? What does it say?' Cal couldn't think of one thing to be nervous about. Andrea would be here soon and they'd be married. That was all he needed to know.

Joe puffed out an exasperated breath. 'Tips and techniques, mate. If I told you what they were, they probably wouldn't work.'

Fair enough. Perhaps one of the tips was to appear nervous enough for both of them.

The last six months had had its share of ups and downs. Cal had watched Andrea's world begin to expand as she started to look beyond the boundaries of her mountain refuge, but still she'd shed a tear when they'd packed up all her belongings, ready to bring them home.

If he hadn't been so sure of her, his own confidence would have wavered. The first few weeks back in London had been difficult; she'd scoured the journals for a job and found nothing that suited her. Cal had wondered a few times whether he really could make her happy, but holding her at night never failed to quell his fears.

Then the right job had come along. It needed a special kind of person to work with children with disabilities and Andrea had agonised for days about whether she could do the job justice. But Cal had convinced her to give it a go and she'd come away from the interview fired with enthusiasm. The job offer had come two days later, and she hadn't looked back.

They were both changing and growing. Cal's new responsibilities meant he travelled much less than before, but when he did he knew that Andrea supported him in what he was trying to achieve. She'd taken time off work to accompany him on a trip back to Africa for a week, and sharing that had added yet another new facet to their happiness.

And he *was* happy. He'd never thought he had a right to anything this fulfilling, but now he could reach out and take it, knowing that Andrea was happy too.

'The cake's in one piece, at least.' Yet another of Joe's needless reassurances broke Cal's train of thought.

'The cake's the last thing we need to worry about. I *know* that's going to be great.' Maggie had insisted on making their wedding cake and Cal had heard that Joe had helped with the decorations. It had been a very special gesture and Andrea had been happy to let their friends decide on the design.

Joe shook his head. 'You might have warned me about this best man business. It's far more nerve-racking than actually getting married.'

'Don't worry. It'll all be over soon and you can relax.' Cal grinned at him. 'By the way, have you met Andrea's maid of honour? Her name's Maggie and I think you'd really like her.'

Joe finally smiled.

The music Andrea had chosen for her walk down the aisle began to play from speakers hidden amongst the foliage. Cal got to his feet, craning round to catch his first glimpse of Andrea, and saw Maggie coaxing the two little flower girls in the right direction.

Then he saw her, dressed in white lace with flowers in her hair. A lump rose in his throat as Andrea hurried down the aisle towards him, her father trying and failing to slow her down to a more modest pace.

And then they were standing together. He bent towards her, whispering in her ear. 'Let's get married, shall we?'

Andrea smiled up at him. 'Yes. Let's do just that.'

* * * * *

A REUNION,
A WEDDING,
A FAMILY

AMY RUTTAN

MILLS & BOON

For all the positive strong women in my life.
This one is for you.

PROLOGUE

Summer, ten years ago
Jasper, Alberta

CANDICE WARNER HAD to put some distance between herself and her brother's antics. She loved Logan, but he was currently running around a campfire buck naked in the moonlight and she didn't need to see that. Especially not on her birthday.

Not that she couldn't understand or empathize with his desire to let loose tonight. In a week he and his best friend, Jimmy, would be leaving Jasper for basic training with the Canadian Armed Forces.

Jimmy. The boy she'd had a crush on forever.

Candice sighed. She was still processing the fact that Logan and Jimmy were leaving and she had no idea when she'd see them again.

You're leaving soon, too. You're going to university.

Even that was hard to process. It scared her. The idea of leaving Jasper was overwhelming. She'd spent her whole life here.

She wandered away from the campsite and sat down on a log by the river, far enough away to get some peace and quiet, so she could think. The only problem was, she couldn't think clearly. Her mind was going a mile a minute—everything was so uncertain.

"What're you doing here all alone?"

Candice glanced up to see Jimmy walking toward her. Her heart skipped a beat at the sight of him, like it always did. He had the reputation of being the love-'em-and-leave-'em type—always a new girl on his arm—which should have stopped her, but she couldn't help herself. There had always been something there—a spark, a connection—and she could talk to him in a way she couldn't with anyone else. She saw Jimmy for who he really was and she considered him one of her best friends.

For so long it had always been the three of them: her, Logan and Jimmy.

Now, with everyone leaving, nothing would ever be the same.

"Can I join you?" he asked, interrupting her thoughts and making her realize she hadn't answered his initial question.

"Sure."

"Want a beer?" he asked, handing her a can.

She cocked an eyebrow. "I just turned nineteen an hour ago."

"Right, so you're legal now. And I thought you might need it after seeing your brother naked."

She laughed and took the can, but didn't open it. "Thanks."

Jimmy took a seat next to her and glanced up at the sky. "Wow. So many stars. I'm going to miss this."

"I'll bet." Candice sighed, hoping her voice wasn't shaking. She wanted to tell Jimmy how she felt, but couldn't find the words. And that was the problem—

she had never been able to find the words. "So you and Logan are really leaving?"

Jimmy nodded. "There's nothing to keep us here."

"What do you mean there's nothing keeping you here?" she asked.

"Exactly that? What's the alternative? Work in my parents' motel and have no life, killing myself for ungrateful tourists? No thanks."

"Your parents worked hard to build the motel into a success."

He snorted. "Right. Which is why I was left alone most of my life."

"There's really nothing that makes you want to stay here?" she asked.

He chuckled. "Come on, Candy. What's here?"

"I am," she whispered, her body trembling as she found the courage to look him straight in the eye. "I'm here."

He smiled at her, his eyes twinkling in the moonlight. "Not for long. You're going off to school to become a doctor, some hotshot surgeon. You won't come back after that. You're too special to waste your life here."

Her cheeks heated. "What do you mean?"

Jimmy reached out and touched her face. She closed her eyes, her body humming with anticipation.

"I think you know what I mean, Candy," he said softly. And then he leaned in and pressed his lips against hers, stealing her first kiss.

She always wanted it to be him. Only ever him.

And in that moment, she didn't care that her brother had told her time and time again that Jimmy was off-limits.

This is what she had always wanted and she wasn't

going to miss her chance. She didn't want him to leave without knowing how she felt.

"I love you, Jimmy," she murmured against his lips.

"I love you, too, Candy. I always have."

Her knees went weak at his admission and she felt like she was going to cry. They kissed again. More fervently this time. They were both leaving but they had this last week together and she was going to make it count.

"Come on," she said, standing and reaching out a hand to him.

"Where are we going?" he asked.

"To my tent."

"Are you sure?" he asked. "Maybe it's the beer talking…"

"I haven't had a drop. Have you?"

"No." He showed her his can, which was unopened, just like hers. "I haven't had mine, either. I haven't had a drop all night."

"Then why did you bring me one?" she asked.

"To give me an excuse to come talk to you." He stood and cupped her face, kissing her again. "Because I couldn't leave without telling you how I feel."

"Come on," she said again, pulling on his hand and leading him to her tent.

"Are you sure, Candy?"

She nodded. "Yes."

She'd never been so sure of anything in her life.

CHAPTER ONE

Present day
Jasper, Alberta

"So glad you're back, Candice!" Samantha greeted her warmly, as she approached the reception desk at Mountain Rescue.

"I'm glad to be back," Candice replied. And she was. After having a flu that had knocked her sideways for two weeks it felt good to be back at work, especially as she knew there was going to be so much to catch up on.

"You'll be happy to hear that the head office in Gatineau hired you a new paramedic while you were off sick. He starts today and should be here soon!"

Candice nodded as the receptionist handed her a file folder on her new employee.

"I told them I would get around to it," she muttered as she took a sip of her now cold coffee. Since she'd arrived an hour ago, she'd been busy trying to get through the thing she hated most: bureaucratic paperwork.

She would much rather be out in nature or in the field saving lives, but since she'd been promoted, she'd found herself stuck behind a desk more often than not. They were approaching the busy tourist season, though, so she was hoping that she could get out more. Just like she had in the winter, when all the skiers had descended upon Jasper and she'd had the chance to fly her helicopter a few times for rescues.

"I know, but they were approached by someone who's served in the Canadian military and had amazing credentials. They couldn't turn him down," Samantha said sympathetically. "I know you would've rather chosen your new paramedic yourself."

Candice's frustration ebbed away. She had a soft spot for anyone who'd served, like Logan had. Though she missed her brother terribly, she knew he would have been honored to have died in service to his country and she was so proud of everything he had accomplished. Her parents had been proud, too, before they passed— her mother a year after Logan was killed in action five years ago, her dad last summer, to pancreatic cancer.

So, yeah, she had a soft spot for those in the military. Just thinking about Logan made a lump form in her throat. It was all she could do to stop herself from shedding a tear right there, but she made a point of not crying at work.

In fact, she never, ever cried in front of anyone.

Her ex-husband, Chad, had always said crying was a form of weakness. She was the boss here at Mountain Rescue. She couldn't afford to show weakness.

"Ex-military?" she asked, clearing her throat and trying to regain control of her emotions.

"Honorably discharged." Samantha smiled. "It can't be all that bad, can it?"

Candice nodded and half smiled. "No, you're right."

Head office knew what they were doing, even though she did prefer to make her own decisions about personnel.

Candice opened the file and was grateful she'd put

down her coffee cup first. If she had been holding it, she would've dropped it right there, all over her paperwork.

Blaring up at her in big, bold letters was a ghost from her past.

"You okay?" Samantha asked.

Candice shook her head and quickly shut the file. "What?"

Samantha cocked an eyebrow. "I asked if you were okay. It looked like you'd seen a ghost."

She tried to muster a smile, but it probably looked a little manic since Samantha took a step back from her.

"I'm fine. Could you let me know when he gets here?" She hoped that her voice wasn't shaking.

"Of course." Candice turned from the reception desk to head into her office, and only when the door was closed behind her did she relax, sitting down and opening the file again to stare at the name.

Jimmy Liu.

Samantha had been right about one thing—a ghost from her past *had* been contained in that new personnel file.

Jimmy was back.

Her first.

First kiss.

First time.

First love.

And her first broken heart. They'd spent a week together, just the two of them, and right before he left, he broke it off, shattering her heart. The memory of that moment came back to her in a painful flash.

"I thought you loved me?" she'd said that day, a decade ago. Her heart had felt as if it was being crushed. It had been hard to breathe.

"I don't." He glanced away, not even having the decency to look her in the eye.

"So that's it?" she asked, her voice trembling.

"Yeah," he'd said, coolly. *"It is."*

Her heart had been shattered a second time months later when she'd lost the baby they had conceived that first night together.

Jimmy had never come back to Jasper again.

It had crushed her. Logan had warned her so many times about Jimmy, but she hadn't listened.

"Candy, Jimmy is my best friend, but he's not right for you," Logan had argued, trying to hold her back from going to see him that last night, after he'd broken things off.

"Let me go," she argued back. *"He loves me. He said he did."*

Logan looked at her sadly and her heart sank.

"Please, Logan. I need to talk to him."

He sighed. *"Fine, but honestly, Candy, you're too good for Jimmy. You have all these high aspirations and I think you need to pursue your dreams. You want to be a doctor. People like me and Jimmy...we'd just hold someone like you back,"* he'd concluded.

Now, Candice shook away that thought, tears stinging her eyes as she thought of Logan. As she thought of the rejection, the heartbreak and the dreams she hadn't followed.

Of the baby she lost.

The family she no longer had.

After losing Logan and her mother in the space of a year, it fell to Candice to stay in Jasper and take care of her dad. Even though he told her to go back to medical school, she couldn't leave him.

So Mountain Rescue had become her family. All she

needed. They'd been the ones there for her when her father passed away last year.

Unlike her ex-husband.

And Jimmy.

Jimmy Liu. Back after all this time.

With a sigh, she set down the file and stood up, stretching and tying back her long, dark brown hair. She wandered over to the window that overlooked the parking lot and watched as an old, beat-up white SUV slowly parked.

An SUV she recognized from ten years ago.

Her pulse began to race, and when the door of the vehicle opened, her heart skipped a beat, just like it always did when she saw Jimmy.

You're the boss. Remember that. You're the one in control this time.

And she would keep reminding herself of that. After Jimmy's rejection and her brief, disastrous marriage to Chad, she was done being rejected and hurt.

Everyone left her eventually, so she would never put her trust in someone else again. She'd never put her heart in someone else's hands.

Jimmy and Chad had both hardened her heart to love. So now her love was her work.

She took a deep breath to calm her frayed nerves. This was not how she wanted to start her Monday.

"The new paramedic is here," Samantha said, opening the office door.

"Thanks, Samantha. Show him in." She tried to keep her tone level.

Samantha nodded and disappeared.

Candice took another deep calming breath and took a seat behind her desk, straightening the papers and folding her hands across his file, her back ramrod-straight and her lips pursed tightly together. Nothing from the waist up betrayed the fact that her leg was twitching under the desk, nervously bouncing, while her pulse thundered between her ears.

Samantha returned, with Jimmy. "Right this way, Mr. Liu."

"You can just call me Jimmy," he said in that suave, charming voice that had won her over. The sound conjured up the image of his smile, the little twinkle in his dark eyes and the inevitable wink.

She'd fallen for that charm once.

But that was then and this was now.

You've got this. You're the boss, remember? You hold the power this time.

She rolled her shoulders as he walked into the room, but the moment he appeared, all that resolve, all the control she had over herself, seemed to melt away, like the morning mist off the lakes when the summer sun hit it.

He looked almost exactly the same, but he had filled out in all the right places. Broad-shouldered and muscular, the grey suit and white dress shirt he wore fit him like a glove. His black hair was short and clean-cut and there was a small scar on his face, but that handsome chiseled jaw and those full lips were just the same as she remembered.

Lips she had often dreamed about in the years after he left. She could still remember their first kiss down by the river so clearly. The night he'd taken her in his arms and she put her heart in his hands, giving herself to him.

Trusting him not to hurt her.

Listening to him whisper that he'd always love her.

Lies.

Don't think like that.

He flashed one last smile at Samantha and then his

gaze fell on Candice, his eyes widening and his mouth opening in shock for a brief moment.

She was very thankful that he couldn't see her leg tapping under the desk. He'd know she was nervous then. She put a hand on her knee to stop herself.

"Candy?"

"Jimmy Liu," she said. "It's been a long time."

Jimmy couldn't quite believe what he was seeing and for one brief moment he was reminded of all those old black-and-white movies that his yéye would watch endlessly when he was kid.

"Of all the gin joints in all the world, she had to be in mine..." Or something like that.

Right now, he was feeling that.

Hard.

Gone was that shy, shrinking girl he'd once known. The one always hiding behind Logan or behind a book. Here sat a confident woman. Her hair was still that beautiful, silky brown and the sight of it reminded him of the few times he'd tucked a strand behind her ear, making her blush.

He couldn't help but wonder if she still bit her bottom lip when she was nervous, something he had always found endearing.

Seeing her brought him right back to that night when they'd first kissed, the night they'd made love.

God, he'd loved her then.

He would've stayed with her. If it hadn't been for Logan.

"You can't see my sister," Logan had snapped, pushing him.

"What do you mean?" Jimmy asked. *"I love her. It's why I can't enlist with you. I want to stay with her."*

Logan shook his head. *"She has dreams, dude. Dreams to become a doctor. You'd hold her back."*

Jimmy sighed. He knew Candice had big plans—it was one of the things he admired most about her. *"But I love her."*

"If you love her, Jimmy, you'll let her go," Logan had said. *"Let her go. For me."*

He shook the memory from his mind and saw the way her dark brown eyes were looking at him confidently, not darting around nervously.

Logan had made it clear that Candice was off-limits, and even though Jimmy knew it was for the best, it had killed him to walk away from her. He'd carried a picture of her—stolen from Logan—with him for years. He still had it. Thinking of her and her better life without him had gotten him through the heartache and loss.

Especially when he'd learned she'd married.

Jimmy may have failed Logan on the front lines—he'd survived that IED attack, but hadn't been able to save his best friend's life—but he could keep that old promise he'd made before they left Jasper ten years go. He'd let Candice go so she could follow her dreams and she was still off-limits. Even if a part of him still wanted her, was still affected by her.

She's married.

Not that he was even in a position to think about dating or being with anyone. He'd sowed his wild oats and he was paying for it now. He had responsibilities and a son who depended on him.

"It's Candice, not Candy," she said, sternly interrupting his thoughts. "And when we're out in the field we address each other by our surnames, so you can call me Lavoie."

His stomach knotted. Lavoie—so that was her married name. He was somehow envious of her husband, while also hating the man's guts.

"That's why I didn't recognize your name," Jimmy said. "Lavoie and not Warner. How long have you been married?"

He knew, of course. She had gotten married just a month before the IED attack in the Middle East. It was a peacekeeping mission that had gone sideways, injuring him and killing Logan.

Jimmy had spent months recovering in a military hospital in Germany, undergoing surgery to remove shrapnel from his hip and learning to walk again as both his legs had been broken.

And the whole time, all he could think about was how his best friend was dead and the girl of his dreams was someone else's wife.

Her eyes narrowed as a blush rose in her cheeks. "I'm divorced, but didn't bother changing my name back."

"Oh." Secretly he was thrilled, but he tried not to show it.

He recalled her words to him… *I love you, Jimmy. I always have.*

He looked at her now, but didn't see that emotion in her eyes anymore. It was all business, which was for the best.

This was better.

Was it?

"Why don't you have a seat and we'll go over some of the expectations," she said, motioning for him to take the empty seat in front of her desk.

"Sure." He sat down stiffly, uneasy about the tension that had descended between them. They were strangers, but weren't.

He was surprised to find how much it pained him

that she was acting so distant, when they had once been so close.

You haven't been home in years. What did you expect?

It still bothered him to this day he couldn't have been here when they buried Logan, but he'd been stuck in the military hospital in Germany. Afterward there had seemed no point in coming back to a Jasper—Logan was gone and Candice was married—so he'd moved to Toronto.

He couldn't blame Candice for being mad at him, or even hating him. He had broken her heart and not been here for her when she needed him after losing her brother.

Candice flipped open his file. "So, you did your paramedic training with the Canadian military?"

"Yes. I was a medic and have my certification in wilderness medicine and surgery. I can perform minor surgeries in some of the roughest conditions."

"What kind of surgeries?" she asked.

"Sutures, removing shrapnel and tracheostomy. I've done a few chest tubes." Not that any of his skills had been useful when it had come to helping Logan in that crucial moment on the front lines...

"Hold on, buddy!" Jimmy had shouted above the gunfire.

They were slightly protected by the overturned truck, but a wall had crushed Logan's lower half and pinned both of Jimmy's legs, making it so he couldn't do anything to help Logan.

"I can't feel anything," Logan whispered. *"I think my pelvis and my spine are crushed. Pretty sure my femoral artery is severed."*

"You need to hold on. We're going to get you evacuated and into surgery."

Logan shook his head slowly. *"Promise me one thing."*

"Anything," Jimmy said.

"Take care of Candy for me."

"You can take of Candy yourself when you get home," Jimmy told him.

Logan had shaken his head again. *"I can't. I know I said keep away from her, but you have to promise me you'll look out for her. Promise me. I know she cares for you..."*

But he hadn't done that. He'd let her be, hoping she was happy.

The only reason he'd come home for the first time in four years was because he was looking for a way to make things right for his son.

Her eyebrows arched and she nodded. "That's impressive."

"Thank you."

"I can see why Head Office hired you." She closed his file.

"Thanks."

"We're headed into another busy season. The summer brings a lot of tourists to Jasper—as you're well aware—and the backcountry camping is now open, as well as the regular campsites. Most of these areas are patrolled by the park rangers, but we do have to help on some of the backcountry hikes."

"Okay," he said.

"A lot of visitors are unfamiliar with how fast the weather can change in the mountain, so it will help that you're a local, even if you haven't been back in... what, ten years?"

He wasn't going to let on he had been here four years ago. That he'd come back because of her, only to leave heartbroken.

"Yeah. Ten years," he said dryly.

She cocked her head to the side. "You okay? You seem to be in shock."

"I am a bit," he laughed nervously.

"Why?" she asked, folding her hands in front of her.

"To be honest, I didn't think that you would be running the mountain-rescue program in Jasper."

"Why?" she asked, those brown eyes narrowing again.

"You always wanted to go to medical school. I thought you'd be a surgeon or something by now."

A strange expression crossed her face, one he couldn't read, but it was obvious by the way she straightened her back that he'd touched a nerve, even though he hadn't meant to.

"Yes, well, circumstances change," she said stiffly. "After Logan died, my mother didn't take it so well and she passed away the following year. It was just me and my dad until last year, when I lost him to cancer. There's no time for medical school when you're trying to hold your family together."

It felt like Jimmy's stomach had dropped through the soles of his feet into the floor. He had heard that Logan's mom was gone, but he hadn't heard that Mr. Warner had passed, too. His parents hadn't told him that. The Warners had always been so kind to him, so welcoming. It was hard to believe they were gone.

"I—I don't know what to say, Candice. I'm so sorry." He meant it.

A half smile appeared on her lips, but didn't extend to her eyes. It was perfunctory. "I appreciate that."

She stood up and he followed, but was still shocked at how calm she'd been sharing just how much she'd lost since Logan had died—her mother, her father, her husband… She was completely alone.

She's your boss.

Candice held out her hand. "Welcome to Mountain Rescue."

Jimmy stared at her outstretched hand. What he wanted to do was give her a hug. Wanted to let her know that he was here for her. That he still cared for her. He wanted to hug her and comfort her, like he used to do. Like he always dreamed of doing every day he was away from her. Only, he couldn't do that. He'd broken her heart and he'd been gone so long that they were effectively strangers.

He took her small, delicate hand in his, reveling in the feel of her soft skin and hoping his palms weren't sweaty as they shook.

"I look forward to working with you." He held her hand longer than he intended and she pulled it away, a pink flush rising in her cheeks, which made his heart beat a bit faster.

"Samantha will show you where your gear is and will give you a temporary uniform…" She trailed off as the phone began to buzz. She answered it and sat down, grabbing a pen and paper to write down the details.

Jimmy stood quietly, unsure of what to do. Or where to go.

"Thanks, we'll be there soon." Candice hung up the phone and glanced at Jimmy. "I would get your gear together and change. Looks like your first assignment is right now. There's an injured hiker in Maligne Canyon, slipped down a ravine. We need to retrieve him. You up for this?"

Jimmy nodded, shaking away all those old thoughts, the sadness—everything that was swirling around his head. "I'm ready."

Candice smiled and nodded. "Then have Samantha show you where to get ready and we'll get on the move ASAP."

Jimmy nodded and opened the door, glancing back at Candice, who was on the phone again. He couldn't quite believe that they would be working together.

Little Candy Warner was his boss.

It's Lavoie now.

She was no longer that girl he had loved. His first love.

He couldn't afford to mess up this job. He needed it to make a life for him and his son. He had to start over, even if it meant he was right back at the beginning again.

CHAPTER TWO

CANDICE DIDN'T KNOW WHY she was so nervous. She'd executed rescues at Maligne Canyon many times, but this was the first time she was doing it with Jimmy by her side.

Even though she was trying to tell herself she was over him, it was clear he was still affecting her. Making her nervous, making her fidget. She usually had good control over her emotions, but they had been all over the place since she'd first seen his name in that file.

She climbed into the back of the ambulance rig so that she could sit next to him. Another member of her team was driving and there was another truck with more gear following—essentials like climbing gear, water, blankets. Whatever they might need.

She didn't normally sit in the back, but Jimmy was new and usually the new employees stuck to her like glue during their first few missions. As much as she wanted to keep her distance from Jimmy right now, she couldn't. He was new and it was her responsibility to train him.

Her team was one of the best in the province and she wasn't going to mar that reputation by letting Jimmy go off on his own the first day. Just because she was uncomfortable being close to him didn't mean she wasn't going to do her job. Things had changed. Mountain Rescue's reputation under her command was all that mattered.

Her feelings did not.

"Where are we headed to, boss?" Stu asked from the front seat.

"Maligne Canyon. We need to park close to the first bridge lookout."

"Sounds good," Stu said.

Candice settled beside Jimmy as the siren sounded and they started on the highway toward Maligne Canyon, twenty minutes northeast of Jasper.

It was awkward sitting this close to him. Usually, it didn't bother her to be crammed in the back of the ambulance with her coworkers, but this was different.

This coworker had seen her naked.

"Did you find everything you needed?" she asked, clearing her throat.

"Yeah, I think so," he replied, going through his rucksack.

She noticed some medical gear she hadn't seen before. It looked like a surgical kit, but she wasn't sure.

"What's that?" she asked, leaning over.

"It's a kit I carry with my own gear. Something I suggested to head office."

Candice was impressed. "Well, we'll make sure you get what you need. Perhaps you can go over the kit with the group?"

"Sure." He went back to organizing his gear.

He was wearing a short-sleeve shirt and she silently admired his muscular forearms and the tattoo she didn't remember him having before. It was a simple geometric mountain with a lone spruce. It wasn't overly large, but she liked it quite a bit.

When they were teenagers, they all had talked about getting tattoos. Jimmy knew it would bother his overly strict parents, but he never went through with it in Jasper. Even when Logan had gotten one.

Even when she had gotten one. One she'd thought about getting rid of from time to time.

"Your tattoo is so sexy," he'd murmured when he'd first seen it, tracing the outline of it on her thigh with his finger.

"It's nothing huge," she said, his touch making her blood heat.

"It's a big deal to me, and that I'm the first you've shown it to."

He'd pulled her close in that tent and kissed her again.

She shook away that thought, annoyed that all these memories she'd thought were locked up were sneaking back in and distracting her.

Don't let him get in your head.

"Do you have bear spray in there?" she asked, trying not to let her thoughts overtake her.

"Ah, no. I think I forgot that." He frowned.

She pulled out a can from her bag. "Here, the bears are busy eating right now after their hibernation, so you never know what you'll come across. It's better to have it."

Jimmy smiled. "Thanks, boss."

It was so bizarre hearing him call her *boss*, instead of Candy.

You told him not to call you Candy. Remember? And everyone else calls you boss or by your last name.

It was just… She wasn't used to *Jimmy* calling her that.

Candice smiled. "You're welcome."

She swayed as the rig rocked and sped along the highway. The RCMP had shut down Maligne Lake Road and the parking lot close to bridge number one, where the hiker had fallen. If it was the spot that she was thinking of, it was a vertical drop down the side of the canyon and they would have to use their rappelling lines to hoist out the hiker.

She only hoped the hiker wasn't too badly injured or hadn't been washed away by the river.

"Do you remember how to rappel?" she asked.

"What?" Jimmy asked, his confusion evident as he looked up from his rucksack, obviously not having heard what she'd said.

"You and Logan used to do a lot of rock climbing and I'm wondering if you remember how to rappel down a rock face?"

He nodded. "I do. I kept it up when I was living in Toronto."

"Good, because if I'm right, the hiker is at the bottom of a pretty steep vertical drop. It'll be slick and the water will be cold. It will be a technically challenging retrieval."

"I'm ready," Jimmy stated firmly. "And I'm familiar with the area."

Candice smiled. "I know you are."

She didn't know what made her say that, because it had been so long since she'd seen him and she'd never witnessed him in an emergency situation. What made her think that he was ready?

Jimmy was a stranger, for all intents and purposes.

He's not a stranger.

She knew Jimmy Liu. A little too well.

Yes, she might be worried about working with Jimmy because of everything that had happened between them in the past, but she had no doubt that he was capable and that he would be an asset to the team. He came with glowing reports from his commanding officers.

She did have a niggling worry, though. Would he take orders from her?

Would he respect her?

If he respected you, he wouldn't have left the way he did.

She was annoyed for thinking that and for doubting herself. She was the head of Mountain Rescue, a first responder, a certified ranger and a pilot. He *would* do what she said.

What she needed to do was stop worrying unnecessarily and focus on the rescue.

That was all that mattered.

The ambulance slowed down and made a right turn onto Maligne Lake Road. They would be at the site soon.

"I can't believe someone climbed over the fence," Jimmy murmured as they arrived at the trailhead.

"People do it a lot, unfortunately, to the point that it's a common rescue—though not always a positive outcome. One wrong move and the river can wash you away."

Jimmy nodded. "I'm willing to learn from you, boss."

Warmth spread through her. Maybe this wouldn't be as bad as she thought.

As the ambulance parked, they grabbed their gear, and Candice led the way to bridge number one. She just hoped that they would be able to get to the hiker easily.

Constable Bruce was waiting to speak to her and she motioned for Jimmy to follow her. Constable Bruce was one of the Mounties she liked dealing with the most. He knew his job well and was easy to work with. Some of the other, older Mounties still remembered her as a kid and didn't treat her with the same respect. Bruce had transferred from Toronto to Jasper and didn't have that shared history, so he treated her like a colleague should.

"Lavoie, I'm glad you're here," Constable Bruce said as she approached.

"Where else would I be?" Candice joked.

He smiled and then his gaze fell on Jimmy. "Ah, your team has a new paramedic, I hope?"

"Yes." Candice turned to Jimmy. "Jimmy Liu, this is Constable Bruce from the Jasper detachment. Jimmy served with the Canadian Armed Forces overseas. He has extensive experience working in harsh conditions."

Bruce raised his eyebrows, impressed. "Pleasure to meet you, Liu."

"Pleasure is all mine, Constable." Jimmy shook Bruce's hand.

"Well, the hiker climbed over the fence near the falls, right at the end of the trails. He was going to rappel down the limestone cliff to the bottom, but was unfamiliar with the porous limestone and his spike didn't hold," Bruce said.

Candice sighed. "Do you know how badly he's hurt?"

Bruce shook his head. "No. He did call out for help, but we haven't been able to communicate with him since his initial distress signal. His partner here tried to stop him—he's the one who called us—and he says the victim was acting strangely."

"Strangely?" Candice asked, alarm bells going off.

"I'll let you speak to his partner."

Candice and Jimmy exchanged glances. She was trying to piece together all the information she had to figure out what might have propelled the hiker to try and rappel down the side of the canyon.

Bruce led them over to the victim's worried-looking partner.

"Dean, this is our first responder Lavoie," Bruce said, introducing them. "Can you fill her in on what happened?"

Dean nodded, still obviously flustered. "Well, we had been up Roche Bonhomme. We decided to take the trail quite quickly because Reggie's training for an Ironman competition and he thought that elevating quickly and descending just as fast would help with his cardio endurance."

Candice groaned inwardly at that decision. It did not improve endurance if you weren't used to it.

"Are you from here?" she asked.

Dean shook his head. "No, we're from Ontario. Reggie wanted to train in the mountains, for some reason. We've been in Jasper a couple of days and have been hitting the trails hard. I don't know what happened on the descent, but he started complaining of nausea and seemed off balance."

"Off balance?" Candice asked, her mind running through scenarios, putting the pieces together.

Ontario was closer to sea level than they were. It could be altitude sickness or something more sinister, like a high-altitude pulmonary edema or a high-altitude cerebral edema.

"Yeah," Dean continued. "He was stumbling and then he wanted to climb over and rappel down the canyon. I was trying to convince him not to do that, but it was like he was drunk and there was nothing I can do to stop him. I tried to make sure his line was secure at the very least, but he moved so quick and the line gave way."

Candice nodded. "Thank you, Dean. I know this is stressful but I promise you we'll do our best to help Reggie."

She motioned for the team to follow her and they made their way along the well-marked trail to the viewing platform at the very end. She shivered as a cold gust of wind blew a mist of glacial water from the waterfalls below over her face.

Taking a deep breath, she steeled her resolve. "Let's get going."

Jimmy fell into step beside her. "What're you thinking?" he asked.

"Why don't you tell me your thoughts based on the info we have."

"A test?" he asked, cocking his eyebrow.

"Yes."

"I think acute mountain sickness, or AMS, based on the irrational behavior and their recent climb."

"Impressive. AMS would explain what drove him to act irrationally. If it's an edema, he'll probably need a hyperbaric chamber and there's also whatever injuries he might have."

The rangers had come and cut the fence so her team would have access to rappel and get a backboard down. She was secretly pleased when Jimmy went straight to work getting his harness and his gear on. She didn't have to explain anything to him, so she could focus on getting ready to head down.

She was going to go down first and assess the situation and then Jimmy would follow.

It was a tricky descent, but she'd done retrievals at the bottom of this canyon before. Some were easy and some hadn't ended well, but she knew this rappel like the back of her hand.

Her only hope was that Reggie was at the bottom on a stable rock ledge and not in the water.

Candice focused on setting up her gear, and as she arranged her harness, Jimmy came up beside her and helped without her asking, or having to tell him what to do.

His hands around her as he pulled on her harness made her move just a bit faster. He was so close she could smell him. It made her skin break out in goose-flesh and she was glad she was wearing a long-sleeve shirt, so he couldn't see how he was affecting her.

"You're secure and I'll secure your line down. You don't want to make the same mistake the hiker did," Jimmy stated. "Limestone won't hold anything."

"I know," Candice said, unable to help herself from staring at him.

He smiled. "What? Why are you looking at me like you're surprised I know what I'm doing?"

Heat bloomed in her cheeks. "I'm not. It's just…"

"You forget I lived here my whole life. I know what kind of accidents can happen in the mountains, too."

"Yeah, but you haven't been home in a long time."

A strange expression crossed his face, and he turned away.

The rest of the team got into place and Jimmy helped to hold her line as she made her way to the edge with her pack. She did know this drop well, but as she stood at the edge and looked down, she still got that feeling in the pit of her stomach.

The one of exhilaration mixed with fear.

Her pulse drowned out the roar of the water tumbling down below her. She knew how damn cold that water was and she really didn't feel like taking a dip. All it took was one wrong move. The elements could shift something. Something might move.

It was nature and it was unpredictable.

Candice took a deep breath and pulled on her rucksack.

"Ready, boss!" Stu shouted from where he was standing next to Jimmy, who was preparing to go down next.

Candice nodded and, looking through the foliage, she scoped out where she wanted to land. She would slowly make her way down, and she just had to hope that she would be able to quickly spot Reggie, and that she had room to safely land at the bottom.

The water had shaped the soft rock in a gorgeously compelling way, but it wasn't exactly even and it definitely wasn't easy.

She made her way over the side and started her slow drop down the canyon wall. Her eyes focused on where she was going as she dangled in the air, slowly inching her way closer to the hiker, who was, thankfully, perched on a ledge.

The only sound she heard was the water. The ice-cold mist was spraying her back, but she was used to it and she'd learned to drown out the sensory overload and just focus on the task at hand. A life was at stake.

The farther she descended, the more her eyes adjusted to the dimness and she could better make out the victim, sprawled out on a rock ledge just inches from the rushing water.

"Reggie?" Candice called out. "Can you hear me?"

Reggie didn't respond, which meant that it was possible he was unconscious, and if he was unconscious it could mean a lot of different things. Her mind was racing as she ticked through everything it could be: internal bleeding, head trauma…

Her feet touched the canyon floor and she got her footing on the slippery rock, being mindful of the moss.

"I'm down," she called up. "Send Jimmy down!"

"Sure thing, boss!" Stu called back.

Candice set her rucksack down where she could access the medical supplies and it wouldn't be washed away.

She carefully made her way over to Reggie. His leg was bent at an odd angle, which probably meant a fracture. She couldn't see any blood, but that didn't mean he wasn't bleeding internally. Reggie was wearing a helmet, but she could see there was blood from a laceration on his face. That was superficial, but he could've also done something to his neck. She didn't know what was underneath him, other than rocks, or whether he'd hit his head on his way down.

A couple of rocks cascaded down the wall and she glanced up to see Jimmy making his descent.

She would be glad when he got down here and the two of them could properly assess Reggie, then get him on the backboard, which would follow Jimmy down.

She worried her bottom lip, watching Jimmy get closer, but it became apparent that she had nothing to worry about. Jimmy knew what he was doing.

After he joined her, they waited as the backboard was lowered down, and then Jimmy did an assessment of the patient's ABCs.

"Pupils are reactive, so that's a good sign," Jimmy muttered.

"He has a fracture in his leg," Candice stated. "We'll have to get that stabilized before we get him on the backboard and out of here."

Jimmy nodded and moved to Reggie's leg, palpating it, and frowned. "It's his femur, so there could be internal bleeding. I'm going to start an IV line of fluids and we need to get up him out of here. He needs oxygen now if we think this might be related to altitude sickness."

Candice nodded. "His fingernails are turning blue."

Jimmy frowned. "Yeah, he needs oxygen treatment."

They set about quickly setting up the IV lines and getting Reggie oxygen. Jimmy stabilized the leg and together they got him onto the backboard and covered him, then secured all his lines and made sure everything was strapped down.

Candice couldn't believe how seamlessly they worked together in the damp conditions down by the edge of a glacier-fed waterfall. It was surreal to see that the boy she'd known from childhood was now a strong, capable man, helping her save someone's life.

And he was doing a damn fine job.

"Pass me that line," he said.

"Sure." She reached across, their fingers brushing.

"I think everything is secure enough to move him," he said.

"Good. Let's get him out of here." She stood and together they lifted the backboard to secure it to the ropes, so Stu and the RCMP officers waiting at the top could pitch in to help get the backboard up the side of the cliff.

"You should go up with, Reggie," Candice said as they continued to hook up the harnesses and make sure that Reggie was stable. "You're the paramedic."

Jimmy nodded. "Okay, boss."

Candice had to help hook Jimmy's harness, and even though she'd done a vertical rescue like this before and had hooked up people on her team to a backboard many times over, having to hook up Jimmy was giving her pause.

Her pulse was thundering between her ears, and she only hoped that he didn't notice that her hands were trembling as she pulled the hooks and tethers across his chest.

Holy cow, he's more muscular than I remember.

She chastised herself for thinking like that as her cheeks heated. She knew that Jimmy was looking at her.

"You okay, boss?" he asked.

She cleared her throat and stepped behind him, tugging on a line. "Fine."

Only she wasn't fine.

What was this hold that Jimmy Liu had on her? She'd thought she'd gotten over this years ago, when he'd left and broken her heart.

She'd cried for weeks and then had found out she was pregnant with Jimmy's child.

She'd steeled herself to be a mother—to go it alone—but just as she'd started to get truly excited, she'd lost the baby. And her heart had broken all over again.

So she'd closed off her heart as a means of getting through—the only way she could function and survive.

She thought she'd moved on, but being here with him, so close to him, touching him, brought it all back and it made her feel like that meek, quiet young woman again. It made her think of all her broken dreams, everything she'd lost.

Get a hold of yourself.

"You're good to go." She stepped back and pulled out her radio. "Stu, Jimmy's good to go and the patient is secure."

"Right," Stu responded.

Over the roar of the waterfall, she could hear the

team at the top, and slowly Jimmy began to ascend the side of the cliff, keeping the backboard stable.

Candice took a deep breath and watched from below, holding the ropes from the bottom and doing her part to make sure that the patient got to the top of the cliff safely.

Once they were to the top and Jimmy was over the side, she slipped on her rucksack and made the ascension herself.

Her climb up was quicker than Jimmy's and when she got to the top the rest of her team were already heading toward the helicopter that would airlift Reggie to the hospital. The helicopter had landed on the main road, because there wasn't much room in the small parking lot.

Jimmy helped unhook her and she took off her helmet, then made her way to the air ambulance. Stu was going to accompany Reggie to the hospital as he was a paramedic and Jimmy didn't have the clearance yet, so Jimmy briefed him on his initial observations.

"Stu, the patient has a suspected broken femur. An obvious laceration to the head, but pupils were reactive. There didn't appear to be any blunt trauma, though the patient did fall, but I'm suspecting AMS. Possibly a high altitude pulmonary edema or a high altitude cerebral edema. The patient is from Ontario and his partner was reporting strange behavior associated with AMS. He was also slightly cyanotic."

Stu nodded. "I'll monitor his oxygen."

Candice helped load the patient on the helicopter and then stepped away, ducking as the helicopter's blades began to whir. She blocked her face from the dust being kicked up and watched as the helicopter rose from the highway and took off toward the hospital.

As the helicopter disappeared in the distance, she saw that Jimmy was giving instructions to Dean and the RCMP was waiting to accompany Reggie's distraught partner.

Candice took a deep breath.

The rescue had gone well, even if Jimmy brought out all those unexpected and unwanted emotions in her.

Emotions she thought had been long buried.

She was annoyed with herself for letting her control slip like that, but she had to learn to deal with it. Jimmy didn't want her back. He'd made it clear when he left, breaking her heart after she'd offered it up to him.

And that was fine.

She had found love after him.

Yeah, and look how that turned out. You're divorced and he wasn't exactly the catch you thought.

Chad had left her when she needed him most.

Just like Jimmy.

Candice shook away that thought. The point was, she'd grown up since Jimmy Liu left Jasper. She'd mourned her brother alone, taken care of her parents.

She'd outgrown her foolish crush on Jimmy and she had to keep reminding herself of that. Except, when she looked at him, it was like no time had passed. Sure, things had changed, but he just brought her back to those happy days together before it all ended.

It was the last time she'd felt truly happy. Logan and her parents had still been alive and she'd thought Jimmy was the one.

You're fooling no one.

"Everything okay?" Candice asked as Jimmy made his way over to her.

"Yeah. The RCMP will take care of Dean."

"We'll have to get you hospital clearance so you can

accompany the patients in future. It should've been you riding in that helicopter instead of Stu."

A strange look passed over his face. Almost like fear, but it was a brief and his expression relaxed, though the smile didn't extend to his eyes. It was forced, like he was trying to hide something. "Right. Sure."

"You sure you're okay?" she asked, puzzled by his behavior.

"Not a huge fan of helicopters or planes, if I'm honest. Don't like flying. Reminds me of…" His lips pursed together as he paused. "Doesn't matter."

She had a feeling that it did matter, but it wasn't her business. When Jimmy had left her, she'd closed her heart to him. The only thing that should concern her about Jimmy now was how he fit in at Mountain Rescue and how he did his job. That's all that mattered.

Nothing else.

A lot had changed in ten years. They both were different people.

She was a different person.

Are you?

If she was going to make this situation work, then she had to keep her distance from Jimmy Liu.

"Well, we better get back to Jasper. I don't have my rig license, but we can take the pickup and we'll go over your first rescue."

"Sure. Sounds good, boss." He avoided her gaze as he walked away to help pack up the rest of their gear.

Candice cursed herself. She should've made him ride in the rig. They had time to go over his first rescue later.

Having him ride with her in the pickup was not distancing herself from him.

She hated that he brought out this irrational side of her.

She hated that she went right back to being that unsure girl who'd lacked confidences.

The girl who had been in love with Jimmy Liu.

CHAPTER THREE

You've got to get a hold of yourself, Jimmy.

He knew that working with Mountain Rescue would involve helicopters. He'd grown up watching them fly past, but since his time in the Middle East and that last mission he'd served there, helicopters had become something he feared—the cause of the explosion that had injured him and killed Logan.

He'd felt good about the rescue today until the helicopter had arrived—he was annoyed with himself, both for forgetting that a rescue like this usually required an air transport and for letting it get to him.

He thought he was over it.

How long had he worked with Kristen, his therapist, to get over his traumatic experiences overseas? Having seen Candice married and happy in Jasper four years ago, he'd wanted to better himself, so he'd started going to see Kristen when he was back in Toronto. He needed help to move past the trauma of his injury.

Past the trauma of Logan's death.

The trauma of losing Candice.

It was a dark period of his life and he'd be the first to admit he'd lived recklessly for a while. But those years hadn't been all bad.

One good thing came out of it.

Marcus.

It's not exactly how he ever pictured his life turning out, but becoming a father had helped Jimmy start to heal the rift between him and his parents. Helped him to understand them in a new light, to experience the drive a parent feels to provide for their child, even if that means making hard decisions. Having Marcus had gotten his life back on track and brought Jimmy back to his family.

He would do whatever it took to continue to turn his life around for his son.

He needed to get control of his fear of helicopters. He couldn't even help load Reggie onto the helicopter, and when he'd watched Candice move with ease toward it, it had made him worry about her.

Made him panic.

Because it brought him straight back to the day Logan died. They'd been trying to evacuate, but the helicopter had been hit by a missile, exploding and sending them flying.

This is not a war zone. Candice is safe.

He thought he had better control. He hadn't had an episode like that in a long time.

At least it wasn't a full-blown panic attack on his first day. He was trying to make a good impression.

There was a thud, knocking those thoughts from his head, and the pickup slowed.

"Dammit," Candice cursed, as she flicked on her four-way flashers and brought the truck to a stop at a lookout on the shoulder of the highway, where the majestic sight of the Athabasca River and the peaks of Roche de Smet and Gargoyle Mountain could usually be viewed.

But you couldn't really make out the peaks in this

mist and fog, so the lookout was empty. There wasn't even a mountain goat or an elk nearby to pique a tourist's interest and compel them to stop.

It was just them.

"Flat?" Jimmy asked as Candice cursed under her breath again.

"Yes." She groaned, shifting the truck into Park. She leaned her head against the steering wheel, banging it ever so lightly in frustration.

"Come on. Surely you know how to change a flat. I mean, your brother and I showed you enough times."

She glared at him. "I'm quite capable of changing a flat tire."

"Then why the cursing?" he teased.

"It's the last thing I need. A flat tire with you in the truck."

He cocked an eyebrow. "What's that supposed to mean?"

She shook her head and mumbled again, undoing her seat belt and opening the door.

Jimmy was confused. He didn't know what he'd done, but this was not the Candice he remembered.

This Candice was stressed.

Unhappy.

Do you even know what happiness is? When was the last time you were happy?

Jimmy sighed and undid his seat belt, sliding out of the passenger side of the truck. He closed the door and made his way to the back, where Candice had pulled out her emergency roadside kit and was busy setting up cones around the perimeter of the truck.

"We're on an overlook. No one is going to hit us," he said offhandedly, watching her methodically place the cones.

"It's also foggy. The last thing we need is some big recreational vehicle slamming into us out of the fog."

She had a point.

"Give me those," he said, taking the rest of the fluorescent cones and placing them around the front of the pickup.

After he finished, he asked, "Well, do you need me to replace the flat?"

"Nope." She said, standing there with her arms crossed.

"Okay. Then are you going to do it?" he asked, confused as to why she was just standing there.

"Nope."

Jimmy scratched his head. "Look, I'm no rocket scientist by any means, but one of us has got to change the tire if we want to get this truck moving again."

"We can't change a tire that isn't there."

"What do you mean it's not there?"

She held up her hands in exasperation. "The spare is not here."

Jimmy checked the flat tire and frowned, realizing what the problem was. "It is here, actually. It's just already on the truck."

"Great." Candice pulled out her phone and called for help. They would need a tow and a ride back to the station, because of the fog, the ambulance was way ahead of them now. She ended the call. "I guess all we can do now is wait."

"Did they say how long they were going to be?" he asked, glancing at his watch. He'd promised his parents that he wouldn't be late tonight picking up Marcus. He didn't want to wait hours by the side of the road.

Jimmy knew deep down that his parents wouldn't care if he was late because they adored Marcus and were so thrilled to be grandparents, but Marcus was going through a bit of a shy stage. When they lived in Toronto, he hadn't see his grandparents much, so he hadn't known them well when he and Jimmy had moved back to Jasper. Now they were here, Marcus was getting used to them, but still preferred having his dad close by.

"Why are you in such a rush?" Candice asked.

"I have to get home to my son," he said firmly, annoyed by the flat tire and the delay it was causing.

Candice's eyes widened. "Your—your son?"

"Yeah."

"I didn't know that you had a son," she said.

"I wouldn't think so," Jimmy teased. "This is the first time I've mentioned him, after all."

Candice crossed her arms and slowly walked over to him. "So your wife is expecting you home?"

"My wife?" Jimmy chuckled and shook his head. "No. I'm not married. Marcus's mother is not in the picture."

Marcus's mom, Jennifer, had been a one-night stand.

Jimmy hadn't even known he was a father until Marcus was six months old—that was when Jennifer had left their son on his doorstep. For a long time he'd resented Jennifer for hiding her pregnancy. He hated that he hadn't been there when Marcus was born, but he was learning to let that go because now he had Marcus and his son was a gift.

"Where is Marcus's mom? Is she from Jasper?" Candice asked as she sat next to him on the guardrail.

"No. She was from Toronto. She served overseas, like me. It was just a one-time thing and about six months after Marcus was born she showed up and dropped him off, almost as though she was discarding him. She had a lot of PTSD issues and I tried to find her, to get her help, but before I could she was killed in an accident. So it's been just Marcus and me for the last year. I'd been trying to better myself for some time and Marcus's birth made me realize I had to do a lot more than I was," he said softly. "I was so angry that she didn't tell me she was pregnant—that I couldn't be there, you know?"

"Right," Candice said quickly, looking away.

He couldn't believe that he was admitting this to Candice. Obviously it was making her uncomfortable.

He hadn't even told his own parents everything that happened since he'd been discharged from the armed forces. How serving had messed him up so completely, the extent of his injuries overseas...

His parents were easily connecting with Marcus, but Jimmy still had a hard time opening up to them. They'd been so distant when he was growing up, always working, so focused on the hotel that it often felt like they'd forgotten they even had a son. He'd never been able to trust in them in the past, so it was difficult to do so now.

Difficult to trust anyone, really.

"I'm so sorry to hear about Marcus's mother. How old is your son?" Candice asked.

Jimmy smiled. "He'll be two in a couple of months. He's a handful."

"Who has him now?"

"My mom. She loves being a grandma."

Candice smiled at him, but there was a sadness in that smile. Something she wasn't saying.

"She's lucky. My mom would've loved being a grandma. I think she was hoping for that when I got married to my ex, but it was never meant to be."

"Why?" he asked.

Candice sighed. "Well, she died a year after I got married, but it wouldn't have happened even if she'd lived… Chad didn't want kids. He said he did in the beginning, but changed his mind after we were married for a couple of months."

"How long have you been divorced?"

"Three years. We were only married for two. We separated when my dad got sick because he wanted to go back to med school, but I couldn't leave my dad alone in Jasper."

"Sorry to hear it didn't work out."

Only, there was a part of him—a surprisingly large part—that wasn't sorry that it hadn't worked out. He looked at her, sitting next to him on the guardrail in the fog. Her dark hair was tied back, the same way she sometimes used to wear it, but she was a very different woman than the one he'd left behind. Not just because she was in a mountain-rescue uniform with big black boots instead of a flannel shirt, jeans with holes in the knees and Converse sneakers. There was so much more that had changed—he could see it in her eyes and hear it in her voice. So much more she was keeping from him now.

Instead of her head down and her dark hair hiding her face, she was looking straight ahead with determination, her arms crossed.

This wasn't the same girl he'd fallen in love with.

He glanced over his shoulder at the Athabasca River. It was moving swiftly, the summer melt making it swell, and this section of the river was so wide it almost seemed like a lake. This wasn't far from where they had camped that night—the night everything changed between them.

"Remember that time Logan went skinny-dipping just over there?" he asked, thinking of that moment when he'd had to bear witness to his best friend's bare ass.

A smile tugged at the corners of Candice's mouth. "I try not to. I mean, I wasn't exactly thrilled my big brother decided to strip off all his clothes in front of me and go skinny-dipping."

"He was drunk."

She forced a smile. "I remember. I painfully remember."

"Come on. It was funny."

"You weren't traumatized by it. You don't have siblings so you have no idea how gross it is when your brother gets naked in front of you." She scrubbed a hand over her face. "You two were always doing nonsense like that and dragging me along!"

"You didn't have to be dragged along. You seemed to go willingly."

A pink blush rose in her cheeks and she quickly looked at him, then averted her gaze. "Well…yeah, I didn't really have a lot of friends. Logan was my best friend, too."

"And what about me?"

The blush deepened and she glanced up at him. "What do you mean, 'what about me'?"

"Wasn't I your friend?"

What are you doing, man?

He wasn't sure what he was trying to do. He promised himself that he wasn't going to treat her with familiarity. She was his boss and she'd made it quite clear that there was nothing between them beyond a professional relationship.

But he found that when he was around her, he couldn't help himself. All those old feelings that he used to have for her came flooding back.

Even though he'd kept away from Jasper—from Candice—seeing her again proved that those feelings had never faded away. Just sitting here with her made his blood heat, his heart race. He reached out and touched her face. He could feel her tremble under his touch.

"No. I thought you were my friend, but you weren't."

She got up and walked away.

Jimmy was disappointed, but really, what could he expect? He's let her down in so many ways over the years.

He ran his hand through his hair.

"Yeah, I suppose I deserved that," he muttered.

She turned on her heel. "Deserved what?"

"Your rejection," he said. "I have a lot to apologize for."

She pursed her full lips together. "Yes, you do."

He stared at the ground, not entirely sure what to say.

She sighed. "Fine. You were my friend, too, I suppose, but you were a crappy friend."

He chuckled in relief that she was letting him off the hook…for now. "How so?"

"You let me see my brother's bare ass and did nothing to stop it." There was a twinkle in her eye. This was the Candice he remembered. She may have been shy, almost like a wallflower when they were young, but there were moments when she could take you down with a one-line zinger. It was one of the many things he'd always loved about her.

"Yeah, I guess that does make me a crappy friend." He hopped down from the guardrail and glanced back out over the water. He could make out Gargoyle Mountain through the mist. "We did drag you to a lot of places that you probably didn't want to go."

"Who said I didn't want to go?" she asked.

"Well, most girls that were your age at the time didn't want to go traipsing through the woods and drag racing and…whatever stupid things Logan and I used to do."

She smiled as she approached him. "I liked those stupid things you and Logan used to do. I never fit in with the other girls, anyway. I guess that's why boys never asked me out. I wasn't girly enough."

"I wouldn't say that," he said.

Candice looked up at him, the pink rising in her cheeks again. "What?"

"Guys liked you, Candy. You just didn't notice." He took a step closer to her and fought the urge to reach out and touch her face. To pull her in his arms and kiss her. "*I* liked you."

There was a flush of pink in her cheeks. "I liked you, too."

Get a hold of yourself.

Only, he couldn't.

All he could think about was that night by the river.

Jimmy's pulse was thundering in his ears as he moved closer to her.

"That night…"

"Don't," she whispered.

"Candice."

She bit her lip and he bent down, unable to resist her.

There was a honk and Jimmy took a step back, the spell of the moment broken as the tow truck came to rescue them.

"I better go…deal with the tow-truck driver," she said awkwardly, not looking at him.

"Yeah."

Candice walked away and Jimmy scrubbed his hand

over his face, annoyed that he couldn't control himself around her. Even after all this time.

Candice stayed late to fill out paperwork. Once they'd gotten back to the station, she hadn't said a word to Jimmy, other than to help get him set up with some paperwork and an online training course. When their shift was done, he left, but she stayed behind.

She tried to focus on work, but all she could think about was the fact that they'd almost kissed and the revelation that he had a son.

It made her heart ache and brought back all the pain of losing their child. The one he never knew about.

You have to tell him.

She knew she did. But he'd mentioned how he was so angry that Marcus's mom hadn't told him about Marcus, so what would he think when she told him about their lost baby?

She was scared.

She was also scared at the effect he had on her.

Her body trembled as she thought of their near kiss.

She was glad that the tow truck had come just then.

Candice sighed. She got up from her desk and wandered to the window, looking out at the distant mountain range. There were a few bighorn sheep wandering in the parking lot, but everything else was quiet and calm.

Except her.

Seeing Jimmy had completely rattled her.

It brought back all these ghosts from her past. Ones that she thought were long gone. She'd been a fool to think that they were.

There was a knock at her door.

"Come in," she called.

Stu opened the door and stuck his head in. "Just got back from Edmonton."

"Oh, Reggie was transported to Edmonton?"

Stu nodded. "You were right."

"Right?" she asked, confused.

"About acute mountain sickness and in particular HAPE. He had a pulmonary edema and is in the hyperbaric chamber. He was given some dexamethasone. Reggie was going up peaks too quickly. His body hadn't adjusted to the altitude."

"Seems odd, though," Candice stated, letting the part of her that wanted to be a doctor sneak through.

"Why's that?" Stu asked, leaning against the door.

"He was in shape."

Stu nodded. "Seemed like it, eh?"

"What do you mean?"

"He wasn't really. His partner said he lost over one hundred pounds in less than a year. He had bariatric surgery. Reggie's heart was weak and couldn't handle what he was putting it through. If he trained for his big race somewhere else, then he could've slowly built his heart muscle up, improved his cardiovascular system. Instead he was here and he pushed himself too far."

"And paid the price," Candice sighed. "That's too bad. Just goes to show you that you can't judge a book by its cover."

Stu nodded. "He should be okay. You got oxygen to him in the nick of time. The emergency doctor praised you for that."

"It wasn't just me. It was our new paramedic, Jimmy, too."

Stu smiled. "Yeah, he seems like a good guy."

"He was…" She shook her head. "I mean he is."

"I'm going to head for home. You should, too, boss.

You're still getting over that nasty flu. Don't push your-self too hard."

"Thanks, Stu. Good night."

Stu left, shutting the door. Candice sighed. She was glad that Reggie was going to be okay. And Jimmy had noticed the cyanosis before she did. She was thinking altitude sickness, but in that moment he'd caught the subtle blue tinge of Reggie's nail beds and they'd got-ten him oxygen.

It was a job well done.

Jimmy had told her that she was too good to waste her life here and she had to admit that there were mo-ments that she regretted that she didn't get to finish medical school. If she had, she'd be a doctor now, like Chad was, but she had stayed behind with her dad. Yes, her dad had insisted over and over that she return to school, but she couldn't bear to leave him.

So what's stopping you now?

Other than work, nothing was keeping her here. But she loved her job and it was days like this—having helped to save Reggie's life—that reminded her that hers was a life worth living.

But you're alone.

She couldn't deny that. She was alone.

It was in times like these she often wondered what her life would have been like if she hadn't lost their baby.

She'd have someone.

Dammit, Jimmy.

She groaned and shut down her computer, then grabbed her purse and jacket. She hadn't been ques-tioning anything about her life when she woke up this morning, but then he came walking through her door.

An unwelcome ghost from her past.

Is he unwelcome, though?

She shook away that thought and clicked off the office light.

She needed to get home.

And she needed to put Jimmy Liu out of her mind.

This was her life and there was no room for ghosts.

CHAPTER FOUR

THE MOMENT SHE pulled into the driveway at home, Candice realized she didn't have anything to eat in the house and she really didn't feel like takeout.

Usually, she did her grocery shopping outside of Jasper, especially during tourist season, when the prices were a bit higher, but the thought of the hour-long drive to Hinton and getting food there wasn't appealing. So she sucked it up, changed, picked up a couple of reusable bags and walked the fifteen minutes downtown to the small grocery store.

Downtown Jasper had come alive. It was a beautiful summer evening and with the summer sun almost at its solstice, it was staying light out later in the evening.

Candice usually liked to avoid the tourist crowds because it got loud at night, which she hated, but tonight it was a welcome distraction.

It got her mind off of Jimmy.

"Hey, Candy!"

She turned around and there he was—Jimmy. And, in his arms, a little boy who looked an awful lot like him, except for the layer of chocolate ice cream around his mouth. He smiled at her with chubby cheeks, then rubbed his eyes, smearing more melted ice cream all over his face. Next he buried his face on Jimmy's shoulder, spreading the chocolate over his white T-shirt.

"Hey yourself," Candice chuckled as Jimmy glanced down at his once clean shirt and rolled his eyes.

"I didn't expect to run in to you here," he said.

Ditto.

"Yeah, well, I had errands to run and felt like a walk." Her eyes tracked back to the adorable boy clinging to his father.

It made her heart melt. It made her long for what could've been.

"So this is your son, I take it?" she asked, hoping her voice wasn't shaking.

"Yeah, this is Marcus and what remains of his chocolate ice-cream cone."

Marcus looked at her shyly from his father's shoulder.

"Hi, Marcus. How are you?" she asked brightly.

Marcus smiled, but still kept his head on his father's shoulder.

"This is Candy, Marcus. She's my boss and an old friend of Daddy's," Jimmy said. Marcus stared up at his father and then smeared chocolate on his cheek. "Thanks, buddy. I appreciate it."

Candice couldn't help but laugh. "It's a good look on you."

"Thanks," Jimmy said dryly. "Do you happen to have a tissue or something? My arms are a bit full."

"Sure." Candice pulled out a packet of wet wipes she carried in her purse and wiped off Jimmy's face. Then Marcus held out his chubby hands and stared at her intently. "You want clean hands?"

Marcus nodded and then giggled as she took his little hands in hers and wiped away the melted ice cream, first off his little fingers and then his adorable cheeks.

"Thanks," Jimmy said. "You really saved the day there."

"You're welcome. What're you doing downtown so late?"

"Well, I took Marcus to the park and then we had some ice cream, obviously, and then we were going to get some groceries for Năinai."

"I was heading to the grocery store, too," Candice said.

"Mind if we join you?" Jimmy asked.

Say no. Say no.

"Sure."

Jimmy fell into step beside her. Marcus was clearly tired, with his head still on his father's shoulder and his thumb in his mouth.

"He really is adorable," Candice said. She couldn't help but stare at Marcus. He was so cute. She never knew if her lost baby had been a boy or a girl, but she often thought it would have been a boy. "He's almost two?"

Jimmy nodded. "Yep. Almost two—right, buddy?"

Marcus nodded his head.

"Looks like the trip to the park wore him out. Although, that chocolate ice cream might wake him back up again later."

Jimmy chuckled softly and shifted Marcus to his other arm. "He played pretty hard. Where we lived in Toronto wasn't the greatest, so it wasn't always safe to play in the park. I made the right decision coming back home."

"I'm sure your mother was thrilled." Candice knew that though Jimmy and his parents had had their issues, Mr. and Mrs. Liu had missed him. He was their only child.

"My mother is over-the-moon happy. She came to Toronto for a while when I found out I had a son and was given custody. I had no idea what to do with an infant, but my mom helped. That's when the nagging to come back to Jasper started. I had to get some stuff together before I could come back home, though."

"I bet your mom begged you to move into her place."

Jimmy laughed. "She did, but I rented a place down the street from your parents' old place, actually. It's a small modular home, but it's good for Marcus and me."

Her heart skipped a beat. "You... So you're my neighbor?"

"You're still at your parents' place?"

"It's my place now, since Dad died."

His expression softened. "Right. Sorry."

"No, it's fine." They walked into the grocery store.

Candice got Jimmy a cart and Marcus whined a bit as Jimmy sat him down in it, but soon was happy when Jimmy began to push the cart around the store.

Jimmy pulled out his list. "Thankfully her list is small and once I get that car seat installed she can make trips into Hinton with Marcus."

"Yeah, it's cheaper to drive out there to the co-op rather than hit the small grocery store, especially with all the tourists."

"Where the heck would nutmeg be?" Jimmy asked, staring at the list and scratching his head. "And what the heck is nutmeg?"

Candice shook her head. "Come on. We'll share the cart and I'll help you."

"Yeah, but that still doesn't answer the question of what a nutmeg is."

"It's not a thing, it's a spice," Candice teased. "Come on. Seriously, how did you survive on your own in Toronto?"

"Takeout," he muttered, picking up a bunch of bananas.

Candice snickered and Marcus smiled up at her. She couldn't help but smile back down at him. Not only was he cute, but he also had the biggest, brightest smile. He had that charm that his father had.

And Candice felt her heart melt when she looked down at the chubby little toddler.

It made her long for their lost baby. A lump formed in her throat and she tried not to think about it. Although it was hard. Marcus reminded her of the thing she longed for the most.

Family.

"So, Stu came back from Edmonton and Reggie is stable," she said, trying to distract herself from being around Jimmy and Marcus.

"That's great to hear," Jimmy said. "Did he have AMS?"

Candice nodded, then picked up a canister of nutmeg and handed it to Jimmy, who examined the bottle, wrinkling his nose as he put it in his cart.

"What do you use this for?" he asked. "It smells strong."

"Baking."

"Bleh." Jimmy shook his head and they continued their meander down the aisle. "What about HAPE or HACE?"

"Pulmonary edema."

"Huh, but he was athletic."

"Ah, it appeared so, but Reggie had lost a lot of weight too fast. Like, over a hundred pounds in less than a year and he hadn't been working too long on improving his cardiovascular health before he went gung ho up the trails."

"Ah, that makes a lot of sense. You've got to acclimatize slowly if you're not in the best of health. People think losing weight fast automatically makes them healthy, but it doesn't. You have to build muscle, too."

"He should be okay."

"Glad to hear it. I guess that explains why he went a bit crazy and decided to repel down Maligne Canyon," Jimmy said.

"You can't always blame AMS on that," she said offhandedly, adding her stuff to their shared cart. "Even people not suffering AMS do that."

"Yeah, but then it's just stupidity."

She snorted. "Welcome to Mountain Rescue."

Jimmy smiled at her and there was that twinkle in his eye. The one that made her weak in the knees. It was so easy to talk to him.

It was easy to be around him in general.

You can be friends with him. You were once before.

"I'm glad to be a part of Mountain Rescue. I'm glad I was able to do what the armed forces trained me to do and that I can do it back in my old hometown."

She couldn't help but think of that night down by the river, when he said that he had to get out of Jasper. That there was nothing for him in this town.

Now he was thankful to be back.

"Maybe you've finally seen the error of your ways then?" she asked.

"What do you mean?" he asked.

"You told me once that there was nothing here."

He looked confused. "Did I?"

"You did."

"When?"

"Right before you and Logan left for basic training. The night we…" She trailed off, not wanting to say it.

"Right," he said, clearing this throat and looking away. "I've realized I was a complete idiot back then."

"That you were," Candice muttered as she walked away from him, into the next aisle.

They finished up their grocery shopping and Candice walked with Jimmy to the downtown parking lot, helping load his groceries in his trunk while he buckled Marcus into his car seat. The little boy had drifted off to sleep on the walk.

"Do you want a ride home? I mean, we are practically neighbors."

"Thanks," she said. "I'm okay."

"It's getting pretty dark," he said. "It's no trouble. Marcus sleeps well in the car. Let me drive you home."

She worried her bottom lip. She should really just say no, but she did buy ice cream and the longer she stood here, it became less ice and more cream.

"Sure. Thanks." She climbed into the passenger seat.

Jimmy go into the vehicle and slowly pulled out of the parking lot. "Now, to remember how to get out of this downtown area."

"Turn right at the end of the street and follow it up to the edge of town."

It was only a five-minute drive from the bustling downtown to the western-most edge of Jasper and her parents' little log-and-stone home that backed into the forest and the vast wilderness of Jasper National Park.

Jimmy pulled into the driveway, behind her SUV.

"Thanks for the ride."

He nodded. "Anytime. I'll see you at work tomorrow."

She nodded. "Yes. We have some training to do up the mountain."

"I look forward to it."

"I wouldn't," she teased.

Candice got out of the car and quickly made her way up the driveway. She didn't look back. She didn't want to look back.

They could be friends, but nothing more. Even if he *was* stirring up all these old feelings inside her. She wasn't willing to put her heart at risk again.

She'd find the courage to tell him about the loss of their baby and then she would keep her distance from him.

Jimmy sat in Candice's driveway for a few minutes, making sure that she got in okay. It was a bit surreal to be back in front of the old Warner place. He'd spent many happy times here with Logan, with Candice.

The little log home made of wood and stone was something he thought about often. He thought about all the times he and Logan would hike through the small woodlot behind the house, down to the little spring.

How you could see Whistlers Peak and the tiny station at the top, where the tourists could ride a gondola up to see Jasper from on high.

How many times had they sat on the porch at night in the summer or played basketball at the end of the long drive?

It was kind of hard to believe that the Warners were gone.

And that Candice was alone.

He should've never left—he'd been a fool.

He should've stayed in Jasper. He could've become a paramedic and stayed with Candice.

You would've held her back.

And if he had stayed, he wouldn't have had those last moments with Logan.

He wouldn't have Marcus.

He glanced in the rearview mirror to watch Marcus sleeping and he couldn't help but smile at him.

The light came on in Candy's front room and he slowly pulled out of her drive and headed back to his parents' place on the other side of town to deliver his mom's groceries. They lived in a small wartime home near the hotel district. His parents had run a small motel, but had sold it off and were now retired.

His mom wanted him to move back home, but for their newfound good relationship to remain the way it was, it was better for Jimmy and Marcus to live on their own.

His mother met him at the car.

"You're late," she said.

"Sorry. I ran in to Candy Warner and she was walking home with her groceries, so I offered her a ride."

His mother gave him a quick smile, but then it disappeared. "Oh. That was nice of you."

"She's also my boss. And I guess she's not actually Candy Warner now. She's Candice Lavoie."

"Yes, but she's divorced," his mother remarked, opening the back door of the car and slowly taking out a bag of groceries, so as to not wake up Marcus.

Jimmy cocked an eyebrow. "That doesn't change the fact she's my boss."

"I know, but you're the one who mentioned her name change."

"Mom, did you know that Candice was going to be my boss?" he asked.

Her eyes widened and she blinked a couple of times. "Of course."

"Why didn't you tell me? You could've warned me."

"What was there to tell? You were friends with her and Logan. I didn't think it would matter." Her mother narrowed her eyes. "Does it matter?"

Yeah.

Only he couldn't say that out loud. His mom didn't know what had happened between him and Candice ten years ago. And though she didn't need to know, it did matter that Candice was his boss.

If he'd known she was going to be his boss...he would've gone in more prepared. He still would've taken the job, but he would've been prepared. He hadn't been prepared to see her.

He had to learn to deal with seeing her. Just like he had to deal with helicopters being used for mountain rescues.

He had to deal with it all, because nothing was going to change.

Candice was off-limits and helicopters were part of his job.

Great. Now you're comparing Candice to helicopters. You need to get a grip.

"Nope."

"Good. Did you get everything on the list?" his mother asked as she walked up the drive and he followed behind carrying the rest of her bags.

"Yes."

"And why is my grandson so sticky?" she asked.

"Ice cream."

His mother made a face and disappeared inside.

Jimmy sighed and dropped the rest of the bags just inside the door. He glanced up at the half moon in the dark sky. It was twilight and soon it would be dark enough to see the stars.

The thought of seeing stars made him think of Candice and that night by the river, and of Candice all alone now, just down the street from him.

But there was nothing he could do about it.

With his son, with his traumatic past, he would hold her back. Just like Logan always said he would.

She was free.

He was not.

CHAPTER FIVE

JIMMY WAS SITTING on the grass with the rest of the Mountain Rescue crew, having just hiked up the Overlander trail. They were supposed to wait for Candice to show up, but Jimmy was confused as to how she was to get there, because was no way to access the meadow with a vehicle.

He had a horrible feeling that she was probably coming by helicopter, so he was bracing himself for that. He had to control his panic, so he wouldn't lose trust with his teammates.

"Is she always this late?" Jimmy asked Stu.

"Sometimes. Depends if she can get her flight plan approved or whether there's cloud cover by the airport."

"Her flight plan?" Jimmy asked, his heart skipping a beat as he sat upright. "She flies?"

Stu nodded. "Yep. Not always, but she does. I think Nigel is flying the helicopter today, though. He's relatively new, as well, but he's been around for four months."

Jimmy couldn't believe what he was hearing.

Candice was a helicopter pilot.

A ball of dread formed in the pit of his stomach. The idea of Candice in a helicopter was a bit too much to bear. The thought of her getting hurt made his stomach churn and twist.

"Here comes Nigel now. I bet Lavoie is with him," Stu said offhandedly as he got up off the ground.

Jimmy was frozen.

He closed his eyes and tried to remember all the tricks that Kristen had taught him to deal with the panic that was currently rising in him.

He told himself that he was standing in a meadow off the Overlander trail—a trail that he hiked all the time with Logan when they were kids.

That he wasn't back overseas...

"Get under cover!" Logan had shouted over the gunfire.

Jimmy made his way to the helicopter, but before the helicopter had a chance to land, it exploded in a fireball and he was thrown back.

More explosions thundered through the air and he covered his head.

But not before he'd seen the crumbling wall coming toward him and Logan...

Jimmy shook the nightmare away as the propellers died down. Candice climbed out of the helicopter and he shook the remnants of the memory from his mind. He had a job to do and Candice was his boss. He had to prove to her he had what it took to do this work.

Candice was handing Stu gear from the helicopter.

He was on edge—the anxiety wasn't abating—but he swallowed his fear and made his way to the helicopter.

"Look alive," Candice said, tossing him a bag.

He caught it and walked away from the helicopter, then put down the bag where Stu was setting up equipment with Kate.

He needed to shake this anxiety.

He needed to focus on his work, but he was struggling.

"You okay, Jimmy?" Candice asked, coming up beside him.

"Fine," he said sternly.

She cocked her head to the side and he knew just from her expression she didn't believe him, but he didn't care. It wasn't really any of her business. Just like it wasn't his business if she wanted to be a fool and fly a helicopter around.

Keep it together.

"I brought you guys up here to go over a rescue in backcountry. Specifically, we're going to look at what was packed and how we would perform basic first aid when we have to hike in and carry out a patient."

"Couldn't you just fly in with the helicopter?" Jimmy asked, annoyed.

Candice's eyes narrowed. "This is in situations where you can't fly in."

"Then why did you fly here? Why didn't you hike in with us?" Jimmy snapped.

Stu, Kate and Nigel all looked at him in shock.

Candice crossed her arms and took a step toward him. "I would like to speak to you. Privately."

"Whatever you have to say can be said in front of everyone. I don't care."

What're you doing? Get a hold of yourself.

"No. I don't think so." Candice turned. "Nigel, can you start?"

Nigel nodded and motioned for Stu and Kate to follow him.

Jimmy sighed, annoyed with himself.

"What is wrong with you?" she asked tightly.

"Nothing."

"Nothing?" she echoed.

Jimmy scrubbed a hand over his face. "I know."

"You know?"

"I'm sorry. That was uncalled for."

"I won't tolerate anyone undermining me in front of the team. I am head of Mountain Rescue and I got here through hard work and firsthand experience. You may have experience in the armed forces, but this is *my* team. This is *my* mountain. Got it?"

"Yes. Got it. It won't happen again."

"See that it doesn't." She held his gaze for a bit longer. "Now, I would like to utilize your experience working in field hospitals by having you prepare a simple surgical kit for the field like we talked about yesterday. Do you think you can handle that?"

Jimmy nodded. "I can. Thanks, boss."

"Good," she said softly before walking away.

Jimmy ran his hand through his hair.

You're a boob, Jimmy Liu.

He wanted to tell her what was bothering him. He wanted to tell her about the PTSD, but then it would bring about talk of Logan and his death. He wanted to explain everything going on inside him, but he couldn't find the words.

He didn't want Candice to think less of him.

He didn't want Candice to see him as weak. It mattered to him what she thought of him, because he was a member of her team and he didn't want to be kept from work because of a stupid helicopter and the way it triggered him.

He wanted to have control of this. He would get control of this.

He couldn't be in the armed forces, but he could be doing what he loved again—saving lives in the place he never should've left.

* * *

Candice didn't know what had come over Jimmy.

He'd seemed fine last night when he dropped her off at her place after grocery shopping. Even though she had promised herself that she should avoid him, she had enjoyed the simple shopping excursion with him and his son.

Really enjoyed it. Which scared her.

She wasn't supposed to be enjoying herself with Jimmy.

He'd been back what, a day, and she was already falling into those old patterns. Old patterns she knew led to heartache and disappointment. Jimmy had left her. He'd told her he wanted more and then ended it. She had to remind herself of that. Jimmy was not the kind to settle down. He'd made that clear when he'd admitted that Marcus's mother was a one-night stand.

Still, she was concerned about his behavior. Something about the helicopter had triggered him.

Candice wasn't a fool. She knew it was most likely post-traumatic stress, which was concerning.

They used helicopters for a lot of rescues and she couldn't keep him aside every time they needed to do so. She wanted him on her team, in the thick of things. He was a competent and knowledgeable paramedic and she didn't want to waste his knowledge or his talent.

In fact, she was a bit jealous of his knowledge, if she was honest.

Why don't you go back to school?

She shook away the lingering thought. There was no way she could leave.

Jasper was her home and Mountain Rescue was her life.

As they were going through their equipment, she

heard the distant sound of an engine. She turned to look and saw one of the Parks Canada vehicles coming toward them. The ATV pulled up and stopped.

"Lavoie, glad you're out here," Ranger Matt said as he parked his all-terrain vehicle.

"We're on a training session. What's up?" Candice asked.

Matt's lips pursed together under his bushy, graying moustache. "There's a been a bear attack."

The rest of the team went quiet.

"I see," she said. Her stomach twisted in a knot. Bear attacks were never pretty. This would be grim.

"Do you need us? I have a paramedic with me."

"Yeah. We could use you both. Do you have your rifle with you?" Matt asked.

A shudder of fear ran down her spine. "I do."

"The bear is still on the loose. I'll help your team load up the helicopter. The trail has been shut down. You and your paramedic can come with me. We'll have to carry him out so we need to be careful."

Candice nodded and turned to her team. "Okay, let's get off the trail. I'll need a surgical kit. Jimmy, I want you to come with me—this will be a good learning experience—and, Nigel, I'll need my gun."

She tried not to pay attention to the worried expression on Jimmy's face as she grabbed her rifle and the gear she thought she might need.

She'd been a park ranger before she took her mountain-rescue training and she knew what to do when a wild animal went rogue, not that she relished it very much. She had no doubt the bear had attacked because it had had too many interactions with well meaning, but stupid, tourists, and had lost its fear of humans as a result.

She loaded her stuff in the back of the ATV and Jimmy joined her.

"I didn't know you knew how to use a rifle like that," he whispered stiffly. It was a Winchester Ranger. It was powerful enough to take down a bear at close range.

"Before I got into rescue I was a park ranger. I've had to put down a grizzly or two," she responded tightly. It was one of the worst parts of her job.

"That sounds awful."

"People don't know how to behave in bear country and they don't know how to give the animals space." She sighed. "I hope you're prepared for this. We're going to have to do as much damage control as we can and then carry the victim out. The helicopter can't land where the mauling took place."

"I've seen scary crap at the front lines. I'll be okay."

Candice didn't even want to begin to think about what Jimmy had seen overseas. She knew he'd been with Logan when he died. There were times she thought she wanted to know what had happened to her brother, but then there were times she realized it was better she didn't.

She remembered how her mother had fallen apart after losing Logan.

Candice had had to be strong for her dad through all of it. And for herself, when Chad had left. As a result, she'd never had the chance to really process Logan's death. Never had the chance to grieve, and now was not the time, either.

Candice had to remain strong and in control.

Like she had for the past ten years.

Ranger Matt came back. "We better go. Your team is ready to leave."

Candice nodded and she climbed in beside Matt

while Jimmy got in the back with the equipment. Ranger Matt headed back down the trail the way he came, and though Jimmy winced as the helicopter started up, he visibly relaxed as they distanced themselves from the rotating blades.

The ride in the ATV was rough.

The farther they got down the trail, the thicker the brush got and she realized that the attack must have taken place close to the road. At least they'd be able to get an ambulance in to take the victim to the hospital.

She also realized that this attack had probably happened not long after her team had passed through here. She glanced back at Jimmy and could see that he was thinking the same thing, the closer they got. His lips were pursed and he looked serious.

Ranger Matt slowed down.

"The victim had been camping in an unauthorized spot and didn't check in with us to let us know he was planning to camp here. I suspect there wasn't proper food storage, but I'm not sure."

"So you don't know what provoked the attack?" Jimmy asked.

"We've been watching this bear as a matter of interest for some time—it's a problem bear—but there hadn't been an attack until now. Thankfully, he was scared off by a crowd of people—the ones who found the victim— and took off. Still, be on your guard. When a bear finds a food source, they come back. And this bear isn't one that's likely to give up free food."

A shiver ran down Candice's spine at the thought of the victim as food. It was her number-one fear living in the mountains.

Once they stopped, they all climbed out and Candice

loaded her gear on her back and grabbed her rifle, following Ranger Matt's lead, with Jimmy between them.

As they drew closer, she saw the group of hikers that had found the victim. They looked startled and upset, but uninjured, as the rangers took their statements.

"This way," Matt said grimly. "The patient was stable when I left to come find you, but it's bleak."

Candice swallowed the lump that had formed in her throat. They ducked under a low branch and she tried not to react to the scene of a destroyed campsite and the state of the attack victim's legs.

"Whoa," Jimmy said under his breath.

"This is bad," she whispered.

"I've seen worse," Jimmy said tightly.

They exchanged glances. Jimmy's brow was still furrowed, his lips a firm line, his jaw locked. Her stomach was doing flip-flops.

"I'm sure you have," she said, quietly.

"We can do this." Jimmy nodded. "Together."

She liked that firmness. That certainty. It grounded her.

"Yep."

She was glad Jimmy was back to his normal self. It gave her confidence that this would go well. They put on their gloves and made their way swiftly toward the patient. The man was only semiconscious, which was probably for the best. The rangers had managed to tie a tourniquet, which was stopping the man from bleeding to death.

"What's his name?" Jimmy asked over his shoulder.

"Ryan," a ranger said. Candice didn't see who the other ranger was, and she didn't care as she started pulling out her gear. She was trying not to let her thoughts overtake her at the sight of the man's mangled legs. She wasn't even sure that they could be saved.

The victim also had lacerations on his face and head from where the bear had grabbed him.

"You've seen worse?" Candice asked Jimmy nervously.

He nodded. "I have. We can only do our best to stabilize him and get him safely to the ambulance. The main thing right now is to stop him from bleeding out. The tourniquet was well done, but it won't hold for long."

"So what're you suggesting?" Candice asked. "We can't exactly sew his legs back on here."

"No, but I'm going to use hemostat. It'll stop him from bleeding out and then we can splint the legs and get him transported. First, I'm going to set up a central line."

Candice's eyes widened. "Here?"

He nodded. "Here."

"Just tell me what to do." She was eager to learn. She had always wanted to become a surgeon—that had been the plan before she'd had to leave school and return home.

All she could do was listen as he directed her. They inserted the central line, then Jimmy attached a bag of saline and Candice gave the victim oxygen, while Jimmy went to work making sure that the patient wouldn't bleed out on the mountain and that they would be able to move him.

Once Jimmy was sure everything was holding, they carefully stabilized the legs and then moved Ryan to the backboard.

"He's stable. We can transport him now," Jimmy called out.

Several of the rangers came and helped. They lifted

up Ryan and carried him down the trail to the road, where the ambulance was waiting to take him to the hospital.

"You go," Candice said once they'd loaded him, taking a step back.

Jimmy nodded. "What about you?"

"I have to go with the rangers to look for the bear."

A brief moment of panic crossed Jimmy's face, but it disappeared. "You're going to go hunt a bear?"

"I'm a trained ranger. I know these woods. You take care of Ryan." She smiled at him with reassurance. "I'll be fine. You did a good job, Liu."

Jimmy nodded, but he didn't look convinced that she would be fine and that annoyed her. She couldn't help but wonder if he still saw her as Logan's little sister.

That girl that used to be vulnerable.

That shy girl.

She wasn't that girl anymore.

Aren't you, though?

Tears stung her eyes, but she held back her emotions. She shut the ambulance door, banging on it to signal to the driver it was safe to go, and then watched it race away.

She was envious that Jimmy had medical knowledge she didn't have. Logan had once said that Jimmy would hold her back, but Jimmy had the skills she wanted. The family she wanted.

She was still that same person she'd always been.

Scared and lost.

CHAPTER SIX

WHAT'RE YOU DOING HERE?

Jimmy wasn't sure.

He'd arrived back at the station, after helping ensure Ryan was stabilized and in the hands of the doctors at the hospital, to find out that Candice hadn't returned from hunting that bear. It freaked him right out.

It was surreal seeing her with that rifle and knowing that she was putting herself in danger up on that mountain. He was worried about her.

When his shift was over, he went back to his parents' place to make sure that Marcus was okay and to spend some time with him, but he was on call for the night and Marcus was staying with his grandparents, so once he made sure Marcus was settled he went for a drive, taking his phone with him.

And the drive ended up at Candice's place.

Now, he was sitting on her porch, waiting for her. At least the neighbors remembered who he was and no one was worried about a stranger sitting on Candice's porch, waiting in the twilight for her to return home.

Headlights turned the corner of the street and he sat up straighter. It was Candice's SUV. He stood up so that she could see him and wouldn't be frightened to find him there.

His heart was hammering. He was nervous and anxious and…he didn't know what else. Only when she parked her car and got out, looking no worse for wear, was he able to calm his anxiety and take a deep breath of relief.

She came up the drive and stopped, looking confused. "Jimmy?"

"Hey!" He waved.

"What're you doing here?"

"I wanted to make sure you were okay. You didn't come back to the station before my shift was over."

"Well, technically your shift is not over since you're on call tonight," she teased.

"I know, but still. You were tracking a bear. A bear! Did you end up finding it?"

"We tracked it, but didn't encounter it. We're hoping it went farther into the interior, but we'll have to put up warnings for the tourists and keep a lookout on the backcountry trails."

She sounded tired.

"I'm glad to see you're okay. That bear did a number on Ryan."

"How is the patient?" Candice asked, coming to sit beside him on the step.

"He'll live. I don't know about his legs, but the surgeons were very hopeful and they were impressed that I used my clamps so well. I explained to them where I learned it."

"I was impressed, too," she said softly. "And, truth be told, a bit envious."

"Envious?" he asked, confused.

"Yeah, you learned all these skills when you served. Skills I wanted to learn, but never got the chance."

"Why not?"

She cocked her head to one side. "You know why. I had my dad to take care of. There was never time."

"I can show you."

"You can?" she asked, perking up.

"Of course. If you want."

"I'd like that very much," she said.

An awkward silence fell between them as they sat there on her step, the sky fading from the purple hues of twilight to darkness.

"You hungry?" he asked.

"I am. I was going to go inside and make dinner."

"How about we go to the diner instead? I saw that it was still there. I can't drink because I'm on call...but we could least have a hamburger or fries or something."

Great. You're starting to ramble.

"Sure. That sounds great."

"I'll drive, because I'm on call."

"I'm aware," she said dryly. "I'm the one who made the schedule."

He chuckled. "Oh, right. So it's you I have to thank for that. I forgot."

Candice laughed. The way she used to when they were together. When they were younger. When they didn't have a care in the world. It made him feel happy. It made him feel like a weight had been lifted off his shoulders. It made him feel free.

He missed that.

Jimmy opened the passenger door for her then climbed into the driver's seat. It wasn't a long drive to the small diner that sat at the edge of town, away from the tourist center and all the chain restaurants, and there were only a couple of cars in the parking lot.

Jimmy hadn't been sure it would still be here, so was glad when he'd come home to find it was still standing.

He parked the car and they made their way inside.

"Candice, good to see you!" The waitress, Kelsey, said with a smile from behind the counter and then her eyes widened as her gaze landed on him. "My goodness! Is that Jimmy Liu?"

"Good to see you, Kelsey. It's been a while."

Kelsey grinned. "It has. I remember you all coming in here when you were kids!"

Jimmy chuckled. He'd missed that familiarity you only got in a small town.

"Sit anywhere you'd like," Kelsey said, before ducking into the kitchen.

He followed Candice to a booth in the corner.

Nothing had changed.

Still the same padded seats in the same blue and red vinyl. Same faux marble tabletops. It even smelled the same, like bacon grease and coffee. They looked out over the highway, the row of trees on the far side occasionally interrupted by a car or a truck passing through.

It was night and the campgrounds were closing down for the evening. The trails were already closed and the tourists were back in their lodgings or in town.

Jimmy was hoping for a quiet night, but usually when he'd hoped for a quiet night while serving overseas, he'd got the exact opposite.

"Marcus is with your mom?" Candice asked.

"He is. So he's safe, but I'm hoping that I don't get a call tonight. I could use the sleep." He crossed his fingers, holding them up for her to see.

"Let's hope not. It's only your first week here and it's been an eventful one, that's for sure. Of course, it's always kind of busy when we have a lot of tourists in town. In winter, ski patrol picks up a lot of the slack, though there are times we have avalanches and some other issues, but summer seems to have a lot more accidents and definitely more encounters with wildlife."

Jimmy shuddered. "I don't remember a bear attack like that when we were kids."

She smiled. "Well, we weren't working and not every attack is reported. Besides, when we were kids we didn't really care what was going on around us."

"My mother would've made me aware of a rogue bear," he said dryly. "She may have been working all the time, but she was overprotective. Still is, just not with me now."

Candice laughed softly. "My grandmother always said that grandkids were her pride and joy. My mother always felt a bit snubbed."

"That could be it," Jimmy said.

"The trouble is that tourists are getting a bit bolder with photos and selfies. It's a shame, really." There was a sadness in her voice. "Every year, it just seems to get busier, and I sometimes long for the peace and quiet. If I didn't love Jasper so much, I'd probably go farther north."

Jimmy cocked his head to one side. "Would you?"

"I've thought about it, but no, this is my home. I'm happy here and I don't want to leave."

He wanted to ask her why she wanted to stay. She always had big plans. Her parents were gone, so what was she staying here for?

She had said how much she wished she could learn more and that she still wanted to be a doctor. So what was keeping her in Jasper?

"Can I get you two something to drink?" Kelsey asked, interrupting his thoughts.

"I'll have a coffee," Jimmy said and Kelsey looked at him like he was crazy. "I'm on call tonight."

She nodded and turned to Candice. "What would you like, Candy?"

"The same. I'm also on call."

Kelsey nodded. "I'll be back with your coffee in a minute."

"I didn't know you were on call, too," Jimmy said.

"You're still fairly new and you're still on probation. When you're on call, so am I." She smiled at him. "So how does it feel to be back home?"

"Strange," Jimmy said. "I never thought I'd come back here, but this is the best place for Marcus."

"How about you?" she asked softly.

"What do you mean?"

"Is this the best place for you?"

Jimmy nodded. "Yes. It is. I was a fool to leave."

He *was* a fool to leave, but both he and Logan had been so convinced that they could take on the world. They thought that they'd come back to Jasper as heroes.

Instead, Jimmy had returned defeated and Logan came back in a box.

His heart sank as he thought of that and he fought back the emotions running around inside him. He could hear the explosions, the gunfire, the screams in his mind.

Get a hold of it.

"You okay?" Candice asked.

"Of course," Jimmy said quickly, shaking the vision of Logan out of his mind. "Why wouldn't I be?"

"You just seemed to go somewhere else."

"I'm fine."

Liar.

"Here's your coffees. You ready to order?" Kelsey asked, interrupting them again.

"Banquet burger and fries," Jimmy said. He didn't

even need to look at the menu to know that he wanted that large, greasy burger that had all the fixings. Just like he and Logan had always eaten, while Candice would have just a small cheeseburger and look at them in disgust as they shoved their fries in between the patty and the bun.

"I'll have the chicken burger, please, with a salad," Candice said.

"I'll get on this right away," Kelsey said as she turned to leave.

"Chicken burger and a salad?" Jimmy asked.

"What? I'm not feeling very hungry and don't want something heavy like your disgusting, greasy banquet burger." She shook her head. "You're getting older, Jimmy Liu—you might not be able to pack away the burger the same way."

"You mean by ramming the fries into it?" he teased.

"Yeah, exactly. You and Logan were so disgusting."

Jimmy laughed. "You chose to hung out with us."

"There was no one else to hang around with. I liked hanging out with my big brother and…" She trailed off and pink tinged her cheeks.

"And me?" Jimmy asked, grinning.

"Sometimes," she said quietly, and there was the hint of something more in her dark brown eyes. Was it a flash of pain? He couldn't be sure…

"Thanks."

She chuckled, shaking off whatever heavy thoughts had rattled her. "It's the truth."

"Well, I'll try not to be too disgusting."

"Good. I appreciate it."

"I can't believe it's still here," he said wistfully. "I remember when we moved to Jasper. I was like…six, and we came here from Toronto. I was so exhausted and it was dark. This place was the only place open and I think Kelsey was working here then, too."

Candice smiled warmly at him. "She probably was. And, of course, this place is still here. This is an institution. Everyone comes here for Sunday lunch."

"Everyone except my parents. They were always working at the motel."

"I believe you came here a few times with us."

Jimmy smiled. "Your parents were always kind to me. My parents had a business to run so I was grateful that yours included me so much. They didn't have to."

There were unshed tears glistening in her eyes. "Yes. They liked you quite a bit."

Jimmy missed them, just like he missed Logan, and he felt so bad that he hadn't been there for any of them when they needed him.

"If I had of known..." He trailed off and shook his head. "About your dad."

"They understood. You were injured, too. Your parents were there. They came to every single funeral. Logan's, my mom's and my dad's. At least my parents are with Logan again."

"I have one banquet burger and fries and a chicken burger with a side salad," Kelsey said, cheerfully putting their plates down before them.

"This looks great, Kelsey. Exactly like I remember." Jimmy lifted the bun to add condiments.

Kelsey smiled. "You're welcome. Glad you're back, Jimmy."

She left them and Jimmy grabbed the ketchup.

"I'm so glad you're not jamming fries in there," Candice teased.

He cocked an eyebrow. "Who said I wasn't?"

In actual fact, he hadn't planned on doing that, but

now that Candice reminded him that he used to do it, he grabbed a handful of fries and started layering them on the top of his hamburger patty.

Candice was grimacing.

"Mmm…" he said, teasing her as he smooshed down the hamburger bun, squishing the fries and causing the ketchup and mustard to ooze out the side. He took a bite. "Yum."

She wrinkled her nose. "You're gross."

He winked and she laughed.

It felt good.

It felt right.

They finished their dinner and paid the bill before heading outside, into the dark. It was a peaceful night. There were stars in the sky, just like that night when they sat down by the river. She hoped it stayed this way. She was exhausted and could use a quiet night.

She hadn't planned for Jimmy's first night on call to follow a day of her hiking over the trails as they tracked a bear.

Even though they'd ridden in the all-terrain vehicle, there were some places the ATV couldn't get to and her legs were aching. And the bumpy trail had been hard on her posterior.

All she wanted was a hot shower and to go to sleep.

She hadn't been expecting to find Jimmy waiting for her on her porch, but she was glad he was.

It was confusing being around Jimmy. One minute they were laughing together, like no time had passed— almost like they could go back to the way things once were—and the next she was remembering the feeling of her heart being shattered when he walked away.

"I need to get home and change before I go back to the station," she said.

"I'll drive you home."

Say no. Say no.

Only, she couldn't. It made sense.

"Okay."

"I don't want to hang out at my parents' place. Marcus is not the best sleeper and it would be better for him to get used to the feeling of waking up at his grandma and grandpa's, because he'll need to stay with them when I'm on call."

"So where are you going to go?"

He shrugged. "My place or the station. Hadn't really thought which."

"Why don't you keep me company at the station for a while?"

She couldn't believe she was saying it, but she was lonely, too, and they were having a good time.

"Sure," he said. "If you don't mind."

"I don't. That way if we get a call, we can ride out together."

"Sounds like a plan."

They climbed into Jimmy's car and he drove them back to her place. When he parked in front of her house, she suddenly felt nervous and she didn't know why.

He'd been in the house before.

Nothing had really changed. She'd updated the decor a bit and added her own touches, but the furniture was the same.

It was still, in essence, her parents' place.

It was an easy way to keep them close and she really didn't have time to think about decorating, anyway. This was her home. This was where she felt safe—cozy and at peace.

"Come on in," Candice said, unlocking the door.

"Wow," Jimmy said in awe. "Nothing has changed that much."

"Why would it?"

"I don't know. I guess I thought you would put your spin on it or…"

"I don't have time for decorating. My dad's only been gone a year and it didn't feel right. This is home."

He smiled and nodded. "I'm glad you didn't change it, if I'm honest."

"Good."

Jimmy kicked off his shoes and jammed his hands in the front pockets of his jeans. He wandered into the front room, staring at the wood paneling that her father had painstakingly cut, stained and put up when her parents bought this house before she was born.

"Still the same," he said with satisfaction as he glanced out the bay window onto the dark street.

"Make yourself at home. I'll be back soon." She dashed up the steps to her bedroom. The only change she had made was taking over the main bedroom. Her father's cancer had prevented him from going up the stairs in the last few years of his life, so the dining room had been converted into his room.

She quickly changed and freshened up, grabbing her phone before she headed downstairs.

Jimmy wasn't in the living room. He had wandered to the back of the house, to the small den, where he and Logan had hung out a lot playing video games. The den had a sliding glass door that opened into a sunroom, and the sunroom had a door that led out onto a deck and into the backyard.

He was standing in the sunroom, in the dark, staring out at the forest. She could sense his sadness and she assumed he'd noticed the pictures of Logan. After Logan had died, her parents had turned the den into a bit of a shrine to him.

"You okay?" she asked quietly.

"Yeah," he said, barely glancing over his shoulder. "I wasn't... I wasn't expecting to see Logan's stuff."

"My parents wanted to display some of his things." She wandered into the room and gingerly touched Logan's picture, trying not to cry as she looked at his happy, smiling face.

Jimmy chuckled nervously under his breath. "I don't know why I didn't expect it. This is... This was Logan's home."

"You miss him?" she asked.

He nodded. "I do. He was my best friend."

"I know. I miss him, too."

Jimmy ran his hand through his hair and turned around. "I know. I wanted to be there..."

"We know you were injured and in hospital in Germany, Jimmy. We understood why you couldn't be here." What she didn't say was: *why didn't you come back after you recovered? Why did you stay away for so long?* But she couldn't make herself ask. "Want another coffee?"

He smiled and stepped out of the shadows. "That would be great."

She turned to head back to the kitchen and Jimmy followed her. She flicked on the light and he took a seat at the kitchen table, in the same spot he always sat in when he'd come over for Sunday dinners, and for one brief second she thought she saw Logan sitting there beside him... Her parents, too. And for an instant, she was happy again.

It felt like it did all those years ago.

It's not the same.

Just because Jimmy was back in her life didn't mean that all that pain disappeared. A lot of water had passed under the bridge between the two of them and she had to remember that.

She shook her head and turned her back to Jimmy. "How do you like your coffee these days?"

"Black."

"Coming up."

"Your dad used to make this coffee that would cause our hair to stand on end. He'd make it when he and my dad would go out fishing and they'd take us. You know, the couple of times my dad would actually go. Grudgingly, but still. I almost wonder if your dad sort of forced him to come." Jimmy laughed. "My dad has hinted that your dad could persuade anyone to do anything."

Candice laughed. "Yes. He was a smooth talker."

"I loved those weekends," he said, reminiscing.

"I never got to go on those fishing trips," she said dryly.

"Well, it was a men's weekend."

She rolled her eyes but laughed. "Yeah, Dad liked those trips."

"So did my dad. We'd hike up to some remote lake, pitch our tents, fish...never catch anything, usually, but the coffee your dad gave us was like engine oil or something. You'd stay awake for days."

"I'm afraid my coffee is not like that." She pulled out a mug from the cupboard. "That recipe went with him to the grave."

"That's too bad, because one cup of that and being on call would be no problem...for a couple of days," he chuckled.

Candice poured him a cup and set it down in front

of him. He blew away the steam and then she poured herself a cup and sat down in the chair across from him.

"So how far did you track the bear?" he asked.

"Pretty far off the trail. We're hoping it stays there, but I doubt it will. It's a problem bear and it's been getting bolder and bolder. I think it's only a matter of time before it comes back and we'll have to put it down."

"It's a shame."

"It is a shame." She sighed, trying not to think about it. "So you said Marcus is having a birthday soon?"

Jimmy nodded. "I did. He's turning two."

"Any ideas of what kind of party you want to have?" she asked, taking a sip of her coffee.

"Theme?" he asked, confused.

"Sure. Kids birthday parties usually have a theme."

"You know, my mom was asking about this, but I didn't pay any real attention to what she was going on about."

Candice chuckled. "What was she asking?"

"Whether he liked some goofy show with a pig or another show with dogs."

"Definitely go with the dogs. I've seen the pig show, it's annoying."

Jimmy laughed. "Yeah. Dogs it is."

"Good choice."

"You know, you should come to his party. It'll just be me, my parents and him, but he took a shine to you and I'd like you there."

Her heart skipped a beat. "You want me there?"

Jimmy smiled. "I do."

She didn't know what to say to that. She was flattered. The little boy was cute and Jimmy was so tender with him. It had melted her heart to see him holding that boy so close, rubbing his back and tenderly kissing his head.

Jimmy was a good father and she was envious of his good luck.

And she wanted to go to Marcus's party...but then there was a part of her that said she shouldn't. That it would be a mistake to go, to get involved, to get too attached when her heart could be on the line. What if Jimmy met someone else? She couldn't be in their lives then. She didn't want to get hurt again.

But you want a family.

"Sure," she said, hoping he wouldn't notice the crack in her voice. "I would love to come. And if your mom needs any help or needs me to make a run into Hinton for supplies, I can do that."

"She'll hold you to that," Jimmy warned.

"I'm sure she will."

"It means a lot to me that you'd come to the party. You're important to me, Candice. One of the few people I know I can count on..." He paused and a look crossed his face that she couldn't quite read—a confusion, a hesitation, almost as though he was making up his mind about something.

Jimmy sighed. "Listen, I want to tell you about my injuries and why I couldn't be there for the funerals. Something my parents don't even know. I owe it to you to tell you the truth."

"Okay," she said calmly, her heart racing.

"It took me a year to recover from my injuries."

She was shocked. "A year?"

"I broke both my legs and had shrapnel in my hip. It took some time to heal and walk properly again. I still have pain from time to time."

"So that's why it took you so long to come home and why you were discharged."

He nodded. "I wanted you to know. You're my boss, after all."

"Is that the only reason?"

His dark gaze pierced into her, mesmerizing her, holding her. "No, but I didn't want you to find out any other way."

She worried her bottom lip.

You have to tell him.

"There's something I want you to know then."

Her heart was racing faster. She got up from the table and started pacing, trying to calm her nerves. "That week we were together ten years ago…"

"I remember," he said hesitantly.

"After you left, I found out I was pregnant."

His eyes widened. She could tell he was in shock.

"What happened?" he asked quietly, clearly trying to process it all.

A tear slipped down her cheek and she brushed it away. "I miscarried. I'm sorry. I had no way to get ahold of you and I was hurt."

And you broke me.

Only she didn't say that. She didn't want to cry.

"Only my parents knew. I never told Logan."

Jimmy got up and put his arms around her. "Hey, I'm sorry."

She looked up at him, trembling, loving the way his arms around her made her feel so secure. So safe.

He touched her face. "I'm sorry I wasn't there, Candice."

She nodded. "Me, too."

Before she knew what had come over her, she stood on her tiptoes and kissed him. And it felt so right to kiss

him again. Warmth spread through her and she melted
in his arms all over again. The kiss deepened.

You need to end this.

Only, she couldn't. She didn't want to.

Her phone buzzed. She broke off the kiss and picked
it up. There was an emergency text and her stomach
sank when she read that the bear had come back. The
message also contained the coordinates for a campground.

"We're up."

"What's wrong?" Jimmy asked, breathing deeply.

"The bear came back."

Her stomach was doing flip-flops on the drive to the
campground. They had taken her SUV because it had
everything they needed in the back.

Nigel had driven the ambulance out to meet them,
even though when they answered the call, she was assured by the rangers that the campers had suffered only
minor injuries and that the bear had been taken care of.

Still, it was Mountain Rescue's job to make sure that
everyone was okay.

Thankfully, the campground was one of the main
ones and they didn't have to hike in. But because it
was a full campground, there were several people mill-
ing about even as the RCMP tried to keep the crowd
under control.

Jimmy wasn't saying much. He had been smart and
carried his first-aid kit in the back of his car, but she
seriously doubted that they would need to do anything
major tonight.

At least, that's what Constable Bruce had said when
he'd called her.

Candice pulled up beside the ambulance as Nigel stepped out.

"Have you been waiting long?" Candice asked.

"Nah," Nigel said. "Just got here."

Nigel was trained to fly the helicopter and to drive the rig, but he wasn't a fully certified paramedic yet, which was why Jimmy was on call. She rotated between her paramedics and the rest of her team.

"They're over here," Nigel said. "Looks like a small laceration and a possible sprain. The bear did more damage to their tent."

"Still, I'll check them out and we'll probably have to take them to the hospital to get checked out if the bear caused the laceration," Jimmy said, slinging his pack over his shoulder. "They'll need antibiotics."

Nigel nodded and Candice followed them over to where a couple was sitting at a picnic table. Jimmy headed straight for the young woman because she was clearly bleeding.

"Hi, I'm Jimmy Liu and I'm the paramedic. What's your name?"

The woman smiled and Candice swore she was blushing a bit, but she wasn't surprised. Jimmy had that effect on women. "Traci."

"Traci, that's a nice name. Can you tell me what happened?" he asked as he set down his pack and pulled out his head lamp and gloves.

"Sure," she said. "We were about to go to bed when this bear charged into our campground. It went straight for the tent and we ran. As I was running I hit my head on a branch and my husband, Derek, slipped and sprained his wrist."

"So the bear didn't cause your cut?" Jimmy asked, gingerly inspecting it.

"No." Her voice shook. "It was too busy tearing up our tent."

"You didn't have food in your tent, did you?" Candice asked.

Derek shook his head. "No. We're from Edmonton— we know what to do in bear country."

Candice nodded. "You got this, Jimmy?"

Jimmy nodded. "Yep. I'm going to clean it and use some dissolvable sutures. It's superficial. Then I'll check the wrist."

Candice nodded and made her way over to Ranger Matt, who was talking to Constable Bruce.

"So you got the bear?" Candice asked.

Ranger Matt nodded. "We did. I happened to be doing my patrol of the campground before the gates were shut and locked for the night just as the bear came through. The RCMP are talking to the other campers, as they're pretty shook up."

Candice could see a tarp and a large shape under it. She was sad seeing it there, but knew it had to be done to keep people safe.

"I'm going to check on my new paramedic. Thanks for keeping me updated," Candice said.

Matt nodded and wandered off with Constable Bruce. There was a truck now waiting to remove the bear.

Candice was just glad she didn't have to fill out paperwork that Matt would have to fill out. She made her way over to Jimmy as he was wrapping a tensor bandage around Derek's wrist.

"How's it going?" Candice asked.

"Good," Jimmy said. "Their injuries are minor and don't require a hospital visit, so Derek and Traci are going to go with the RCMP, who have arranged accommodations for them in town."

Candice nodded. "Good."

"Now, if the wrist is still throbbing tomorrow or, if you notice any kind of oozing or redness, please make your way to Jasper Urgent Care, okay?" Jimmy said.

"Sure thing. Thanks, Jimmy," said Derek as he put his good arm around his wife.

Jimmy cleaned up his stuff and then disposed of his gloves in the garbage in the back of the ambulance.

"I guess we should head back to the station and make our reports?" Jimmy asked.

"Yes."

As Candice turned to head back to her SUV, she heard something go "pop" and felt pain shoot up her leg. She crumpled to the ground, seeing a few stars before she passed out.

CHAPTER SEVEN

ALL SHE COULD FEEL was pain. In her ankle, her elbow and her face, but there was something else besides the pain—the awareness that she was floating in the air. As her eyes adjusted to the blurry darkness, she realized that not only had she lost a contact, which is why everything was blurry, but she was also being held by someone.

And that someone was Jimmy.

"Jimmy?" she asked.

"You fell," he said, his voice shaking a bit.

"How? It's flat here."

"You must've rolled your ankle and, in those boots, I'm worried you broke it. Your ankle has started to swell. We need to get you to the hospital."

She groaned. The side of her face and the back of her head were both hurting.

Of all the injuries she could've sustained in her job, of course, she had to trip over her own feet and fall flat on her face in a campground.

She was humiliated.

And she was embarrassed that Jimmy was here to see it. At least she couldn't really see with one contact now missing.

Jimmy carried her into the back of the ambulance

and set her down on the gurney. She winced, but kept her one eye shut.

"What's the matter?" Jimmy asked, his voice rising an octave, but she couldn't tell if he was panicked or worried or angry. He was just a blur—a navy uniform, flesh and a dark blob of hair on top. "Why are you keeping your eye closed like that?"

"I lost a contact and it's really hard to see. I also think the contact in my other eye is scratched, because it's pretty useless to see out of. You're a blur, and I'm getting a bit of double vision going on." She tiled her head and tried to make out his facial expression. It looked like he was frowning.

"Can you take out the other contact?"

"I will, but you need to get my spare glasses—they're in the glove compartment of my SUV."

"Cool, but right now I'd like to look at that ankle."

"I'll get them, boss. You said the glove box?" Nigel asked. She hadn't even realized he was there, too.

"Yes. Thanks, Nigel," Candice said. She winced and sucked in a breath as Jimmy gently palpated her ankle through the boot.

"Yeah, it's swelling. We need to get this off." He undid the laces and gently removed the work boot, but it still hurt and she moaned a bit. "Sorry."

Next he took off her sock and even without good vision she could see the redness, the swelling of her ankle, and feel that it was hard to wiggle her toes without excruciating pain. She only hoped it wasn't broken and it was just a sprain.

"We're going to need to get this X-rayed to be safe," Jimmy said. "And your double vision is worrying me."

"What if it's just to do with the missing contact?"

she asked, even though her head was throbbing and things were spinning.

"I seriously doubt that," he said dryly.

"Here are your glasses, boss," Nigel said, coming into the ambulance and handing the big, black frames to Jimmy.

"Thanks." Candice took out her one remaining damaged contact and tossed it into a garbage bag. Jimmy handed her glasses to her, but she had a hard time putting them on. "Dammit."

"Yeah," Jimmy chuckled gently. "It's just the contact."

He took the glasses from her and helped her slide them on gently. Everything kind of came into focus, but she still had a bit of double vision and the change in her focus made her stomach do a flip-flop.

"I'm going to be sick," she moaned.

Jimmy grabbed a kidney bowl just in time.

"Oh, God," she moaned, lying back and closing her eyes. It was better to close her eyes and she just wanted to sleep. She felt woozy.

"Hey," Jimmy said and she felt a cool cloth on her forehead. "Hey, don't sleep."

"I'm not," she murmured. "I feel awful. It hurts."

"I know it does," he said gently, touching her face. "I know."

Jimmy hated seeing her like this. When she rolled her ankle and fell, he'd dashed forward, trying to catch her, but he'd been too late and she went right into the gravel. He was furious with himself that he hadn't made it to her in time and was worried she had hit her head too hard. He was anxious about what it would mean if he was right.

Her ankle was turning an awful color and he was worried she'd broken it. From what he could tell, there was a small depression in the road and she'd stepped in it the wrong way and twisted too hard. It should never have happened. He should have been beside her, should have protected her. But once again he'd let her down.

He had to put that out of his mind. Right now he had to focus on taking care of Candice. He hadn't been there for her in the past, but he could be here now.

Guilt and panic drove him as he investigated her wounds. All he wanted to do was take care of her, to make the pain disappear.

"Nigel, could you get us to the hospital?" Jimmy asked as he carefully strapped Candice onto the gurney.

"Sure thing, Jimmy." Nigel climbed out of the back of the rig and shut the doors while Jimmy finished securing everything inside.

"Where are we going?" Candice murmured.

"To the hospital," he said calmly. The last thing he wanted to do was agitate her.

"Right."

"Do you have an emergency contact I could call?" he asked.

"Nope," she said. "They're all gone."

His heart sank a bit. "You don't have anyone? Not an uncle or cousin or anything?"

"Nope. No one left," she murmured. "I have a couple of friends in my phone. Not a lot of time to make friends when you're the boss, though."

"You have me," he whispered, but she didn't respond. He didn't expect her to, but it was true. Sure, he'd been gone for a long time, but he was here now and he wasn't going to leave her.

Nigel turned on the lights, but he didn't put the siren

on. They didn't have a dire need to get to the hospital, as Candice had Jimmy looking after her.

Jimmy sat watching Candice carefully as she drifted in and out of consciousness and it was freaking him out a bit.

He leaned over the gurney and touched her gently. He smiled as he watched her.

He'd always thought she was beautiful. Before Logan had died, he'd asked Jimmy for one thing—to take care of Candice—and that was what he would do right now.

I know I said keep away from her," Logan had whispered all those years ago, when they'd been trapped, *"but you have to promise me you'll look out for her. Promise me. I know she cares for you."* He was repeating himself again.

"You can take of Candy yourself when you get home," he said frantically.

Logan shook his head and Jimmy saw the light fading from his best friend's eyes, the chaos of war going silent as he had watched his best friend slip away.

"Tell her... Tell her I love her and take care of her."

"I will, Logan. But hang on. Just hang on."

"I can't. I can't..." his friend had repeated...

"I'm here," he whispered again now, his voice catching as he touched her face gently. "I'm here and I'm not going anywhere."

She opened her eyes and sort of smiled at him. "You're where?"

He chuckled. "Here."

"Good," she sighed, drifting off again.

"Hey, you need to wake up."

She groaned. "If I wake up I'll be sick."

"I'll catch it," he teased.

She laughed a bit. "Gross."

Jimmy chuckled softly to himself.

The ambulance pulled into the bay, so Jimmy got up and grabbed everything as Nigel opened the back doors.

Together, they lifted the gurney out of the ambulance into the hospital.

Thankfully, it wasn't busy, and Candice was immediately taken into an emergency-room pod, where Jimmy helped move her off the gurney into a bed.

"You going to stay?" Nigel asked.

"Yeah. We can call a cab to come get us when she's discharged. You okay to get back to the station?"

Nigel nodded. "No worries. The next shift will start soon. I'm almost off duty, but if you're okay to stay...?"

"I'm okay to stay. She doesn't have anyone else."

Nigel nodded. "I'll see you later then."

"Thanks, Nigel."

Nigel left and Jimmy took a seat in the chair beside the bed as they waited for Candice to be triaged and assessed.

"Where is my SUV?" Candice moaned.

"At the campground. It's fine. We can get it tomorrow. Ranger Matt knows what's going on."

Candice sat up, wincing and touching her head. "What is going on? Where am I?"

"In the emergency room. You rolled your ankle and I think you have a concussion. We need to get it checked out."

She glared at him in disbelief, her black glasses sliding down the bridge of her nose. "As if."

"Really." He tried not to laugh at her bizarre behavior, which was a classic sign of a concussion. It would take time for her brain to heal if that was the case, and her being alone worried him. She would have to be monitored.

"I'm Dr. Zwart—what seems to be the problem?" Dr. Zwart looked up from his clipboard. "Oh, Lavoie, I didn't know it was you!"

"Hi," Candice said brightly, before lying back down, obviously dizzy again.

"I'm Jimmy Liu. I'm a paramedic with Mountain Rescue."

"Pleasure—can you tell me what happened?" Dr. Zwart was already staring at the ankle, which was bruising.

"We responded to a call about a bear and I tended to a minor laceration and a sprained wrist. Candice went to speak to the rangers, stepped in a hollow, rolled her ankle and face-planted onto the gravel road. She's had some double vision, nausea, dizziness and peculiar behavior."

"So she needs to be checked for a concussion," Dr. Zwart stated. "Tell me about the ankle."

"She can't put weight on it and it started swelling fast. I removed the boot and elevated it the best I could. I did do a palpation, but it's so swollen I'm not sure if the bone might be broken."

Dr. Zwart nodded. "We'll do an X-ray. You can head back to your rig, Liu. We've got it from here."

"With all due respect, Candice doesn't have anyone else. She's not only my boss, but a family friend. We grew up together and I would like to stay."

Dr. Zwart nodded and tilted Candice's head to look at the scrape. "Sounds good. I'll order some tests and I'll have the nurse clean up the facial laceration, which appears to be a superficial scrape, but still, as it was the gravel road in the campground we better get it checked out."

"Thanks, Dr. Zwart. Is there a phone nearby?"

"You can use the one there by the nursing station. Just dial nine to get an outside line."

"Thanks, Doc." Jimmy got up and headed to the nursing station. Picking up the phone, he dialed home to speak to his mother.

"Hey, Mom," he said.

"Jimmy? Is everything okay?" his mom asked, panic in her voice. "It's almost midnight."

"I'm okay, but Candice is in the hospital. She might have a concussion and a fracture. She doesn't have anyone else, so I've got to stay with her to monitor her for the next twenty-four hours if it's a concussion. Unless the concussion is bad, they won't keep her here."

"I understand," his mom said gently. "She's a good girl. Don't you worry about Marcus. He'll be fine with his *năinai*."

"Thanks, Mom. I appreciate it." He hung up the phone and headed back to the curtained-off bed, where a nurse was cleaning Candice's face.

"You're Candice's emergency contact?" the nurse asked.

"I am. I'm Jimmy Liu."

"Good. She's going to have to take off her uniform to have the X-ray because there's metal in it. Could you step out while I get a gown on her?"

"Sure."

"Good." The nurse finished cleaning up Candice and closed the curtain, opening it a few moments later. "We're going to take her to get an X-ray. You can wait here." The nurse lifted the side bar of the bed, preparing it for the journey down the hall.

"Jimmy, are you coming?" Candice asked.

"No. I'll stay here," he said. "I'll be waiting for you."

"Okay." She frowned.

Jimmy stepped out of the way as they rolled the bed out of the curtained room and off to X-ray.

He wished he was going with her. It pained him to let her out of his sight.

He was worried about her, worried he had let her down again, worried he'd let down Logan by not honoring his promise to look out for her.

And he was also worried about himself.

He still wanted Candice after all this time and that was a worrisome prospect indeed. She was single and free, yes, but she still had dreams to fulfill, dreams Jimmy still worried he would hold her back from.

He promised Logan he'd take care of Candice and he would do that by making sure she fulfilled her dream. Which meant setting aside his feelings for her.

The hospital called Jimmy a cab once all the tests on Candice were completed. He managed to help her get dressed, but the giddiness was wearing off and it was quickly replaced with exhaustion. He was feeling it, too.

He was relieved when Dr. Zwart announced the ankle was just a bad sprain and should be right as rain in a couple of weeks, and that the concussion was a grade one and she would only have to be monitored for forty-eight hours before her follow-up appointment.

It could've been a lot worse.

And he was glad it hadn't been.

He paid the cab driver, leaving Candice in the car while he opened the front door of her house, and then picked her up out of the taxi and carried her up the porch and into her house.

He shut the door with the heel of his boot and the slam roused her.

"Where are we?" she said weakly.

"You're home." He didn't know where to put her, and then he saw a bedroom in what used to be the dining room and remembered her saying that her father had used that room. "I'm going to put you on the couch and then I'm going to make up your dad's bed, okay?"

"Okay."

He set her down gently and then made his way upstairs. The linen closet was still in the same place and he pulled out a spare set of sheets, then headed into her room to grab her pillows, but her old room was empty. It was only then he remembered she said that she'd moved into the master bedroom.

While the rest of the house was still her parents' home, this room was hers. And it suited her. It was modern and clean, with soft colors, and looked comfortable and calming.

When he picked up her pillows, he could smell that vaguely vanilla scent that was distinctly hers.

Focus, Jimmy.

He piled up her quilt and pillows on the sheets he'd grabbed, then found an oversized nightshirt and grabbed some of her toiletries. Everything was precariously perched, but he managed to get downstairs without dropping anything.

He set everything on the spare bed and made quick work getting the room prepared for her. Once it was ready, he went back into the living room and picked her up.

"Can I sleep now?" she asked.

"Soon. Let's get this uniform off," he whispered.

"Okay." Then she giggled. "But usually men buy me a drink before that."

Good lord.

"Would you just cooperate?" he asked firmly.

Candice stuck out her bottom lip. "Okay."

It's not like she's getting totally naked. Just out of her uniform.

That's what he had to keep reminding himself as he helped Candice out of her shirt. He kept his eyes averted, but her silky hair brushed his cheeks. Her hair still smelled like vanilla, but just faintly.

Exactly the way he remembered.

Focus.

Now came the tricky part. He had to get her out of her trousers.

"Do you think you can stand?"

"No, but I can try."

"Put your arms around my neck." He reached down to undo her belt.

"Okay."

His blood heated as his hands skimmed her soft skin.

She's concussed. Get a hold of yourself.

He was inwardly cursing every deity of bad luck he could think of for putting him in this situation. A few hours ago, they had been kissing in her kitchen, and now Candice was swaying back and forth and laughing.

"What's so funny?" he asked, frustrated.

"Jimmy Liu is undoing my pants!"

He rolled his eyes, glad no one else was around to hear this.

"Jimmy Liu's hand is on my butt!"

"My hand is not on your butt. Not right now, anyway. Step out of your trousers slowly."

She stepped out, one leg at a time and he caught sight of the tattoo. The sexiest tattoo of a feather he'd ever seen. Well, it wasn't so much the tattoo, but the placing of it on her inner thigh and the fact it was Candice.

He remembered how much he liked to kiss that tattoo.

Focus.

He helped her put on her nightshirt and then climb into bed, gingerly lifting her swollen ankle up onto a pillow. She was watching him petulantly and he couldn't help but smile at her.

"Thanks," she said.

"You're welcome, but you owe me a drink or something," he muttered, folding her uniform.

"I'll never remember that."

"I know."

"Sorry."

"What?" he asked.

"I need the bathroom."

He rolled his eyes. "Okay. Let's get up. You're worse than Marcus, you know."

He helped her to the bathroom and waited outside while she cleaned herself up. When she opened the door, he carried her to bed. He settled her against the pillow and arranged the pillow at her feet to elevate her leg, before doing a final tuck of her quilt.

"There. You're snug as a bug in a rug."

She smiled dreamily at him. "I never understood that."

"What?" he asked.

"The bug in a rug."

He chuckled. "Me, either."

"Are you going to leave?"

"No," he said. He wasn't going to leave her—not tonight. And there was a part of him that didn't ever want to leave her. "I'll sleep on the couch."

"Can you stay for a bit longer?" she asked, patting a spot next to her on the bed.

"Okay." He sat down gingerly.

"Thank you for being with me tonight."

"You're welcome."

"You know how I feel about you," she said.

His pulse quickened. "Pardon?"

"I loved you and you left. It hurt, but it's okay that you don't feel that way about me."

Jimmy could tell that she was a bit out of it. That this was the concussion talking and Candice probably wouldn't remember any of this in the morning.

"I cared for you," he said gently.

"You did?"

He nodded. "Logan didn't want me to hold you back."

"Hold me back?" she asked, confused.

"From going away to medical school, but I've always cared for you." He reached down and touched her face, brushing his knuckles over her soft, silky cheek.

Candice leaned forward and touched his face, too. "I wanted you to be my first. I'm glad you were."

And before he could stop her, she kissed him, gently, and then it deepened into a longing, lingering kiss. He cupped her face, not wanting the kiss to end, reveling in the feeling of her soft, full lips against his.

The kiss broke and he let Candice lie back down, her eyes closed as she drifted off into sleep.

His blood sang with unrequited longing. He wished that their kitchen kiss could have continued and that she might remember this conversation.

He certainly wouldn't forget.

CHAPTER EIGHT

CANDICE WOKE WITH a start. She'd been having a lovely dream, where she was kissing Jimmy and could still feel his lips against hers. But the sensation faded as her aches and pains claimed her attention—her pounding head, her throbbing ankle.

As her eyes adjusted to the light, she realized she was in her father's old bedroom and she was in one of her pyjama shirts, but still wearing her bra and underwear.

What the heck happened?

She tried to roll over and get up, but couldn't.

Candice managed to grab her glasses, which were sitting on a side table, and as she put them on the world came into greater focus. As she looked around the room, she noticed that Jimmy was slumped over and snoozing in her father's old recliner by the window. Her heart skipped a beat and she touched her lips. Had it been a dream or had it really happened?

"Jimmy?" she whispered.

He woke with a start. "Hey, you okay? You need something?"

"Answers," she said and cleared her throat. "And maybe some water."

"Well, you're due for some acetaminophen. Hold on, I'll be back." He got up and quickly left the room, returning a few moments later with medication and a big glass of water. "Take two. Dr. Zwart said you have a grade-one concussion and you're going to need a bit of time to heal."

Well, that explained the hazy memories and the bizarre dreams. Since he wasn't mentioning their kiss, it must've been a dream, but there was a part of her that suspected it hadn't been. That it had really happened and even though she would be mortified if that was the case, she was hoping it had.

"A concussion? I can't take time off for a concussion. I'm supposed to do the backcountry loop on the weekend."

"Yeah, even if you didn't have a concussion, your ankle is kind of really sprained. I doubt you're doing a hike on the weekend."

Candice groaned as she got a closer look at her purple-and-red swollen ankle.

"What the heck happened?" she asked.

Jimmy sat down on the edge of her bed. "You stepped into a hollow the wrong way, rolled your ankle and face-planted onto the road in the campground."

Candice groaned. "Are you serious?"

"Yes, and we've had this conversation before."

She winced and vaguely remembered bits and pieces of last night, but a lot of it was a blur. "Where's my car?"

"Ranger Matt drove it to the RCMP office. It's just down the street, so I'll grab it later."

"You stayed here all night?" she asked.

He nodded. "I did."

Heat bloomed in her cheeks as she looked at her state of undress. "You—you…undressed me?"

"Yes." There was a twinkle in his eyes. "You were a bit, uh, sick…on your uniform."

She groaned and lied down again. "I'm so sorry."

"You weren't sick on me," he teased.

"I'm so embarrassed."

"Don't be."

The thought of him undressing her brought a blush to her cheeks. Her body thrummed and she wished she could remember more of it. She had no doubt he was a gentleman about it, and she was still a bit embarrassed, but there was another part of her that was slightly thrilled at the idea of Jimmy undressing her. His hands on her again.

She only wished she remembered it. And that she could have been a willing participant, undressing him, too. The thought of undressing him slowly, running her hands over his body, exploring that tattoo and his muscles, made her heart beat faster, her blood heat.

Don't think about him like that. You don't want to get hurt again and he's not in to you.

"What about Marcus?" she asked, changing the subject and getting her mind off of Jimmy naked with her, his hands on her.

"I told my mom what happened and she has Marcus. He's fine. You need someone to stay with you for the next couple of days and I can do that."

"Why?" she asked.

"Is there anyone else?" he asked quietly. "My place is small. It's better for you to stay put here."

"What about Marcus?"

"I can bring him by, if that's okay? And besides, my mother would love to clean my place thoroughly and finish my unpacking so she can root out secrets." He was teasing and winked at her.

She smiled. "Yes. I'd like it if you'd bring Marcus by."

And that brought her right back to reality. No, there

was no one else in her life. She was alone and it was something she'd never really allowed herself to think about, instead keeping herself busy with work.

Her parents had been only children. She didn't have any cousins or aunts or uncles or anyone. Logan and her parents had been her family and they were gone. It scared her to think of being vulnerable and alone, with someone she didn't know making decisions for her.

"Thank you for taking care of me," she said soberly, shaken to her very core by the simple realization that she had no one.

It hurt.

"Hey," Jimmy said, softly inching closer to her. "It's okay."

She brushed away a tear. "Sorry."

"You've been through a lot. You have a grade one concussion and a bad sprain. Yeah, it's not an ideal time to take time off of work, especially with an annoying new employee, but I'm here for you, okay?"

She nodded, sniffling. "Thanks, Jimmy. I really appreciate it."

"No problem. Now, sit back and relax." He stood up and placed a set of crutches close to her bed. "Since you have a concussion, I'm afraid you can't watch television or read or look at your phone, so… I thought you might like to listen to a podcast or an audio book or something?"

"No thanks," she said, her head pounding. "I think I'm going to try and make it to the bathroom and then come back and rest."

"Okay. I'm going to run up the street and get your SUV. I'll be gone twenty minutes. You going to be okay?"

She nodded. "I'll be fine. Go."

"Okay." Jimmy slipped out of the dining room and left the house. She craned her neck to see him jog down her sloped driveway in the direction of the RCMP station.

Candice sighed and leaned back against the pillows.

She tried not to cry, but it was hard not to. There were so many emotions playing with her. She blamed her head injury on her inability to keep it under control and then she laughed as she thought that only she could manage to get a concussion rolling her ankle and doing a face-plant on a gravel road.

She sat up and grabbed the crutches. It took a couple of tries to get herself up, but once she was up she moved easily to her father's bathroom.

After cleaning herself up and finding a change of clothes neatly laid out for her, she managed to make her way out of the dining room and to the kitchen, just as Jimmy pulled up in her driveway.

He came bounding up the steps and back into the house.

"Where are you going?" he asked when he saw her creeping down the hall.

"I'm hungry."

His eyes widened and he smiled. "Well, that's a good sign."

"Yeah, the pain in my head is dissipating. So if I take it easy the next few days I should be okay."

"You're still not cleared to drive or anything. Dr. Zwart wants you to follow up with him in forty-eight hours."

She nodded. "I understand."

He followed her into the kitchen and made her sit at the table. "What would you like?"

"Just some toast. I better take it easy."

Jimmy nodded. "Toast, it is."

He found her half loaf of bread and popped two slices into the toaster.

"What about Marcus's party?"

"Well, I do have to relieve my mom later, but she promised to come sit with you. She wants to take you up with your offer to help with the party, but no reading or writing. Nothing that requires too much thinking power."

Candice chuckled. "I'm not the best party planner, but I'd love to help and to keep busy."

"You picked the right theme. Dog over pig."

"That's pretty easy. I told you, that pig is annoying."

He grinned at her and her heart skipped a beat. "You know, I can't believe you're still wearing the same glasses."

"They're in fashion again, but they're not the same glasses," she said. "They're upgraded and not out of the discount bin, where my dad liked to shop."

Jimmy chuckled. "Well, they do suit you. I always liked those type of frames. They scream 'sexy librarian.'"

Heat bloomed in her cheeks and all she could think about was the kiss she'd dreamed about. But was it just a dream?

"Jimmy, about yesterday… Did we…? Did I do anything out of the ordinary once we got back from the hospital?"

He turned his back to her as the toast popped up. "What do you mean?"

There was an odd tone to his voice and she knew that something had happened. Maybe her dream wasn't a dream. Maybe they had actually kissed.

Oh. No.

"I mean, you did suggest I buy you a drink when I was trying to get your pyjamas on," he teased.

"I mean, did we kiss?"

"Before or after the concussion?"

She moaned. "I know we did before, but I'm not sure about after."

He chuckled. "It's okay. Like I said, you were a bit out of it."

"Still."

She was embarrassed.

She didn't want to get hurt by him again and she was his boss—kissing him once was unprofessional, but twice? Inexcusable.

He set down the toast in front of her and then got her some butter. "There you go."

"Are you going to sit around here all day watching me like a hawk?" she asked.

"Pretty much."

"I appreciate it, but I think I can manage."

He shook his head. "Don't be stubborn. Dr. Zwart said that you needed to be watched closely for the next forty-eight hours, so that's what I'm going to do. I have to leave you for a bit today to be with Marcus, but like I told you, my mom will come sit with you. Thankfully she's bringing me a change of clothes. I'm about ready to ditch this uniform."

"I wish I had some clothing to offer you, but I doubt you'd fit in anything of mine."

"Purple isn't really my color, but thanks," he said, pouring himself a cup of coffee he'd brewed earlier.

"I'm sorry that I'm taking you away from Marcus." She meant it. A kid needed his dad around.

"It's okay. He's young and you need help. It's the least I can do. You're my friend and Logan was my friend."

He frowned and then poked at his coffee cup, pushing it slightly. The mood shifted and she could feel the sadness permeating the air.

She felt it, too, whenever she thought of Logan.

Candice set down her toast, which now tasted like sawdust in her mouth. Her head started to throb.

"I think I'm going to lie down again. My head is hurting." She stood up and grabbed her crutches, making her way out of the kitchen. "Thank you for the toast."

"No problem. If you need anything else, let me know."

"I will," Candice called over her shoulder as she hobbled down the hall and made her way back to her father's old room. She really needed to put some space between them.

After Candice went back to bed, Jimmy stepped out onto the deck and made his way down to the forest. He could hear the water from the edge of the property and he made his way through the trees to the small clearing where he and Logan used to sit down by the spring's edge.

The two stumps they had once sat on were still there, though a bit overgrown now with long grass and moss.

He sat down on his stump and stared out over the water.

"I know you said you didn't want me to start anything with her, but it's not easy, Logan. She's a great person." Jimmy scrubbed his hand over his face, annoyed that he was talking to himself.

Things would have turned out so differently if he had known that Candice was pregnant before he left. He would've stayed. Would have been there for her, experienced all the excitement at the prospect of a baby, and held her in his arms when that dream was shattered.

Instead, he'd been thousands of miles away and had had no idea any of it was happening. But maybe that was for the best. If he'd stayed, there was always the chance that Logan would have been proven right—that Jimmy would have held back Candice and she would have ended up resenting him.

Jimmy took a deep breath and got up from the stump. He wandered back to Candice's home and made his way back inside. He went to check on her, but she wasn't sleeping, like he thought she might be.

Instead, she'd gotten dressed with the clothes he'd laid out for her and she was sitting on the couch with another cup of coffee.

"There you are," she said when he came back in. "Where were you?"

"I thought you were sleeping so I went for a walk in the woods. Sat on the stump chairs that Logan and I used to chill at."

"I'm glad you found them. Dad always refused to get rid of them."

"I'm glad he didn't. How did you get another cup of coffee?" he asked, taking a seat on the coffee table by the couch.

"I made it?" she said, confused.

"You're supposed to be resting."

"I'm not an invalid, Jimmy. You can't stay here forever. I can manage on my own—I have to manage on my own."

"I don't plan on staying here forever," he snapped. "But you need to rest and someone is supposed to stay with you for forty-eight hours."

"You have your son. You can go. I can manage," she said stiffly.

Of course she didn't need him. She'd been on her own for so long.

"You need me now," he responded. "You needed me yesterday, when you hurt yourself and you were out of sorts. You told me that you needed me."

Her eyes widened and the blush rose in her cheeks as she sat up. "What?"

Jimmy kneeled in front of her. "I'm happy to be here, Candy. I made a promise to Logan. When he died, he asked me to take care of you."

Tears filled her eyes and one slipped down her cheek. "What? He said what?"

He brushed away the tear. "I'm here for you."

Candice trembled under his touch and all he could think about was kissing her again. His pulse was thundering between his ears and he recalled the way she had kissed him last night. She didn't remember that and he wanted her to remember it.

He wanted her to remember their kiss.

He cupped her face and leaned in.

"Jimmy? Candice?"

Jimmy jumped back and Candice wiped the tears from her eyes as Jimmy's mother walked in, carrying a bag of groceries.

"Mom, what're you doing here?" Jimmy asked.

"It's one o'clock, you told me to come by." His mother's eyes flickered between him and Candice and he swore he saw a secret little smile. "I brought Candice some lunch. Some of my broth, too."

"Thank you, Mrs. Liu," Candice said, her voice shaking. "I appreciate it."

"Call me Liena," his mother said, smiling warmly. "I'll just put these into the kitchen?"

"That would be great, Liena," Candice said.

"I'll be back," Jimmy said. He followed his mother into the kitchen. "Is Marcus with Dad?"

"Yes," Liena said, puttering around Candice's kitchen. "Marcus loves being with his *yéye*, and Yéye loves being with him, but Marcus is missing you. You go spend some time with your son and I'll take care of Candice."

As much as Jimmy wanted to stay with Candice, he wanted to check on Marcus. Though he was a bit terrified at the prospect of his mother watching Candice, someone had to stay with her and his mother was the only person who had offered.

His mother had always had a soft spot for Logan and Candice Warner.

And it would also be nice to change out of his uniform and shower.

"Okay. I'll be back by this evening," Jimmy said.

His mother waved. "Go. Don't worry about it. I'll take care of her like she's my own daughter."

Jimmy paused as his mother began to hum and put things away. If he didn't know any better, he would assume that his mother was plotting something. Sometimes he could never be sure what Liena Liu was thinking, and he knew his mother was a persistent force to be reckoned with on the best of days.

Jimmy left the kitchen to find Candice sitting upright on the couch.

"How's the ankle?" he asked.

"It doesn't feel as swollen. The elevating is working."

"Well, let me check before I go." He kneeled down

in front of her and unwrapped the tensor bandage. The swelling had definitely gone done, which was good.

"I was going to attempt a shower," Candice said. "Do you think you can leave the bandage off for a bit?"

"Okay, but I'll wrap it tonight before you go to bed."

"You're coming back?" Candice asked.

"I know you can manage on your own or whatever," he teased, trying to make light of the awkward situation from before. "I'm just following Dr. Zwart's advice. I'll just be here a couple of nights and then you'll be on your own."

Candice smiled. "Okay. Fine."

"Glad you're accepting your fate," he quipped. "Not like you had much of a choice, though."

"Go spend time with your son," she said. "I'll see you later."

Jimmy stood. "Okay. By the way, my mom is stocking your kitchen. I'm sorry."

She smiled. "It's fine. It'll be nice to spend time with her."

"Try to sleep or she'll talk your ear off." He left Candice sitting on the couch and his mother in the kitchen. His stomach flip-flopped with anxiety, but he had no choice.

He needed a shower and he needed some space from Candice before he tried something utterly foolish, like kissing her again.

CHAPTER NINE

As much as she fought Jimmy coming to take care of her at first, she was glad that he had and grateful to Mrs. Liu for staying with her while Jimmy was spent time with his son. She did her best to help Liena with planning Marcus's birthday party, but she kept dozing off. She only hoped she'd be well enough to attend.

Jimmy came back that evening and she convinced him to spend the night sleeping upstairs in her room instead of cramped on the couch or in the chair by her bed again.

The next day Marcus came over and she got to enjoy watching the little toddler run all over her backyard. Jimmy's rental didn't have much of a yard to play in, so Marcus was in his element, running and stretching his little legs, and Candice got the pleasure of watching Jimmy interact with his son.

She only wished she could join them.

After forty-eight hours, she was able to get around okay, and when she had the checkup with Dr. Zwart, he cleared her to drive and do some other stuff, but to do those things slowly. He wasn't ready to clear her for work, though, and told her she couldn't go back for a week.

Jimmy, on the other hand, had to return to work, so

she made sure that Stu and Nigel would take him under their wings. Jimmy was a capable paramedic, but he was still a new member to Mountain Rescue. Stu, her second in command, was a competent trainer, but she'd feel so much better when she got back to work and could see Jimmy's progress for herself.

When Jimmy was done his shift for the night, he would come by and check on her, and she quickly got used to how nice it felt to have someone look in on her. To have someone that cared.

She just didn't want to get used to relying on that particular human connection, because if Jimmy found someone else, started dating someone else, he wouldn't make time for his late best friend's little sister.

Who said he's going to date anyone else?

She ignored that little thought in her head.

A man like Jimmy Liu wouldn't stay single for long. She'd seen how the other girls in their school had re-acted around him. He was handsome, charming and smart. And he'd only gotten more appealing with age— being a first responder meant that he was in good shape, and he was a good father. Anyone who wasn't obtuse could see the way he doted on his son.

He was a catch.

Why can't he be your catch?

That, she didn't know. Other than she was afraid of the toll that losing him would take on heart again.

"Hey!" Jimmy said, coming into her house after his shift. He paused when he saw her sitting on her steps. "What's up? You look really angry."

"I'm going stir-crazy," Candice muttered. "My foot is still a bit too swollen to get on my sneaker, but I don't like driving in my flip-flops to Hinton."

"Why are you going to Hinton?" Jimmy asked.

"I need to go into a larger town for supplies."

"Should you be doing that?"

"Dr. Zwart said I could, but I wasn't going to go until I got my foot to fit my sneaker, which it doesn't." She tossed away the sneaker. "I wanted to get Marcus a present and there's a better selection of stuff in Hinton."

"Well, why don't I drive you?"

"You just came off an overnight shift."

He shrugged. "I'm not tired and, anyway, my mom tasked me with going into town to get some stuff for the party. We can pick up Marcus and take him out to lunch, or to a bigger park. And best of all, you can wear your flip-flops!"

Say no.

Only, she was going stir-crazy and she liked spending time with Jimmy and Marcus. She'd been off work for a week and she'd seen them frequently. She was getting used to having them around, glad they lived down the street and she saw them often.

"Okay." She smiled. "Let me grab my purse and we can go."

"Sounds good. I'll meet you at the car."

She grabbed her things and locked up her place.

Jimmy was waiting at the bottom of the porch steps and he helped her down, as she was still limping a bit.

She wasn't used to hanging around at home.

She was used to working, or flying in the helicopter, or being up on the mountain doing a rescue, or doing her rounds with the rangers. It kept her busy. It kept her mind off everything else and spending the last few days just sitting there, unable to do anything, her mind had bombarded her with a lot of stuff she thought she'd locked firmly away.

So even though this was putting her heart on the line, she was thankful for the errand and the excuse to go out. Jimmy took her hand and they ambled to his car.

"You're walking a lot better."

"I've been working hard on some stretching and physio. I plan to be going back up my mountains by next week."

"You're ambitious."

"I have a backcountry loop to walk. I had to switch. I was supposed to be doing that last weekend when I got hurt."

"I know. And Stu still wants me to go with you."

"We can't have two paramedics on the loop. We always need a couple in Jasper. That's why he doesn't want you to go with him."

"And Stu doesn't want to take a 'greenhorn,'" Jimmy said sarcastically, making air quotes, "up the mountain. Whatever that means."

Candice chuckled. "A newbie, I think."

"I know these mountains, too. I know I've been gone for a while, but I grew up here. Did Stu?"

"No. I believe Stu is from Canmore. So, still the mountains, just different ones."

"Exactly." Jimmy shook his head. "But you're the boss lady, too, and I suppose he wants the 'greenhorn' to go with the boss lady."

"Stop air-quoting 'greenhorn,'" Candice said, laughing. "You look like a chicken when you do that."

Jimmy cocked an eyebrow. "How is that?"

"You stick out your neck like a chicken."

"Okay then. You sure you're over that concussion?" He was grinning, his eyes twinkling.

"Pretty sure." She climbed into the passenger seat and buckled up while Jimmy climbed into the driver's side. They drove across town and Candice stayed in the car while Jimmy ran inside to grab Marcus and Marcus's bag. It was just an hour's drive to Hinton, but they would need provisions, especially for a toddler. She may not have kids, but she knew that they required a lot of stuff.

Stuff that she wished she had.

Yes, she had big aspirations to become a surgeon, but she also wanted a family. She wanted a couple of kids.

Jimmy came out of the house with a diaper bag slung over his shoulder and Marcus in his arms.

Jimmy opened the back door and set Marcus down in his car seat.

"Hi, Marcus!" Candice said, smiling at the little boy.

Marcus was drinking out of his sippy cup, but he smiled behind it, his eyes crinkling and twinkling with recognition. Jimmy finished strapping in Marcus and then passed the diaper bag to Candice over the seat.

"Here, you better man the bag. There's snacks and stuff in there and if I left it back here with him he'd lay waste to it. Wouldn't you, Marcus?" Jimmy teased his son, who laughed at him from behind his cup.

Jimmy finished making sure that Marcus had what he needed and then climbed into the front seat.

"You got everything?" Candice asked.

"Yes. And a list from my mom. There's some stuff she wants us to pick up for the party. It's all in the diaper bag. As well as some extra things to keep him occupied, but honestly, he's due for a nap so hopefully he'll sleep on the way to Hinton and then be ready to go when we get to the superstore."

"Does he sleep well in the car?" Candice asked.

"He does. When we drove from Toronto back home, my mom came with us. She flew to Toronto and helped me pack up what little we had into the trailer I rented and then we made the trip out west together. She kept Marcus busy in the back and I was able to focus on driving. When I moved back it was spring and there were still parts of northern Ontario and the prairies that were getting late snowfalls."

"Yeah, it was a weird winter," she said.

"And driving around Lake Superior with a trailer and a baby was no picnic. I was glad my mom was able to help, but really, she'd do anything for Marcus. If it was just me, she'd make me fend for myself," he quipped.

"That's not true and you know it."

He nodded. "Yes. I'm joking. I would've thought that in the past, but Marcus has really opened up my eyes, and though it's still not perfect, my relationship with my parents is better than it's ever been before. I'm glad they have a good relationship with Marcus."

Candice chuckled. "Your mom sure does love him."

"And I don't?" Jimmy teased.

"You do. That's not what I meant."

"I know what you meant. And, yeah, it's true. Marcus is the light of her life."

As they pulled out of town, leaving Jasper behind them, Marcus started to drift off to sleep, and held tight to his little sippy cup full of water. Candice smiled at him.

"He really is cute," she said.

"I think so." Jimmy grinned at her.

"Do you think he'll sleep the whole way there?" Candice asked.

"He should."

"I'll never understand how little kids can sleep in such odd positions."

Jimmy chuckled. "I think adults can, too. I mean I

remember sleeping in some crummy, tight spaces when I was a teen. Especially after a bush party."

Candice winced. "Yeah, I remember some of those bush parties. You and Logan really were the worst influences."

"What? It gave you an appreciation of nature, I bet." He winked at her and she laughed.

"I suppose it did. It's why I love Jasper so much."

And that was why Chad had left her. He didn't want to spend his life in Jasper. He didn't want to take care of her father when he got sick.

He didn't want a family.

And truth be told, he was never much of an outdoors person. She should've seen it earlier, but she hadn't. She had met him in university when her family members were all alive and well, and he had dazzled her with his charm. And then she'd lost Logan, and her mom, and her dad had closed in on himself a bit, so she'd clung to Chad like a lifeline because she didn't want to be alone.

"That's probably why my marriage ended," she said quietly.

"Yeah, you never really told me about…what was his name?" Jimmy asked.

"Chad."

"That's a horrible name." Jimmy made a face. "Who names their kid Chad?"

"Chad is not a horrible name. Our marriage didn't end because of his name."

"Fine. So then why did it end?"

"We wanted different things. He didn't want to stay in Jasper, unless we were going to upgrade to a condo or a lodge where we could ski and host parties. Fancy parties. He didn't want to stay and help take care of my dad when he first got sick. He also really detested the outdoors. unless it was clean, sanitary and socially acceptable."

Jimmy cocked an eyebrow. "What did you see in him?"

"He was nice. We had a good time when we met in college. I loved him and we both were focused on medicine. And to be fair, he was supportive of me when Logan was killed and my mom started going downhill, but he wanted to go back to school. He wanted to be a doctor. He wanted a life in the big city and I wanted to stay in Jasper."

"You really wanted to stay in Jasper?" he asked.

"I did." She smiled. "It was hard to give up medical school. It hurt, but it was the right thing to do at the time. I love Jasper. Chad didn't, so he left."

And it had hurt more than she had expected. She thought she'd built walls to protect herself, but when Chad left those walls had crumbled more easily than she could have imagined. She had barely survived Jimmy leaving and that second abandonment forced her to realize that the only way to protect herself was by never letting anyone close in the first place. So she'd closed off her heart, thrown herself into looking after her dad, and after that into work, and she had been just fine.

Until Jimmy came back and upset her carefully ordered existence.

"Since I told you about Chad, why don't you tell me about Marcus's mom. You told me she passed away."

"She did," Jimmy sighed. "I met her after I got back from Germany. She had served, too, and she had some problems with PTSD that she never dealt with. I couldn't see it at the time—I was still coming to terms with what had happened with Logan—and we grew close and got together one night. Then she left. I didn't love her. I cared for her, she was my friend, but I wouldn't call it love. Then, six months after Marcus was born, he was left on my doorstep. She couldn't handle it. It broke me not to know about him until six months later, but still I tried to get her help with her PTSD. She didn't want it, though, and there was nothing further I could do."

"That's too bad." She felt even worse that she hadn't told him sooner about their baby. That it had been kept from him for so long.

Jimmy nodded. "It sucked. She had no one, and one night she drank too much..."

"I'm sorry. And I'm sorry that Marcus won't know his mother."

Jimmy gave a sad smile. "Yeah, me, too. I did manage to locate her father, but he didn't want anything to do with Marcus, or me, for that matter, but he did give me a picture of Jennifer in her uniform. So I have that put away for when Marcus wants to learn about his mother."

"Have you ever thought about getting married?"

"Nope. Never thought about it," Jimmy said quickly. "All I've been focused on is moving back to Jasper to give him a great place to grow up and to give him the chance to be close to his grandparents. I'm trying to rebuild my life after a rough couple of years. Marriage is the last thing on my mind."

Candice didn't know why she was disappointed when he said that.

She certainly wasn't looking to get married again, but the way he so quickly dismissed the idea gave her an unexpected surge of sadness—for him and for Marcus. They deserved all the happiness in the world. She couldn't give it to them—she couldn't risk her heart again, wouldn't put herself in that position—but she wanted it so badly for them both.

The rest of the hour-long drive to Hinton was unremarkable. She was used to this stretch of road and she never really tired of just staring out the window at the mountains, trees, rocks and occasional animals.

It was a bright, sunny and clear day.

The water sparkled, flashing a brilliant blue from the mineral runoff and the springs underneath that fed the various lakes.

Marcus continued his nap and only woke up once before Jimmy pulled into the parking lot of the superstore, where they could grab everything they needed from Liena's list and where Candice could find Marcus a birthday present.

Jimmy parked and they got of the car, Candice grabbing her purse and the diaper bag. Jimmy got Marcus out, locked the car and carried him over to a shopping cart, sitting him down in the baby seat.

"I'm going to have to change him when we get inside," Jimmy remarked. "He's quite ripe."

Candice laughed and put the diaper bag in the cart. "It'll give me a chance to pick out a present for him without him noticing."

"He won't remember, even if you pick it out right in front of him. As long as you wrap it in garish-colored paper or a giant box he can destroy, he'll be happy. This is what I've learned about kids since Marcus turned one—much like cats, kids like playing with the box itself a lot more than what's inside the box."

Candice laughed. "Okay then, but we'll have to distract him with something small so he won't cry when I take away the present to wrap it up for him."

"This is true. We'll have to get some ice cream!"

Marcus squealed and clapped his hands. "Ice cweam!"

"That's right," Jimmy said. "Ice cream, but first shopping for Năinai and then ice cream. Okay, buddy?"

Marcus nodded and then grinned at Candice. "Ice cweam, Candy!"

"That's right!" And her heart melted as Marcus giggled and squirmed in the shopping-cart seat. He was so excited about the prospect of ice cream—it was adorable.

"Now you know why I bring extra clothes," Jimmy said.

"I have friends who have kids. I get it."

Once they got in the store Jimmy picked up Marcus and took him to get changed while Candice shopped for the stuff on Liena's list.

Jimmy and Marcus came back a few moments later, Jimmy holding Marcus's tiny, chubby hand in his as Marcus toddled beside his tall father.

Her heart skipped a beat as she saw them.

Marcus smiled and waved and she couldn't help but smile and wave back at him. Then he pulled free of his father's hand and ran toward her, his chubby little legs barely supporting his body as he ran down the aisle, squealing and laughing.

Candice kneeled down and he ran into her arms, throwing his arms around her neck and hugging her— he wanted her to pick him up. Her heart swelled and she completely melted, holding him in her arms as she stood.

Jimmy looked a bit shocked as he approached her. "I have never seen him warm up to someone so fast before."

"Well, that's because he knows that Candy rocks. Right, Marcus?"

Marcus nodded.

Candice placed him in the cart and he happily squirmed as she pushed the cart up and down the aisles.

This felt like how it always should have been. It made her happy and yet it scared her. Her heart was slipping into Jimmy's hands again.

And she hated that it felt so right.

That she wanted it to be right.

They finished up their shopping after Candice found a present for Marcus and they distracted him with an ice-cream cone when they were leaving the superstore. He was happily making a mess while they loaded up the back of Jimmy's car with everything that would be needed for the birthday party in a few days.

"It's a beautiful day," Candice remarked. It was sunny, warm and clear. There would be so many people out on the mountain and her mind immediately went to what was happening at work.

"Where are you?" Jimmy asked as he kneeled down and wiped off Marcus's sticky hands.

"What do you mean?" she asked. "I'm here."

"You were thinking about work, weren't you?" Jimmy teased.

"Maybe. The park will be packed. There will be a lot of people out and about."

"That's pretty pathetic you're thinking about all the rescues you could be doing because there will be more people in the park." He winked at her and put Marcus back in his car seat.

"It's not that!"

"No?" he asked.

"No. Well, it's partly that, but I've been running

Mountain Rescue for three years and I'm wondering how they're getting along without me."

"It'll be okay. Stu is good."

She shot him a dirty look. "What?"

He threw up his hands. "You're better. Obviously, boss."

Candice sighed. "It'll be good to get back next week and I'm looking forward to getting out on the trail."

"Actually, I'm looking forward to that, too. It's been a long time since I did a backcountry hike."

"Well, we're going to do the Skyline Trail. It's one of the busiest backcountry trails, but the most problematic. It's going to be a pain hiking with all that emergency climbing gear. It might be needed, but hopefully not."

"Let's hope not. So what do you say we get some lunch and make our way down to the Beaver Boardwalk and walk some of it? See if we can see some beavers."

"That sounds fun."

It had been a long time since she'd gone walking along the boardwalk through the wetlands. Actually, she couldn't even remember the last time she'd been down there. When she came to Hinton, she was usually on a mission to get her groceries and leave.

This would be nice.

They picked up some sandwiches and a grilled cheese for Marcus, then drove to the trail and parked. They walked for a bit, letting Marcus stretch his legs along the boardwalk, which meant they had to stop every few minutes so that the boy could squat down and stare at the water and the marsh.

It was adorable.

They didn't walk too far before they found a nice picnic spot near Maxwell Lake and sat down to eat.

Marcus couldn't walk the length of the trail and neither could Candice. Her ankle was bothering her a bit, but she was glad for the stretch. She would make sure to ice and elevate it tonight.

"I forgot about this place," she said. "My parents used to bring Logan and I here when we were younger. I don't know how many times Logan threatened to feed me to the beavers."

Jimmy chuckled.

"Logan liked to bring his dates here to make out."

"Gross."

"What?" Jimmy asked.

"It's bad enough I had to see my brother streak from time to time, but I really don't need to know about where he brought girls to score."

Jimmy chuckled. "Sorry."

"Why did he bring them to a swamp?"

"Wetlands," Jimmy corrected, grinning at her. "And I thought you didn't want to know. I thought it was gross."

She rolled her eyes. "It is, but still I'm curious about the choice of destination."

Jimmy shrugged. "It's quiet here and pretty. It's different from the river or the mountains, I suppose. This wasn't his only spot."

"Yeah. I'm good." She smiled, thinking of her brother. He'd been so well-liked by everyone. She missed him. He was the best big brother a girl could have had—even if he was a complete contrast to her—and it seemed unfair that his life had been cut so short.

"I didn't bring girls here," Jimmy said. "I was too classy."

"Where did you bring girls?" She couldn't believe she was asking him this.

Jimmy shrugged. "Usually to the river, but honestly

I never really had the same amount of girls that Logan had. There was the odd one or two, but not really."

"I find that hard to believe," she said.

"It's true."

"You always had some girl on your arm."

His gaze was intense, and it made her pulse quicken. "Just because the girls were on my arm doesn't mean anything happened. There was only ever one girl I wanted to take out. You were my first, too, Candice."

Her cheeks heated. "I know."

Her heart was hammering against her chest, feeling like it was going burst out.

"You were the only one I ever wanted," he whispered.

She leaned forward, wanting to ask him so many things, but they were interrupted by a loud screech.

"Daddy, I made a mess," Marcus shouted.

Jimmy broke their shared gaze and looked down at his son. "You sure did, buddy. That's a lot of ketchup."

Candice leaned over and tried not to laugh. "Oh, my. Yeah that is."

"I'm going to take him to the restroom and clean him up." Jimmy picked up the diaper bag.

"I'll clean up here. You done with your lunch, Marcus?" Candice asked.

"Yes, Candy. I done."

"Oh, good."

Jimmy took Marcus by the hand and Candice watched the two of them walk away. Her heart skipped a beat again.

You can have this.

All she had to do was not be so afraid and take the plunge, but she was scared of being hurt and losing it all.

"You have a beautiful family there."

Candice spun around to see an elderly couple walking past the picnic table.

"Pardon?" Candice asked, shocked.

The elderly woman smiled. "Your family. You have a beautiful family. How old is the little boy?"

"He'll be two soon," Candice answered stunned.

"Ah, the terrible twos. Although not so terrible. Enjoy it." The elderly woman smiled and continued on her way with her husband.

Candice stood there for a few moments, her hands full of garbage. She didn't correct the older woman and she should have.

Jimmy and Marcus were not her family.

But she wanted them to be. If only she was brave enough to take the chance.

CHAPTER TEN

THE RIDE HOME was quiet, with Marcus sleeping in the backseat, completely played out. Jimmy looked over at Candice and even she was dozing, her head resting against the door.

It brought a smile to his face as he took his time and made his way back to Jasper.

He really didn't want this moment to end.

It was peaceful.

And it felt right.

All he'd ever wanted was Candice.

Nothing about that had changed.

After he had cleaned up Marcus from the ketchup incident, they'd strolled around the boardwalk for a while and then found a park so that Marcus could run around. It was close to dinner and they had had a quick bite to eat and then made their way back to Jasper.

It was only six o'clock in the evening, but it had been a long day for both Marcus and Candice. He was surprised Candice had managed to make it so long through her first real outing after her accident.

He slowed down as they approached the park gate and Candice woke up.

"Are we home?" she asked.

"No, we just made it to the gate. You can go back to sleep if you want."

She winced. "I don't think that I can. It's not very comfortable sleeping in a car, to be honest."

"No. I know."

Jimmy showed their pass at the gate. There was hardly anyone on the road—it was just them, the mountains and an odd goat that had ambled down to eat grass along the highway.

"That was a good day," Candice sighed.

"It was."

She looked back at Marcus. "He's fast asleep."

"Car rides are magic for him." Jimmy laughed and then frowned at something he saw in the distance—flashing four-ways and a woman waving her arms frantically from the shoulder, where there was a small dirt road that led to one of the recreation areas off the Yellowhead Highway.

"What's going on here?" Jimmy murmured. He pulled off the road and parked the car close to the woman's van, then rolled down his window as the woman lurched over, her hand on her very pregnant belly.

"Thank God," the woman whispered breathlessly. "I need help."

"Sure. What's wrong?" Jimmy asked, shutting off the ignition.

"My husband, he was driving and he just passed out! I don't know what happened. I had to steer the car the best I could and managed to pull off here, but he's not waking up."

"Have you called an ambulance?" Jimmy asked calmly.

She shook her head, trembling. "No. I didn't…think."

"It's okay. We've got it and I'm a paramedic. I can

help." Jimmy turned to Candice, who was already pulling out her phone and calling emergency services from Hinton, since it was closer to where they were, between Jasper and Hinton. "Stay with Marcus."

Candice nodded and took the keys from him as she gave their coordinates to the first responders in Hinton.

Jimmy got out of the car and grabbed his medical kit from the trunk. He pulled on his gloves and followed the terrified woman to her van.

"What's his name?" Jimmy asked.

"Steve," she whispered.

"And what's yours?" Jimmy asked as he reached in and felt for a pulse.

"Mary."

"Mary, I'm going to get your husband out of the van and I'm going to check his airways, okay?" Jimmy was trying not to alarm her, but there was a faint, sluggish pulse. The cause of Steve's unconsciousness could be as simple as low blood sugar or as serious as a stroke. He needed to get Steve on his back so he could check his airways and elevate his legs.

Candice got out of the car. The windows had been opened and the doors were locked, so Marcus was safe, asleep and close by.

"Ambulance is on its way," Candice said. "Thirty minutes out."

Jimmy nodded. He moved and extracted Steve from the front seat, lying him on the ground. He positioned Steve on his back and then loosened his belt and unbuttoned his shirt a bit—anything to keep restrictions of blood flow to a minimum.

He then checked to see if anything was blocking the airway, it wasn't.

"Steve? Can you hear me?" Jimmy asked as he

checked the ABCs, but there was no response. He raised Steve's legs at least twelve inches off the ground, hoping for some response, but there was none.

Dammit.

He was going to have to do CPR. He looked at Candice and shook his head. Candice nodded in silent response and moved to Mary, to keep her occupied.

"Mary, I'm Candice and I'm a first responder. Can you tell me what happened?"

"He was driving me to the hospital. My water broke about an hour ago." Mary winced and breathed deep.

"You're in labor?" Candice asked, stunned.

Jimmy whipped his head around from where he was doing CPR. "She's in labor?"

"How far apart are your contractions, Mary?"

Mary shrugged. "I don't know, less than a minute. This is my fourth baby."

"Candice, you need to get the emergency blanket out of my trunk and get Mary set up in the back of her van. Okay?"

Candice nodded and moved quickly. She opened the hatch of Mary's van and set up the emergency solar blanket, then had Mary sit down on it.

"Do you feel any pressure, Mary? Any urgency to push?" Candice asked.

"Oh, yeah. I wasn't paying attention before…but I feel it." Mary winced again. "I just want to push."

Candice grabbed gloves from Jimmy's vehicle while he continued his compressions.

"I've never delivered a baby," she said under her breath.

"You can do this. This is her fourth, remember your first aid and your basic training," he said. There was no way they could switch. Jimmy had to keep up with compressions, and with Candice just getting over a concussion, there was no way she'd be able to keep up with the CPR.

Candice nodded and he watched her make her way back to Mary while he kept the CPR going on Steve. He was hoping he'd hear that sweet sound of a siren soon.

"The baby is crowning," Candice called out.

Come on, Steve. Wake up and see your baby being born.

That was when he heard Steve gasp.

Jimmy rolled him on his side. "Breathe for me. Breathe."

He finally heard a siren in the distance and he breathed a sigh of relief.

"You're okay, Steve. You're okay. I'm Jimmy Liu, a paramedic. You were unconscious."

"Mary?" Steve croaked.

"She's okay," Jimmy reassured him as the ambulance pulled up, its sirens off, but with the lights flashing. Jimmy glanced over and Marcus was still out like a light.

The doors of the ambulance opened and Jimmy spoke with the paramedics, giving them all the information he'd gathered while examining Steve.

"Jimmy, I need your help!" Candice called out.

"We've got this," the paramedic said.

Jimmy nodded and headed over to help Candice.

"The baby is not coming. A shoulder might be stuck," Candice said calmly.

"Okay. We need to get Mary into the McRoberts maneuver." Jimmy climbed in behind Mary. "Mary, I need you to bring your legs up toward your tummy. Candice, try to move the baby to free the shoulder."

Candice nodded, but he could briefly see the concern in her eye.

Jimmy sat behind Mary and helped hold her legs. If this didn't work during the next contraction, he'd push on her belly.

"Okay, Mary, when you feel the next contraction, push!" Jimmy ordered.

Mary cried out and Candice moved the baby gently. That was all it took and the baby was quickly delivered. Candice held the infant in her gloved hands.

"It's a girl!" Candice said, her voice shaking.

The baby let out a cry and Jimmy congratulated Mary as Candice laid the baby down on her belly. They wouldn't cut the cord here in the back of the van.

A second ambulance pulled up and paramedics came rushing over. Jimmy climbed out of the back of the van and noticed that Marcus was awake, staring at the lights.

Candice covered Mary and the baby with another blanket, and she seemed to be gazing at the happy mom and healthy baby with longing.

It caused a twinge of longing in him, too, and made him pause, thinking about the baby they had lost. It broke his heart that he never got to share in the joy of the pregnancy with Candice, hadn't been there to comfort her in the sadness of the loss. They'd never met their son or daughter, never have the chance to watch their child grow. The thoughts and emotions threatened to overwhelm him, but he forced himself back into the present moment. His son needed him. And, right now, he really needed his son.

He removed his gloves and disposed of them in one of the biomedical waste containers the ambulance had. He sanitized his hands, then got Marcus, lifting his little boy out of the car and holding him tight.

"Daddy, look!"

"I know, right, buddy?" Jimmy said, kissing him.

Mary was being put on a stretcher with the baby and Candice was cleaning up and giving the paramedics information on the birth.

She came over and shut the back door of Mary's van, making sure it was secure.

"We have to wait for the tow truck," Candice said. "I have all their information."

Jimmy nodded.

"Candy, look!" Marcus said, pointing to the ambulances.

"I know!" Candice smiled. "There's a tow truck coming soon, too!"

Marcus made a face, his eyes wide, as Jimmy looked at him.

"Sounds fun, right, buddy?" Jimmy asked.

Marcus nodded. "I sit."

"Okay." He set Marcus back in the back seat with his toys and a cup of juice, making himself comfortable to wait it out, "reading" a book that was upside down.

Jimmy sighed and leaned against the car, Candice next to him as they watched the ambulances pull off the side road and head out onto the highway, back to Hinton.

"That was…something," Candice said, laughing nervously.

"It was." Jimmy smiled down at her. "You did a good job."

"That was the first time I delivered a baby."

"Your first time?" he asked. "I would've never guessed it."

"Yeah, you don't get many pregnant women up on the mountain passes."

"You did a good job for your first time."

"Thanks." She nodded. "So did you, knowing that move to help the baby and helping the father."

"You kept your calm, too. We make a good team."

A strange look passed on her face. "Yes. We do."

"But what?" he asked.

"Well, helping Mary deliver that baby just makes me want to go back to school even more. I mean, what's keeping me here, really? What's stopping me from packing up and going? There's nothing for me in Jasper anymore...is there?"

Jimmy's heart sunk down to the soles of his feet.

You can't be the one thing that holds her back.

"Yeah. You should do that." He turned and looked down the highway, watching as the tow truck finally came into view.

"I'll give the driver the information and then we can head back to Jasper." Candice walked away and Jimmy sighed.

He couldn't be selfish. She should go back to school and follow her dreams. She was smart and had a clear, calm presence. She would make an amazing doctor. Look at how well she'd handled unexpectedly having to deliver a baby. He had been so proud of her in that moment.

He couldn't hold her back from seeing what she was truly capable of.

Even if he wanted her to stay with him more than anything in the world.

CHAPTER ELEVEN

"Answer the door, Jimmy!" Liena shouted from the kitchen.

"Okay." Jimmy really hoped his mother's shouting didn't wake up Marcus. They weren't quite ready for his birthday party. At least the couple of other kids who were invited—mostly neighborhood families his parents knew—hadn't arrived yet, so it was still pretty quiet.

He was so behind schedule.

He opened the door and was relieved to see Candice standing there.

Jimmy hadn't seen her in a couple of days, not since they went to Hinton.

He'd been keeping his distance since she mentioned wanting to go back to school, but it was such a relief to see her.

He'd missed her and she looked so nice. Her dark hair was tied back and she was wearing a pretty floral blouse and denim skirt. It was summery and casual, and she looked so beautiful. It was all he could do not to stare at her in appreciation.

"Thank God it's you," he said in exasperation, the balloon he'd been trying to hold closed deflating with a horrible sound.

Candice watched the balloon zoom out of his hand and across the room. "Problems?"

"Marcus didn't sleep last night. I had to attend a rescue and I'm behind on blowing up balloons. It's not going well."

"Well, your mom called me and asked me to come early." Candice handed him a brightly colored package. "For Marcus."

"Thanks. I wonder what it could be," he quipped and then stepped aside to let her in. "How have you been?"

"I'm good," she said quickly, barely looking at him.

Yep. It was definitely awkward.

"You sure?" he asked.

She looked at him like he was crazy. "Why wouldn't I be sure?"

"You just seem on edge," Jimmy said, closing the door.

"If you must know, I am anxious about returning to work tomorrow. I'm worried about what's waiting for me and how much paperwork there's going to be."

"Well," he finally said, "I could use your help decorating. Hopefully that will take your mind off work and the horrible mess that Stu made."

He was teasing, hoping to bring levity to the situation. Hoping to get a rise out of her and take their relationship back to the way it was.

What relationship?

He didn't have a relationship with her and he had to remind himself of that.

"Sounds good."

His mother came out of the kitchen and smiled. "Candice, I'm so glad you're here!"

"Glad to be here, Mrs. Liu."

"Liena," his mother said. "Can you come help me finish decorating the cake?"

"Of course." Candice moved past him to the kitchen.

"Mom, she's helping me with balloons," Jimmy protested.

His mother looked at him. "I don't know why you're struggling with this—you're full of enough hot air."

His father, who was sitting in the living room doing nothing but reading a newspaper, laughed.

Jimmy glared at him. "You know, you could help, Pop."

His father raised his paper higher and said, "You're doing a fine job, son."

Jimmy rolled his eyes and went back to blowing up balloons, trying to rush through the decorating he was doing so that he could speak to Candice before the rest of the guests arrived. He watched her in the kitchen with his mother, helping get the food ready for their neighbors, and it warmed his heart to see Candice working so well with his mother.

She wanted to go back to school and he had to let her. It was her dream.

He couldn't hold her back.

He had to let her go.

Again.

When Marcus woke up, Jimmy's father scooted upstairs to get him while Jimmy finished the last touches on the decorations inside as the first of the guests arrived.

He didn't think that this would be so much work, but Marcus had made friends with a few of the toddlers in the neighborhood and his parents had insisted on giving Marcus a proper birthday, even though Jimmy couldn't remember his parents ever giving him a birthday as elaborate as this. He'd get a cake and Logan would come over, but it would be brief.

And usually it was just his mom who would be there, as his dad had to run the motel.

Jimmy didn't know who half these people were, but they knew his parents and Marcus, and several of them seemed to know Candice.

As Jimmy navigated the crowd, he watched Candice from a distance.

He couldn't help himself.

And the more he watched her, the more he wanted her.

His blood heated as he thought of their kiss before her accident. It was all he could think about these days. In fact, he hadn't stopped thinking about her since he'd first returned to Jasper and run in to her again. She was like a ghost coming back to haunt him.

Taunt him.

"It's time to sing 'Happy Birthday' to the birthday boy," his mother said, interrupting his troubling train of thought.

"Of course," Jimmy said, shaking thoughts of Candice from his head.

He had to focus on his son.

He found Marcus running around with a couple of kids in the backyard. Candice was also outside, talking with one of his neighbors—another single father, about their age—and a pang of jealously hit him.

Focus.

Jimmy picked up Marcus. "Time for cake!"

Marcus clapped his hands and Jimmy sat down with him at the picnic table.

His mother came out of the house carrying a cake in the shape of the ugliest dog Jimmy had ever seen, but it made Marcus happy and everyone sang "Happy Birthday."

Marcus squealed in delight, and with his help, they blew out the candle and his mom took pictures, blinding them all.

"Come to Yéye," his father said, holding out his hands. "We'll have cake together."

Jimmy handed over Marcus to his dad while his mother began cutting the cake. Looking around, he noticed that Candice had headed inside, so he got up to follow her. It was much quieter inside.

"You need help?" he asked.

Candice jumped, startled. "Why did you sneak up on me like that?"

"Sorry. I didn't mean to."

"I'm trying to find the ice-cream bowls your mom said were in here. I found the tray and the spoons, but not the paper bowls."

"They're in the dining room." Jimmy headed into the dining room to grab them from the hutch, where his mother had squirrelled away party stuff. "Here they are."

"Great." Candice took the bag of paper bowls from him.

"Are you avoiding me?" he asked.

"What?" she asked, shocked.

"You've been acting weird."

"I don't know what you're talking about. You've been avoiding me!"

Jimmy shut the door to the dining room so they'd have some privacy.

"I'm not avoiding you." Only that was a lie. He was.

"Really?" she asked, unconvinced. She took a step closer to him.

"I've been busy."

"Something changed after that rescue," she said.

"Nothing has changed except…" His pulse was thundering in his ears. All he wanted was her. All he could think of was that kiss they shared.

"What, Jimmy?" she asked, a blush in her cheeks. "What's wrong?"

"Candice." And before he could think rationally about where they were or why it was a bad idea, he pulled her into his arms and kissed her, like he'd wanted to ever since the last time he'd kissed her.

The bag of paper bowls dropped to the floor and her arms were around him. All he could think about were her lips on his. His blood was singing and his body burned with desire for her.

He wanted her.

Only her.

He wanted to taste her, to touch every inch of her.

He wanted to be lost in her kisses.

"Candice? Where's the ice cream?" his mother called out.

Candice broke the kiss. "That shouldn't have happened. I'm your boss… I… That shouldn't have happened."

She picked up the package of bowls and opened the door, scurrying out of the room, leaving Jimmy standing there, stunned.

He shouldn't have kissed her. He didn't know what he was thinking and he was angry at himself.

Hadn't he convinced himself that he wasn't going to hold her back? That he wasn't going to ruin her dreams?

He shouldn't have kissed her. He had to put a stop to this once and for all.

Because the only dreams that he was willing to ruin were his own.

Candice couldn't get that kiss out of her head.

The first one she'd thought about a lot, but this one was heated. Urgent. Her body still thrummed with need.

She couldn't believe that she had lost control like that.

It had been so hot.

She had to get control of herself, had to figure out what she wanted. Yes, she wanted to go back to school, but she wanted Jimmy, too. She wanted both him and Marcus in her life, but could she put her heart on the line again? Could she walk away from the guarantees of medicine for the uncertainty of Jimmy's love? She was so scared of being hurt, of losing it all, of ending up alone, again.

After Marcus had opened his gifts, she left discreetly, telling Liena she had a headache and saying nothing to Jimmy.

She had to put distance between them. She had to think.

When she returned to work the next day, she had a lot of paperwork waiting for her, so she spent her time doing that, because she wasn't cleared to fly quite yet and she didn't want to go out into the field until she did her round on the Skyline Trail.

Stu kept Jimmy busy so they didn't have to say much to each other.

Which was perfect.

Was it?

She was missing him. Missing their talks. Before he'd come back into her life, she'd been lonely, but used to it. Now, she felt that absence, that ache of isolation, too keenly.

So she threw herself into her paperwork, hoping it would take her mind off everything.

It didn't.

Candice knew that she was fooling herself. Especially as they were getting ready to go on their back-country round. She was going to have to make amends.

She worried her bottom lip and rubbed her temples before pushing the intercom to the ambulance bay.

"Jimmy, can you come to my office?"

"Sure thing, boss."

She cringed at him calling her *boss*.

No, this was better. This was normal.

Only a part of her couldn't help but wonder, was it?

Jimmy knocked and entered her office.

"You wanted to see me?" he asked. She could tell he was uncomfortable, too.

He looks so good in his uniform.

"Tomorrow, you ready for our backcountry trip?" she asked.

"I am. I packed a basic medical kit."

"Most of the injuries, if we encounter any, are minor. Major rescues are usually called in and we do a helicopter rescue if we can. The Skyline Trail is well populated and slots of time, with the number of hikers all on, always fill up."

He nodded. "I remember."

"Stu will drop us off at the Maligne trailhead and we'll walk toward Signal Mountain before being picked up again."

"You're not going the opposite way?" he asked.

"No, I like to go that way because starting at Maligne, you've already gained a lot of elevation and can go downhill."

He smiled. "That sounds smart."

"Look, I know that things have been weird—"

"I know. And it was my fault. I'm sorry for what happened. I want you to know it won't happen again. I want to be friends, Candice."

She knew it was for the best, but still felt the stab of disappointment, and was angry at herself for being disappointed. She shouldn't care. She wouldn't care. If he could walk away, then so could she. "I want that, too."

"Good." Jimmy nodded. "Do you need me for anything else?"

"No. I'll meet you here tomorrow morning about seven a.m., that way we can get a start on the trail and get to the Snowbowl site in the first day."

"Sounds good. I'll see you bright and early tomorrow." Jimmy left her office and she released the breath that she hadn't known that she was holding.

It was better this way.

Was it really though?

She shook her head, trying to dispel the niggling thought in her mind. Trying to ignore the voice in her head telling her to take a chance on Jimmy Liu, like she wanted to.

It was a want that terrified her. Terrified her of being hurt again. After Jimmy, and then Chad, she couldn't handle another broken heart.

It was going to be a long four days indeed.

CHAPTER TWELVE

STU DROVE THEM out to the Maligne trailhead. They weren't the only hikers that were about to start on their journey and there were already other hikers on the various points of the trail, judging by the way the parking lot was full.

Every slot of the Skyline Trail had been booked for July and August, while September and October were almost full, too. It was one of the most popular backcountry hikes in Jasper so you had to claim your spot well in advance and there were always hikers waiting in town to see if someone canceled.

There was one lodge at the halfway point of the trail that catered to people who had the money to pay for a night or two of all-inclusive lodging and, thankfully, they were going to stay at the lodge for one night, because it was included in their rounds. They wouldn't reach the lodge until their second night, though, so they'd be camping out tonight.

She had her list of everyone that should be on the trail and she knew what to do if they found someone on the trail who shouldn't be there, though she hoped that they wouldn't have that problem.

Their plan was to get to the Snowbowl campground before nightfall, and the ride to the trailhead had been quiet, with Jimmy going through his pack and Candice trying not to think about everything she was feeling and the fact it would be just be the two of them out there.

At least they would have their work.

That would distract her.

You're here to do your job and train Jimmy. That's it. After this, you won't have to hike the trail with him ever again if you don't want to.

Stu parked the truck. "Got everything you need, Lavoie?"

Candice nodded. "And I have my satellite phone ready in case we have to call in a helicopter. Hopefully we won't."

Stu nodded. "When I did the Tonquin trail you were supposed to do, we didn't encounter anything really worrisome, just some bog foot from walking too long in wet gear and minor injuries."

"Let's hope we have the same luck," Jimmy said from the back.

"Thanks, Stu. See you at Signal Mountain in four days," Candice said.

Stu nodded and Candice climbed out of the truck. She grabbed her gear and slipped it on her back. Jimmy clipped his pack on and handed Candice her walking poles. With all the gear they were carrying and her ankle just recovered, she was happy to have the walking poles for support.

Stu drove out of the packed parking lot with a wave.

"It's busy here," Jimmy remarked.

"It is. It's one of the most popular trails. That being said, there won't be a ton of people on it. Or shouldn't be. I'm hoping we don't have to issue fines."

"Let's hope not."

They made their way to start of the trailhead, with

Candice leading the climb, as she'd done this route before. She liked hiking the Skyline Trail and it was a good hike to test Jimmy on, even though she knew that he and her brother had done this hike on their own before.

Still, it had been some time since Jimmy had been here and she wondered if he'd struggle with the elevation climb after spending so much time away from Jasper. She wondered if he had any residual pain in his legs or hip that would affect his hiking. It had been five years since his injuries, but it was possible the pain still flared up now and again, especially as he'd said it took him a year to recover, but so far he was doing well.

As they kept walking, she kept turning around to check on him, but he was keeping up with her.

After an hour and a half of hiking, they came to the Evelyn Creek campsite.

"We didn't hike very far," Jimmy said as they sat down on a picnic table.

"No, we'll stay here for half an hour, check on the campers that are here or come through and fill our water bottles. Then we'll continue on."

Jimmy nodded and set down his pack. "I always thought it was strange to have a campsite so close to the trailhead."

"Well, it depends which way you're coming and how late you started. Some people start from Signal Mountain and end up at Maligne. Personally, I like this way better."

He nodded and then sat down next to her on the picnic table. "How is your ankle?"

"It's fine." It ached a bit, but she didn't want to worry him and it was nothing she couldn't deal with. She had a tensor bandage to wrap it tonight, when they got to the Snowbowl campsite.

And she was looking forward to getting to the lodge near the Curator campground tomorrow night.

Even just to have a bed for one night would be great.

"Do you want me to make the rounds and see if anyone is camping?"

"Sure. I'll stay here and watch the trail."

Jimmy nodded and slipped off the picnic table to check the campsite. She seriously doubted anyone would be there. If anyone was, they'd likely left and started off early up the trail. Still, they had to make their rounds.

Jimmy came jogging back. "There's a camper with a swollen hand. Probably a sprain, but I said I would look at it."

"Okay." Candice jumped down off the picnic table. "Let's go."

They picked up their packs and made it down to the hiker's campsite.

Candice checked to make sure he had a permit and he did. He told them he was on his way down the trail, having started at Signal Mountain. He planned to finish a bit early, but slipped and fell, spraining his hand the previous night, so instead of finishing early he spent his last night camping and was having a hard time packing up his gear. Joshua Mooney was a young man from Jasper and liked to do the Skyline at least once a year.

Jimmy checked out his hand.

"Do you have someone picking you up at Maligne?" Candice asked. "You can't drive with that hand."

"Yeah. I have my satellite phone to call my ride. Told them I'd be down there in a couple of hours, but I'm having issues packing up and getting out of here."

"We can help," Candice said.

"You might have a dislocated knuckle," Jimmy said. "Once you get picked up you should head to the hospital in Jasper and get it checked out. I'll wrap it, but you definitely need an X-ray and some splints."

"Thanks," Joshua said. "This is the first time I've hurt myself on a trail. Or hurt myself this bad. Glad you guys came by."

"Glad to help," Candice said, and she shared a smile with Jimmy as he finished taking care of Joshua's hand.

After Joshua was all wrapped up, they packed up his gear, got his food down from out of the tree and helped him get his gear on his back, ready to make his way to his ride.

"Please check in with Mountain Rescue when you get to the trailhead. I want to make sure that you're okay. I'm going to be calling in your last coordinates," Candice warned.

Joshua nodded. "Thanks, Ranger Lavoie. I will."

Candice and Jimmy watched as Joshua continued his way down the trailhead.

"Well, if that's the worst of it, I'll be happy," Jimmy said.

"For sure." She shook her head. "Come on, let's make sure the campsite is cleaned and we'll continue on to Snowbowl. It's still another two or three hours before we can stop for the night."

Jimmy nodded.

They packed up the rest of their gear, Candice made the call about Joshua and they made sure they left no trace before continuing on their ascension of the Skyline Trail.

Jimmy walked behind Candice, trying to show her that it wasn't hard for him. That he could handle mountain rescue, but it had been far too long since he'd done this hike with Logan. And even then, he didn't remember it being so brutal.

But then he'd been younger. Not over thirty and unused to the altitude in the mountains. His hip was hurting a bit, but he could manage. He was glad when they took their breaks, or when they met someone else along the trail and checked in with the other hikers—so far, everyone they'd run into had a permit—and there was a couple of times they had to stop because Candice spotted a bear and pulled out her binoculars. That's when they had to give wide berth and make sure the bear knew that they were coming.

One thing Jimmy had forgotten was the spectacular vista as they made their way up from the trailhead toward the snow-covered notch.

There were times when he'd stop to catch his breath, and also just to marvel at the wonder of the place where he'd grown up. High peaks and slender trees, blue glacier-fed lakes. Granite and earth, blue and gold. It really was beautiful.

It made him forget about all the horrors he'd seen while serving. It made everything else seem so small in comparison.

They had spent some time in the Little Shovel campsite to check on hikers before they could continue on to the Snowbowl, so the hike took longer than Candice's estimated two to three hours.

Once they got to Snowbowl, one of the busiest campgrounds on the trail, they went around to check on everyone who was camping before setting up their own campsite. It was then that it hit Jimmy—he and Candice would be sharing a tent.

There wasn't room enough for two tents on their site, as they had to minimize the impact on the environment.

He could tell by the way that Candice was worrying her lip that she hadn't thought of this arrangement, either.

"Do you want me to sleep outside?" He had done that with Logan.

"No. We can make this work. We're adults."

"Right." But he knew that she wasn't completely convinced.

They pitched their tent on the tent pad, grabbed what they needed for their dinner and Jimmy made the small campfire out of the dried brush that was on the ground and homemade fire starters he'd packed, while Candice made her rounds to the six other campsites that were occupied.

It actually shocked Jimmy how busy it was, but then, he probably shouldn't have been surprised.

Summer was a popular time and it was a nice night. There were barely any mosquitos hanging around near the tree line and there wasn't much wind, but it was a bit cold and he was thankful for his warm clothes and his sleeping bag.

Candice came back when he had the fire started.

"Everything good?"

She nodded and pulled out her little folding camp chair, setting it up so she could sit in front of the fire. "Everyone is healthy and they know you're a paramedic should there be any issues in the night."

"Good." He pulled out a couple of bags of freeze-dried meals and added water to them before heating them over the fire. It was food that was easy to pack in and out. It tasted horrible, but it was only for a couple of days.

The sun was beginning to set and it was a clear enough night that he was hoping to see a few stars, though he didn't plan on staying up too late because he was exhausted from their hike.

"Tomorrow night at the lodge will be nice," Candice said. "It's my favorite part of doing the Skyline hike."

"Why's that?" he asked.

"It's a bed to sleep in, indoor plumbing and they feed us. No freeze-dried food for the night."

He grinned. "I can go for that. Your freeze-dried chicken is ready, by the way."

"Yum," she said, making a face, and he laughed.

"At least you don't have to do this hike in the winter."

"No, this trail is shut then, thank goodness, but there have been times when people still barged their way through and we've had to do winter rescues. Not too often, but still. You have to wonder about some people."

"For sure." Jimmy sat down on the ground in front of the fire and tried to pretend that his freeze-dried meal was something better than it was. "What's been your hardest rescue since you started here?"

"Hardest?"

Jimmy nodded. "Tell me about it, so I can learn. I mean, I'm still the newbie here."

She chuckled softly. "Avalanches are always hard. And mudslides. Mudslides are hard."

"Have you ever been in an avalanche?" he asked.

"Once. I was doing a rescue for someone who had been skiing at a high peak—one of those helicopter drops—and before we could extract him, an avalanche struck. I was tethered to my team and we just swam to the side—that's the best you can do." She frowned. "We lost the victim, though. There was nothing we could do and that was my toughest moment. It took so long to let that go." She sighed. "I blamed myself for the longest time."

"You blamed yourself?"

"Of course," she said. "It took a long time for me to realize that some things are out of my control and now I just keep trying to improve, so that I don't lose the next one."

Jimmy pondered that admission for a few minutes.

"What was yours?" she asked.

"What?" he asked.

"You served in the armed forces, you were a paramedic, so what was your hardest moment?"

"My hardest loss was…" It was even hard to say the word. "Logan."

She looked at him then, across the firelight. "Tell me."

And even though he hated talking about it, he just couldn't hold back anymore. There was something about being here with Candice, in a place that had also meant so much to him and her brother, that finally unlocked something inside him. He'd been carrying around that burden for so long. He wanted to be free.

"Our unit was attending a patrol that was down. Logan was the commanding officer and we were working together to get his men out. But then there was an air strike and the helicopter coming to take out wounded men was shot down. Logan and I were blown back by the explosion. When I came to, he was trapped under a wall next to me. The lower half of his body was being crushed and I tried everything—everything I could to save him—but…"

Candice didn't say anything for a few moments. The only sound was his pulse thundering in his ears and a few snaps from their fire as he relived that moment.

"There was nothing you could do," Candice finally said softly.

"No. Nothing. He just slipped away from me." Jimmy tried to hold back the tears.

"I know, Jimmy. We never blamed you. I hope you know that."

He nodded. "Thanks. It was hard to let him go."

"But you were there with him in his final moments and that matters," she said gently. "He had you beside him and I know that would have helped. It would have made him feel like things were going to be okay. There was no one he knew he could count on more than you. You were his best friend."

He glanced up at the sky, trying not to lose control of his emotions in front of her. The stars he'd been looking forward to seeing had started to come out.

"I never get tired of seeing that," Candice whispered, following his upward gaze with her own.

Jimmy glanced at her. She was so kind, so under-standing, and it meant a lot to him that she didn't blame him for Logan's death.

He loved her so much. Even after all this time.

"I think I'm going to head to bed." Jimmy picked up the remnants of their meal and the utensils, desperate to busy himself before he did something he would re-gret. "I'll get our packs up on the pole as soon as I'm done cleaning up."

"Sounds good. I'm beat." Candice put out the fire, covering it with dirt.

Jimmy silently watched the trail of smoke disappear into the darkening sky.

As soon as her head hit her tiny camping pillow, Can-dice fell asleep. She didn't hear Jimmy come into the tent and get into his own sleeping bag, but she did wake up when she heard him murmuring.

She sat up and glanced at her watch.

It was one in the morning.

It took her a moment for her eyes to adjust to the darkness and she could see that Jimmy was thrashing and sweating in his sleep.

Not that she blamed him.

She had seen the pain in his face as he talked about Logan's death. It had been hard for her to keep her composure. She knew what had killed Logan—his cause of death had been explained to them at the time—but she didn't know that Jimmy had been right there when it happened.

She also didn't know about the helicopter, which at least explained his aversion to them and why he'd acted so weird.

Candice couldn't even begin to imagine the pain he was going through, or had gone through. It almost broke her to see him grieving her brother still.

She unzipped her bag, scooting out into the coldness of the tent.

"Jimmy," she whispered.

He continued to thrash, locked in his nightmare.

"Candy," he called out, still asleep.

"I'm here."

"I'm sorry," he said. "Logan, I'm sorry. I let you down."

"Shh, no, you haven't." She touched his head and gently stroked his face. "You haven't. I'm here. I'm here."

"Candy?" he murmured, now half-awake.

"Yeah. I'm here."

"Good. Stay with me," he whispered.

"Okay." She pulled her sleeping back closer, snuggling up against Jimmy, her head close to his.

"Candy, I'm sorry."

"I know." She brushed the hair back off his face. "I know and it's okay."

"Good." And he drifted back into sleep.

She knew he wouldn't remember this and that was okay. She was here right now with him and she'd been a fool to think that she wouldn't be.

It was risky putting her heart on the line like this, but she couldn't stop herself.

She was still in love with Jimmy Liu and she always would be.

He'd always had her heart.

Always.

CHAPTER THIRTEEN

IT WAS A long hike to Curator campground and Candice made sure she got up and had her stuff packed before Jimmy knew that she had spent the night curled up beside him. She didn't want him to know that she had been privy to one his nightmares.

They had a long hike of forty-six kilometers ahead of them and she was looking forward to getting up closer to the notch and to the lodge, so she could have a decent night's sleep and some good food.

They had a quick breakfast after Jimmy retrieved their gear from the top of the pole used to avoid bears being attracted to the site.

After finishing packing everything up and filling their filtered water bottles from the stream, they made their way onto the trail. They were the last to leave their campground, as the other hikers had already made an early start after checking in with her.

Some were heading in the same direction, toward the Signal Mountain trailhead, and others were going back down toward the Maligne trailhead. They were still ascending, but tomorrow, as soon as they crested the notch, they would start their descent toward Signal Mountain.

They were right on track to finish on time, provided nothing bad happened, which she was really hoping wouldn't.

Candice was exhausted after a sleepless night, but it was worth it and she knew she was going to sleep well when they got to the lodge later on.

Jimmy was keeping up, and both of them were wearing dark sunglasses to protect their eyes from the sun. The UV rays were a wee bit stronger the higher they ascended. Even though that sun was hot, they wore long sleeves to protect themselves from the sun and the wind.

It was windier today, which slowed their hike, and it was just the two of them on the trail. Them, the mountains and the sky—which was the beauty of backcountry camping in Jasper.

They stopped after four hours to have a drink by a stream and eat something, taking off their packs and sitting down by the trickling water.

"I can see the notch. It's getting closer," Jimmy said, taking a deep breath.

"You're breathing hard. Are you okay?" Candice asked.

Jimmy nodded. "I'm getting used to the elevation again, but don't worry, I'm not showing any signs of AMS. My hip is stiff, but I'm good."

She cocked an eyebrow. "You could be delusional—let me check your hands."

Jimmy smiled and held out her hands. She lifted her sunglasses and examined his nail beds for the signs of cyanosis.

"You're good, but you will tell me if you're having issues, got it?"

"I'm okay, Candice. I swear." He took a bite of his

granola bar and looked out over the meadow. "Haven't seen a bear yet today."

"They're still fattening themselves up on shoots, dandelions and grass, and I believe it's caribou calving season still, so they'll be wherever the caribou are." She pulled out her binoculars and scanned the area. "There's nothing as far as these binoculars can see. So that's good."

"I've been watching for tracks, but nothing."

Candice sat down and handed Jimmy the binoculars so he could take a look.

"How long do you think until we get to the lodge?" he asked casually as he looked around with the binoculars.

"A couple of hours. I don't see any hikers on the horizon at all." She finished her granola bar and packed her garbage away.

"So you mean we might actually get to relax at the lodge tonight?" he teased.

"We got to relax last night. No one was hurt and everyone had a permit. It was all good."

"I forgot to ask yesterday if Joshua made it safe off the trail?"

Candice nodded. "When you were using the facilities, Stu called and told me Joshua got to the hospital."

Jimmy snorted. "Facilities. Sure."

She laughed. "Yeah, they're not the best and not really private. It's rustic."

"Rustic? I think the word you're looking for is primitive."

"What do you expect? This is a national park and this is backcountry camping. If you want facilities you have to get yourself a camper or a recreational vehicle and camp down outside of town or rent a cabin."

"Don't think I haven't thought about it. I'm getting a bit old to be sleeping on the ground."

She rolled her eyes. "Hardly. Shall we go?"

"Yes! Let's get to the lodge." Jimmy handed her the binoculars and she slung them around her neck.

They clipped their rucksacks back on and headed up the trail. The lodge and the Curator campground were a bit off the Skyline Trail, but both were popular places to spend the night.

When they arrived, they made their rounds in the Curator campground to make sure that everyone there was allowed to be there, and then Jimmy tended to a minor wound on someone's calf that was a bit infected.

After that they hiked to the lodge, where the last little cabin was waiting for them.

Candice's heart sank when she saw it and its one double bed. Her pulse began to race at the thought of having to share a bed with Jimmy tonight.

It's no different than sleeping next to him in the tent.

That was how she had to rationalize it in her mind. It was for one night.

"Tight quarters," Jimmy remarked.

"Yeah." She worried her bottom lip.

"It'll be okay. I'm just glad it's a real bed and we don't have to even use our sleeping bag. I saw the propane tank, which means heat, right?"

Candice laughed, his enthusiasm breaking the tension that only she, apparently, was feeling. She was relieved about that.

"Yeah, it means heat," she said, dropping her pack into the corner. "Let's wash up and get some dinner."

"Sweet!"

She laughed again and poured the water out of the pitcher into the washstand. She cleaned herself up, trying to keep her back to Jimmy for some privacy, but she couldn't help but peak over her shoulder to watch him change his shirt.

Focus.

She brushed out her hair, braiding it into two braids because it was the easiest to deal with. Once they were both presentable, they made their way out of their private lodge to the main lodge to have dinner.

They passed the stables where the pack animals were kept, then made their way up into the larger lodge, where they joined a group of fifteen other hikers for a home-cooked dinner.

This was Candice's favorite part of the Skyline Trail and it had been some time since she'd been able to come up here and experience this.

Jimmy charmed his way into conversations with the other hikers, a few of whom they had met the previous night at the Snowbowl campground.

The dinner was simple and filling, and soon they made their way back to their lodge. The sun was setting behind the mountain range and they both sat out on their little private deck to enjoy the quiet.

"I could stay here for a few days," Jimmy said with a sigh. "This is a nice way to end a day of hiking."

"It is. It's a nice perk." She glanced over at him and couldn't help but smile. It was nice to sit here with him. She hadn't realized how lonely she'd felt all these years—it was only since Jimmy's return that she'd seen how empty her life had been. Even when she was with Chad, she had been lonely.

She'd been keeping her distance ever since that kiss at Marcus's birthday party, but she missed Jimmy and Marcus. Life was empty and quiet without them.

Logan had been her best friend, but so had Jimmy. And she had missed her best friend.

"What?" Jimmy asked.

"What do you mean?"

"You're smiling at me."

"Is that wrong?" she asked.

"No, I guess just a bit odd since we didn't seem to part on good terms at Marcus's party."

She sighed. "Yeah, I know. I was dealing with a lot of emotions."

"I get that," he said quietly. "I've missed you the last few days."

"Same." Her cheeks heated even more. She got up. "I'm going to go change."

She rushed inside the cabin, embarrassed but also thrilled to hear that he had missed her, too. That he'd been thinking about her.

The door opened and closed behind her.

"Candice, I've never stopping caring for you. I came back to see you once, but you were married and looked so happy. I didn't want to disrupt your life, so I left."

Her heart skipped a beat and she spun around. "You came back?"

"You looked so happy with your husband. I didn't want to intrude." Jimmy reached into his pack and he pulled out a photo. It was worn and crinkled, like it had been viewed a thousand times. "I carried this with me. Logan told me I'd hold you back so I left, but I've never stopped thinking about you."

She couldn't believe it.

He gripped his hand over hers so they were both holding the photo. "Your photo saved me, Candice. So many times."

She handed it back to him so he could pack it away.

"If it hadn't been for Logan…you would've stayed in Jasper?" she asked, emotions swirling through her.

"Yes."

Jimmy couldn't believe that he was admitting this, but he couldn't help himself. Not when it came to Candice. She got under his skin and he was terrified by what it meant, but he wanted to be with her.

Even if it was just for one night, for one moment.

He never wanted to hurt her, but he needed her. Now.

"I can't believe it," she whispered.

"What?" he asked.

"I can't believe that you carried that around."

"Of course I did. I wanted you, too, Candice."

"And now?" she asked.

"I care for you—I always will—but I still don't want to hold you back."

"You're not," she said.

He touched her cheek and ran his hand down her neck. Her pulse was racing a mile a minute—he could feel it under his fingers. She moved closer to him, her fingers lightly brushing over his face, which made him feel like he was on fire.

He closed his eyes, trying to regain control over his senses, knowing it was Candice touching him. Something that he'd dreamed about for so long.

"Jimmy," she whispered, her voice catching in her throat.

He cupped her face and pulled her close, tight against his body.

He wanted to kiss her again, like they had before. Only he didn't want this kiss to end. This is what passion with Candice tasted like. He remembered it so keenly. It was sweet and honeyed and he wanted it all.

It rocked him to his core. He didn't want this moment to end. He wanted more.

Oh, God.

"Candice, I don't know if we should," he said, even though he wanted to.

"Do you not want me now?" she asked breathlessly.

"I do."

Candice touched his chest. "I think we should, because I want you, Jimmy. I always have."

"I want you, too. I can't help it. I've always wanted you."

And it was true.

He wanted Candice.

She was here. He was here.

And he wanted her.

Candice melted in his arms again.

This was what she wanted—to be swept up in his arms.

She wasn't one-hundred-percent sure he wouldn't hurt her, but tonight she was willing to take the risk. Just like she had the night they first made love ten years ago.

She was ready and wanted to be with Jimmy in this moment. Again.

Righting a wrong.

She'd always wanted Jimmy and had never felt for another man what she felt for him. It was fierce, overpowering. It scared her and thrilled her how she burned for him after all this time. He woke her up when she hadn't even realized she'd been asleep.

"Candice, if you're sure."

"I am."

She shrugged out of her shirt. "Touch me," she whispered.

"Oh, God. Candice." Jimmy scooped her up and carried her the short distance to the bed, lying her down, pressing his kisses over her body. Over her lips, her neck and lower.

"You make me feel alive again," he whispered and then kissed her deeply, their tongues entwining.

They made quick work getting out of their clothes so they could be skin-to-skin. She ran her hands over his body, touching him, reveling in the sensation of being with him again. Even if it made her vulnerable. She ran her hands over his scars, and it made her breath catch in her throat to see what damage had been done to him.

He caught her hand. "I'm okay now. I'm here."

She nodded. "I know."

She opened her legs for him to settle between her thighs. She was already wet with need and she arched her hips toward him, wanting him to touch her.

To take her.

Wanting to feel all of him.

"I don't have protection," he groaned.

"I'm on birth control."

"You're sure?"

"Yes." She bucked her hips, making him moan. "I'm sure."

Jimmy kissed her again, deeply, his hands on her body branding her skin where he touched her. His touch making her blood sing.

"You're so beautiful," he murmured against her neck. His hand slid between her legs, stroking her and driving her wild with need.

"I want you inside me."

"Oh, God, I want that, too."

He covered her body with his and thrust.

Candice cried out. She couldn't stop herself. Being with him was overwhelming. It's what she had always wanted.

"You're so tight," he moaned.

She moved her hips, urging him as he moved slowly at first, when all she wanted was it hard and fast.

She wanted Jimmy to possess her, to take her.

Only him.

He moved faster, making her cling to him as he took her with urgent need. The sweet release built deep inside her and she succumbed. Pleasure overtook her as he continued thrusting until he stilled, his release coming shortly after hers.

He rolled to the side and she curled up next to him, listening to him breathe in the darkness. It was comfortable. Safe.

And that safety scared her.

The last time she'd felt this way all the people she cared about were still alive.

"Candice?" he asked. "Are you crying?"

"No."

She sat up and brushed away the tears. "I'm fine."

Only that was a lie. She knew she couldn't trust him with her heart…but she'd lost it to him, anyway.

CHAPTER FOURTEEN

LOUD BANGING BROUGHT her out of her slumber.

She didn't know when she'd fallen asleep, just that she'd fallen asleep curled up against Jimmy and they didn't have their clothes on.

"Ranger Lavoie!" The frenzied shout came from outside.

Candice jumped out of bed and threw on her glasses. It was five in the morning, and the light was just tinging the sky.

The banging continued.

"What's going on?" Jimmy asked groggily.

"Ranger Lavoie!" the urgent voice yelled.

"Coming!" Candice shouted. She frantically began pulling on her clothes so that she could answer the door.

She opened the door. "What's wrong."

"A hiker fell in the lake—we don't know how long they've been there, so we're doing CPR."

"Okay. We're coming." Candice scrambled and grabbed her satellite phone.

"What's going on?" Jimmy asked as he pulled on his gear.

"Hiker fell in the lake. I'm calling the helicopter."

A strange look passed on Jimmy's face. "What?"

"They're doing CPR down by the lake. See what you can do," she said.

"On my way." Jimmy grabbed his pack and headed out the door to follow the manager of the lodge to the lake.

"Mountain Rescue," Stu's voice said over the phone.

"Stu, it's Lavoie. I need a helicopter stat to Shovel Pass."

"I'll dispatch one right away."

Candice was glad the lodge was well known so she didn't have to give her coordinates and that the helicopter would have lots of room to land.

She pulled on her boots and grabbed her pack, heading to the lake. It was foggy out and she could see how a hiker making one wrong move might stumble off the path into the lake. She moved along the path she knew so well and came across Jimmy, who had taken over CPR for the hiker.

"What can I do?" Candice asked, kneeling down on the opposite side of the hiker.

"I brought a defibrillator. I need that."

Candice nodded and went into Jimmy's pack, finding the defibrillator at the top. He was still doing compressions and breathing in the women's mouth.

She could hear the helicopter. It wasn't far out.

"Take over compressions for me," Jimmy said as he began to attach the defibrillator.

Candice took over.

"Okay. Clear, Candice."

Candice moved and Jimmy used the defibrillator.

There was a flutter of the woman's eyes.

"It's working," Jimmy said. "Continue with compressions."

Candice continued and then there was a cough and

gurgling as the woman tried to bring up lake water. They rolled her into the recovery position.

"Good, good," Jimmy whispered. "You're going to be okay."

Candice pulled out a blanket from the bag and they wrapped the woman up to prevent hypothermia.

The woman's husband was close by. "Is she going to be okay?"

"We're going to take her to the hospital in the helicopter," Candice said. "You can come with us."

The man nodded.

Jimmy was frowning.

She knew that it had to do with his fear of helicopters, but now was not the time to placate him. The had a job to do.

The helicopter landed, and the blades kept running.

Stu got out with a backboard and they worked to get the hiker ready to be taken down the mountain. They loaded her and her husband in the medical helicopter and Candice tossed in their gear to Stu. When she looked back, she saw Jimmy standing at a distance.

Frozen.

He still had his gear.

"We've got to go, Jimmy," Candice said.

"I can't."

"You have to. I know you're afraid, but you can do this."

His eyes narrowed. "What do you know of my fear? You don't know anything. You weren't there. You don't know how it feels."

"You're right. I don't, but Jimmy, we have to go *now*," she said firmly.

Jimmy pursed his lips and nodded. He climbed on board, but she could tell that he was on edge. That this was too much for him as he took the noise-canceling headphones and buckled himself in.

"All good, Nigel!" Candice shouted.

Nigel gave the thumbs-up and the helicopter rose off the mountain and made its way down the rest of the trail, heading toward Jasper rather than Signal Mountain.

Candice was a little disappointed they wouldn't get to finish the trail, but this was what they were here for. She'd let the rangers know when they landed that they were unable to finish the rest of the trail from Curator Lake down to the Signal trailhead, and the rangers would take care of the rest.

Jimmy wasn't looking at her and she knew that he was having a hard time with this. She tried to get him to look at her, but he couldn't.

Or he wouldn't.

Her heart sank. This reminded her of what had happened that night ten years ago, when he'd left. He became distant, cool, and wouldn't look at her. She'd had no idea what he was feeling.

She was angry that she was being made to feel so uncertain, that she was losing control of her rational thought and letting her anxiety take over because of him…again.

She hated this. She swore she'd never let anyone make her feel this way again. And yet here she was.

This was a mistake.

The helicopter landed on the helipad, where doctors were waiting to take the patient and her husband straight into the hospital. The patient was breathing on her own, but they had to make sure her lungs were clear and that she overcame her hypothermia.

Jimmy told the doctors what he had done and passed off the case.

Candice climbed out of the helicopter with their gear. They could head back to their homes from here, and Nigel and Stu could head back to the airfield. They walked silently off the helipad toward the parking lot as Nigel flew the helicopter up and away.

Once it was in the distance Jimmy turned toward her. It was clear he was angry.

"I didn't appreciate that."

"What?" she snapped.

"Ordering me on the helicopter, especially after I told you what happened."

"You're a paramedic. You had to come."

"So is Stu and he was there."

"You worked on the patient!" Candice snarled. "See sense, Liu. You had to get on that helicopter. There wasn't time to be afraid. And you knew beforehand that helicopters were part of this job!"

He glared at her as they walked away from the hospital. "It's nothing to do with fear. I have post-traumatic stress disorder, Candice. I couldn't get on that helicopter."

"Is your PTSD going to continue to affect your job like this?" she asked, knowing how harsh she was being even as she said it.

"So now here comes the boss hat." He shook his head.

"Jimmy, it's important. If it is going to be an obstacle, you need help."

"I've had help. I know how to deal with my PTSD and I disclosed this information when I was hired for the job. I got on the helicopter, didn't I?"

"You did get on, but not without a fight. I'm worried about you, Jimmy."

"You don't need to worry about me," he said quickly.

"Not anymore. I won't hold you back, Candice. It's clear you can live your life just fine without me."

She was taken aback. Her heart skipped a beat and her stomach sank like a rock. This was exactly how it had happened last time.

He was letting her go. Again.

"You're not holding me back," she said.

"No. You're right. I'm not," he snapped. "You're holding yourself back!"

"What's that supposed to mean?"

"Why did you stay here, Candice? There's nothing for you here. Go, make your dreams come true. Don't be so afraid to leave."

It was like a slap to the face.

"You're here, Jimmy," she said. "What if I want to stay?"

He shook his head. "Don't stay for me."

"Well, I'm not the only one hiding from the world." Her voice trembled. "Have you even dealt with Logan's death? Have you even gone to see him since you got here? You say you're not free, but you are. You have a family, a child. You can go anywhere with him."

"Yes, I have a child. I had another one, but you didn't bother telling me about that, did you? You were afraid to tell me about our baby, but I had the right to know."

A tear slid down her cheek. "Yeah, you did have that right, but I had the right to know why you left me. Logan may have thought he did the right thing telling you to leave, but he didn't. It was my life. My choices."

"Then go live it, Candice. Go."

She didn't know what to say to that.

"I'll see you at work." She turned on her heel and

walked away from him, trying not to cry. Candice was angry she'd given her heart to him again and been burned once more.

Jimmy watched her walk away as it began to rain. He was getting soaked, but he didn't care. He hated himself for what he'd done.

For breaking his promise to Logan by falling in love with Candice.

For ruining things with her a second time.

Jimmy didn't go after her. Instead he headed home. He needed to have a hot shower and he needed to get into a change of clothing.

When he walked into his house, his mother was shocked to see him.

"You're soaked through!" she exclaimed.

"Yeah," he said, exhausted. "Where's Marcus?"

"Napping. You weren't supposed to be home yet."

"We had to airlift someone off the mountain."

His mother pursed her lips. "Did you get on the helicopter?"

"I did."

"That's progress."

"Is it? I almost didn't, Mom." He scrubbed a hand over his face.

"But you did," his mother said. "Go have a hot shower and dry off. You're dirty and soaked and things will seem clearer once you're clean and dry."

"Will they?"

Liena smiled. "They will."

Jimmy wasn't so sure of that. He headed upstairs and went to have a shower. It felt good to rinse off the mountain.

As he stood there with the water rolling down his

skin, all he could think about was Candice and what she had said.

That she was still here.

What was he so afraid of?

He wasn't a burden.

In the end, he'd been the one Logan had asked to take care of his sister.

Promise me one thing. Take care of Candy for me.

Logan's voice was so clear in his head.

He got out of the shower and dried himself off. He had to find Candice. He had to make things right. She was the one for him. She always had been. He'd go anywhere, do anything, to make a family with her. He couldn't walk away from her again.

Logan had been his best buddy, but Candice had also always been there for him.

She was his best friend.

And he couldn't live without her.

As he dressed, his phone started vibrating with a call from Mountain Rescue.

"Candice?" he asked, answering the phone.

"No, it's Stu, there's been a mudslide and the helicopter Candice was piloting went down."

"What?"

"I'm coming by with the rig. It's all hands on deck."

"I'm ready."

Jimmy's stomach sank to the soles of his feet, his heart hammering. And as he glanced at his phone he saw the messages that had come through while he was in the shower.

He cursed.

And he prayed she was okay.

I can't lose her.

He'd lost her once before, he wouldn't lose her again

He was ready and out the door as the rig pulled up, his gear in his hands.

"What happened?" he asked quickly. "The details in the message weren't clear."

Stu looked worried. "There was a mudslide on the highway. Candice went to check it out and after she took off to head back to base we got word of the mayday and lost contact."

"What about the mudslide?"

"Thankfully no one was involved as there was no one driving along that section of the highway."

Jimmy worried his lip. "Was she alone?"

"No, Nigel was with her, but not flying. Kate was on board, too."

Stu raced along the highway out of town and down the Icefields Parkway. It took them a good twenty minutes to get to a point where Jimmy could see a plume of smoke rising from the ground.

His stomach knotted and his pulse raced.

Oh, God.

As they rounded the corner, he could see a wall of mud and where the RCMP had barricaded off the road. They moved to let them through.

The helicopter was a mess and on fire, smoking. He could make out Kate and Nigel sitting off to the side of the road, but he couldn't see Candice.

"No," Jimmy whispered.

His stomach sank and he felt like he couldn't breathe. Like the wall of mud was suffocating him.

No, he couldn't lose her.

Stu pulled over and Jimmy bolted from the ambulance, panic driving him as he made his way through the mess of debris and smoke.

Nigel was bleeding from a head wound and Kate was lying on a tarp with other paramedics dealing with her.

"She's over there," Nigel said, seeing his frantic face.

Jimmy nodded and made his way through the crowd. Finally, he saw Candice, soaking wet with a makeshift sling, talking to an RCMP officer.

"Candice!" he shouted above the sound of the drizzle.

She spun around, her face scratched up. "Jimmy?"

Jimmy stopped in front of her, resisting the urge to pull her into his arms. "Are you okay?"

"I could be worse. You should be looking after Nigel. Where is your gear?"

"Stu has Nigel and Kate. I was worried about you."

She smiled, but her face was guarded. "I'm fine."

"You could've died."

"But I didn't. I landed the helicopter when I saw there was engine trouble. It was a rough landing and as we were getting out the helicopter it caught on fire and we got caught up in another small mudslide. We have to get to the hospital. Nigel has an open wound."

Jimmy sighed. "Thank God you're okay."

"I think I sprained my wrist, but, yeah, I'm okay." She smiled. "You weren't answering your page."

"I was in the shower." He looked up at the sky. "Fat lot of good that did me."

She laughed gently. "Don't let this accident interfere with your job. Look, I know I was hard on you, but you're a good paramedic. I don't want to lose you."

"I don't care about the damn helicopter," Jimmy said. He took a step toward her. "It was you I was worried about."

"Me? Why?" Her eyes were wide and he could see that she was trembling.

"Because I love you, Candice Lavoie. I always have. And when I heard your helicopter went down, I thought

I'd lost you. I can't live without you. I was a fool. I'll go anywhere, do anything to be with you. I'm sorry, but I won't leave you again. I need you."

Candice took a step back, her breath catching in her throat. She couldn't quite believe what she was hearing. Tears stung her eyes.

"You—you what?"

"I love you, Candice. I always have. Logan was my friend, but you are my best friend. You always have been and I was too blind to see it. I walked away from you once before, but I can't walk away this time. I can't. I need you in my life. You're my family and I want you to be a part of Marcus's family, too. I can't lose you."

Tears started streaming down her face. "You love me?"

"I do. I've never stopped loving you. I was a fool to take so long to realize it."

A lump formed in her throat and she began to cry. "I… I've been so alone and… I've always loved you too, Jimmy. I've never stopped loving you. I was just… I was so afraid of getting hurt and losing the only family I have left in this world. I was afraid of losing you."

Jimmy cupped her face in his hands and wiped away her tears in the rain. "You'll never lose me. You'll always have me, that is, if you still want me?"

Candice smiled, her heart skipping a beat. "I do. I want you, Jimmy. I always have and I always will."

Jimmy bent down and kissed her, and though she never liked to let her guard down when she was working, she couldn't help but melt in his arms and kiss him back.

This was where she belonged. With him.

She was finally home.

EPILOGUE

One year later

CANDICE PARKED THE car in her driveway and saw that Jimmy and Marcus were sitting on the front steps, waiting for her to come home, like they often did. Especially when she and Jimmy weren't working together.

Not that they had been working together since they'd gotten married.

Candice had stepped back from her job as head of Mountain Rescue to take online courses and finish her degree. And they had plans to spend the winter in Edmonton so that she could finish her premed course and enrol in medical school.

Of course, now that might have to postponed, but Candice was quite okay with that.

"Hi, Candy," Marcus shouted from the porch.

"Hey, how was your day?" Candice asked as Marcus ran over and gave her a big hug.

"Good. Năinai and I went to the park and did crafts!" Marcus showed her the painting he made. "It's us!"

"Although there's an extra person in our family," Jimmy teased.

Marcus glared at him. "Năinai said the number was just right."

"It's a great picture." Candice kissed the top of Marcus's head and took the picture from him while he went back to playing.

Jimmy chuckled and came down the steps to give her a kiss. "You're going to give our son a complex. And clearly my mother is having some issues with counting."

"Maybe not," Candice teased.

Jimmy cocked an eyebrow. "What's going on?"

"I had my check up with Dr. Zwart today. Regular physical stuff."

"Right…" Jimmy said, taking a step back.

"Your mother is quite perceptive. She obviously knew before I did."

Jimmy looked at the painting and then looked at her. "Are you serious?"

Candice smiled. "Yes. So I'll have to delay medical school for the time being. Stu said he'd have me back in a heartbeat to do the paperwork at Mountain Rescue since he hates it so much."

"We're going to have a baby?" Jimmy asked, still stunned.

"Yep. Should come early next year."

"A winter baby in Jasper," Jimmy groaned and then he grinned. "A baby!"

"I know, but I do have the best paramedic in Jasper as my husband," she said, putting her arms around his neck.

Jimmy grinned. "That you do."

"So are you happy?" she asked.

"I am." He kissed her gently and then touched her belly. "Very happy."

"Me, too."

"So why don't we go tell Marcus that his *nǎinai* was right and there is an extra person coming?"

Candice chuckled. "I'd like that, but you know he's not going to be surprised. He'll just call you out on it. He's exactly like you."

Jimmy sighed. "I know, and I hope our next kid is just like you."

"You know he or she will probably do the same."

Jimmy laughed. "I hope so. I certainly hope so."

They walked hand in hand up the porch to share the news with Marcus and let him know that he was going to be a big brother.

Candice was happy. She was no longer alone. She had her family.

And, together, they were home.

* * * * *

MILLS & BOON

Coming next month

MISTLETOE KISS WITH THE HEART DOCTOR
Marion Lennox

Oh, she wanted him. She ached for him. Her whole body felt as if it was surrendering.

She was being kissed and she was kissing. He didn't need to balance on his bad leg because she was holding him.

Maybe it could count as therapy, she thought, almost hysterically. Helping patient stand. Maybe this was a medical tool designed to make him feel better.

It was surely making her feel better. Every sense seemed to have come alive. Every nerve ending was tingling.

More. Every single part of her was screaming that she wanted this man, she needed this man, that she wouldn't mind in the least if they fell back on the bed and…

Um, not in a million years. Not!

Because this was a hospital ward and any minute the door could open as a nurse arrived for routine obs. This was a patient and she was a doctor and…

Shut up, Elsa, she told her inner self fiercely. Just let this moment be.

So she did. Her mind shut down and she let herself just kiss. And be kissed.

The kiss was deep and long and magical, and as it

finally ended it was as much as she could do not to weep. But Marc was still holding her. He had her at arm's length now, smiling into her eyes with such tenderness that…

No! She made a herculean effort to haul herself together. This was way past unprofessional. She could just about get herself struck off the medical register for this.

But right now she was having trouble thinking that it mattered, whether she was struck off or not. For Marc was smiling at her, and that seemed to be the only thing that mattered in the whole world.

But this was still well out of order. This man's life was in Sydney. It could only ever be a casual fling.

Oh, but his smile…

'About that date…' he ventured, and she needed to shake her head but all she could do was look up into his deep eyes and sense went right out the window.

But then reality suddenly slammed back with a vengeance. The hospital speaker system cracked into life and she heard Kim, one of the hospital's junior nurses. Even through the dodgy hospital intercom she heard the fear in Kim's tone.

'Code Blue. Nurses' station. Code Blue.'

Continue reading
MISTLETOE KISS WITH THE HEART DOCTOR
Marion Lennox

Available next month
www.millsandboon.co.uk

COMING SOON!

We really hope you enjoyed reading this book.
If you're looking for more romance, be sure to
head to the shops when new books are
available on

Thursday 26th November

To see which titles are coming soon, please visit
millsandboon.co.uk/nextmonth